A Distant and Beautiful Place

A Distant and Beautiful Place

Yang Kwija

*Translated by Kim So-young
and Julie Pickering*

UNIVERSITY OF HAWAI'I PRESS
HONOLULU

Library of Congress Cataloging-in-Publication Data
Yang, Kwi-jia
   A distant and beautiful place / Yang Kwija ; Translated by Kim So-young
and Julie Pickering.
       p. cm.
   ISBN 0-8248-2192-0 (hard cover : alk. paper) — ISBN 0-8248-2639-6
(pbk. : alk. paper)
   1. Yang, Kwi-ja—Translations into English. 2. Short Stories, Korean—
Translations into English. I. Kim, So-yong. II. Pickering, Julie. III. Title.
   PL992.89.K85 K55 2002
   895.7'34—dc21
                                                                        2002007125

This book has been published with the support of a grant from the Korea
Literature Translation Institute.

The poems quoted in "The Wonmi-dong Poet" are by Kim Chŏnghwan,
Yi Hasŏk, and Hwang Chiu.

Earlier versions of "The Wonmi-dong Poet" and "The Tearoom Woman"
appeared in *Seeing the Invisible*, a 1996 *Manoa* feature issue on contemporary
fiction by Korean women, and in *Korean Literature Today*, respectively.

Designed by the University of Hawai'i Production Department

Printed by The Maple-Vail Book Manufacturing Group

Contents

Acknowledgments

THE TRANSLATION OF this book was made possible by a generous grant from the Korea Literature Translation Institute. The translators also thank the many colleagues and friends who have provided much-appreciated advice and support. Special thanks to Bruce and Ju-Chan Fulton for their helpful suggestions, and to Kim Younguk, Suzannah Oh, Song Kyusun, and Yu Youngnan for their assistance and encouragement. The translators are also grateful to Pamela Kelley and Sharon Yamamoto at University of Hawai'i Press for their assistance, and to Yang Kwija for her gracious cooperation.

Introduction

SINCE HER LITERARY debut in 1978, Yang Kwija (b. 1955) has garnered a critical and popular following enjoyed by few Korean authors. Yang grew up amid South Korea's breakneck drive for industrialization and economic development. Not surprisingly, her writing explores the modern urban experience in a changing society: the opportunities and disappointments of the new economy and the social mobility that it seems to promise; the deterioration of traditional ties of trust and reciprocity; and the underlying, yet ubiquitous, atmosphere of violence and fear that characterized South Korean life prior to democratization in 1987. Throughout her work, Yang explores these themes with straightforward prose, compassion, and humor.

Yang Kwija started out writing short fiction, as do most Korean fiction writers. She is remarkable, however, for her consistent productivity. Beginning with her debut work, which won the Newcomers Award from the prestigious literary journal *Munhak sasang* in 1978, she has published a steady stream of stories, first from the Chŏlla region, where she was born and raised, and then from Seoul, the South Korean capital, and its environs, where she settled in 1980. Since the mid-1980s, she has added dozens of novellas and full-length novels to her body of work, publishing best-selling and prizewinning works on a regular basis.

As with so many of her contemporaries, Yang's roots are in the provinces, but she has lived most of her life in and around the nation's large urban centers. Her early works draw on this experience, examining the lives of ordinary people struggling to survive with dignity as their society shifts from a traditional rural way of life, where community and family are paramount, to an urban-centered lifestyle, where individual needs and ambitions reign.

The protagonists in her early stories are often "salary men," faceless office workers struggling to overcome the alienation and loneliness of Korea's newly industrializing cities. The short story "Rust"* chronicles the dismal existence of a would-be journalist sidetracked in the advertising department at a metropolitan newspaper company. The melancholy protagonist is frustrated and angry at what seems to be the broken promise of modern Korea's remarkable growth.

This theme of middle-class alienation is one of several running through *A Distant and Beautiful Place,* Yang's best-selling collection of linked stories published individually in literary journals from 1985 to 1987 and as a collection, *Wonmi-dong saramdŭl* (The people of Wonmi-dong), in 1987. *A Distant and Beautiful Place* documents the lives of those on the periphery of Seoul, struggling to find refuge, if not prosperity, somewhere between the modern metropolis and traditional society.

Wonmi-dong (literally, a distant and beautiful neighborhood) is located in the satellite city of Puch'ŏn, Kyŏnggi Province, just west of Seoul. Yang, her husband, and their newborn daughter moved there in 1982, after housing costs drove them from the capital, where they had lived for two years. Her portrayal of the community is based on personal experiences and observations.

In *A Distant and Beautiful Place,* Yang captures the essence of modern Korea in transition. Once a traditional agrarian community, Wonmi-dong was swept up in the storm of change generated by South Korea's forced march toward industrialization and economic development in the 1970s and 1980s. As the population of the Seoul metropolitan area grew, housing prices in the capital rose beyond the reach of the average citizen, driving hundreds of thousands to seek shelter in the surrounding suburbs.

The resultant population and real estate boom shook long-

---

*"Rust," trans. Ahn Jung-hyo, in *Reunion So Far Away* (Seoul: Korean National Commission for UNESCO, 1994), pp. 149–178.

established rural communities. Local families sold farmland to housing contractors who, in turn, built inexpensive apartments and shops to accommodate new arrivals from Seoul and the hinterlands. The newcomers had no place in the traditional network of reciprocal obligations maintained by the local people and instead pinned their hopes on industrialization's promise of upward mobility and a better life. However, like the frustrated journalist in "Rust," many found that promise was too often broken.

In *A Distant and Beautiful Place*, Yang weaves these themes of alienation amid change, a lost sense of community, the deterioration of traditional values, and the subtle undercurrent of violence and fear into a tapestry of vivid characterizations and rich dialogue. The middle-class protagonists in the first two stories struggle to find a place for themselves and their families in an unfamiliar world that makes alluring yet ultimately empty promises. In this volume's title story, "A Distant and Beautiful Place," Seoul's skyrocketing housing costs drive Ŭnhye's family to a small apartment in Wonmi-dong, hardly the answer to their dream of a better life. Hamstrung by competing responsibilities and expectations, the protagonist, a middle-class office worker, father, and dutiful son, skeptical about his family's prospects in the satellite community of Puch'ŏn, laments that "hope was everywhere. It just wasn't for him."

The unwilling door-to-door salesman in "The Spark" struggles with similar frustrations as he tries to shake off the humiliations of unemployment in Korea's new economy. He, too, has a family to raise, but he must operate in a society where promises are meant to be broken and sympathy is hard to find.

The working class is not immune to the uncertainties of this new world. Im, the good-natured repairman in "On Rainy Days I Have to Go to Karibong-dong," sells his land in nearby Kyŏnggi Province in hopes of building a better life in the city, but he, too, finds prosperity elusive and is forced to take odd jobs to make ends meet. Like the factory worker in "The Underground Man," Im is a good person, committed to doing the right thing, despite the deceit of others. However, in the new world of Wonmi-dong, goodness is of little worth.

The story of Old Kang, the cantankerous protagonist in "The Last Land," illustrates the deterioration of traditional values as South Koreans embrace the dream of prosperity. A native of

Wonmi-dong, Kang collides headfirst with the realities of his changing community when he persists in spreading night soil on a field wedged among newly built apartment buildings and shops. Observing the uselessness of his feud with the newcomers he calls "damn Seoulites" regardless of their origins, Kang's wife and children prefer the proceeds of the sale of his land to its harvest.

Old Kang's dilemma is also one of many examples of the interpersonal conflicts that arise when relationships of reciprocity and responsibility, dearly held in the traditional village, clash with city dwellers' need for work and dreams of upward mobility. Divided as it is among newcomers and old-timers, Wonmi-dong enjoys a certain sense of community until a new grocery store encroaches on the turf of Captain Kim, proprietor of Brothers Supermarket and head of the local neighborhood association. In "Our Daily Bread," Kim joins in a cynical alliance with one competitor to drive out another, in the end undermining fragile community ties.

"The Wonmi-dong Poet" also portrays the deterioration of community and the threat of violence that characterized South Korean life under military rule during the early 1980s. When the Bachelor Ghost, a would-be poet, is attacked by thugs, his supposed friend, Captain Kim, abandons him, leaving seven-year-old Kyŏngok to wonder about the meaning of friendship and community.

What Kyŏngok describes as the Bachelor Ghost's "unfortunate mental state" may be the result of the political repression and threat, if not outright use, of violence so common in pre-1987 South Korea. In "A Vagabond Mouse," the man who abandons his family and disappears on Wonmi Mountain is scarred by memories from a May spent in "that southern city," a not-so-subtle reference to Kwangju, site of the South Korean military's massacre of citizens in 1980. In "Bellfinch," the idealistic husband is incarcerated for his beliefs. Given the time in which Yang was writing, her references to political repression can be abstruse, but she clearly portrays the effect of this era's heritage of fear and violence on individuals, their loved ones, and the larger community.

Rich in its sense of place and history, *A Distant and Beautiful Place* established Yang as a major writer, respected in the literary community and admired by readers from diverse social backgrounds. Since the late 1980s, Yang has concentrated on longer works, including the award-winning novella *Hidden Flower* (*Sumŭn kkot*, 1992) and the best-selling novels *I Long To Possess That Which Is Forbidden Me* (*Nanŭn somang handa, naege kŭmjidoen kŏsŭl*, 1992), *A Thousand-year Love* (*Ch'ŏn nyŏn ŭi sarang*, 1995), and *Contradictions* (*Mosun*, 1998).

These more recent works reflect Yang's acute awareness of the contradictions faced by Korea's intelligentsia and newly emerging middle class since the inauguration of a civilian government in 1987 and the collapse of socialism on the world stage. In *Hidden Flower*, honored with the 1992 Yi Sang Literature Award, an author struggling with writer's block searches for answers in a world where long-accepted absolutes no longer apply. This semiautobiographical work probes the meaning of literature in modern Korea, the role of the writer in a democratic society, and the value of compassion and self-examination.

The wildly popular *I Long To Possess That Which Is Forbidden Me*, a psychological and political portrayal of a feminist's revenge against a symbol of male oppression, broke new ground for Yang as a writer and in society at large. It was the first Korean novel to examine the persistence of gender roles in contemporary Korean society and the alienation of the modern woman, and, in doing so, to transcend the stereotyped depiction of *han*, that mysterious blend of resignation, longing, and resentment so often attributed to Korean women, past and present.

Today Yang remains one of Korea's most successful authors, commercially and critically, with the publication of *A Thousand-year Love*, *Contradictions*, and the novella *Bear Tale* (*Kom iyagi*, 1996), which won the 1996 *Hyŏndae munhak* Award. She also has become a popular cultural figure, frequently featured in women's magazines, newspaper columns, and other mainstream media and respected for her personal character as much as for her writing.

A Distant and
Beautiful Place

AS THEY SQUEEZED the wardrobe out the narrow door, a fragment the size of a coin chipped off the side. The same thing had happened when they moved in. Gasping under the weight of his end, Ŭnhye's father had no time to examine this new blemish. He could only imagine the inner layers of wood gleaming like ivory and the angry scab that would eclipse the older scars on the rough surface. The ten-foot-long wardrobe was already scratched in several places. It couldn't be helped. After the initial annoyance passed, the scratch would establish itself as yet another mark of time.

Because of the weight shifting forward and his own plodding gait, he soon forgot the scratch. The wardrobe resembled a huge coffin as it slowly emerged lengthwise through the cramped doorway. "Shift it to the left now, to the left!" the mover directed, the words straining to escape his clenched lips. Ŭnhye's father summoned all his strength and leaned slightly to the left. Only then did he see the mover's red face, veins bulging, on the other side of the door. A feeling came into his right wrist, like a spasm from bearing the weight in one position for so long. The fear that he might lose his precarious grip at any moment made him tense.

How much more energy do I have to put in before we get the rest of this thing out the door without another scratch? He squeezed his eyes shut, despairing that the effort would require his last bit of strength. A pained cry, more agonizing than any groan, was about to burst from his throat. "Slowly now, pull it back slowly. No, no, back!"

The mover sounded as though he was gritting his teeth. Ŭnhye's father was gritting *his* teeth. "Back now, to the left." It was only a matter of time before his right hand gave out. Cold sweat dripped down his back as he felt himself losing his grip. *I can't . . . I can't hold it any longer,* he was about to cry to the dirty cotton gloves on the other end of the wardrobe when at last the mover set his end down on the hallway floor, and the weight suddenly lessened. They had made it into the hall. The mover leaned out the door and shouted. "Hey, Chang! Get in here! I need some help with the wardrobe. The owner's not up to it."

After carrying the wardrobe down the steep flight of thirty stone steps that led from the house, the mover and the driver leaned against the truck, smoking. Carrying the wardrobe down those steps was enough to exhaust anyone. At the bottom was an empty lot, just large enough for a truck to turn around. The sight of his family's shabby belongings piled in the open saddened Ŭnhye's father. Not that they hadn't always been shabby. He tried to ignore the props of their poor existence poking from the small bundles and fumbled in his pocket for a cigarette. The wind was fierce and the cigarette was difficult to light. It was a smarting cold, harder and sharper than a knife blade. The cold wave that accompanied the winter kimchi season each year had started blowing a few days earlier. *Temperatures will drop to ten below zero, the coldest of the year.* Last night's weather report had been right: It was going to be the coldest day of the year.

His mother must have noticed the new chip on the wardrobe as she passed with several light bundles. *Tsk, tsk.* He could hear her cluck in disapproval from where he stood in the yard. The sound was so penetrating that he tossed his cigarette to the ground and crushed it with his foot before he had smoked even half of it. For some reason, the sound of the clucking old woman, weighed down by her layers of clothing and with a muffler wrapped around her head, sent a chill down his spine. *Maybe it's the cold,* he thought. Maybe that's why he felt that chill as the wind blew up over their little bundles in the vacant lot.

There was no one to help them move, no one except his immediate family—his wife, his mother, and his young daughter—the mover, and the driver. It was the suddenness of the move, he tried to persuade himself, and it was a weekday. Still, he wouldn't have asked anyone to help even if it was a weekend and they had planned well in advance. They had moved too often for that. They had been at this house less than two months.

What? You're moving again?

Director Cho, the head of his division, scowled quite in spite of himself. Ŭnhye's father shouldn't have cited the move as his reason for missing work that day. But what could he say? Just two months earlier he had stood at Cho's desk offering the same excuse for his absence the next day. He should have known better. The same question had popped out of Cho's mouth last time. *Moving again? How come you move so often?*

Director Cho had this habit of asking one question after another. *Why can't you? Have you forgotten that work begins at eight? Don't you know what we do here in the sales division? Don't you realize what day this is?* He never knew how to respond, and when he did, Cho always came back with another question. *Oh, and why is that?*

There was no way around Cho's impossible queries. All he could do was push on, threading his way through the ridiculous riddles in silence. Hardly daring to breathe. His breathing—maybe it wasn't even his own anymore. Like everyone else in the world, he was bound by the tenacious ties of this complex thing called family. The fatigue he felt after a day at his desk in that office, where even the air was heavy, was the same fatigue one might feel after a duel for one's life. There was no need to explain why he couldn't give up the duels he fought six days a week. After all, everyone has their own bloody battles to fight.

Come to think of it, it was only natural that Cho should scowl. According to Pak Ch'ansŏng, who sat at the next desk, there was no need to take a day off work every time he moved. Leave household matters to the wife and take life easy, he advised. All Pak needed on moving day were the address and location of the new house. He even described the rare feeling he had when he entered an unfamiliar neighborhood in search of the new house where his family waited.

"And if that doesn't work, you could move on Sunday and lend the wife a hand."

A Sunday move was the obvious compromise, but it was out of the question. His mother would never agree to move on the Sabbath. There was no crossing her belief that Sundays should be devoted to the Lord. She had been a Sunday school teacher for many years now.

"They wouldn't fire you for taking a day off to move, would they? But the Lord, he'd drive you away if you moved on the Sabbath. What choice do we have? You know which is more fearful!" Having rested long enough to smoke a cigarette, the mover began toting the larger bundles down from the house. It didn't look as if there was much left. His wife was with their daughter, collecting things in the kitchen. The child leaned against her mother's back, rubbing her eyes and whimpering.

"Look at Ŭnhye," his wife called. "She wants me to carry her on my back!"

The poor kid must be sleepy, he thought. She had been up since dawn because of the move. His wife pushed back her own unkempt hair and tried to comfort the child. Her nose was red, and she held one hand to her lower back, as if to support her enormous belly. Her frozen hands were swollen after several days of hard work. The mover, who had been traipsing in and out of the house in his winter boots, now picked up the rice chest in the front of the kitchen and headed for the truck. Ŭnhye continued to whimper, and her mother attempted to mollify her in a voice as brittle as straw. "What's wrong, Ŭnhye? Mommy's busy, too. I'm going to spank you if you keep pestering me."

Ŭnhye's father looked in the bedroom, but everything that needed to go had now been taken. The room was empty except for some trash lying on the floor. Footsteps echoing, he stepped inside and glanced around. A few rusted nails and Ŭnhye's scribbling were all that was left on the blank walls. The door to the attic was wide open, and long ribbons of dust marked the spot where the wardrobe had stood. They had only to sweep up now, and then his weary respite in this room would be over. It felt strange somehow, looking around the room he had occupied, the room he had returned to each night to lean against the wall and read the newspaper. And it felt strange confronting the few scraps of memories, the few remnants of the past.

There on the wall was the tape measure made in boredom one Sunday. He had carefully marked off the inches and stuck it to the wall with Scotch tape. He had planned to record Ŭnhye's growth but had marked off only a yard and ten inches because he hadn't expected to live there long enough for her to grow much past three feet. At first the child had wanted to be measured every five minutes. He recalled her solemn expression and the way she stood at attention, pressing her thin shoulders against the wall. She didn't seem to grow very quickly. Neither the marks of time nor the hatchmarks on the tape change if you keep watching them. But time clearly does pass. He looked at the carefully spaced marks once more. He could imagine the child's thin shoulders superimposed on the tape. Now all that remained on the barren walls was the tape, and it would leave only a tattered scar when it was torn down.

A cold wind seeped down from the attic, and when he closed the door he discovered another remnant of the past. When was that? It had happened late one night when he had returned home drunk. He remembered the occasion clearly because it had happened quite recently. There had been a get-together of the old-timers in the sales division, a kind of pep rally. According to Pak Ch'ansŏng, the oldsters, now entering their thirties, were being pushed aside by the younger generation, and the group had consumed an assortment of drinks on the pretext that they should unite to protect themselves. He didn't remember how they had decided to gain supremacy over the newcomers. In any case, he had arrived home well after midnight, collapsed into bed, and fallen asleep.

In the middle of the night, he woke with a terrible thirst. The curtains were drawn and the room was pitch dark. *I need some water,* he thought, fumbling through the dark toward the door. But for some mysterious reason, the door wouldn't open. And the doorknob felt strange. Instead of a round knob with a button in the middle, a long thin handle wiggled in his hand, then fell off altogether. Thirsty and convinced the door wouldn't open, he brought his fist down on the wood with all his might. The thin plywood door, good for decoration and nothing else, gave in with a thud, and his wife jerked awake. "Why are you trying to open the attic door?"

He ran his hand over the cracked door and touched the broken handle. There was a simple explanation for his scuffle with the attic door: In the house they had lived in before, the door to the kitchen had been on that side.

Wherever they went, it was always several days before he was startled out of the habits of one house and came to grips with having moved again. Now he remembered—he was the one who, when

Ŭnhye started crawling up the stairs, had installed the hook on the attic door. The door that wouldn't open. The thirst and raging impatience. He turned away, fuzzily recalling a shadow breaking off the handle and smashing its fist into a door that wouldn't open. But now the sound of Ŭnhye sobbing shook the empty house. Her mother must have finally given her a swat.

"What are you doing to that child? We can't have no crying on an important day like this!" His mother lifted Ŭnhye onto her back and stood at the threshold of the main room. "Mighty cold, ain't it, Ŭnhye? Yes, but I'm feeling good. Finally bought our own house, after all that wandering."

The child screwed up her lips, trying to control the distress that welled within her. Streaked with tears and snot from a lingering cold, Ŭnhye's face was blue from the chill wind, but her grandmother kept repeating how good she felt, though she, too, looked haggard.

"Thank you, Father. Thank you for giving us a house to live in." He recalled his mother's prayer earlier today at the breakfast table. "Thank you for helping us on our way. Lord, you promised Abraham generations of prosperity and bestowed a wonderful land on him. This family has suffered great hardships with no house to call its own, but now, thanks to your blessings, Father, we, too, are leaving for Canaan. Lord, who has given us a fine house, please watch over us in our new home and help us live in accordance with your ways . . ."

Her prayers were always so articulate. As she often said, it was only natural after more than forty years of believing in the Lord. But this morning's prayer was particularly eloquent. Her strong accent disappeared without a trace, though the rough intonation remained as she prayed for nearly ten minutes. This was the second time she had spoken of the land of Canaan in her prayers. An eighteen–*p'yŏng* apartment in Puch'ŏn was Canaan to her. For him, it was the first house he could call his own in four years of marriage, but for Mother, it was the first since Father's death. In fact, it was her first house in twenty years.

"So how are we going to do this? Are you two going to go ahead in a taxi?" she asked. The cab of the moving truck had room for only two more people.

"It would cost too much to take a taxi all the way to Puch'ŏn," his wife replied. "We'll ride in the back of the truck. That way we can give the driver directions."

After scraping together the money for their new house, his wife wasn't going to squander on a taxi. "Go get a blanket. We won't get cold if we wrap up," she said as she waddled into the kitchen again. "Will that be enough?" his mother asked. "You in the family way and all? Maybe I should ride in back."

He couldn't let his mother ride in the truck bed. And he could hardly ask the mover to sit back there. People who earn a living by the sweat of their brow can get nasty when they think they are being treated unfairly. Besides, it was a long ride.

He suddenly realized he was no longer a citizen of Seoul. He didn't even know how long it would take to get to Puch'ŏn by anything but the subway. He was used to moving in circles around Seoul, from Miari to Hwagok-dong, from Hwagok-dong to Ssangmun-dong, but this move, across the boundary to Kyŏnggi Province, was downright foreign to him.

We'd better hurry, he thought. *We may own a home now, but Puch'ŏn is completely new territory.* He reached down with both hands to sweep the trash into a pile. That's when he kicked something. It flew through the air, banged off the wall next to the kitchen, and tumbled to the floor with a crash. Its red back and four rotating feet startled him. Leaning over, he picked it up cautiously. It was a seal, a crude plastic toy he had bought for a pittance from a street vendor at the subway entrance last summer on his way home from work. Wind it up by the spring in its abdomen, and its feet paddled furiously. The seal had spent the entire summer paddling around a tub of water; now its unsightly red back was peeling and faded.

His wife must have thrown it out. Except for the rattle it now made because the seam connecting the back and abdomen had come loose when it hit the wall, the seal still worked. It didn't matter whether he threw it away or kept it, so he slipped it into his jacket pocket. He could always throw it away later, so there was no harm in keeping it a little longer.

His mother was down below on the street with Ŭnhye on her back. Every time the driver lifted a bundle onto the truck she warned him to be careful of the breakables inside. Ŭnhye lay flat against her grandmother's back. The cutting wind blowing from the top of the hill hit her square in the face. The weather was ominous; it might even snow. The mover rushed past with a large wooden tub filled with the last pots and pans from the kitchen. "That's it," he called out, not bothering to look back. "Let's get out of here before we freeze to death."

"He's right," Ŭnhye's mom murmured as she leaned against the hallway door to catch her breath. "I'm freezing. Let's go."

From the bedroom to the hall he wandered, and from the hall to the yard. Then suddenly he realized something. He had finally bought his own home and was headed for Canaan, the land of milk and honey, just as his mother had said. So why was he feeling so lost?

Well, even Abraham would have been daunted at the thought of moving all the way to Puch'ŏn with a pregnant wife on the verge of giving birth, a mother nearly seventy years old, and a whimpering daughter.

The movers began throwing ropes across the truckload of bundles. At his wife's insistence, they had left a space for the two of them beneath the window at the back of the cab. "It'll be hard to keep the furniture in place if you sit there." The driver was reluctant, but Ŭnhye's mother won in the end. "You know, we could get stopped for this," the driver added.

The driver was nicer than the other man, though. The mover glared at the pregnant woman as she crawled in among the bundles. "I guess it won't be as cold in there as at the very back," the man snarled. Ŭnhye's mother pretended not to hear and began spreading the blanket and pieces of clothing in the narrow space left in the bed of the truck. The cab and the sections of the wardrobe to the left and right would block the wind.

His mother climbed into the passenger's seat with the sleeping child wrapped in her sweater. "Go up and see if we've left anything behind," she said. "Can't come back for anything once we're gone. Go have one last look."

"Pull! Pull it tighter! Good! You got it?" The air was thick with steam pouring from the men's mouths. He dashed up the stairs, his own breath puffing in clouds. He didn't expect to find anything; he was simply taking another look because his mother had asked. All that remained was a blunt coal pike in the storage room where they kept the *yŏnt'an* briquettes used for heating and cooking. There was nothing worth taking. As he turned to go, he noticed a note wedged in the door of the back apartment where a young working couple lived. *I've taken the grill you borrowed. Ŭnhye's mom.* His heart warmed at the small, precise writing. If she had gone to the trouble of retrieving possessions from other people's kitchens, nothing had been left behind.

He headed down the stairs, slowly this time. His wife, wedged amid the furniture now bound in a tangle of ropes, waved at him to hurry. A long drive ahead of them, the two movers stood with their backs to the truck, relieving themselves. Now the only thing left to do was depart. When he reached the bottom step, he turned. The front gate, with its peeling watermelon–green paint, swung in the wind. All morning, not a soul had looked out from the scattering of large Western–style houses nearby, and now, with only a glance, he bade farewell and jumped into the back of the truck.

It was cozier among the bundles than he expected. As the truck headed down the hill, they had to brace themselves to keep from slipping, but after that, they had only to endure the vibrations of the rumbling truck. He pulled his wife's thick coat up over her head, hoping to protect her goosebumped face from the wind. "Not yet . . . I can't breathe." She pulled the coat down and draped it over his knees instead. At first glance, they must have looked like just another bundle. And even if someone did look more closely, they would see only a shabby lump of humanity, nothing more.

As the truck wove its way out of the city, they pulled the blanket up around their shoulders and huddled in silence. From time to time his wife shifted under the weight of her large belly. He wadded up some clothing and stuffed it behind her back so she could lean against the truck's cab. The distant sound of a pop song filtered from the radio inside.

The truck had to pause frequently for traffic lights, so eventually they decided to put on extra sweaters. Whenever the truck stopped, people in the cars behind them would notice them. His wife was practically lying down now, buried beneath the clothes and blanket; he covered his face with a sweater and pressed closer to the wardrobe. His wife remained silent, even when the truck stopped for long intervals. If she hadn't stirred each time the truck jerked to a halt or accelerated abruptly, he might have wondered if she were still alive. Stretching his leg toward her, he felt her warmth, and she shifted once more. A bundle of quilts bound by a rope wobbled on top of the desk, and somewhere dishes rattled incessantly.

He shouldn't have moved them into that old house, knowing the owner had put it up for sale. He had never imagined anyone buying a house in the middle of winter, but that is just what happened, and so they had to pack up and move just days before the baby was due. He had been naive to believe the real estate agent. The house had been on the market for three years, the man said, and not a single person had come to look at it. It would never sell! The ugly old house was wedged between several luxurious mansions. What could anyone do with a tiny property at the top of a steep hill? What's more, the house was in such a terrible state of repair that no one would dare take it on. The owner had long since given up on selling and now planned to fix the house up and pass it on to his son, the agent explained. The rent was extremely low considering you had the main wing of the house—two bedrooms and a living room—and were removed from the other wings. And so he had signed the rental agreement, despite his misgivings. Winter was coming and they had no time to dawdle, what with the date they were scheduled to vacate their old house fast approaching.

No prospective buyers, and yet scarcely two weeks after they moved in, wouldn't you know it—the house was sold. And by the very same realtor who had arranged for them to rent the place. The owner, the one who had said he was going to give the house to his son, signed the sales contract without a word to them, then demanded that they move out. The people in the lower wing could stay, but the buyer wanted the main wing for himself. And he wanted to move in before the year was out because he felt it was bad luck to move during the new year.

They were in a difficult position, with the baby due at the end of the year. He might have stood his ground, had they moved in without knowing that the house was on the market, but such was not the case. And the owner had, after all, offered to pay their moving expenses.

At first he couldn't accept what had happened; they had just started a new life, and the forced move was so abrupt. A dizzying array of strategies, which could hardly be called ingenious, flashed through his mind. He had nothing to offer as proof of their rights, however, just a few feeble facts: they had reported their new address to the district office only two days before; they had barely figured out the bus routes; they still hadn't unpacked all their things.

There was no getting around it, though, so he decided to clear his head and accept the situation. The most sensible solution was to resign to reality as soon as possible. There was nothing more fool-hardy than resisting with youthful bravado, he decided. And so they began another depressing round of real estate offices.

"Oh, look! The Han River's almost frozen!"

He hadn't noticed his wife's face poking out of the blanket, but now she was shaking him. The truck was crossing the Han. The wind from the river surged over him. The edges of the river were beginning to freeze. A paper–thin film of ice connected the dark green water and the thicker ice along the banks. They could see those migratory birds with the black backs—what were they called? Mallard ducks? The birds flapped their wings, preparing for flight. Several boats were frozen in the water near the banks. His wife craned her neck the entire span of the bridge, as if she had never seen the Han before.

"Aren't you cold?"

"No. Well, just a little . . ."

Once they had seen the frozen river, the cold seemed to intensify. *Just a little,* she had said, but he felt quite cold now. She slipped her hands under the blanket and began rubbing her icy feet. The cush-ions they had laid on the bed of the truck hadn't warmed from their body heat, and the cold enveloping their legs threatened to chill them through. "Come closer." He pulled her near and slipped his arm around her shoulders.

"We still have a long way to go, don't we? It's already so cold. What are we going to do?" she asked in a small voice as she pulled the clothes around them. The covers slipped down each time the truck moved.

We still have a long way to go, don't we? Her question reminded him of that Saturday when the sleet had come down so hard. They had taken the subway from City Hall station to a place called Puch'ŏn. They had never been there before. They had gone on the advice of his wife's high-school classmate. The woman had made a tidy profit building a couple of houses there, and she said they could buy an apartment for the price of the key money on a few rooms in Seoul. They were already exhausted by the search for a house to rent, so they could hardly ignore her advice. He wouldn't have been so worried if they could put off moving until Christmas, the deadline the new owner had given them, but the baby was due Christmas Day. They had to move at least ten days before the due date, just to be on the safe side.

Each time he ducked out from work to go house-hunting with his wife, he worried that she might go into labor. His heart jumped whenever he got a call from home. They were desperate, but a suitable house simply didn't present itself. They couldn't find a place that fit both their budget and moving schedule. A decent house would turn out to be too expensive, and when the price was right, the house was unspeakably small and uncomfortable. On occasion, a house would seem just right, but invariably the date was wrong. His pregnant wife waddled around looking at houses, too. Every Saturday and Sunday the whole family had to go out on house-hunting expeditions to neighborhoods where rent was cheap. And then they heard about Puch'ŏn. There was no reason to delay. Determined to sign a contract on the spot, he counted the days until the next Saturday when he and his wife boarded the Seoul–Inch'ŏn subway, which ran through Puch'ŏn. It was a cold, wet day in early December.

He wouldn't forget their first trip to Puch'ŏn for a long time. His wife trailing after him, gasping under the weight of her belly . . . the watery beef soup they had in an alley somewhere as they wandered through the unfamiliar neighborhoods. The roads were difficult to navigate, and the unpaved side streets were muddy from the sleet. It was winter, but construction was in full swing in some places, and the neighborhood around the subway station was dotted with empty lots piled high with spent *yŏnt'an* ash. Every house and shop had the same face, but they didn't look the least bit cheerful or friendly; rather, they all emitted an air of indifferent laxity. The city looked brand-new one moment, as if it was starting out fresh; then the next instant it seemed old, as if it was already feeble and broken. Wandering the streets of the unfamiliar city, where new beginnings coexisted with decay, they shivered, lips blue, in winter's first cold spell.

After snooping around a collection of squat apartment houses painted loud colors, they finally signed a contract. A sales contract, not another rental agreement with a key money deposit. It was an eighteen-*p'yŏng* apartment on the second floor, about four bus stops from the subway station. All they had to do was add 3.5 million won to the key money they already had. Two million was from a long-term bank loan that the previous owner hadn't paid off. And they could cover the rest if they closed their savings account and sold off their wedding jewelry. Best of all, the moving date was soon. He was encouraged by his wife's calculations: They would have time to unpack, lay in a winter supply of kimchi, albeit a bit late, and still have a week to recover before the baby was due. The apartment had three rooms, including a space that could be called a living room, and a *yŏnt'an* boiler that supplied hot water as well as heat. His wife beamed as she toured the apartment. "It's like a dream! Look at this! Remember Hyŏni's house over in Chŏng-nŭng? It's eighteen *p'yŏng*, but it goes for more than thirty million won! No, it must go for over forty million now! Oh, come look at this! The bathtub's made out of marble! It's so elegant!"

The truck stopped at the rotary in Yŏngdŭngp'o. Vehicles lined the roads in all directions, waiting for the light to change. *Time for a smoke,* he thought, digging slowly through his pockets. "Where are we?" his wife asked. Only her eyes were visible.

"Yŏngdŭngp'o. I think we're halfway there. Cold, aren't you?"

"Yes, a little."

She started rubbing her feet again. He tucked the blanket around her shoulders, then stretched his legs cautiously and tried to stand. The front and sides of the truck bed were blocked, leaving only the rear open to view. There was nothing behind them but a long line of taxis waiting for customers. He wanted to smoke, but unfortunately, his cigarettes were in his pants pocket. He retrieved them and was about to sit down when he realized his matches were in his pants pocket, too. As he rose a second time, his eyes met his mother's through the glass partition at the back of the truck cab. *Cold, eh?* That was what she seemed to be saying. He shook his head as he watched her wrinkled lips open and close.

Ŭnhye must have awakened; her head popped over the back of the seat. *Daddy!* she seemed to say. He tried to smile, but he felt as if his lips were cracking. The child's small hand tapped on the glass. Then another face suddenly appeared beside hers: the driver. He gestured downward with his hand. *Wants me to sit down, I guess.* Like an obedient student, he quickly crawled back among the covers.

The light changed and the truck leaped forward with a violent cough. The wind, which had subsided momentarily, began to whip around them once more. He postponed the cigarette and shoved his hands into his jacket pockets to thaw, but something blocked his way. *What's this?* he wondered, pulling out the faded red seal. Annoyed that he was still carrying the silly toy around in his pocket, he squeezed the seal until it creaked.

The seal reminded him of the office. "You know that Director Cho? In Yŏngdong there are probably a dozen bar girls that he calls mistress. The man worships women. He's always saying stuff like, 'Do you realize what day this is?' He picked it up from those girls. Didn't you know? Women have a patent on expressions like that. First step to becoming a nag. Basic technique for getting on someone's nerves."

Pak Ch'ansŏng loved analyzing and deciphering Director Cho. It was Pak who once told him about seals. Of course, it was in reference to Cho.

"Did you know that a male seal can have as many as fifty wives at a time? Just lines 'em up and bang, bang, bang! You never heard that? Boy, are you ignorant! Why do you think people eat seal penises for stamina? Now, fifty would be too many for our Director Cho—considering his age and all—but I'll bet he can handle ten. Ha, ha, ha. We could call him Cho the Seal Dick. Cute, huh?"

"Seal Dick" kept the office crew entertained for some time, and the nickname gave them the perfect excuse for a good laugh as they stumbled from their too-short slumber and headed to work each morning. Director Cho had a subtle way of getting on people's nerves—jerking them around, piling on work without them realizing it, then sneaking off, pretending he was fed up with it all, only to return at the last minute to take credit for the finished product. Still, they tolerated him. A man in his position needed a few faults. *Director Cho's no better off than any of us,* he sometimes thought. Except for a little more pay, a few more years under his belt, and a slightly higher position in the firm, he wasn't any different from the rest of them. He went around in the same endless circles with nothing particular to brag about, except perhaps that nickname.

"Directors are nothing special. They get together and complain about their superiors and whine about their expense accounts, just like us. Seal Dick loves badmouthing the executive director, but in the presence of the old man, he's always bowing and scraping. That's just the way it is."

For all intents and purposes, Pak was Director Cho's right-hand man, so he knew more about all their superiors than the others. It was through Pak that the staff learned that Mrs. Seal Dick had just bought a new wardrobe inlaid with mother-of-pearl. Now they entertained themselves by exchanging views on the price and beauty of such furniture. And at the end of their conversation, they would add a "shit" or a "damn" for good measure.

That was it. The "damns" that punctuated the lives of the entire staff, himself included, required no further comment. It gave him some pleasure to be able to call Director Cho Seal Dick. What else could he do? Everyone glared daggers at their superiors: the staff at Cho, Cho at the executive director, and the executive director at the president of the firm. Those living in a perfect world, where there was no need to glare, would never understand the simple pleasure hidden in that look.

He sat the seal on his knee and gazed at it as he smoked a cigarette. The truck was racing along a road lined with ash–gray cement buildings. Black smoke belched from a towering chimney. The truck had picked up considerable speed compared to its hesitant progress earlier in the journey, and the wind blew harder as a result. He shuddered and took a long draw on the cigarette, tapping the ash off with quivering fingers. The wind swept away the ash, and he bounced along with the vibrations of the wheels.

Factories appeared as dark gray bodies, blackened by the smog. It looked like they had passed through Kuro and were heading for Kaebong-dong. They seemed to have traveled so far, yet Seoul showed no sign of ending. Even the concrete walls of the factories seemed to stretch on forever. He thought of the people working inside. He imagined another Director Cho who would serve as fodder for the workers' complaints. Recalling the families who depended on those workers, he looked at his wife. Once again she had wedged herself inside the blankets and clothes, so even her face was buried. *Cold always brings sleep. But it's dangerous to sleep in the cold*, he thought, reaching over to wake her. Then he stopped. The rise and fall of her round belly were clearly visible through the layers of clothing. He could only hope that she was dreaming of their new house with its elegant marble bathtub. He took another long draw on his cigarette, melancholy at the thought of moving, with his aging mother and young daughter in the truck cab and his pregnant wife in the back with the furniture. He lifted his arm to discard the cigarette, which had burned down to the filter now. *Is this still Seoul?* Gazing at the buses weaving busily through the traffic, he marveled at the city's enormity.

He didn't want to dwell on the fact that he couldn't find a place for himself within the boundaries of the huge metropolis. He had begun this roaming from one rented room to another years ago, back when a key money rental agreement lasted only six months. His mother had left his sister's place down south during his last year in college and had come to Seoul to cook and clean for him in his rented room. It was after he got married and needed more living space that he began to feel that his life was a desperate struggle just to find a place with two bedrooms and a small living room. Sometimes the rooms drove them into the streets, and other times they abandoned the rooms for another place. In most cases, it was the rooms that sent them packing. After those countless moves, he had come to one conclusion: There was no hope without your own house. Hope, especially for those living in Seoul, meant a house.

Now he was leaving Seoul to fulfill that hope. He couldn't shake off the feeling that something wasn't quite right. After all his years in that enormous city, he had never owned a house. That was the same as saying he had lived without hope. But now he had bought a house. The only difference was, it was in Puch'ŏn, not Seoul. So in this case, was the house synonymous with hope? He hadn't found an answer. *No,* he told himself repeatedly, *I'm not being driven from Seoul.* Crouched in the bed of the moving truck, watching his wife shiver in the cold, he heaved a low sigh. He felt so depressed now that he couldn't believe he had been so excited about the sales contract, pouring over it again and again. He was already nothing; he was insignificant. His mother's pitiful suggestion that he was Abraham, leading his clan across the plains to Canaan, was nothing more than a defense against a sad premonition. Abraham? He would never be Abraham. Because he couldn't escape his mother, house, daughter, or wife. Monthly installments at the bank, overdue payments, his pathetic salary and bonus, all the little debts to be paid off, the electronic toys his daughter begged for. No, he couldn't imagine leaving Seoul like Abraham, not with those chains jangling around his ankles.

How many years had he been living this life? The kind of life where you wake up asking, "What day is it?" As the nineteenth of each month passed like all the nineteenths before it, he longed only for some other day. Today the nineteenth and tomorrow the twentieth— he knew all too well what those days entailed. There had been so many mornings when he had awakened knowing it was the twentieth or the eighth—it didn't matter—he just wished it was another day. Only when he realized that today was that faraway day that had always eluded his grasp did he come to his senses and get up to shave.

But hope was everywhere. It just wasn't for him. There was one solace, though. When the nineteenth passed, a Sunday would sometimes follow and bonus day would soon draw near. There was no harm in considering the threat of falling if he could hope for something different and go after it on the off chance that he might succeed.

From Oryu-dong, the truck spent more time standing still than it did moving. The narrow two-lane highway couldn't accommodate the endless stream of traffic. When the tires' vibrations stopped, his wife woke from her fitful sleep, turned, and rolled herself into a tighter ball. And each time he pulled up her covers, he looked away for fear he might encounter her swollen face. Piled at her feet were several *ramen* boxes bound with green nylon twine tied in the shape of a cross. FRAGILE. DISHES. The warnings were scrawled in red crayon. Some boxes bore special warnings, complete with exclamation marks: EXTRA FRAGILE. GLASS! On their first few moves, his wife was near tears at the sight of the inevitable breakage; she had cried when two of the crystal glasses she had splurged on when they got married were broken. Since then, however, she had mastered the art of moving and now marked each bundle with its own special warning. Still, each time she found a new scratch on the wardrobe or dressing table she was upset and nearly shrieked in horror.

There was no end to the stories about that wardrobe. When he married her, he was immediately obliged to find a place for the ten-foot-long wardrobe she had brought with her, but it simply wouldn't fit through the door. The shabby rented room was the problem. It had no real door with one of those push-button locks, just a flimsy plywood thing only slightly larger than a trapdoor. They tried tipping the wardrobe on its side, they tried standing it on end, but nothing worked. The room didn't even have a window. For several years he had worked hard to save money for a house, but the rent on two rooms was still more than he could afford after paying off the wedding expenses. He had no choice but to leave his new bride's wardrobe in the landlord's hallway.

In their next house, they couldn't fit the whole wardrobe in one room; they put the larger section and one of the small sections in one room and the other in his mother's room. During that move, the wardrobe, still new for all intents and purposes, got a long, thick scratch across the front. Each time they moved, the cumbersome wardrobe brought nothing but complaints from annoyed movers. And wherever they went, the room turned into a long, cramped box as soon as the wardrobe was brought in. "Well, we can't let a wardrobe rule our lives," his wife said finally. Then she, too, began to scowl at the wardrobe that had been beyond her means in the first place. Still, it was thanks to her devotion that the wardrobe was in such good shape.

When she found out about this morning's damage, she was sure to let out another scream. But who knows? Maybe she had seen it already. Maybe she was too exhausted to let a chip off a wardrobe bother her. He looked at her. She was awake because of the frequent stops. And she probably couldn't sleep anymore because of the cold. It hurt to see her huddled form. "Where are we?" she asked in a thin voice from the depths of her blankets. At first it sounded like a moan, and he was startled. For a brief instant, before he heard her repeat the words, all manner of catastrophes ran through his mind. The most alarming was the image of this woman—no, his wife—giving birth in the back of a moving truck.

"We're almost there. Hang on just a little longer. It's cold, isn't it?" She stuck her mussed head out first, then struggled to sit up. The truck was slowly climbing a low hill toward the boundary where Seoul met the province. She seemed to shiver, then sneezed suddenly. "See! Sleep hunched up in the cold and you catch a chill." Lacking an alternative, he stared at her red nose.

"You could trade places with Mother if you're too cold." She shook her head. "I'm all right. We're almost there . . ." Her weary voice was drowned in another sneeze. She gathered herself and leaned against the wardrobe.

"Did you remind them to keep the boiler burning?" They had asked the real estate agent and his wife to keep the heat on in the new house, but now he felt anxious because he hadn't called to confirm this before they left.

"The rooms are nice and big, so we'll have no trouble getting the wardrobe in . . ." He searched for words to console his wife, but all he could think of was the wardrobe. "That stupid wardrobe! Who cares where we put it," she snapped. Her indifference left him speechless. They had agonized so over the wardrobe in Seoul. Did she realize there was a difference between a Seoul wardrobe and a Puch'ŏn wardrobe? Her hair tousled and her lips cracked by the wind, she smiled weakly.

"Look! There's the statue of the guardian beast. That means it's not Seoul anymore."

The truck had finally crossed the border into Kyŏnggi Province. With nothing more than the meaningless GOOD-BYE! on the back of the stone border marker, Seoul was gone. They watched in silence as the stone beast faded into the distance. A few moments later his wife murmured, almost as if she were reciting the refrain of a song. "It seems colder here. My feet are freezing."

He reached under the blanket and fumbled for her feet. His hands felt as if they were touching ice, and he began to rub. As he thawed her icy feet, he looked into his wife's face. She in turn stared into her husband's haggard face.

It seemed like her feet would never warm up, and the truck rattled on and on. "That's okay," she said, tucking her feet under her body. As he smoothed the blanket over her legs, the truck passed beneath a huge arch welcoming them to Puch'ŏn, but the furniture blocked his view. WELCOME was all he saw. GOOD-BYE! and WELCOME! The greetings made him feel lonely. Seoul had shoved them aside. It had gathered all its forces to drive them out, only to bid them a treacherous farewell. Loaded in the back of a speeding truck, they were greeted by Puch'ŏn: "Welcome!" What tricks lay hidden behind that slick hello? He gazed at the passing landscape, shivering with apprehension, or was it just the cold?

He was to blame when the truck driver got lost and they ended up in Sosa-dong. It was only at the entrance to Sosa-dong that he remembered the real estate agent telling him to find City Hall and drive straight down from there. The truck started up again and began following the signs to City Hall.

"Sosa. Isn't that where Sosa peaches come from?" His wife seemed to have recovered, relieved, no doubt, that they were almost there. "The very mention of peaches reminds me of when I was pregnant with Ŭnhye. Boy, did I eat a lot of peaches! I couldn't stand to eat anything else! Remember what you said? 'Looks like that baby's destined for a life of leisure in the Peach Blossom Paradise.' "

He smiled bitterly. Why did she have to drag up that old story at a time like this? From Canaan to the Taoist Peach Blossom Paradise. At the end of a long journey in the back of a moving truck, she had managed to discover one more ray of hope.

From City Hall, he had to give directions to the driver. As they passed the white building, imposing as all government structures are, the road narrowed abruptly and the truck driver was forced to blast his horn to alert passing pedestrians. After several minutes barreling down a quiet street lined with an awkward combination of indistinguishable spec houses and empty lots, he saw their new neighborhood unfold in the distance. Next to the residential area was an industrial complex, dark and gray, with soot pouring from its chimneys. On the hill that stretched the length of the neighborhood like a silk-screen painting were a few sparse patches of snow, fading now under the dark sky like dust.

At last the truck stopped, and he, his aging mother, young daughter, and pregnant wife finally became residents of that distant and beautiful place, Wonmi-dong. The owner of the Kangnam Real Estate Office was the first to stick his head out; then a handful of kids dashed out to surround the truck. The woman from the beauty salon paused from the permanent she was giving to open her door and look, as did the man leaving the wallpaper shop for another job. And from the third floor of the apartment house, a young man with sunken eyes watched them unload their belongings from the truck.

The Spark

HE HAD JUST LIT a cigarette when he heard the blast of the signal and the churning of wheels from one of the cavities in the dark upper reaches of the station. "The train is now arriving. All passengers please step behind the safety line." *Damn, of all the rotten luck!* He jammed his cigarette into the sand-filled ashtray on top of a garbage can and smacked his lips at the bitter aftertaste.

Moments earlier, just as he stuck his ticket in the turnstile, the signal blast had announced the arrival of another train. As he rushed down the stairs, he had stumbled and in a short, faltering instant, dropped his ticket. The stairs and the ticket were strangely similar in color, and by the time he located the ticket, the Inch'ŏn-bound train had departed. *The later it gets, the more crowded they are,* he thought. Regretfully, he watched the train glide away, its cars looking empty enough for a man to spread open a newspaper, even if he did have to stand.

But that was out of the question now. The gush of passengers onto the platform boded ill. And this, after all, was City Hall Station: It was bound to be packed with an endless stream of office workers heading home.

Perhaps he should have eaten a more substantial lunch. He was hungry and his legs hurt. That cigarette would have helped steel him for the thirty-minute battle that lay ahead, but no sooner had he lit it than the next train arrived.

The whole day had been that way. Beginning that day, he had decided he would sacrifice all else in order to find the one person who would pry open his stuttering lips. It had been a day spent in the cold, exposing his frozen body to a bitter north wind that lurked between the buildings, swooping down as he haltingly examined face after face. He had poked his head into this shop and that but was never able to approach a single person, and now his haphazard orbit continued on the subway train.

Although he was standing in a bad spot, smack in the middle of the car, constantly jostled and shoved, he was able to observe the other passengers in amazement. *All these people, you'd think in the course of a day, I'd be able to find the one I've been looking for.* Even though the train was so crowded he could hardly breathe, he felt empty and lonely. If only he had found one person, if only he had been able to sputter out the words locked inside of him.

As the train dashed through the tight web of night, its windows were etched with human figures in a contrast of dark and light more distinct than any mirror's reflection. He could see only the backs of the people in front of him, but the windows revealed their faces perfectly. From the patches of white hair on the back of his head, the man standing to his left appeared to be forty or fifty, but the face in the windows was clearly that of a youth in his twenties. The large, bright eyes and the mouth, still too young to hide his feelings, were strangely hardened. No, this fellow definitely wasn't the one he was looking for. First of all, he wasn't the right age. And so he eliminated the head to his left.

In the shadows locked in the black canvas of the window, he couldn't find a single man over forty, although one woman seemed about that age. She looked as though she was trying to conceal the fact that she was chewing gum. She didn't chew overtly, but occasionally she moved her mouth, and in unguarded moments she even emitted a small, startling *snap*. Her large pocketbook, subtle eye movements, short, well-kept permanent wave, gray coat, and bright lipstick suited the woman's plump figure and suggested dignity. But she, too, was eliminated because she gave the impression that, while a great deal of money might go into that pocketbook, none would ever come out.

Of the people in the glass, by far the most conspicuous was a fellow dozing with a manila envelope clasped to his chest. The man's shoulders slumped from time to time, distorting the composition of the glass canvas slightly, but he always came back into focus. One of his hands hung from the strap suspended from the ceiling, and the other crossed his chest, clutching the envelope. A beige coat hung carelessly over his thin frame, open in front to reveal a wrinkled wool shirt covered with lint and a shiny pair of dirty pants held up by a loose belt. The reflection off his belt buckle produced a brilliant flash in the canvas. If only he could see the face buried in the arm hanging from the strap. But the man did not reveal himself. He was leaning so far to one side that he looked as though he might collapse on the person next to him. And then, just as the composition of the canvas was about to go awry, the man righted himself and settled into another round of exhausted sleep.

Only a few months earlier he, too, had hung from a subway strap in the same weary posture, forcing his body to remain erect when it wanted only to collapse, struggling against the sleep that snuck up as he tried to catch the names of passing stations. Since losing his job, though, he rarely felt drowsy on the train. He couldn't fall into a comfortable sleep, not even for a minute. Who knows, but that sleeping man might one day lose his sweet slumber, too? *Falling is so much easier than taking flight,* he thought. To be able to sleep like that, with a manila envelope clutched to one's chest—that may be what happiness is all about.

As the sleeping man's shoulders threatened to collapse onto the passenger next to him once more, another figure appeared in the dark window. At first he didn't recognize the familiar face. Its brief appearance, with its narrow, somewhat weak forehead and scowling eyebrows, was profoundly meaningful. Whenever he, who should have hidden behind the others' wooden faces, appeared in the window, the sleeping man disappeared. The fact that the sleeping man and he, who knew the pain of insomnia all too well, couldn't appear in the same canvas was also profoundly meaningful to him.

As always, the entrance to his neighborhood was dark and cold, though it was still early. On winter nights it was difficult to guess the time. The shopkeepers got lazy about keeping their signs lit and signaled their early closure by leaving only a single fluorescent bulb on inside. When the lights of the cars on the expressway passed from sight, the wintry night in Wonmi-dong felt more desolate than ever. He looked at the smattering of lights leaking from windows here and there and shivered. After the warmth of the subway, and then the bus, slipped away, an aching cold passed through him.

The Chinese pancake wagon stood at its usual spot on the corner of the road leading to the industrial complex. A carbide light flickered under its red canvas awning. Some nights the shadow of the woman frying stuffed pancakes danced in the light until nearly midnight. She hummed hymns as she flipped the pancakes, never returning home until her batter was gone.

He had been a resident of Puch'ŏn for nearly five years now. He and his wife had agreed to start out there when they got married. At the time, the headquarters of M Foods was in Yŏngdŭngp'o, and they decided the daily commute wouldn't be too much for him. They cut costs on their wedding ceremony and with the extra money bought a thirteen-*p'yŏng* apartment in Puch'ŏn. It was a good start, and by the time M Foods moved its headquarters to a new building near Seoul Station, they had saved quite a bit.

Looking back now, he could see that his bad luck began with that new office building. His wife decided to start her own business and used their savings to open a small clothing shop in the underground arcade in downtown Puch'ŏn. She struggled along bravely for more than a year, but maintaining a well-stocked shop and keeping inventory proved too much for her. She finally gave up the business, losing the entire security deposit.

Next he was transferred to the Pup'yŏng factory because he lived nearby in Puch'ŏn. A demotion of this nature did not bode well, but he buried himself in work without another thought. Then a few months later he was fired without a word of warning. The reason was simple: the elimination of unnecessary staff in the course of structural downsizing. It all happened last spring, the worst luck in his entire life. And the bad luck had continued into the new year.

Just beyond the Chinese pancake wagon was the Wŏnmi Wallpaper Shop. During the summer, the shop's owner, Mr. Chu, and Mr. Ŏm of the Happiness Photo Studio next door dragged a low bamboo platform out front and played *go* everyday. He often sat at one corner of the platform and watched their game, partly to escape the exhausting heat and partly to evade the nervous anticipation of the future that threatened to suffocate him. The interaction of black and white stones didn't clear his head, but it helped pass the time.

His own house was on a street to the left, past Sunny Electronics, Kangnam Real Estate, and Im's Butcher Shop. Past a steel gate that always stood open and through the narrow path to the back was the kitchen door. An incandescent bulb cast a faint glow over the backyard. He called his son in a low voice. "Chinman!" The latch on the kitchen door rattled, and the door opened. His wife always kept the door locked; the darkness of the backyard frightened her.

The next morning he sat down in silence to an early breakfast. He was used to eating at dawn now. He couldn't afford to miss breakfast, if only because he knew how it would affect him as he wandered the streets later. In the old days, he never could work up an appetite for breakfast. He used to rush off to work, still groggy from a lack of sleep or a hangover, leaving his rice all but untouched. These days his wife seemed astonished by her husband's silent appetite; she remembered his lethargic movements and nauseated expression as he left for work each morning. She slipped her cold hands under the quilt covering the warm spot on the floor and gave him a troubled look. The feeling that he might never recover his indifferent eating habits—when food was nothing more than a tiring formality, when he felt as if he were chewing on rocks—was another one of the things suffocating him.

Chinman was still fast asleep, breathing regularly, as his father dressed and got ready to step outside. He smiled bitterly as he looked down at the boy's face, a face that was never free of fading scars and newly acquired scratches. He recalled his wife telling him that the boy had broken a neighbor's soy sauce jar the day before while playing Superman, a pastime that had already caused numerous complications, large and small. She had detailed the soy sauce jar incident from start to finish as soon as he got home the night before.

His wife had been sitting in their room, immersed in the piecework she sometimes took in, when she heard Chinman scream. By the time she rushed outside, it was too late. The boy had knocked over the soy sauce jar when jumping down from the low wall that separated their place from the house behind. He had tried to avoid the jar but ended up howling and screaming, with two badly scraped knees. When Sora's mom, the jar's owner, and his own mother appeared, Chinman wailed even louder, but Sora's mom was unrelenting in her anger. Last summer, when the boy jumped in her plastic tub and shattered it, she had restrained herself, but this was too much! She shrieked, rapping him on the head with her knuckles.

Fearing that she might be blamed for spoiling the child, his wife gave Chinman a thorough spanking and rushed off to the potter's shop. Her heart was still pounding with anger when she returned with a jar that she guessed to be the right size. She seemed to have salvaged her pride by blaming even this, the shabby treatment of her son over such a minor incident, on their present state of poverty.

Of course, Sora's mom protested vehemently and refused to take the jar. She waved her hands and insisted that she had cracked the boy on the head because he and Sora were such good play-mates, not because she was angry with him. Sora's mom was known as a sharp dresser, the local beauty queen. He had seen her wearing yellow shorts and sunglasses several times during the sum-mer. Her husband ran a shop called Reliable Equipment and did household repairs, but her fingernails were always beautifully mani-cured in violet nail polish. As the woman at the Brothers Super-market once snickered, Sora's mom was wasted on Wonmi-dong. No, she was wasted on Puch'ŏn!

The fashionable woman came out, in the midst of a cold-cream massage, and made a fuss, joking that Chinman's mom must really be angry if she thought she had expected her to buy a new jar. His wife couldn't help chiding herself for her own narrow-mindedness, but she set down the jar and turned to go, offering one last apology.

"I hope it's not too small. It looked about the right size."

Sora's mom gave the jar a quick once-over.

"It's a little smaller, but . . . that's all right. Still, I shouldn't be taking this."

"I know you can't judge a book by its cover, but for heaven's sake!" his wife clucked that evening. Chinman was standing on top of the desk with a scarf over his shoulders. Previously he had bro-ken his arm jumping off the slate roof of the coal shed. The child climbed up on everything so he could jump down. The front gate, the wall around the yard—all he needed was something to climb on and he would give a squirrel a run for its money. He wanted to be Superman. Black cape flapping as he flew between the city and outer space, the child was piling up endless flying hours. Of course, he had learned all this from the cartoons on television.

For Chinman, Superman was the hero of every cartoon. After a night dreaming of Supermen soaring dizzily through space, the child was even worse in the morning and spent the entire day with a scarf around his neck. Chinman believed there was no reason why he couldn't fly if only he worked at it. His father thought the boy might actually be turning into Superman, breaking an arm here, shattering a jar there, and generally causing trouble along the way. While he struggled to lift his own feet from the ground, his son just might fly into space. The boy would fly up, up, up, while he sank deeper and deeper until he was completely submerged. The thought of being weighed down by stones dangling from his body, never to rise again, made him feel as if he were suffocating.

"The little I'd saved for a rainy day went to buying that jar. We're really broke now. You've got to ask for an advance on your salary today. I can't keep buying on credit."

His wife was near tears as she followed him out the gate. Passersby scurried into the bitter cold wind of the winter morning. The clatter of shop shutters opening rang through the air. When he reached the butcher's shop, he turned to look back, and she was still there, standing by the gate. "Go back in. Chinman's all by himself." Reluctantly, she turned. There was a reason why he hadn't answered when she demanded he get an advance. An advance? Another day of rushing about, just like yesterday, spread before his eyes, and it hadn't even begun.

His first job after more than six months of idleness was not showing the slightest progress. Actually, when he thought of the game of hide-and-seek he had played with those hints of jobs, of the awkwardness of going around résumé in hand, of the pride he felt when he got his own desk again at a temporary job that lasted only one month, he didn't feel like he had been idle at all. Despite an avalanche of hardships that he had never imagined possible before losing his job, he couldn't give up hope that next year would bring him a new position. He couldn't give up hope that a job similar to the one he had grown accustomed to and shown some skill at—drafting documents, overseeing purchases, and balancing the department's monthly accounts—would come his way again, partly because he believed the irresponsible words of others.

"Wait just a little longer. We're not hiring right now, but let's see what comes up in the New Year." Worse still were the ones who said "You'll be hearing from us in a day or two. Let's go for it!" Some of them even offered to shake his hand, as if the job started right then and there. He knew that their words were nothing more than simple courtesy, but what alternative did he have? All he could do with his long white fingers, used to nothing but writing with a pen and affixing seals to documents, was record the story of his life on the résumé forms he was given.

After filling in his date and place of birth and when and where he graduated from university, all that remained were his six years in the acquisitions department of M Foods. He flinched each time he encountered the vast blank space remaining on the form. It was frightening to imagine what unknown experience he might write there next. He would always feel uneasy not knowing what he might record there in the future. Another college graduate, who had been fired from M Foods at the same time, was now working as a night watchman. Stranger still, because that type of position had the charm of permanence, few were available and competition was stiff. There was no guarantee that he wouldn't some day be writing down a similarly low-level job below his years at M Foods' acquisitions department. It was only a matter of time. Six months of unemployment were enough to make him recognize the harsh reality that he might have to take a laborer's job, carrying things on his back and soiling his white, uncallused hands, in order to make a living.

It was no coincidence that he'd seen the newspaper advertisement for an organization with the dubious name of Traditional Culture Research Association. Since his dismissal, he had been combing the want ads in practically every daily newspaper. Whenever an advertisement showed the slightest promise, he cut it out and stored it carefully in his wallet. At first he believed the colorful phrases and visited each and every firm, résumé in hand. The results were obvious. In the ads, they said they were hiring midlevel management, but what they really wanted were salesmen. Every company was the same in the beginning. For a couple of days they trained applicants in what they called orientation, insisting all the while that the job had nothing to do with sales. Orientation included a section on sales, but that was simply part of the training program for new employees, they said. After going through three or four such training sessions, naively believing the adamant assertions that they were not for door-to-door sales, he finally grasped the technique for deciphering newspaper want ads.

It was quite simple. If an ad said "Managers wanted. Guaranteed monthly salary of 300,000-plus. Apply at office," it was obvious. And if it included the proviso "Desk jobs guaranteed," they were definitely looking for salesmen. It wasn't long before he learned not to be taken in by the ads. He didn't want to be a salesman, absolutely not. He held out some hope for the applications he had submitted, and at that point he was still willing to wait. That was his final act of defiance: He was not going to be a salesman. He didn't want to imagine himself going door-to-door selling dubious natural food products or freshly patented insoles to slip into shoes. Everyone had a job to which they were specially suited, he thought. He had never believed that any job except the efficient planning of acquisitions, the prompt balancing of monthly accounts, and the preparation of the next month's budget was right for him.

And so the months passed. He had no choice but to go back to the newspaper ads, however, because during that period he had finally been reduced to selling his apartment and moving into a rented room. The money slipped away like water through a gunnysack. The dazzling image of the life he had worked so hard to achieve over the last several years lost its brilliance and was ruined in the space of a few months.

The ad for the Traditional Culture Research Association, which he could find no fault with, despite his newly acquired skills of discrimination, ran in a metropolitan newspaper. With the '86 Asian Games and '88 Olympics just around the corner, there was an acute need for systematic research dedicated to the propagation of traditional culture, the ad began in small print. In response to the needs of our time, the association was recruiting individuals interested in promoting traditional culture. Successful applicants would be invited back for interviews, and a dozen or so finalists would be given an opportunity to tour museums in various countries in Europe and the Americas. For this reason, those disqualified from overseas travel need not apply.

He passed the initial screening and interview and was included among the dozen or so finalists. The office was located on the second block of Chongno Avenue in downtown Seoul. It was on the third floor of an old building whose heating and sewage pipes were exposed on the outer walls after numerous remodels. On the first day, fifteen researchers had gathered in the office. They were all men, in their late thirties to mid-forties. While the newly hired researchers milled around the *yŏnt'an* stove, the senior researchers were next door, behind a partition, having their "monthly research meeting" under the supervision of the association's president. On the thin plywood door was a piece of paper: Quiet! Meeting in Session.

The president wore gold-rimmed glasses, but he looked much younger than the researchers. Training began with the president writing his name, Chŏng Pongnyong, on a portable chalkboard. The researchers sat in simple plastic chairs and listened earnestly to the president's lecture. Phrases like "brilliant cultural heritage" and "resurrection of national pride" came up several times, and every sentence was prefaced and punctuated with the words "in preparation for the upcoming Asian Games and Olympics." He even dropped the names of several well-known corporate presidents and vaguely suggested that the association had been founded at their urging.

"That's it for today. I'll save the gist of our training for tomorrow. If I explain too much the first day, it only confuses matters. You are present here because you passed a difficult examination and are qualified to become gifted researchers. This most definitely is *not* a commercial enterprise. We're conveying culture. You are charged with the solemn task of disseminating our brilliant cultural heritage to the general public. I ask you to carry out your task with pride. Tomorrow there will be a more detailed discussion to help you go out and enlighten the ignorant masses. Listen carefully to tomorrow's program, carry out our instructions, and I am sure you will be more than adequately compensated for joining our association."

As he sat in his plastic chair that first day, the focus of his research was whether he should quit. Despite the lofty language, this was clearly another door-to-door sales job. Except for the fact that he would be selling culture, everything else was exactly the same. The energy drained from his body. Run as he may, there seemed no escaping the trap he was in. It seemed easier just to give up and walk straight into the trap. The problem was, the choice was already out of his hands.

The next day, he attended the main training session, despite his misgivings. In the course of one day, four people had quit. Seemingly oblivious to the deserters, President Chŏng spoke with passion. It was time to overcome the general bias favoring ceramics as national cultural treasures, he began. Then he launched into a eulogy to the beauty of traditional metal crafts. Korea's metal culture had surpassed that of other countries by the Three Kingdoms period, he explained. To make a long story short, the Traditional Culture Research Association had developed several bronze imitations of cultural treasures. They were crude reproductions of candlesticks, incense burners, bottles, and miniature pagodas, with expensive price tags, capitalizing on the fame of a certain "Human Cultural Asset."

"Take pride in your work. We must drive ceramics from the display cases and replace them with our association's products. The government has promised its active support in an effort to introduce Korea's rich traditional culture on the occasion of the '86 Asian Games and '88 Olympics."

The training session didn't end there. That afternoon President Chŏng gave a detailed introduction on various strategies for successful customer relations. He also offered several techniques to earn the customer's trust through intelligent and dignified dialogue. Each product had a separate script. President Chŏng instructed them to memorize the script as a supplement to the simple explanations printed in the association's pamphlets. In conference with a customer, inept explanations of the product or any conduct unbecoming to researcher were absolutely forbidden. President Chŏng repeatedly emphasized the importance of well-honed conversational skills, for they were the only weapon with which to capture the customer.

The training session ended, and he stepped out onto the street, a researcher who wasn't really a researcher. He had finally become a salesman. The New Year had arrived, but no one had called him back. The New Year that everyone had promised would never come. He had thought of his wife, up late into the night, rubbing her eyes as she trimmed loose threads from coveralls. The work brought 500 won for a bundle of twenty, but she could work all day and finish only three or four bundles. Now that he thought about it, his work wasn't so bad. If he were to believe only half of what President Chŏng Pongnyong said, he could earn more than 200,000 won a month. His most urgent task was pulling back from the precipice.

More than 200,000 won? He jerked to a stop as he climbed the narrow, dingy staircase. The contract didn't say that they would pay him 200,000 won a month just for showing up at the office and punching the time clock. But he faithfully climbed the stairs each morning to punch in. It may have been President Chŏng's secret conceit, his desire to control his subordinates, that forced them to punch a time clock, but as a subordinate who had already spent several years punching in, he, too, needed a time clock.

On the sofa reserved for guests sat several haggard-looking middle-aged recruits, waiting for the president to arrive. They must have hoped for something, coming to the office so early. In another corner were four or five others leafing through order cards for items to be delivered that day. The researchers were responsible for over-seeing the whole process, from the signing of sales contracts to de-liveries. There were bill collectors whose sole responsibility was collecting monthly payments. Payment in hard cash brought the highest commission to the researchers, but it was hard enough mak-ing sales on the installment plan. Some researchers sold even the least expensive 20,000-won items on ten-month installments. Of course, he hadn't. He hadn't succeeded making even a 20,000-won sale. Among the researchers who had participated in the same ori-entation session was a man who had already handed in seventeen order cards. Not seven, but seventeen! He felt as if he were witness-ing the work of Superman. A Superman who flew from building to building, snapping up customers with nothing more than a three-inch tongue.

He grabbed several brightly colored pamphlets and slipped out of the building. Run into the president and you spent at least two or three hours in his office getting supplementary training. "How do you do? I would like to introduce a new service being offered by the Traditional Culture Research Association. As a researcher, it is my responsibility to point out a few problems facing us today." He'd had enough of the president's training sessions. The diffi-culty was developing the gift of gab needed to carry out a consulta-tion that flowed smooth as water. Not everyone had that skill. He hadn't managed to pull all those words out of his throat even once.

"It won't be easy at first. The words won't come. Yes, it's true. No matter how many times you tell people you are trying to pro-mote traditional culture, they'll treat you like some kind of snake-oil salesman, and that can glue any beginner's lips shut. At best, you may go to someone you know, but most of the time you come away without explaining a thing, much less asking them to buy something. To researchers experiencing this problem, I always offer this advice: Clear a blocked drain and the water runs clean.

That's the key. You have to unclog those lips. Just once, for practice, say what you have to say. Your worries will drain away, leaving you fresh, and from that moment on, you'll feel the courage rise within you. Just once. The first time's the hardest. You must choose the person you practice on very carefully. Forget for a moment that you're trying to sell anything. Just talk, following the script that I've given you. Then success will be yours. It's only a matter of time."

His lips had been glued shut for nearly two weeks, just as the president had said. At first, he made up a list of friends and acquaintances with the idea of selling to them. Visiting M Foods was out of the question, but he spurred himself on by recalling that he was in no position to be choosy. Rolling the phrases around in his mouth, gathering up the confidence that, if possible, he would sell one of the more expensive items, he headed toward his first customer, an old high school classmate. They were quite close, so he would have no trouble bringing it up, he thought.

"Hey, how've you been? Have you had lunch yet? Oh, you have? Gee, I'm sorry. I've got an appointment. I've got to go out. Hey, you're looking good. You son of a gun, you're a lot better off than I am. You wouldn't believe the stress I'm under lately. Oh, look at the time! I've got to run. I'm really sorry. Drop by again, you hear? Promise? I'll buy you lunch."

Firing away like a machine gun, his friend rushed off to attend to his business, exiting before the curtain even went up. There was no point reciting his pitch to the man's back. Next he went to visit a friend who was a year or two behind him in college. They had belonged to the same school club.

"You know Hŏ Sulman, that old fellow who was designated a Human Cultural Asset? This is his work, but people say it's even better than the originals."

"Really? There are a lot of incredible reproductions these days, but these look kind of corny. Hey! Don't you have anything better to do? How'd you end up like this?"

The friend made it clear he had no intention of becoming a customer.

He visited several others, but the results were always the same. He blabbered on about something else and never got around to his sales pitch. He couldn't even spit it out with a friend who, judging from his personality, clearly would have bought something if he just said the word. He watched and waited for a chance to speak, but always turned away in the end. His friend expressed concern about his unemployment and repeatedly offered to look into a job for him, but he refused, explaining that he still had enough to get by on. In fact, he ended up consoling the friend. Friendship, which only took a few words to cement, was always in great abundance. It was even more difficult bringing up his sales pitch with people who didn't know that he had been fired. They looked at him searchingly when he suddenly appeared after such a long period of silence.

"Old buddies come to see me all the time these days. It's such a headache when they insist on selling me stuff I don't need. Things must be getting pretty tough if people have to resort to door-to-door sales. We are lucky, aren't we? At least we've got a regular salary."

What could he say? "A regular salary?" He chuckled hollowly and said his goodbyes, pretending that he had just dropped by to say hello.

From the very beginning, he recognized the need for a customer on whom he could practice his sales pitch, as President Chŏng had suggested. According to the other researchers, the products were a cinch to sell. Compared to some newer products that didn't attract consumers, theirs were targeted at the upper income bracket and therefore easier to market. With luck, you could snag an order for 1 million won or more from apartment-dwelling housewives concerned with interior design. Whenever he heard people say such things, he got nervous all over again. Once he got his sales pitch down, there was no reason why he couldn't fill out order cards, too. If only he could learn to speak so convincingly that customers couldn't resist buying from him. That was the main reason why he hadn't given up his job at the Traditional Culture Research Association. Every time he passed an apartment complex packed with row after row of tall buildings, he paused. The belief that all those women would be his customers, once he got his sales pitch down, kept him going.

The struggle to open his mouth continued through the day. If there was any difference from yesterday, it was that he was no longer aimlessly wandering the streets in search of someone. He spent the morning poking around Paradise Shopping Center and the afternoon at East Gate Market. He was on the verge of getting started dozens of times, but he always gave up. At a dry goods shop, he actually put down his envelope and swallowed, ready to let it fly. If only the shopkeeper hadn't kept asking him what he wanted. But that was it. His mouth wouldn't open.

He pulled his tired body together and set out for home. He was quitting early because he didn't want to get on a crowded subway after wandering the whole day without making any money, like yesterday. East Gate station was quiet. He finally got a seat with warm air flowing from the heater beneath it and stretched out. A man selling what he claimed were the finest quality stainless steel scissors and knives for only 1,000 won appeared at Chongno Fifth Block station. The man set his black plastic bag down on the floor and launched into his pitch.

"I am very sorry to bother you on this crowded subway. Please allow me a moment to briefly introduce the fine 100 percent stainless steel scissors and hiking knife, with sheath, put out by the Hanjin Trading Company. These two items cannot be compared to the blunt and rust-prone products now on the market. I could sing their praises all day, but just one demonstration will show what fine products they are. Look! The blade cuts at the slightest touch. You must keep these products out of the hands of children. Just one touch and it cuts and slices. As you all know, it is impossible to find a pair of scissors for less than one-thousand won. However, during this promotional period, we are offering these scissors *and* this knife for just one-thousand won. Yes, just one-thousand won. Be careful to keep these products out of the hands of children. They are made of deluxe stainless steel and cut at the slightest touch. Here! Take a look. If you like them, you can have them both for just one-thousand won."

The man laid packets of scissors and knives on the knees of the passengers, all the while slicing white paper to bits. Several people handed him 1,000-won bills, and the man quickly retrieved the unsold packets and headed for the next car. He watched the salesman in breathless awe, taking in every word of his elegant patter and lightning-fast movements.

That evening, he sat on the warm spot in their room and smoked several cigarettes in silence. Meanwhile, his wife spanked their son for jumping off the top of the refrigerator. The boy had no trouble climbing up there, using the wardrobe drawer as a stepping stone.

"Daddy, I saw the baby at Ŭnhye's house today. The baby—it was cute."

The sulking child crawled into his lap. "Who's Ŭnhye?" he asked, looking around at his wife.

"The little girl who moved into the apartments about a month ago. Her mom was as big as a house when they moved in. They had another girl. You know how Chinman plays on the apartment stairs. All he does is try to fly. And you know what? He jumped from the third-floor stairs to the second."

The boy was thrilled with the opportunity to describe his self-taught flying technique. "You raise your arms up high, yell like Superman, then lean back and jump," he explained with elaborate movements of the arms and legs. "You try it, Dad. You can fly! Fly through the sky! Try it, Dad!"

"It's getting to be a real problem. What if he breaks his arm again? We don't have any money. And we don't have medical insurance anymore. I'm thinking of locking him inside tomorrow."

His wife glared at the child. The boy scowled in return and hid behind his father. "No!" he cried, "Superman doesn't stay inside!"

"Ŭnhye stays inside all day long and her skin's so white and clean. Look at Chinman! He looks like a beggar child."

Suddenly his wife clamped her mouth shut. He glanced around at the sudden silence and saw her lips screwing up. Then a single tear rolled down her cheek. "Now what's wrong?" he demanded brusquely.

"We're no better than beggars ourselves. We've run up bills everywhere, at the rice shop and the store on the corner. And I've already borrowed more than thirty thousand won from the woman at the real estate office. I promised to pay her back now that you've got a job, but I don't think she believes me anymore."

Once she got started, the complaints went on for nearly an hour. He was lucky, she said, because he was never home. How about collecting their key money and starting a small restaurant or something? She had heard that the greasy spoon in front of the industrial complex brought in more than a million won a month. The company where Ŭnhye's father worked gave out more than 600 percent in annual bonuses. She envied Ŭnhye's mom. She couldn't remember ever living like that. He had to come up with some money to pay off the electricity and water bills, Chinman's shoes were falling apart, and on and on. . . .

He hit the streets again. It was no different from yesterday or the day before. His determination to open his mouth was nothing new, just as his wife's tears the night before were nothing new.

The weather was cold and the roads were slippery. He wandered from place to place, sometimes staring at the white steam drifting from his mouth, sometimes kicking the ice that lingered in the shadows. When he discovered a pharmacist in a white gown, standing at his counter with nothing to do, he stopped. He could ask for a bottle of tonic and explain traditional culture. He reached out to the glass door tentatively, but at that very moment, someone walked up briskly and shoved through the door ahead of him. The patient and pharmacist consulted in whispers, heads drawn close together. He couldn't interrupt.

He wasn't discouraged, though, and started walking again. He passed a bookstore, a hamburger shop, and a shoe store, then discovered another likely shop. It was a jewelry store that sold watches and gems. A large bronze bird, wings poised for flight, was perched in the display window. Now he had an opening line. He took a deep breath. The shop was empty, except for a clerk in a white shirt looking out into the street. A heater burned bright red; on top of it was a boiling kettle.

He glanced once more at the gems in the immaculate display window, then stepped inside.

"Hello. Welcome to our shop."

"Errr . . ."

"Yes, are you looking for anything in particular?"

"Well, actually . . . I have something to tell you."

"Yes?"

"I see you like bronze sculptures."

He pointed to the bird in the display window. The clerk frowned. Confident with the smooth delivery of his first line, he stepped closer. The telephone rang just at that moment. He waited in silence. The clerk answered the telephone and looked across the counter at him without bothering to mask his suspicion. The call was long, and during it, the clerk seemed to place him. Before he could open his mouth again, the man cut him off.

"You're obviously trying to sell something. Come back some other time. We don't need anything right now."

"No, it's not that. I'm a researcher promoting traditional culture. As you'll see from this—"

As he reached in his envelope to take out a pamphlet, the clerk stepped out from behind the counter and cut him off. "What do you think you're doing? We haven't made a single sale this morning. Please leave. Come back another time." He turned and left before the man pushed him. *I don't want to stay out on the streets any longer,* he thought. His frustration was unexpectedly profound. The courage that had kept him going seemed to melt in a single instant. He came to a bus stop and jumped on the first passing bus. Fortunately, there was an empty seat. That first line had gone really well. He closed his eyes and tried to console himself. If someone would just listen to him, if someone would just keep still for a few minutes, for his sake. He chewed on his lip as the bus bounced along. The speech he had prepared seemed to rise up inside his throat.

"Ceramics are out of fashion now. Look at this intricate craftsmanship, the subtle luster of the metal, the dignified shape. Everything by Hŏ Sulman, even the smallest piece, goes for at least one hundred or two hundred thousand won, but he's given these works to us at a special price in order to propagate Korea's traditional culture. Just look at this incense burner. It's from the thirteenth century, the reign of the Koryŏ king Ch'ungnyŏl. It's truly magnificent. Silver-plated! The original is National Treasure number 214, and this one looks just like it. See how the dragon and phoenix are positioned. Aren't they lovely? Put something like this in your living room and the atmosphere of your home will be transformed. Ceramics are no comparison." He mumbled the script to himself as the bus sped along. It was perfect, as long as he didn't say the words out loud.

"This is a gilt-bronze pagoda, National Treasure number 213. The original stands one meter, fifty-five centimeters, but we've scaled it down to fit in your living room. This one was made by Hŏ Sulman, too. In this one pagoda you find the architecture of the entire tenth century. Look at this refined Buddhist figure, the stairs, and the door. Doesn't it make you feel like you're seeing the real thing?" He was reciting the script for the bronze pagoda to himself when someone asked him something. "Excuse me, does this bus go to Kangnam Bus Terminal?" A pallid young woman with long hair was looking at him. Until he heard an old man's voice say, "Yes, it does," from the seat behind him, he didn't know where this bus was going.

He followed the young woman off the bus at the express bus terminal. She paused for a moment, as if she wasn't sure where she was going, then started to walk in the direction of the waiting room for buses bound for the Honam region. Since he, too, was not sure where he wanted to go, he decided to follow her. Besides, there were sure to be plenty of people in the waiting room.

The waiting room was even more crowded than he had expected. The public address system whined, the ticket collectors shouted, and on top of that, a television was playing a kung fu movie in the middle of the hall. The waiting crowd marveled at the long, glistening knives, the loud cries, and the warriors' lightning-fast swordplay.

The area around the snack booth by the entrance was quiet by comparison. There were even a few empty chairs, and he sat down in one of them, facing the entrance. The wind blowing through the open door was cold but not unbearable.

He was relieved to find an empty chair. Now all he needed was someone to sit down in the chair beside him. And if that person had just twenty minutes to spare, he would be even more relieved. Who should it be? He carefully scrutinized the people around him. The red necktie on a young man chewing gum was the first thing to catch his eye. Several high-school girls were giggling together, and an old woman with a rabbit stole wrapped around her neck sat nearby. The girls laughed merrily, sharing a secret. The old woman kept checking the ticket in her hand and looking around nervously, as if she were waiting for someone. *Not what I'm looking for,* he thought, shaking his head. They weren't quite right. They were definitely not the type who would simply listen to his pitch, to be his practice partner, nothing more.

And then, a man flopped down in the chair next to him and let out a long sigh. Pulled down over his ears was a brown fur cap that didn't match his navy-blue work clothes. No sooner had he sat down than he began rustling through his pockets for something, then he looked up and asked for a light. The cigarette looked so thin and white in his thick, rough hand. On second glance, he realized the man was a porter who carried baggage from the platform to the bus stop outside. Printed in large letters on the back of his jacket, plain as day, was the name of the company he worked for. The fact that the man was nothing more than a porter did not disappoint him. In fact, now that he thought about it, this man would make an ideal practice partner. Suddenly he felt nervous. The man heaved another long sigh and rubbed his hands down his chest.

"I hurried through lunch because I was late. Maybe that's why I'm so short of breath. Thanks. It's cold here. Why don't you go sit in there?"

The man pointed toward the center of the waiting room. He looked about fifty, though he may have been much younger. It was hard to guess his age because the fur cap covered his head. He studied the porter carefully. The man burped several times, perhaps because of his late lunch, and smiled sheepishly when their eyes met. This could be the one. He drew closer and, in a trembling voice, asked the man if he was busy.

"Busy? No, not really. I mean, I have to take a break some time, right?"

"Well then, could you give me a bit of your time? It won't take long. All you have to do is listen."

He was afraid the man might say no.

"Listen to what? Go ahead. Try me."

The man urged him on. At last! The instant it took him to reach into the envelope for a pamphlet seemed like an eternity. He moistened his dry lips and began to recite the first line of his script. The words that until then had only rattled inside his own mouth burst out one by one. The man had an excellent attitude. He listened seriously, nodding now and then. Sometimes he even asked questions. It wasn't difficult to respond to his questions in a manner that the customer could easily understand.

The words poured forth in a torrent. President Chŏng Pongnyong was right. As difficult as it was to begin, once you got started, the words streamed out on their own, forming a river that flowed proudly. Sweat began to gather in his clenched fist. He had long since ceased to feel the cold. When he reached the part where he described old Hŏ Sulman's magnificent skills, his chest felt like it would burst with the radiant sensation that his words were floating like butterflies.

The practice session ended. He hadn't skipped a single line. Slipping the pamphlet back into the envelope, he wiped the perspiration from his brow. The man pulled his cap down over his ears and prepared to get up.

"Thank you for listening to my boring speech. I really appreciate it."

He offered the man a cigarette. The man waved his hand and protested loudly. "What do you mean? I feel sorry for putting you through that whole speech without buying anything. Well, good luck. I hope you sell a lot."

The man headed toward the entrance. The practice session was finished. He looked around, dazed, as if he had just awakened from a dream. The kung fu movie hadn't ended, and the gates leading to the buses were still crowded. He hadn't yet escaped the feeling that something was missing, when someone sat down beside him. He turned to see the porter again.

"I thought about it on my way out, and I just didn't feel right. I'll take one of those candlesticks or whatever you call them. They're just the thing for our family ancestral rites. I can't afford anything too expensive, and they're the cheapest thing you got—just right for my budget. I may not look like much, but I am the eldest grandson of the Kwon clan, so I hold ancestral rites every three days."

He was speechless. Here was a customer who had just ordered a candlestick to place on the table used for ancestral rites every three days. The words that had flowed so freely just moments before disappeared without a trace, and now, the porter began reciting his own speech.

"I may carry baggage for a living, but I've always treated my ancestors with respect. After I lost all the farmland left to me, I came to Seoul to give my children a proper education if nothing else, and look at what I'm going through! I used to be a big man in our village. Born to a rich family, I threw my weight around. But now, I'm ashamed to say I'm fifty and I don't even own my own house! I've tried everything, just to earn a bit more money. The kids keep growing and I don't have any property. You know, everyone in the village used to know my full name, but here in Seoul, I'm just Kwon, the porter."

Kwon's speech was long, but he listened to him carefully and nodded with enthusiasm, as the porter had done for him. The crowds came and went, and the porter's story continued over the sound of a nasal female voice asking so-and-so's mother from Kimje to come to the public address booth as soon as possible.

The Last Land

FOR NEARLY TEN DAYS the wind blew relentlessly. The spring cold snap had arrived. Pedestrians scowled at the plastic bags and candy wrappers that littered neighborhood streets. Garbagemen collected the rubbish and burned it in the vacant lot, producing black smoke that rode the wind and ashes thinner than rice paper that fluttered through the air like swarms of moths.

Once the garbagemen had lit the fires and left, it was the children's turn. Sangsu, eldest son of the wallpaper shop people, Kyŏngok, youngest daughter of Kim who pushed a garbage cart, and that little rascal Chinman swarmed out to throw stones in the fires and toss cinders into piles of dry grass. The children of Wonmi-dong never had learned to play quietly at home. They dashed outside each morning as soon as they opened their eyes, and played until dark, filling the streets with the sounds of their rollicking and crying. So you could hardly expect them to remain calm when presented with the thrill of playing with fire. Their faces soon were black with soot. Occasionally a child would singe a hand and burst out crying, at which point Mr. Chu from the Wonmi Wallpaper Shop appeared. Originally, Chu had made his living as a plasterer in Pusan, but somehow he had ended up in Puch'ŏn's Wonmi-dong, right next to the empty lot. One spark on the spring wind and his wallpaper shop would go up in smoke, so when Chu dashed out to scold the children, they skittered away in an instant. Invariably one of the smaller kids, like three-year-old Mi, youngest daughter of the Happiness Photo Studio, would trip and lose a shoe and start wailing breathlessly. Mr. Ŏm, the proprietor of the photo studio, had three daughters and proclaimed himself a happy man. It had been his own idea to name the girls Chi, for wisdom, Sŏn, for goodness, and Mi, for beauty.

After stamping out the fires, Chu returned to his shop, and then one final character made his appearance: Kang Mansŏng. Everyone in the twenty-third precinct knew Old Kang. Actually, he was better known as the local landlord, and if you weren't aware of the uproar that occurred in his field every summer and winter, you didn't deserve to be called a resident of Wonmi-dong. Old Kang, nearly six feet tall and sturdily built, always dressed like a farmhand. His unusually large nose seemed to take up half his face; it was lumpy and red as a strawberry and somehow suited his ruddy complexion. From his vigorous stride and bulging forearms, which were always exposed beneath his rolled sleeves, it was hard to believe he was nearly seventy. His voice was hearty as well, and when Old Kang paused from his work and bellowed "Yongmun!" his youngest son came running from their back-facing two-story house across the street, some one hundred yards away.

According to the woman from Kohŭng—wife and business partner of Mr. Pak, who owned the Kangnam Real Estate Office—the old man was so terribly strict with Yongmun that not once to this day had she seen him exchange a kind word with the boy. By "not once to this day" she meant in the history of the twenty-third precinct, for Kangnam Real Estate had been there longer than anyone, except Old Kang, of course. Pak and his wife had contributed brilliantly to the recent skyrocketing of Wonmi-dong's real estate prices. If Pak was to be believed, he had once been a big shot in real estate circles back in Seoul's Kaep'o-dong and this side of the Kangnam district, but he had lost all his property in a certain scandal, which he was not at liberty to discuss. Pak left Seoul after that and moved, empty-handed, to Puch'ŏn to become a small-time land broker. He called himself small-time, but no one would dispute the fact that Pak had accumulated a considerable fortune in Wonmi-dong.

The empty lot where the garbagemen burned rubbish had belonged to Old Kang before he sold it under a contract drawn up by Kangnam Real Estate. Four two-story shops had already been built on the land, but the new owner had left the section closest to the road vacant for now. A building would go up in the next few months. Old Kang still had three strips of more than one hundred *p'yŏng* each to the left of the fire road. He leased one to the lumberyard; it was filled with piles of cement, sand, and the like. On the rest of the land, Old Kang grew vegetables with his son every year. It didn't bring in much income, but it was a tidy plot that produced enough for family consumption.

Old Kang had come out to the empty lot, now covered with nothing but ashes, because of that plot of land. Whenever he saw something—anything—that looked like it might make good fertilizer, he swept it into a dirty old sack and took it to his garden. Two of his sons were already married and living on their own, but neither chipped in to support his father. The old man lived off the rent he collected from the lumberyard and from the people who rented the second floor of his house. His land may have been worth several hundred million won on the current market, but he was a poor landowner, barely covering expenses, as long as he planted red peppers on the property. The trouble was, Old Kang persisted in growing vegetables on that expensive piece of land. Over the past few years, several investors had inquired about the land, but they were no match for the old man's pigheadedness, and so he continued farming on either side of the two-lane road leading to City Hall. Spring had come again this year, and Old Kang reappeared in his field wearing the same tattered clothes and black rubber shoes on bare feet.

It was hard work driving a hoe into earth that had been frozen all winter, and removing every one of the burnt-out *yŏnt'an* briquettes embedded in the field like stones meant it took a long time to turn over just a row or two. Yongmun had spent the last month removing *yŏnt'an* from the field and said the land was practically cleared. "Seoul bastards," Old Kang muttered as he took a pack of Hansando from his pocket. The wind was strong; it looked like he would have to use the spindle tree planted in front of the Rose of Sharon apartments as a windbreak to get his cigarette lit. He threw down his hoe and was walking to the edge of the field when Mr. Pak from the real estate office came out and greeted him.

It pained Old Kang no end to see Pak, a small man with black-rimmed glasses and slicked-back hair. Whenever they met on the street, Pak hinted that Kang should sell his land, and last winter the realtor started visiting him at home, trying to sweet-talk him into selling. He said the buyer would construct a pair of buildings on either side of the street. Puch'ŏn's newest landmark, he said. The whole neighborhood would brighten up thanks to the luxurious recreational facilities in the buildings. The plan for the buildings—on the first floor, shops, on the second, a sauna, the third, a health club, and the fourth and fifth floors rented out as offices—didn't appeal to Old Kang in the first place, but since he had no intention of selling the land, he could hardly criticize the investor for counting his chickens before they hatched.

"I hear that businessman Mr. Yu is looking at land over in Shimgok-dong. You know, I've worked so hard for you and our community, and now . . ." Pak gave him a disappointed look; then the woman from Kohŭng, who had followed Pak out to the field, took up where he had left off.

"It's true. My husband has been working on this since last winter. We get by well enough brokering rented rooms, but we're trying to clean up the neighborhood and make it a better place to live."

Old Kang didn't say anything one way or another. "It's not too late," Pak continued. "Please reconsider. It won't be easy getting more than one million won a *p'yŏng* if you keep stinking up the neighborhood with that manure every summer. And prices simply can't go up much more. I mean it. Haven't you heard? The newspapers and TV all say there's a good chance the North Koreans will attack before the Olympics in '88. Things just aren't selling these days, not even the cheaper houses that go for twenty or thirty million."

"Old Kang, you've got to stop being so greedy. Sell while you can get a decent price. Don't you understand? The price isn't going to go any higher, no matter how long you wait. Besides, your wife is dying to sell."

The Kohŭng woman just had to drag his wife into it. Old Kang snuffed out his half-smoked cigarette, carefully slipped the butt into his pocket for safekeeping, and returned to his work without a word.

"I think Mr. Yu is still interested in your land," Pak called after him. "I'll try to get a price that suits you, but you have to make a decision first!"

Old Kang had repeatedly expressed his unwillingness to sell, whatever the price, but Pak didn't let up. Stupid Seoulites, the old man sputtered as the couple returned to their office. He knew they were from the Chŏlla region originally, but to Old Kang, everyone in Wonmi-dong was a lousy Seoulite.

They were all such ill-mannered boors, waving their hands in horror at the smell of a little compost in the fields. Kang brushed the dirt off the handle of his hoe and set to clearing the field again. When he thought of the Seoulites' fiendish habit of piling used *yŏnt'an* on soil that was just trying to get a winter breather, he detested them all the more. The Seoulites he knew were all like that. Over the past few years, he hadn't been able to use all the fertilizer he had collected so painstakingly, the urine he liked to sprinkle on the red pepper field and the nicely fermented night soil he used on the winter kimchi cabbages before hoeing in the summer. It was all because the Seoulites made such a fuss. And as a result, the harvest from the dry and lackluster land had been poor for the last several years.

What's more, each winter the field turned into a garbage dump. He had Yongmun keep an eye on the land over the winter months, and sometimes he went out himself to see who was dumping used *yŏnt'an* at night, but it was useless. This spring he spent his own money for a truck to cart off the discarded *yŏnt'an*. With all the two-story shop-apartments, apartment buildings, and multifamily houses lining the streets of the neighborhood, most buildings housed more than four families. The garbage truck came daily, carting off trash one day and used *yŏnt'an* the next, but there were always more *yŏnt'an* to be disposed of, and people dumped them in the most convenient place they could find. Convenience he could understand, but Old Kang figured plenty of folks threw their *yŏnt'an* into his field out of spite because they hated the way it reeked of night soil all summer.

The fact was, living through the hot summer months with the smell of manure right under your nose, night and day, wind or no wind, was miserable. And Old Kang was a glutton for manure. He kept a pile by the edge of the field at all times and tended it lovingly whenever he had a chance. Folks couldn't live with their windows shut, and they could hardly think of the stench as perfume. What's more, the smell attracted all kinds of pesky bugs; the mosquitoes from Kang's field were especially ferocious. Behind the field was a three-story apartment building with a long row of balconies facing the field; in front was the new road leading to City Hall, with the photo studio, electronics shop, beauty salon, tearoom, and chicken restaurant on either side; and smack in the middle, completely out of place, was Old Kang's field. There was no denying it looked out of place.

Old Kang didn't care if what the neighbors called that shit smell was on the agenda at every monthly neighborhood meeting; he just twitched his big nose and kept working, pulling weeds, thinning vegetables, and training vines, silently and with loving devotion. He didn't bat an eyelash when they marched to his field in protest. And come winter, he suffered their revenge in the form of the discarded *yŏnt'an*. Now it was time to get to work again: He would prepare the soil today, and tomorrow he would spread the night soil and compost he had collected. Old Kang hadn't forgotten the threats made by the residents of the eighth subprecinct. Last year they had filed a petition saying they wouldn't tolerate another year of the manure, but he wasn't the least inclined to forgo the next day's task. Whether he was carting manure from the pigsty or simply spreading compost at plowing time, the stupid Seoulites got worked up and insisted that they could smell what they called shit.

Yongmun must have been tired after hauling away all those *yŏnt'an* last week, because he couldn't get out of bed today. The boy had always been puny, lacking the physique for tilling the earth. He didn't like studying, either, and hadn't gone to university, so his father was frustrated and concerned that Yongmun might never make a living for himself. Old Kang had four other children—a daughter and three sons—all even more hopeless than Yongmun. Old Kang had long since forsaken his eldest son, Yong-gyu. After graduating from college, the boy had dabbled in a variety of enterprises, dragging Kang's second son, Yongmin, in on every one, but nothing came of any of their schemes. Old Kang once harbored great hopes for his third son Yongch'ŏl, an excellent student, but the boy got involved in the student movement—demos or whatever they're called—was expelled from school, and ended up in the military last year. Of his four sons, Yongmun, the youngest, who loathed studying, was the best behaved, treating his father with respect and doing as he was told.

So much for his sons. And what about his daughter, Hŭija, who lived in Seoul? Her husband Ch'oe was the one who had sown the seed of deep mistrust for Seoulites in Old Kang. That miserable wench Hŭija was a lost cause from the moment she graduated from high school and insisted on getting a job in Seoul, instead of keeping house and thinking about marriage. If you could call that a job, of course. She was a clerk in the accounting department of a glove factory in Seoul's Ch'ŏnggyech'ŏn. Some factory: It was really a house with a few sewing machines and four or five workers stitching up gloves. Less than a year had passed before Hŭija and the president of the glove factory fell for each other. When Old Kang found out that they had moved in together, he pushed them to get married, only to discover that his new son-in-law was an out-and-out crook.

It was the early 1970s, when Puch'ŏn had been upgraded from county to city status, and Old Kang was forced to sell off plots of land that had been rezoned during the transition. His son-in-law wheedled some money from the sale, insisting that he was on to a sure thing, but nothing came of it. The glove factory remained much the same size, and Ch'oe developed a taste for gambling, then women. That miserable Hŭija, mother of two by then, tormented her parents by wailing about her adulterous husband day in and day out. Then five years ago, when Old Kang sold off some more land, Ch'oe appeared again, this time begging for 30 million won. Who knows how he had gotten wind of the sale? Later, Hŭija came knocking on her father's door herself, crying for a 30-million-won loan so she could make a new man out of her husband. In the end, Old Kang gave her the money, but he made her sign a loan agreement promising to pay two percent in monthly interest. He felt sorry for his daughter. She was the only child of his first marriage to a woman who had died when Hŭija was still small. He had no way of knowing if Hŭija and her husband used the money to good purpose, but his present wife went to Seoul each month and wrung the interest out of them. Recently they had been quite prompt in their payments, but in the beginning, they kept him waiting each month, and Old Kang had to endure his wife's nagging every time the interest was due.

The task of spreading animal manure and night soil on the carefully tilled field was carried out on schedule. Yongmun was still recuperating in bed, so Old Kang and his wife set to work at the crack of dawn and finished by lunch. His wife may have grumbled, but she had no choice but to help, and after working in the wind all morning, the two returned home exhausted. They had just changed out of their smelly clothes and were about to lie down on the floor, still warm from the morning firing, when someone began ringing the bell at the front gate. No sooner had they returned from the field than the first of their troubles began. His wife reluctantly went out to see who it was, then returned, lay down with her back to him, pulled the covers over her head, and snarled.

"You go. It's that woman. You deal with her. I want nothing to do with it."

At the gate stood a woman in a belligerent pose, holding the hand of a girl who looked to be about seven. As Old Kang stalked from the house, the girl lifted her still-moist eyes and stared at him in undisguised curiosity.

"How dare you do such a thing, right here in the middle of the city!"

Recognizing the woman's shrill voice and tinted hair, Old Kang hawked up a wad of phlegm and spat into the corner of the yard. It was Chŏngmi's mother, the one who hung around with that trendy woman, Sora's mom, imitating everything she did with earnest zeal. Chŏngmi's mom was the one who had stirred up the neighborhood last year; she lived on the first floor of the Hyŏndae Apartments. With the field right under her nose, she was more exasperated with Old Kang than the others, and she wasn't the sort of woman to put up with something offensive to her. It seems her husband was an assistant manager at an insurance company, and she drove her own maroon Pony. On several occasions, Old Kang had seen her sitting at the steering wheel with sunglasses perched on her nose. In other words, Chŏngmi's mom was a self-described "Seoul woman" whose eyes, behind those sunglasses, plainly indicated that she was sick and tired of living in a filthy burgh like Wonmi-dong.

"Look at this child! I dress her in new clothes, and she comes home covered in shit. What is this neighborhood coming to?"

Only then did Old Kang take a close look at the girl. Unlike the kids who hung around in the streets, she was a neat-looking child he had seen occasionally among the class of children that restricted their play to the front of the apartments. She wore a dress with lacy frills and a bright flowered ribbon as cute as a butterfly, but her white socks and red shoes were covered with lumps of what was clearly manure.

"What did you go in there for? Why'd I even bother putting up a fence?"

"What was she supposed to do? Their ball bounced over the fence. How many times have we told you? You're old enough to understand. Do you think the problem will just go away if you're stubborn enough? If you must farm there, use chemical fertilizer. Why do you insist on the old-fashioned—"

"Yongmun!" The old man bellowed suddenly, and the woman's mouth snapped shut before she had a chance to finish. Even the child flinched at his booming voice. "What's the point of tilling the land and planting seeds if you're going to kill the soil with chemicals?" he muttered, oblivious to the woman. He turned away, as if their business were finished. Old Kang didn't even like the idea of using pesticides unless the field was teeming with insects, so there was no way he would use chemical fertilizers that reportedly ruined the soil.

"Go into that field of shit one more time and I'm throwing you out of the house. Do you hear me?"

Chŏngmi's mom cracked the hapless child on the head and turned to go, still angry.

"I told you. I told you we'd have trouble from the very beginning this year. You should have left the field fallow. Or sold it!" His wife had been hiding behind the hall door, but now she began to nag. "I don't have a friend in the neighborhood. They treat me like some kind of pariah, and it's all because of that damn field. Why are you so greedy about land?"

"Shut up, woman! What's all this talk? You should be getting my lunch," Old Kang shouted, but the nagging continued long after he had gone inside. What harm was there in selling the land to help their children? Other people doted on their youngest, but that old coot Kang made Yongmun work in the fields, ruining the poor boy's prospects. He thought nothing of giving money to his daughter, but he wouldn't part with a scrap of land for his sons. Humph! Farming in the middle of the city just didn't make sense. And who used night soil on their land in this day and age? Dumber than an ox, he was. Didn't he realize how much a *p'yŏng* of that land was worth? Sowing pepper and cabbage seeds and fertilizing it with manure. . . .

A *p'yŏng* of that land. Even his wife hadn't imagined the price jumping this high.

It was true: A virgin bride, she had come to the widower and his baby daughter because she was impressed with his prospects as a young landowner with plenty of property. She was born and raised in Inch'ŏn. Her father was a produce broker at the city market who had come to know Kang Mansŏng as a diligent farmer. Kang was young, already possessed quite a bit of land, and most importantly, was hard working, so her father offered his daughter's hand in marriage.

It wasn't that Old Kang had inherited much land. He and his dead wife, Hŭija's mother, had accumulated it through hard work, adding to the small plot his forebears had farmed for generations. Hŭija's mother wasn't very strong to begin with, and she finally died from the work, leaving a small daughter behind. His present wife had endured her share of hardships building their land holdings, but Old Kang firmly believed that she did not compare to his first wife.

Apparently the neighbors gossiped about Old Kang being a rich man because he owned three houses and several pieces of land, but his present holdings were nothing compared to what he had once owned. The first few years had been difficult, but by the age of thirty-nine, after the birth of his second child, Yonggyu, he could see that land bought more land. At the time, land was worthless, and Kang bought every piece he could get his hands on until he owned nearly everything from the foot of Wonmi Mountain to the house where Yonggyu was now living.

It was only after Puch'ŏn became a city that the neighborhood was named Wonmi-dong, for the mountain. Before that, it was called Chomaru, the "Cho Village," or Chochong-ni, the "Cho Clan's Neighborhood," because so many members of the Cho clan lived there. After working his entire life as a farmhand in the Cho clan's Chomaru, Old Kang's father finally managed to save enough money to buy a few *p'yŏng* of paddy land before he died. He was a farmer who had tilled the soil his entire life, all because of his burning greed for land. "Boy, when you grow up, I want you to turn Chomaru into Kangmaru," he said as he dragged young Mansŏng across field and paddy.

After the Korean War, Old Kang began to buy up paddies and fields as the people of Chomaru sold off property to send their sons and daughters to study in Seoul. Landowners with the surname Cho had been leaving the village one by one for some time, and when Old Kang was finished, there wasn't a Cho left. Then Seoul's suburban development boom swept in, and Kangmaru, which Old Kang had worked so hard to create, began to suffer.

Forced land sales, the revision of land use regulations, the development of new housing sites—Kang was stunned as he watched the land sold off piece by piece. He struggled with all his might to hold on to his land, but prices rose and his might was helpless against the power of money. The increase in land prices was so rapid that his own wife and children fretted over his unwillingness to sell for what seemed like such easy money.

His wife was one of the first to understand the situation. Gone were the days when she was simply the wife of a farmer whose land was plentiful but cheap at a few thousand won per *p'yŏng*. It was laughable to think she had been content tilling the soil, now that they were owners of land far too valuable to be used for something as lowly as farming. It was the same land, and yet today's land was different from the land of old. Her husband may have deplored the fact, but they never could have lived this well, for this long, if they had depended on farming alone, especially after spending so much on their sons and daughter. Of course, if the children had taken care of the money instead of squandering it all, they might have been running their own conglomerate by now. Still, when she thought how she could be a millionaire simply by selling their remaining land, new vigor coursed through her body. The problem was, Old Kang refused to accept the land's transformation. She was ready to die of frustration because of his stubborn insistence that they plant cabbages and peppers on that golden land.

After that first episode with Chŏngmi's mother, several days passed without incident. The manure soon dried in the cold spring wind, and since even Old Kang's big nose detected nothing, he assumed there would no further trouble. March raced by as he and Yongmun, who had finally recovered, planted pepper seedlings in the hotbed and covered several strips of land with plastic to grow spring vegetables. Normally, they could almost hear the sprouts growing in the spring showers that fell every other day, but for some reason, there was no rain this year. Unable to stand by and watch the furrows of freshly turned soil harden and dry, Old Kang took up his hoe and broke apart every clod to pass the time. As the drought wore on, his face grew even redder.

There was no trouble over the field, but that didn't mean all was quiet in Wonmi-dong. The entire neighborhood was stunned when Chinman, an expert at causing trouble, was seriously injured jumping out a window on the second floor of the apartment house. The boy bragged that he could fly like Superman, but he ended up in a cast. Luckily, he landed in the spindle tree and broke only an ankle. Otherwise, he would have been killed. It was truly an unfortunate incident, aggravating the already difficult circumstances of Chinman's family, since his father had been out of work for some time. Old Kang heard that Mr. Ŏm of the Happiness Photo Studio paid part of the hospital bill and that Chinman's father had been reduced to working as a day laborer, installing boilers with Sora's father over at Reliable Equipment.

No one told Old Kang such things. Even his wife was snubbed by the neighbors, so she got the local news from their eldest daughter-in-law, Kyŏngguk's mom. The woman from Kohŭng complained about Old Kang, who had a reputation for being a tightwad who cared only for his land, but he knew nothing of this, of course.

"The old coot doesn't bat an eye when something happens in the neighborhood. Why, he wouldn't sell his land for ten million a *p'yŏng*! He's always hoping for a better price. When the time comes, all he'll need is a plot of land for his grave. What's he gonna do? Take it with him?"

If only the sale of Kang's land worked out, the woman from Kohŭng could use the commission to marry off her own well-ripened daughter, but the old man refused to listen, and she despised him for it. The sale of his land might be Kangnam Real Estate's last big deal. No wonder her blood boiled when she saw him tending his field again this spring and realized that there would be no sale this year, either. Still, she had to keep after Kyŏngguk's grandmother. Who knows? If the old man's wife nagged him enough, they might just get that fat commission after all.

As spring blossomed, the wind lost its bite, but still there was no rain, and soon it was mid-April. The sun was hot as summer, so sweat flowed with the slightest movement, but the earth was so dry it took flight on a puff of wind. *Damn!* Old Kang sighed as he stood in the field stretching his back. Chinman's father passed with his son in his arms and nodded in greeting. They must have come out for some air. Chinman's leg was still in a cast, and his face was pale from his confinement. As he watched them pass, Old Kang clucked to himself. *If they're so hard up, why don't they go down to the countryside, take up farming, and be done with their worries?* Old Kang would have thought the same even if he had known Chinman's father was a college graduate who had once been a manager in a major company. When he first heard of Chinman's accident, Old Kang had casually suggested his wife buy a pound or two of meat and take it to the boy, but all he got was a scolding for the suggestion. "That's awfully generous after the way they've treated us. Those young mothers over at the apartments are up to something. They're always getting together and whispering, but when I pass by, they clam right up. Do you think a piece of meat will change anything?"

Old Kang was not particularly interested in what they might be plotting. He had already resigned himself to what looked to be a difficult year. He was more concerned about the crops wilting in the spring drought. After transplanting the pepper seedlings, he had stuck forsythia twigs the size of chopsticks in the ground to support the delicate stems. The pepper leaves had grown well enough, but on each forsythia twig sprouted yellow flowers the size of his thumbnail. Old Kang enjoyed a good mallow soup in early spring, so he also planted a few rows of mallow and covered them with plastic sheeting. The seeds sprouted despite the drought; he poked some holes in the plastic and touched the delicate green leaves. There weren't enough to sell, but he could share them with his sons, and after harvesting the mallow, he would plant lettuce and crown daisies, which they would eat for a long time to come. He used plenty of compost for fertilizer but didn't spread any night soil on that patch.

His fastidious second daughter-in-law wouldn't touch pumpkin leaves, or even ripe pumpkins, grown in a pile of shit. She had been all smiles when she started her married life in the two-story house that her in-laws had given her, but lately she treated her husband with such disrespect that when her father-in-law stopped by for a visit, she greeted him with a terse "hello" and little else, as if she saw him morning and night.

Old Kang's sturdy house, built of carefully matched glazed bricks, was a rarity in that neighborhood. He had torn down the old house that his family had lived in for decades and built a new one during the construction boom. It broke his heart to see the money from the sale of his land disappear down one hole or another, so he came up with the idea of expanding the house. Next to the old man's place was another two-story house, though not as fine, that he had built for his eldest son, Yonggyu. Yonggyu and his wife lived on the second floor with their son Kyŏngguk and rented out the first floor. The land next to his house was zoned for a combination of shops and housing, so he built another house with two shops on the ground floor and living quarters on the second.

As soon as construction was finished, his second son, Yongmin, married the girl he had been seeing, though he was still unemployed, and set up housekeeping on the second floor. Old Kang registered the house in Yongmin's name and told him to collect the monthly rent from the shops on the first floor, but Yongmin, imitating his older brother's example, no doubt, changed the monthly lease contracts to a key money arrangement, determined to use the deposit he collected from the tenants to start an abacus school or some such thing. He promptly went bankrupt, however, and now was scraping by, doing odd jobs for Yonggyu.

From the very beginning, with the used car dealership in Chang'anp'yŏng Market, the factory that manufactured automobile parts, the electrical contracting business, and now, the electronic parts factory, Yonggyu had no luck in business. He always ran out of capital, but Old Kang couldn't bail him out forever. Last time, with the electrical contracting business, Yonggyu had put his own money into a project and was caught in a vicious circle of debt when he wasn't repaid months after construction was completed. In the end, he simply gave up. He didn't think of jumping in to scrape after every penny he could. Yonggyu had a special talent for washing his hands of situations that got a bit tough. He shamelessly stuck out his hand for more money, insisting it was the last time, but his father paid him no heed. When it became clear the old man wouldn't sell off another piece of land no matter how he begged, Yonggyu mortgaged the house he was living in and borrowed off of it. Old Kang's wife took her son's side, and Kang got the feeling that she was going to Seoul to retrieve the money they had loaned to Hŭija. Their son-in-law Ch'oe wasn't one to part with money easily. He made a big deal of appointing Old Kang executive director of his shadow of a glove factory and promised to pay off the interest he owed on the 30-million-won loan in the form of a 600,000-won monthly salary. Kang's wife's heart melted at the mention of an executive directorship, and she gave up her junkets to Seoul.

The house may have been registered in Yonggyu's name, but Old Kang was disgusted with his son for mortgaging it without consulting him first, and he avoided all contact with his eldest son and daughter-in-law these days. By the look of things, they couldn't even pay the interest on their mortgage, so his wife was giving them the money each month, but Old Kang feigned ignorance. Fortunately, Yongmin hadn't asked for a handout yet. Not that Old Kang didn't feel somewhat uncomfortable with his second son's circumstances, too. Since his marriage, that rascal Yongmin clearly had been living off money given to him by his in-laws. It seems his wife's parents, who lived in Seoul, were quite well-off, and that made it all the harder for Old Kang to face his cocky daughter-in-law.

A fine crop of sons his turned out to be. Old Kang sighed in spite of himself as he stroked the healthy green mallow leaves. He had worked hard to raise his children, just as he worked hard to grow vegetables from the land, but they had been a disappointment, offering none of the satisfaction he felt when he brought in the harvest each year. Still, his wife kept after him, urging him to sell the land to help their sons. *Tsk, tsk,* he sputtered as he looked around the neighborhood. Hastily built apartments and worthless shops stood where there had once been fields, and in the distance, black smoke poured from the chimneys of the industrial complex. The changes had all taken place in ten years' time. City Hall had been moved nearby, the fields were rezoned and transformed into residential sites, and building contractors from Seoul swarmed in, slapping up house after house in a month or two with just a few bangs of a hammer. In no time, the neighborhood was packed.

Nowadays, with the neighborhood bustling with people, it was easier, but back when Kang was young, every household tended its outhouse with great care in order to collect night soil. His workday began at the crack of dawn when he slung a sack over his shoulder and headed out to collect dog shit; but no matter how far he wandered, he always raced home to his own outhouse if he felt the need for a bowel movement. Before plowing the cabbages for winter kimchi, he spread a layer of night soil over the fields. He felt great when he smelled that ripe aroma under the summer sun, and back then no one was so silly as to complain about the smell. It didn't matter how many fancy fertilizers and pesticides there were; Old Kang refused to grow green things that looked nice but hadn't been fertilized with night soil. Even today his passion for manure was insatiable, although now he farmed for his own enjoyment, planting only enough peppers and cabbages for the family's winter kimchi. Etched in his bones was the secret that had enabled him to accumulate all that land: His greed for good fertilizer had transformed that barren soil into fertile farmland.

Perhaps he'd planted the seedlings too early this year. Old Kang shook his head, checking the tender shoots one by one. No one waited until the fifth lunar month to transplant seedlings anymore. He could have put up a plastic greenhouse and had fresh green peppers in the middle of winter, but there was no need to go that far. He had moved his seedlings from the hotbed to the field as soon as the spring sun shone. The sun was fine; the lack of rain was the problem. Drought. Old Kang was staring at the wilted leaves when the owner of the beauty salon, who rented her shop from Yongmin, called to him.

"Kyŏngguk's grandfather, there's going to be a neighborhood meeting at my place tonight. I don't think Chŏngmi's mom's going to keep quiet this time. The people from the Rose of Sharon Apartments came over a little while ago and made a big ruckus. Someone from your family will have to come. How about Kyŏngguk's grandmother?"

The woman from the beauty salon was the head of the neighborhood association for the sixth subprecinct. Kim of the Brothers Supermarket was the head of the neighborhood association for the fifth subprecinct across the street, but Im from the butcher shop always led their attack on the shit smell. The head of the seventh subprecinct neighborhood association was much friendlier to Old Kang, in part, because he rented a shop from Yongmin. Im, on the other hand, resented Old Kang for refusing to give him the spot where the beauty salon now stood when the shops were first parceled out. He still couldn't look the old man in the eye without recalling the incident two years earlier when Kang had called him a lowly cow slaughterer. The fifth subprecinct had fewer problems with the smell and insects than the sixth subprecinct, but they were the ones who had filed the petition with City Hall last year. Old Kang knew it was the work of the butcher, but now that the Rose of Sharon Apartments from the fifth subprecinct had joined forces with Chŏngmi's mom from the Hyŏndae Apartments, it was clear that Im was stirring up the local homeowners again this year. The whole neighborhood knew City Hall had said nothing could be done about someone growing a few vegetables on idle land. After all, it wasn't as if he was raising pigs or chickens in large numbers, but Im still hollered about launching a signature campaign next year.

"They all say they've got to stop you before you get started. And they're sure City Hall won't look the other way anymore."

After the woman returned to the beauty salon next to the piano school, Old Kang suppressed his anger with another cluck of his tongue and stared down at his dried-up excuse for a field. Now that he thought about it, the smell wasn't the only thing angering Chŏngmi's mom and the other residents. Except for Im the butcher and the folks in the fifth and sixth subprecincts, the argument centered around the homeowners. Chu from the wallpaper shop and Ŏm from the photo studio rented shops right next to the field, but they treated him with the respect due an older person. Chinman's father, another tenant, was the same, and Kim the garbageman nodded respectfully when their paths crossed during the course of the day. They had never acted rudely toward him.

The homeowners, on the other hand, had reason to make a fuss. Old Kang's land had to be sold if respectable buildings were to be built and their street made presentable. What's more, his landholdings lined the main road, and it didn't speak well for the neighborhood to have the land along the main road covered with shit and vegetables. Real estate prices would increase only if the neighborhood's fortunes improved, and as long as Old Kang's fields remained in that condition, the homeowners would clearly be discontent because they couldn't get a fair price.

Neighborhood meeting or not, Old Kang returned home to get Yongmun and water the fields. Yongmun had been in bad shape since catching a spring cold on top of the exhaustion from which he already suffered, but when Old Kang returned home, his youngest son was nowhere to be found. The boy used to obey without complaint and help on the land, but no doubt even he had gone bad now. Lately he was as slippery as a mudfish and quick with excuses to avoid working in the fields. He found Yongmin at the house, conferring in whispers with his mother, so Old Kang decided to send him out to do the watering instead.

"It'll take three or four trips," Old Kang said.

"Yongmin's going to Seoul. I'll do it," his wife volunteered.

However, when Kang glanced back on his way to the pump, he noticed she was scowling and looked troubled.

"Seoul? What for?"

"He's going on an errand for Yonggyu. To borrow money from his in-laws. Yonggyu hasn't been able to make payroll for several months now. Why don't you help him out? It's not like they're strangers! Your own sons are in trouble, and you act as if it's somebody else's business!"

Old Kang went out back and started to pump without sparing her a second glance. What could he say? It was like pouring money down the drain. The brats knew nothing but spend, spend, spend. They'd never earned a cent, just started up their grand businesses and continued to expect him to clean up afterwards. They refused to take jobs and work for monthly salaries like other people, and they were obsessed with striking it rich in one stroke. They didn't care whose money they used in the process, because, in the end, they knew that his land would cover their bills.

Neither Old Kang nor his wife attended the neighborhood meeting that evening.

"Why should I have to listen to that fuss about the shit again?" his wife snapped when he suggested she attend. Before eating his dinner, Kyŏngguk came running to report that his mother was going straight to the neighborhood meeting on her way back from borrowing money. Old Kang and his wife turned out the lights and went to bed early, certain that they would hear the news from someone.

The next morning Old Kang went to the field at dawn as usual. He stopped short, his mouth hanging open. How could this be? In the field where peppers as long as his finger had grown were the burnt remains of hundreds of *yŏnt'an*. He could put up with the dumping in winter when the field was empty, but throwing *yŏnt'an* ash on a field where living plants were growing—it was barbaric. In an instant, he knew it was the work of the angry residents after the neighborhood meeting, but Kang had never imagined it coming to this. In every row, peppers had been crushed by a *yŏnt'an* bombardment. *Uncivilized brutes!* He ran into the field, lumpy nose flaring, and began tossing the *yŏnt'an* into the street. Only those Seoul bastards would ruin a living, breathing field. Anyone who understood the land would never risk the wrath of heaven with such an outrage.

It hurt to see the innocent sprouts cloaked in white ashes. He didn't know what to do.

Kim the garbageman was on his way home for breakfast when he saw Old Kang dashing around the field, hauling *yŏnt'an* with his bare hands, oblivious to the fact that his shoes had fallen off. Kim didn't notice what had happened to the field overnight, so his greeting was especially surprising.

"I hear you've put the land up for sale, so why are you working so hard? It'll be sold any day."

"What? Who told you that?" bellowed Old Kang, the blood rising to his face.

Kim flinched and stepped backward.

"Your daughter-in-law said so at the neighborhood meeting last night. My wife told me."

Old Kang headed straight home without another word, his shoes on the wrong feet. His wife was trimming winter cabbages and young radishes in the front yard. She stood up, startled at her husband's agitation.

"She didn't say that. I heard she said that you were getting older and thinking of selling the land since you wouldn't be able to farm much longer. I'm sure she just said it because people were giving her a hard time."

"'Just said it'?"

"Well, you can tell how angry they must have been from that field this morning. And besides, it's true. If you sell the land and help our sons, we can live quite comfortably off the interest that the rest of the money earns at the bank."

How could she be so calm when the field looked like that? Old Kang was speechless. Recalling the profound advice of Pak, the real estate agent who called on her the day before, his wife sensed this was as good a time as any to press her point.

"Do you really think they'll let you keep farming like that when everyone's all fired up about road beautification for those games in '86 and '88? I heard there's already a plan to build a bank and a hospital here before the '88 Olympics. Do you think the city will pay us what it's worth if we end up selling to them? Let's get a good price before it comes to that."

"Shut your mouth, woman!" Old Kang bellowed and returned to the field. He wanted to save as many pepper seedlings as possible and hadn't a minute to waste. The repercussions of the neighborhood meeting didn't end there. As news of the meeting spread, Ŭnhye's mom, who lived in one of the apartments, came and asked Old Kang for the 500,000 won that Kyŏngguk's mother had borrowed from her a month earlier. Now that they had sold the land, he could pay her back from the down payment he must have received, she reasoned. The old man's nose only got redder at her suggestion. They were new to the neighborhood, she explained. Her family had moved there from Seoul only last winter, and she had made the loan from money that she had received from a neighborhood loan club. She had come to know Kyŏngguk's mother through the Evada Piano School where her daughter studied, and she had never imagined there would be any trouble, since Kyŏngguk's mom was the eldest daughter-in-law of the largest landowner in the neighborhood. But since then she had learned that Kyŏngguk's mom owed money to several people in the area. That's why Ŭnhye's mom decided to settle the matter directly with Old Kang.

"Do you realize what that money means to us? We were sick of living as tenants in Seoul and finally managed to buy a little apartment here. We've only been here six months." Ŭnhye's mom had planned to repay the one million won she owed on the apartment with the loan club money, plus her husband's summer bonus, but she had gotten greedy for the extra interest she could make by loaning out the money for the intervening months, and now she was nearly out of her mind, worrying that she might never get it back from Kyŏngguk's mom.

As rumor of the sale spread, other neighbors who had loaned money to Yonggyu and his wife came looking for Old Kang. There were eight altogether, including Ŭnhye's mom. Among them were Kim Yŏngjin, a day laborer who had come to Puch'ŏn from Mokdong, where he had received money from the government as compensation for the demolition of his home in an urban renewal project. Kim had handed over the money to Kyŏngguk's mom because the woman from Kohŭng had promised he would get a monthly return of three percent. They all insisted that they had loaned her money on the basis of their confidence in Old Kang and his land, and therefore he had to take responsibility. No one believed him when he said he hadn't sold the land.

"That fool Yonggyu even mortgaged his factory! He said the

money would come pouring in once he's installed the latest equipment, but now the loan's due and they got a warning from the bank."

Realizing she had nothing to lose now, his wife revealed everything. If Yonggyu was that bad off, she warned, then things for Yongmin, who lived off his in-laws, must be even worse.

"Not the land. I won't sell the land!"

"Stop being so stubborn! Let's start by selling the land out front. That'll get the neighbors off our backs for a while. I just want to help the children. What's wrong with you?"

"Don't you see? We've lost all our land trying to help those brats!"

His wife shed a few tears, then went to Yongmun's room, exhausted by the quarrel. Old Kang tossed and turned for hours. He had long since abandoned any hope for his children, but it wasn't so easy giving up the joys of planting seeds and reaping the harvest. Thanks to the bastards from Seoul who had pushed their way into the neighborhood, land prices had gone crazy, and in the process, his children had grown up to be spoiled brats. How could anyone sell the land and use that money to buy rice and vegetables when they could plant seeds and live off the harvest? A vast fortune—something that a simple farmer like him never would have dreamed of—had come their way, but Old Kang felt hollow and lonely when he saw how his children frittered it away as easily as it had come to them. The comfort he got from holding on to that last piece of land was a source of great strength for Old Kang. When he thought of how he would still have plenty of land if the Seoul reconstruction boom hadn't turned his village into a half-baked city, he got even angrier, but what was the point?

It disgusted Kang to think of Yonggyu and his daughter-in-law pretending not to notice the creditors beating at their door, but now there was nothing left for him to do but give in.

The next morning Old Kang left home later than usual. He didn't tell his wife anything. However, his steps took him to the field as always. He pulled a few weeds pushing up between the furrows, then looked back to see Wonmi Mountain, by now covered with green and looking beautiful. It was a fine mountain. It had been called Mŏlmoe, Mt. Faraway, because it looked beautiful from a distance. His sweat permeated every ridge of that mountain from the days he cut firewood there as a young man. How long ago that seemed. *I've lived far too long,* he thought. He glanced down at the weeds, already wilted in the sun, then looked vacantly around the field.

Come to think of it, he hadn't watered the pepper seedlings for the last two days. The mallow was doing well enough, but the tough outer leaves were taking over without his wife to keep an eye on them. And the yellow blossoms of the forsythia twigs had dried up in the drought like grains of rice. The sun shone down brightly, and the neighborhood children had gathered next to the wallpaper shop, where they were engrossed in a game of capture the flag. Old Kang cleared his throat and walked in the direction of Kangnam Real Estate. Then suddenly he turned and rushed toward home. *The least I can do is get a bucket of water and give these poor things a drink,* he thought.

The Wonmi-dong Poet

PEOPLE PROBABLY THINK I'm just an ordinary six-year-old girl, but I'm far from ordinary. While you might say I was conceited if I claimed to know the ways of the world, I can, with some certainty, say I know what's going on at home and how our neighbors' minds work. You see, I'm really seven, maybe even eight.

It seems my parents put off registering my birth because I was such a frail thing and they weren't sure I would survive. I guess I'm lucky to be on the family register at all, even if they have me down as a six-year-old. I always knew Mama secretly hoped I wouldn't make it. Father wasn't quite so bad, but Mama used to snarl at the very sight of me. She'd never dreamed of having another child but went through with it, just in case, and out I came, another miserable girl. She still grumbles about it all the time—but just out of habit, so I don't let it get me down.

It's not that I'm particularly mature for my age; that's just the way our family is. The year I was born there were already four daughters. My eldest sister was over twenty, a full-grown woman, and the youngest was in her last year of middle school. At forty-two, Mama didn't even know she was pregnant until she was four or five months along. She finally decided to have me after consulting several distinguished fortune-tellers. You see, the fortune-tellers "unanimously" agreed I'd be a boy. Under the circumstances, I must have been mighty embarrassed to enter the world with nothing between my legs. I guess that's why I took so long coming out. I nearly killed Mama in the process, so I can hardly blame her. Still, she shouldn't go around saying I'm seven one minute and eight the next. She may think I'm no good at adding and subtracting, but it's obvious: Mama waited until I was two to register my birth, hoping I might die.

I don't want to go into a long explanation about how terrible my family treats me. What I really want to talk about is the Wonmi-dong Poet. Now, I may know a lot of things, but frankly I can't tell you what poetry is. As far as I can tell, it's a bunch of fancy words you spew out with your eyes half-closed on a moonlit night or on the beach with the waves crashing around. But judging from the Wonmi-dong Poet, I guess that's not always the case.

Here in Wonmi-dong, we've got our neighborhood crooner, our neighborhood beauty queen, our neighborhood know-it-all, and our neighborhood poet. Mr. Ŏm, the owner of the Happiness Photo Studio, is the Wonmi-dong Crooner, but he didn't even make it to the Puch'ŏn preliminaries of the national singing contest, so he can't be that great. Sora's mom is the Wonmi-dong Beauty Queen. That's for sure. She's the only one in our neighborhood with violet nail polish and dyed hair. As for the Wonmi-dong Know-It-All, I'm ashamed to say it's my own mother. I say "ashamed" because I know "know-it-all" is an insult that people use about someone who interferes in other folks' business and fights all the time.

The Wonmi-dong Poet has another nickname, thanks to Kyŏngja, the beautician down at the Seoul Beauty Salon. She was the first one to call him the Bachelor Ghost. With his sunken eyes and bushy hair, and the army surplus jacket and faded blue jeans he's always wearing, that's exactly what he looks like when you run into him at night. Kyŏngja isn't the only one. Everyone in the neighborhood seems to look down on him, almost as if he were a child. I guess it's because they all think he's a little touched in the head. I'm not sure when or how he got that way, but one thing's for sure: He's not like ordinary people. He lives on the third floor of the Rose of Sharon Apartments. There are a whole lot of potted plants and three birdcages on the balcony, and come summer, his is one of the few households with the money to keep an air-conditioner whirring all day. His father, who runs an Oriental medicine shop downtown, got himself a young wife and was having the time of his life when his youngest boy left the married son's home to come live with his old man. The lady from Kohŭng, who runs the Kangnam Real Estate Office, said that alone proved the Bachelor Ghost was a fool, but I can't understand what's so foolish about a son living with his father.

If the Bachelor Ghost has one friend, I guess it's me. He's twenty-six, twenty years older than me, but we really are friends. You probably won't believe this, but I have another twenty-six-year-old boyfriend—Captain Kim, the owner of the Brothers Supermarket next door. He is head of the fifth subprecinct of the twenty-third precinct and a lot more fun than anyone else around here. I used to spend nearly every day sitting under the beach parasol in front of his store. We'd laugh and joke, but lately he's gotten kind of short with me. He doesn't tell me jokes or give me ice-cream bars like he used to. I know why he's acting that way, but I have to pretend I don't. It's all because of my third sister, Sŏnok. Last month she just up and left for our aunt's house in Seoul. The whole neighborhood knows Captain Kim and Sŏnok liked each other, but she got kind of edgy and finally went to Seoul to work in our aunt's clothing shop. Sŏnok is really pretty. People often say she's like the proverbial dragon rising from the sewer, and it's true: She is too pretty for our miserable family, and she's always moping because we are so hard up.

I'd rather not have to tell you this, believe me, but our father is a garbageman. He rummages around in other people's trash all day— that's his job. He smells something dreadful when he gets home at night. It's not just my dad I'm ashamed about; there's something else I'd rather keep to myself. My oldest sister married a farmer who lives in Yangp'yŏng, out in Kyŏnggi Province. She's no problem. It's my second sister that I am ashamed to talk about. She started out as a bus girl, then she went to work in a sausage factory. After that, she was a waitress in a tearoom, and now, true to her zeal for profit-making enterprises, she is running a tavern somewhere in Kuro-dong. Imagine! Running a tavern at twenty-five, and with no husband! I went to see her once and found her leafing through a magazine, alone in a room with some beanpole of a man sleeping without a shirt. I could figure out what was going on from that.

Mama and my garbageman dad figure girls need just enough education to get married, so none of my sisters got beyond middle school, except Sŏnok for some reason. She graduated from high school, though in the end, that caused more trouble than good. She's always sulking, saying she doesn't want to work in a factory because she's a high-school graduate. She'd rather be an actress. There's no way she'd be satisfied with Captain Kim's snot-hole store.

You probably think it's strange for a mere six-year-old—but remember, I'm actually older than that—to be hanging around with a couple of old bachelors, but it's not my fault. My best friend Sora and several other kids from the neighborhood all started grade school the last two years. The only other kids old enough to play with have started kindergarten, so each morning when I step out onto the streets of Wonmi-dong after breakfast, there's no one left but a bunch of runny-nosed two-year-olds. It's the same story in the afternoon. The school kids hang around together, never including me in their games, so I'm left all by my lonesome, like some kind of alien. Our neighborhood has two piano schools and plenty of kindergartens that don't cost much, but Mama doesn't even think of sending me. Everyone else rushes to get their kids off to kindergarten in the morning, even the families living in one tiny room, but I have yet to learn a single game properly. My father has brought home plenty of picture-books and broken toys from other people's garbage cans, but I lost interest in them long ago. I guess that means I'm all grown up.

It was this spring, just when I was beginning to feel like an alien, that I became friends with the Bachelor Ghost. I was hanging around Brothers Supermarket, waiting for Captain Kim to come over and talk to me, when I realized the Bachelor Ghost was standing right behind me, waiting to talk to Captain Kim, just like me. He took a crumpled piece of paper from the pocket of his army surplus jacket, stumbled over to the chair next to me, and called my name, "Kyŏngok," as he sat down, and I swear I nearly fainted. I'd always figured he was kind of stupid and a little touched in the head, and once I even yelled, "Hey there, Bachelor Ghost!" right to his face. But now I just sat there, my mouth gaping open, and he said something even more amazing.

"You are calling me a son of bitch, a son of a bitch . . ."

I opened my eyes wide. I admit I had called him the Bachelor Ghost, but cross my heart and hope to die, I never called him a son of a bitch. I just shook my head, without even knowing it, and he kept talking, as if he didn't see me. "You are calling me a son of a bitch, a son of a bitch . . ."

Even now as I think back, I'm still amazed that was a poem! Apparently Captain Kim had heard the Bachelor Ghost was a poet and had asked him to write a poem. The poor guy struggled all night but couldn't come up with anything, so he copied something from a famous poet, and that was the last line.

"What are you talking about? When did I call you a son of a bitch?" Captain Kim said, whacking him on the shoulder as if he had been expecting this all along, but I was speechless. I almost felt as if I *had* called him a son of a bitch and just couldn't remember it. The Bachelor Ghost spent the next few days reciting the son-of-a-bitch poem, and I decided I had to be pals with him, too. After all, it's a lot neater being friends with a poet than being friends with the owner of some hole-in-the-wall store.

Still, I wasn't so adventuresome that I wanted to spend a lot of time with a man who was a bit off his nut. Besides, when the spirit moved him, Captain Kim could give me a piece of candy or an ice-cream bar, while the Bachelor Ghost was completely useless in that respect. All he ever did was talk about poetry, think about poetry, and ask me to recite poetry with him. Poetry was everything to him. On a breezy day, his heart ached at "the wind whispering through the grass," and a passing nun was "imprisoned in a row of seventeen buttons, or sometimes twenty-one." He could spend the whole day reciting the works of famous poets. And that's not all. He told me he could talk for hours simply using the phrases he had memorized. "Poetic conversation," he explained. That was why he stayed up reading every night. He lay in bed memorizing poetry, and the next day he spoke in poems.

Take away his poetry and he was as bored as I was. Stuck in an apartment all day with that young stepmother, he roamed the neighborhood endlessly to pass the time. I would be sitting with Captain Kim, talking about nothing in particular, and the Bachelor Ghost would wander over and plop down beside me, looking as if he wanted to be Captain Kim's friend even more than I did. We would pass the time, lolling in our chosen positions, reading the newspaper, or dozing in the hot midday sun, and when customers showed up looking for *makkŏlli*, we would jump from our chairs and watch Captain Kim fuss over them. Captain Kim changed the subject if the Bachelor Ghost even mentioned poetry, so the Bachelor Ghost never had a chance to discuss it with him. Instead, I was the one who listened to the Wonmi-dong Poet's endless stream of "poetic conversation."

Back then, I preferred Captain Kim to the Bachelor Ghost. I

couldn't help smiling when he whacked my bottom with that big hand of his, exclaiming, "Hey, it's my sister-in-law, Kyŏngok!" The girls walking to piano class gawked in envy whenever they saw me perched on the back of his motorcycle as he made deliveries. The lady from Kohŭng, who knew how well Captain Kim got along with the neighborhood gossips and made a tidy profit by selling vegetables, even fish, often sneered at my sister Sŏnok's poor judgment. "She may be pretty, but with her family she'd be lucky to get Captain Kim." Ha! I could tell what the lady was thinking. Her daughter was a year older than Sŏnok and not much to look at, so the lady from Kohŭng was pretty upset. But when Ŭnhye's grandmother told her to hurry up and find herself a son-in-law like Captain Kim, the lady snorted in contempt.

"Nowadays kids don't care what their parents think. My Tonga has such high standards, she won't even let me suggest a man to her! Why, just the other day a matchmaker offered to introduce her to a clerk down at the bank and she wouldn't even look at the poor fellow! I know it's only junior college, but with more than a year of advanced education, she knows a lot."

Whenever I heard her talk like that, I just itched to say something. You see, I've got a secret. An extra hush-hush top secret. And if the lady from Kohŭng found out about it, well, I don't know what would happen.

I'll bet I'm the only one who knows who Tonga is going with. I found out, quite by accident, last spring when I went over to Sora's house to play. Sora doesn't even know, because I've had to keep it all to myself, and every time I run into someone from the real-estate office I'm on pins and needles. I'm not sure I should tell you because I've never told anyone before, but what the heck, I might as well since I brought it up. Tonga has been seeing the young construction worker who helps Sora's father over at Reliable Equipment. And things are getting pretty serious. One day last spring I went over to Sora's, and when I didn't find her, I went around the corner to look in the side window of their shop, without even thinking, and what should I see but two people glued to each other doing these strange things. Never mind what Tonga was doing, the young man was hugging her head really tight and sweating up a storm. It was kind of scary.

I've gotten off track again, but anyway, it's too bad Sŏnok gave a prospective groom like Captain Kim the brush-off. Apparently he hasn't given up all hope, though, because he still asks after her whenever he sees me. Nothing's changed, though, because when Sŏnok does stop by to visit, she doesn't give the Brothers Supermarket a second glance. "That fool's no better than a beggar's foot-wrappings," she says. Sŏnok is gnashing her teeth ever since Captain Kim somehow got hold of my aunt's phone number and started calling the shop all the time. It looks like Sŏnok has a new man in her life, because nowadays she takes off her clothes and tosses her underwear just anywhere, and that underwear is so scandalous-looking, it makes my eyes pop. If I so much as try to touch them, she slaps my hand.

"What do you think? Pretty, huh? I'll bet you've never seen anything like this before. They're all presents."

Anyone who'd give a gift of panties held together by a piece of string has to be out of his mind as far as I'm concerned, but given her bragging, I think my sister is even more hateful, and that makes me feel sorry for Captain Kim, who doesn't understand what she's really like.

In some ways, Captain Kim's stock has risen thanks to the Bachelor Ghost. I'm only a kid, so no one blames me for hanging around under the parasol at the Brothers Supermarket, but the neighbors often cluck in disapproval at the sight of the Bachelor Ghost poking around the store with nothing to do or sucking on an ice-cream bar like me.

"They say he wasn't like this before he went to college. Seems he was expelled, though. It's obvious why, isn't it? College kids these days! Anyway, he went straight into the army and he's been like this since he was discharged. He's not completely crazy, but he's always mumbling poetry. Oh, I could just die!"

The Bachelor Ghost's stepmother was a regular customer at the Brothers Supermarket. She was always complaining to Captain Kim. "I could just die!" was her favorite expression.

"If only he'd put on some clean clothes, for my sake if nothing else. Oh, I could just die!"

In fact, the Bachelor Ghost did dress just like a supermarket errand boy. It got boring lounging in our chairs all day, so we tried to help out. The best thing the two of us could come up with was sprinkling the ground in front of the shop with a hose—no better way to keep the dust down and beat the summer heat. Captain Kim would stand by, watching with satisfaction, and when we finished, he would toss each of us a bottle of yogurt drink.

The Bachelor Ghost's share of the chores gradually increased. Soon he was cleaning up in front of the store, taking empty boxes down to the storeroom in the basement, even running errands for the customers who drank out front. It was strange, but as the Bachelor Ghost's workload increased, Captain Kim grew more pompous and the Bachelor Ghost seemed more pitiful than ever. Captain Kim must have realized this. So he took the Bachelor Ghost firmly by the shoulders and gave him a serious talk.

"I'm sorry to make a poet do such menial chores. You are a poet, that's for sure, and sometime when I'm not so busy, I'd like to read your poems. You know, when I was in school I helped the other kids write letters to soldiers on the front lines. I was quite the writer!"

After that speech, the Bachelor Ghost worked even harder, trimming vegetables and scrubbing the wooden cutting board used for cleaning fish. However, Captain Kim has yet to read a single line from his poetry notebook. The Bachelor Ghost's poems weren't good enough to read yet so he would take out the crumpled sheets of paper and ask Captain Kim to read the work of a famous poet, and Captain Kim would make some excuse and dart off, drawing a circle at the side of his head with his finger when the Bachelor Ghost wasn't looking. Unaware of this, Bachelor Ghost went around with his pockets full of wrinkled scraps of paper because he wanted to be prepared when the opportunity arose. By that time, I was so fed up with his "poetic conversation" that I was avoiding him and drawing circles at the side of my head, too, just like Captain Kim. But the Wonmi-dong Poet, who was a little, no, really touched in the head, continued to work like an errand boy at the Brothers Supermarket without a word of complaint.

Now, there is something I want to make perfectly clear: Until that incident two weeks ago I secretly hoped Captain Kim would become my third brother-in-law. My eldest brother-in-law, the farmer, is old enough to be my father, so I don't care much for him, and my second sister is still officially single, so there isn't much hope there, so if I'm to have a real brother-in-law, Sŏnok, my third sister, has to marry, and I was hoping for someone like Captain

Kim. It's true, my fourth sister has a thing going with a man at her factory and she's taking longer to get ready each morning, but that's ridiculous because it would mean cutting in front of the two older sisters. If Sŏnok and Captain Kim got married, I would have the right to hang around the supermarket as much as I liked. What would it matter if I ate a 300-won Bonbon Deluxe? The very thought of those neatly arranged packages of cookies and chocolates and candies all at my fingertips made me feel warm inside.

But exactly two weeks ago today, I gave up Captain Kim and all those delicious snacks at Brothers Supermarket. I'm sure I'm doing the right thing . . . I think. I'm the only witness to the whole incident, but I haven't told anyone what I saw. I don't know why, but I don't want to breathe a word of it to anyone. I've simply removed Captain Kim from my list of potential brothers-in-law. I've also made a point of firmly resisting him when he slaps my bottom and calls me his sister-in-law, although it takes some courage. And of course, I no longer accept the ice-cream bars he offers.

The incident occurred a little after ten o'clock one night in early summer. My parents had been arguing since the afternoon, and by evening they were having a knock-down-drag-out fight. My fourth sister doesn't get home from the night shift till midnight, so I was the only convenient outlet for Mama's anger, and I had taken my fair share of curses by sunset. They weren't fighting about anything particularly important. It all began when Mama started nagging Father about drinking four bottles of beer he had gotten in exchange for an eighteen-karat gold necklace he had found in someone's trash. There is no point in going into the details now. The gist of it was, Mama was angry because Father had traded the necklace for four lousy beers without a thought to his poor wife. What really bugged her was missing out on a chance to match the slightly discolored eighteen-karat gold ring Father had fished out of the garbage on an earlier occasion. The argument stretched into the evening when the curses began to fly, and Father belted her. That's when I slipped out of the house, as always, and went to sit in one of the empty chairs in front of Brothers Supermarket. I knew it was only a matter of time before Father gave Mama the old knockout punch and conked out, snoring. Then Mama would drag herself out to the street, nose running and tears wrung dry, and yell "Kyŏngok!" at the top of her lungs. Only then could I follow her home, dawdling on purpose, and go to bed knowing a new day would dawn the next morning.

I'd left the house around nine, and Captain Kim was so busy watching the evening news on the black-and-white television he kept in the room off the store that he didn't even notice I was there. I slipped off my shoes and sat cross-legged on the chair, glancing occasionally at Captain Kim's back as he watched television. He made do with the black-and-white set because he figured his bride would bring a new color television with her when they got married. I figured I could put my head down on the table and sleep if I got tired, and I squirmed in the chair, rubbing my drooping eyelids. The streets were quieter than usual, and the lights on the acrylic signboards at the wallpaper shop and photo studio were already off. The butcher shop must have been closed that day because its shutters were down. Kyŏngja of the Seoul Beauty Salon next to the butcher's shop commuted to work, so her lights were always off by nine. The road stretching from the supermarket toward the industrial complex was lined with empty lots and pitch black as usual. All that was visible was a light shining from the dry cleaners about a block up, and along the bumpy fire road were several piles of gravel and bricks.

Suddenly I heard a sound, like a scream or someone getting sick, coming from the dark road from the industrial complex. Actually, I'm not sure what I heard since I was half-dozing at the time. Now that I think about it, I must have been fast asleep. Maybe I just thought I heard something because my parents were bickering right there in my dreams. Anyway, I heard this ear-splitting scream in my dream or in reality. When I opened my eyes, someone was dashing out of the darkness, heading desperately in the direction of the supermarket. And hard on his heels were two young men, puffing like a pair of trappers after a roe deer that had escaped their trap.

Luckily, they didn't see me because my chair sat outside the circle of light in front of the store. Even more luckily, there was no one else near the store. On occasion, the place overflowed with people looking for a drink, usually factory workers heading home after work. And people from the neighborhood often sat in the chairs, enjoying the evening air. But not that night. As I sat dazed by the unexpected turn of events, the fugitive ducked into the store, and I got a pretty good look at the other two—one in front of the store and the other as he pushed his way inside.

"Get out here, you son of a bitch!" the man shouted as he rushed through the door. He was wearing a sleeveless red undershirt, and his shoulder blades, glistening with sweat, were quite impressive.

"Come out before I rip this place apart!"

Panting for breath, the man out front wiped the sweat from his brow with one hand; in the other, he held two jackets. He, too, wore only an undershirt, but his was white and had sleeves, giving him a somewhat gentler appearance.

What's going on? I wondered. Unable to curb my curiosity, I peeked through the side door at the corner of the store. The man in red had kicked the fugitive to the floor, and Captain Kim was shouting something as he moved crates of beer into the side room just in case things got really rough.

"Brother Kim, Brother Kim . . . Help me!" the man on the floor said in a thin voice. Red Shirt bore down on the man's back with his foot.

"So you know this guy? Maybe you'd like a taste of this, too!" the man shouted, brandishing a beer bottle. Captain Kim blanched with fear.

"Wh-what do you mean? I don't know him! I don't want to get involved. It's none of my business. Please, take him outside!"

The man on the floor finally clambered to his feet. His face was covered with blood running from his nose, and believe it or not, it was the Bachelor Ghost! Come to think of it, with those faded jeans and that dull old shirt he always wore under his old army surplus jacket, who else could it have been? He had run into the store so quickly, I hadn't gotten a look at his face.

"You bastard, where do you think you're going? You deserve a good thrashing!" Red Shirt snarled, revealing two rows of white teeth. The Bachelor Ghost dashed toward the room where the television was whirring. He knew it had a separate exit. But someone had gotten there first and was blocking the door. It was Captain Kim.

"Get out of here! Hurry up and get out, both of you! Fight all you like, but don't wreck my store in the process!"

Red Shirt grabbed the Bachelor Ghost by the scruff. When he saw the Bachelor Ghost being dragged from the store like a dog, White Shirt spewed a stream of spit through his teeth. The two men were drunk; their faces were red and their eyes gleamed menacingly. I quickly slipped into a dark corner. It was really scary! I had to do something to help the Bachelor Ghost, but what? My heart was pounding so hard I couldn't breathe, but Captain Kim was cleaning up the mess in his store and didn't even look outside.

Of the two men, Red Shirt was clearly more vicious. He grabbed a fistful of the Bachelor Ghost's hair and jerked him around like a piece of luggage. When the Bachelor Ghost struggled to escape, Red Shirt kicked him mercilessly in the shins and ribs. Several passersby stopped to gawk, their faces frozen in fear.

"I'm going to turn you over to the cops, you bastard! Come on!" Red Shirt shouted when he noticed the onlookers.

Under the light from the Kangnam Real Estate Office, the Bachelor Ghost made one final attempt to escape. He broke free, but Red Shirt caught him by the hair and slammed his head into a concrete post at the side of the building. *Thud!* I closed my eyes at what sounded like his head splitting in two. I felt like I was suffocating. After the Happiness Photo Studio and the wallpaper shop was a dark empty lot, so if I was going to save the Bachelor Ghost, I had to do it now. The Bachelor Ghost kept struggling toward the brightness of the shops, so this side of the road was completely empty. A handful of people stood watching, but they didn't want to butt in and simply clucked at the miserable fix the Bachelor Ghost was in.

"Get moving, you lousy punk! We're going to the police station."

Red Shirt jerked him by the hair, dragging him on all fours across the pavement like a dog.

"Why are you doing this? What did I . . . do?" As they passed under the bright lights of the photo studio, the Bachelor Ghost howled and tried to shake his head free from Red Shirt's grip. That was when Red Shirt began grinding his foot into his face, and finally I began to run. Fists clenched, I raced like the wind past them and into the wallpaper shop. It was empty; the owner, Mr. Chu, was lying in the room off the back watching television, oblivious to the commotion.

"Hoods . . . Some hoods are killing the Bachelor Ghost!"

He may have looked slow, but Mr. Chu was quick to understand what people said. He shot out the door, and at the sight of the Bachelor Ghost being dragged past his shop, he shouted.

"If the man done wrong, call the cops! What you beatin' on him for? Hey you! Get your hands off him!"

Red Shirt paused at Chu's thick Kyŏngsang accent.

"Keep your nose out of this! The guy deserves to be locked up."

"So call the cops and be done with it! Who's stoppin' you? Why beat the crap out of him? It only takes a minute for a cop to get here on a motorcycle."

"Hey, wait a second! Do you know this guy?"

"You bet I do. What did a nice fella like him do to deserve such a beatin'? What happened?"

Only then did Red Shirt slowly release his grip on the Bachelor Ghost's hair. The Bachelor Ghost staggered to Mr. Chu's side.

"I didn't do . . . anything . . . I was just passing by . . . and they started beating me," he stammered, pausing between words to spit blood.

Mr. Chu shouldn't have taken his eyes off Red Shirt to try to decipher what the Bachelor Ghost was saying. All of a sudden one of the spectators watching from a distance called out, "Hey look, they're running away!"

It happened in an instant. The two men had already disappeared into the darkness of the road leading to the industrial complex, leaving only the clattering of their footsteps behind.

"Hurry! We have to catch them. We can't let them get away!"

Out of nowhere, Captain Kim had appeared, stamping his feet impatiently, as if he were about to run after the two men. It made me want to throw up.

"What's the point? You'd never catch them."

"Can you believe that? They say they're taking *him* to the police station, then *they* run off!"

"So they just picked him at random to beat the shit out of him! And here we were, thinking they'd caught a thief!"

"It's so bright here with all the lights. I'll bet they were going to drag him out where it's dark and beat the shit out of him."

"You're right! A little while ago, up the street, I saw them call this young man over and pick a fight with him. Oh, look at him. He's lucky to be alive."

"So why didn't you say something?"

"Well, I never thought it would turn out like this. I was on my way to the drugstore, and when I saw them fighting I was so scared I took the other road. When I got back, they were still beating him and saying how they were going to take him to the police."

Everyone began talking at the same time. Suddenly the road, vacant just moments before, was bustling with people who had poured out of this house and that to get a look at the battered victim. With his snarled hair, dusty clothes, and bloody face, he really did look like a Bachelor Ghost.

"World's a vicious place. How could anyone do such a thing? They don't deserve to be called humans!" Mr. Chu sighed.

"You're right!" said Captain Kim. "We should have caught those two. Hey, are you all right? What a mess! Let's get you home. Here, I'll take you."

Captain Kim helped the Bachelor Ghost to his feet. *Man, this guy has no pride,* I thought. Powerless to refuse, the Bachelor Ghost struggled home on Captain Kim's arm.

I next saw the Bachelor Ghost again a few days ago, exactly ten days after the incident. Don't ask me how I spent those ten days. I hadn't realized it when we were hanging around together, but once the Bachelor Ghost was gone I nearly went nuts from boredom. The days felt like they were forty-eight hours long. Every once in a while I sat in the chair in front of Brothers Supermarket, but I didn't go too often because I felt uncomfortable around Captain Kim. Unaware that I had been watching that night, he acted no different than before.

"Kyŏngok, how come my little sister-in-law hasn't been visiting me lately? Remember, you have to tell me the minute your sister comes back from Seoul, all right? I'll give you one of these if you do." Then he waved a Yokkang at me. Yokkang are 200-won beancakes with the words NUTRITIOUS CANDY on the side. Captain Kim knew I loved them. But no way! When my sister Sŏnok came home, I intended to tell her every last detail about Captain Kim's cowardly behavior, and nip any lingering attachment in the bud. But, for whatever reason, Sŏnok hadn't shown her face for nearly a month.

Some time ago Mama had gone to Seoul to see her, and she said my sister didn't have the slightest intention of coming home for a visit, even when the shop closed for its regular holiday twice a month. She spent her days-off on the town and didn't crawl in till late at night. What's more, my aunt said Sŏnok had been getting calls from several men. "Why, the phone at that shop keeps ringing all day. Sŏnok can hardly answer all of the calls!" she complained. When it comes to talking, my aunt takes after her sister, so Mama no doubt got an earful of complaints about Sŏnok while she was in Seoul, and by the time she got home, she had decided to deal with Sŏnok as only the Wonmi-dong Know-It-All would.

"The girl's already running around, so we might as well let her try her luck at acting on TV or in the movies. You know, Sŏnok's a lot better looking than what's-her-name, you know, Chang Mihŭi." "What? Are you nuts? Come to your senses, woman. Do you think *anyone* can be an actress?" Father countered, but then he laughed as usual. Clearly, he was laughing because with all his daughters, he didn't mind one of them making some money off her looks.

Now Mama, she can tell the most outrageous lies when she meets that lady from Kohŭng. "People in Seoul know a good-looking woman when they see one. Why, when Sŏnok goes downtown, producers line up to ask her to take a part in their movies. She says she's fed up with being beautiful, though."

Not to be outdone, the lady from Kohŭng, still convinced that Tonga has such high standards when it comes to men, had to brag about her daughter in return. "Our Tonga is so busy lately, what with learning to play the piano and studying flower arranging. She says such bridal lessons are a must in today's world."

Mama is Mama, but that lady from Kohŭng is a genuine embarrassment. If Tonga marries that guy down at Reliable Equipment, she'll never lay a finger on a piano, and she'll be lucky to have a pumpkin blossom for her flower arrangements! When push comes to shove, grownups can be so stupid. They can't see past their noses. Just look at what they said about Captain Kim after that fight.

"That Kim, salt of the earth, he is! Why, just the other day he went over to the Bachelor Ghost's with a can of peaches. He really worries about him. Imagine goin' to all that trouble for a goofball like that. Just goes to show you, Kim's a good man."

That's what Mr. Chu said to Mr. Ŏm from the photo studio. Because Chu was three years older, Mr. Ŏm had always treated him with brotherly respect, and now he nodded in agreement. I thought I would burst when I heard the two of them, but for some strange reason, I couldn't tell anyone what I had seen that night. In that sense, you could say Kim Kyŏngok is the salt of the earth, too.

I got off track telling you what happened after the Bachelor Ghost got back on his feet, but let me say, that Bachelor Ghost is one strange fellow. It was a few minutes past noon, because Sora had just rushed home to get ready for school. She had afternoon classes that week. I was heading home, too, when I happened to glance over at Brothers Supermarket, and there was the Bachelor Ghost stacking soda crates in neat columns in front of the store, sweat pouring from his brow and him looking awful pale. After all, he had taken a dreadful beating and had been on his back for ten days. Still, there he was—lugging those crates back and forth with that sweet smile on his face. At Captain Kim's store! I couldn't believe it, but it was him. I saw him with my own two eyes. I knew he wasn't quite right in the head, but how could he work there, unless he had completely forgotten what Captain Kim had done that night.

Did he forget? I mean the part about Captain Kim shooing him out of the store. Was it erased when he hit his head? Stranger things have happened. There was this soap opera on television about a woman who had amnesia or something like that, and she didn't recognize her own son. When it comes to imagination, I can't be beat, that's for sure. My head's like a beanbag, always packed with wild ideas. I used to pretend I was the daughter of a rich family, abandoned by my parents, but I graduated from those childish imaginings long ago. Nowadays, my fantasies are much more, well, advanced: romances between an alien father and an earthling mother, things like that. Anyway, thanks to my amazing imagination, I decided that the Bachelor Ghost was suffering from partial amnesia. All I needed to do was confirm the diagnosis. As it turned out, I didn't have to wait long. He had finished with his chores and was sitting in a chair under the beach parasol, reading—one of those pieces of paper he carries around in his pocket, no doubt. What a sorry sight: reading those stupid poems when he wasn't right in the head, and him suffering from amnesia to boot. I went over to talk to him.

"What's that? Not another poem?"

"Yes, a sad poem. Very sad . . ."

His face pale, he looked up and smiled happily. A sad poem and he was smiling. I frowned and sat down next to him.

"Are you all better?" I asked in a quiet voice.

"Yeah. Just stayed in bed reading poetry and I was better in no time."

In no time? What did he mean, in no time? It was ten days already. Once again I was disappointed by the Bachelor Ghost's unfortunate mental state.

"I was sitting here that night. I saw the whole thing."

"'The whole thing?'"

"Captain Kim shooing you out of the store."

For an instant, his face darkened and he glanced at me. His eyes weren't dull anymore. They were shiny and black. But only for a moment. He looked down and pretended to pick a scab on his arm, as if he intended not to look at my face again. I pulled my chair closer.

"Captain Kim's a bad man, isn't he?"

He slapped his arm and replied, "No."

But I pressed him. "Isn't he?"

He just rubbed his arm, pretending not to hear. What an idiot. And he doesn't even have amnesia. I couldn't control my anger, but he acted like nothing had happened.

"I've got a sad poem. Wanna hear it?"

Geez, who'd want to hear one of those stupid poems? I stuck my bottom lip out in an angry pout, but he began to recite.

"Drawing the wind into its body and mind with its dry branches,
The silver spindle tree is a persecuted martyr.
But look again,
And it is a martyr longing for persecution . . ."

"You know how to read, don't you? Here, take it. I've already got it memorized."

He pressed the crumpled scrap of paper into my hand. It's a really sad poem, he'd said. It didn't seem a bit sad to me, and yet I kept feeling like I was going to cry. What an idiot! He knew what happened. . . . That Bachelor Ghost is such an idiot.

A Vagabond Mouse

SUMMER NIGHTS in Wonmi-dong usually started around nine. That's when the low bamboo platform was placed somewhere between the Wonmi Wallpaper Shop and the Happiness Photo Studio, and the game of *go* began. The platform, which spent the daylight hours moving back and forth in search of shade, was the latest of many projects belonging to Mr. Chu of the wallpaper shop. Chu had a hobby of disassembling things, then taking twice as long putting them back together. The bamboo platform had been taken apart and reassembled three or four times already, but one leg was still shorter than the others, and if you looked closely, you could see it wobble constantly. The platform was occupied by neighbors chatting from morning till night, so Chu was marking time, just waiting for an opportunity to remove all four legs and fix it properly.

The light from the photo studio display window was enough to illuminate the *go* board. In the window were a couple of birthday photos of one-year-old boys, nude, with their little peppers proudly exposed. At center was a torso picture of a young woman, larger than life, wearing a low-cut yellow blouse, and flanking her were portraits of Namgung Won and Mun Hŭi at the height of their movie careers. The pictures had been in that spot from the day the shop opened. Whenever a Wonmi-dong resident wanted to describe someone, they invariably referred to Namgung Won's square jaw and handsome lips or Mun Hŭi's large, beautiful eyes and shy smile.

The *go* game was usually a tedious standoff between the wallpaper shop's Mr. Chu and the photo studio's Mr. Ŏm; the others rarely had a chance to break into the game. Every once in a while Mr. Pak from the Kangnam Real Estate Office or Captain Kim from Brothers Supermarket would mount a challenge, but when the four men got together, it was more often an excuse for a drinking party than a game of *go*. Kim would produce a plastic container of *makkŏlli* that was due to expire the next day and offer them all a taste. From there it was easy. Neither Chu nor Ŏm was the type to worry about money spent on drinks, and if they wanted more, Brothers Supermarket was right across the street, piled high with all kinds of booze. The party usually began with a vow to have just one drink, and then Pak would launch into his tales of valor during the Korean War. By the time he had shown them the scar where a bullet had embedded itself in his thigh during that famous battle of the Naktong River and set the stage for the rest of his stories, a whole *toe* of *makkŏlli* was gone without a trace.

Then came Ŏm's heartbreaking account of his love for a girl in Saigon when he was a member of the Blue Dragon Corps. The girl, a secretary named Tuang Ti—or was it Tuang Wi?—had sobbed at his rendition of "I Love You." They had heard the story so many times their ears ached. "Lucky Seoul" was the favorite song of Pak, who was now over fifty, but Ŏm's was "I Love You." A self-described "common man," Chu was of the opinion that "Regrets While I Cry" was the only song worth listening to lately. Kim, the youngest of the four, was busy rushing back and forth between his store and the drinking party, keeping careful tabs on how many bottles of *makkŏlli* had been consumed and who was paying. Despite its fancy name, Brothers Supermarket was just a hole-in-the-wall store. Kim was twenty-six and still single, but people called him Captain Kim because he was head of the local subprecinct.

It was one of those summer nights. There were just four of them gathered on the bamboo platform. The drinking had started well after ten when the children who had been playing nearby were dragged home to bed. Chu, who had lost at *go* earlier in the evening, brought out an enormous bottle of *soju*, an indicator that the party was going to be a long one. The bottle was almost half-empty when someone brought up "that fellow."

"There's a cave at the foot of Changdae Peak. They say he's living there," Pak said with some certainty. Changdae Peak was the highest point on Wonmi Mountain.

"What in creation? Brother Pak, I can't imagine anyone lastin' a single day in a cave." Chu dismissed the suggestion of his elder, Pak, with a wave of the hand. He insisted the fellow was dead and buried in an unmarked grave somewhere.

Ŏm thought differently, however.

"A man can live anywhere. One of my customers said he saw him in an abandoned thatched house on the road leading down to Yŏkkok. People around here aren't familiar with that area, so who knows? He might be hiding there."

Kim shook his head now. When it came to rumors, the young supermarket owner couldn't be beat.

"We scoured the whole mountain last year around this time. He just wasn't there. We met some people living up there in a tent, but they said they hadn't seen anyone matching his description. He was long gone."

The four men each downed a shot of *soju*, as if to prove their respective points, then frowned.

"But Brother Pak, how come he went up there in the first place? They say he made a good livin' and had a couple kids."

Chu looked puzzled. No one knew the neighborhood goings-on better than Pak.

"Seems he worked for a company in Seoul. He even had a college degree. A good-looking fella, too. Well, maybe not as good-looking as old Namgung Won over there."

That was all Pak could say with certainty. Of course, a day would have been too short for all the things they *could* have said, but they knew nothing for certain. According to one account, the man had lost his job; another suggested he and his wife were sexually incompatible and she had frightened him off. Somebody came up with the theory that he had squandered his salary and run himself into debt. And still other folks insisted he was fleeing from some terrible but unnamed crime.

"You know, they say there's a soldier ghost on Wonmi Mountain. He died during the Japanese invasion of 1592. Eats one person each year. Remember that old woman who died on her way back from the mineral spring earlier this year? I'll bet it was the ghost."

Ŏm was always hatching bizarre theories.

"Ah, come on! Old folks can kick off anywhere, anytime . . . Hey! Now that I think about it, that fella started frequenting Wonmi

Mountain to get water from the spring and to do that, that—what's it called?—jogging or whatever."

The four men stared up at Wonmi Mountain as if on cue. Its dark outline was visible against the night sky, but for some reason, its thick forest seemed menacing. The people of Wonmi-dong sitting on the bamboo platform that summer night shivered.

The woods smelled fresh in the morning. It had taken him a full month to get used to the smell of the woods at dawn. The first few times out, the musty odor had nauseated him. He could tolerate it until the narrow trail from town reached the ridge and entered the thicker woods; that's when it suddenly turned horrible. The forest was cool and so damp he could wipe the condensed moisture from his face. The trees' breath, spewing forth from their stigmata, was almost visible.

It was strange. He had started going up the mountain because of the marvelous scent of acacia flowers that streamed through his window one evening. When he turned off the lights and lay down, he felt as if clouds of acacia flowers were floating around him, and he couldn't lie still. *I have to go up there,* he thought. Wonmi Mountain— it was right there, but he had never been up. Once he decided to go, he felt as if he had rediscovered an urgent and long-forgotten task.

He soon learned that the scent of the mountain differed from morning to evening. Not only the scent but the colors, too, changed with the hour. And the transparent sound of the leaves trembling in the morning mist became a gentle breath by afternoon. The myriad faces of the mountain captivated him each time he went there.

Since last Sunday he had been going up twice daily nearly every day. He was no longer satisfied by dashing out at dawn to bring back a container of water from the mineral spring. He also enjoyed leaving work early and climbing the mountain at sunset. The mountain's darkness spread from the east, finally enveloping Changdae Peak, where banners warning of forest fires fluttered in the wind. He made a game of the descent, choosing untraveled paths through the darkening forest. If he descended from this side of Changdae Peak, he always emerged in Wonmi-dong, whichever trail he took. Wonmi-dong spread like a flowing skirt around Wonmi Mountain.

The mountain had been there all along but he had only just discovered it. Gone were the dreary days when he scowled at the prospect of giving up a few moments of sweet sleep each morning. The alarm clock was set for five, but he was always awake by then. It took just ten minutes to cross the streets of the sleeping city and reach the path leading up the mountain. Many people passed him along the trail, all with their own water containers and towels emblazoned with a name or slogan around their necks. And occasionally someone would be making his way down already with a bottle of water, moist with dew.

There was more than one spring on the mountain. Halfway up the hill, water dripped from two slender bamboo pipes. Most people from Wonmi-dong went there, but he knew of another place. If you continued up to the ridge that runs along the top of the mountain, there were two paths: one to the left leading to Changdae Peak and another to the right used by people coming from downtown. Over that ridge was a vast forest; it took more than fifteen minutes to pass through it, even at a brisk pace. Beyond the forest was another spring. Maintained by the Mountain Spring Association, a group of a dozen or so elderly men, the spring ran strong, and the surrounding area was clean and well kept.

He drew water from that spring solely for the pleasure of crossing the forest. When he returned through the woods carrying his container of water, magpies fluttered through the air behind him. Sometimes he even heard a cuckoo.

How could he describe the world he saw from the ridge, his pant legs wet with the morning dew? The clean light of the newly risen sun shone over the city, but its tangled streets were stained with filth and reeked of sticky sweat. He felt like he was smelling the stench of an animal's cage. This was completely different from the forest he had just passed through. He felt wretched, like an animal returning to its cage. He wanted to turn back into the forest, if only he could. It wasn't impossible. If he gave up on going to work—no, if he was prepared to be late—he could wander in the woods a bit longer.

But he wasn't so foolish as to be late and do something rash. He had a family of three depending on him. His older daughter, now five, pestered him to buy a piano. "Look how long her fingers are! She must have plenty of natural talent," his wife said. But a whole month's salary wouldn't buy even the smallest piano. His wife was paying into three neighborhood loan clubs, large and small, to save for the house they hoped to buy in the near future. One of them wasn't due to pay out for another year. If they were going to keep up their payments to the loan clubs and raise their long-fingered daughter properly, he couldn't afford to do anything foolish.

"Hey, Captain Kim! Bring on another small one!"

The roasting heat of day gradually subsided, and now the *soju* tasted good. Kim jiggled the bottle to make sure it was empty and stood up.

"The rest is on me. My treat, since I won today," Ŏm said.

"Wait a minute! Didn't you just say you had a slow day at the shop? I paid this far, so I'll pay the whole bill," Chu declared as he stroked his hairy calves. Pak, who had gone to find some fried anchovies or something else to eat, returned with a tray of cucumbers and a bowl of red pepper paste.

"Did you hear this? Around the time that fellow was up on the mountain, they say a milky white light shone from there at night. Happened more than once, according to the people who live at the foot of the hill."

"You're right, Mr. Ŏm. That black mountain lit right up, white as milk. That's how you could tell he was spending the night there."

"Ah, come on!" Chu said. "Sounds like piffle to me. Someone's just makin' a big deal about a full moon, don't you think?"

"Not so," countered Kim. "You could see that light toward the end of the month when there wasn't any moon," he said, as if he had seen it with his own eyes.

The people who had first seen the light said the entire mountain began glowing gently the moment the man entered the woods. His wife stared at the mountain enveloped in light and waited for him to return. Some said he stopped speaking after he began spending the night there. When he returned at dawn, his mouth was clamped shut, and it stayed that way. All he did was look around, eyes sunken but sparkling.

"Must have driven his wife crazy, the way he clammed up like that. Wasn't like he was mute or anything. I think he'd quit his job by then. The days he went up in the morning, he came back at night, and when he went up at night, he didn't come down till the next morning. They asked him why, but he didn't say a word. Must have made her hopping mad, I'll wager," Pak said, shaking his head.

"Then he's a lunatic, clear and simple. The guy's nuts," Kim declared as if he had made an important discovery.

"No," Ŏm said. "He wasn't crazy. You're too young to know better, but some people are just like that. I've been taking pictures and analyzing people's faces through that camera for thirteen years now, and I've come to know something about reading faces. Let me tell you, there are all sorts of people out there."

"You're right. It's the same with me. I can tell if a customer's serious just by looking at him. One look and I know if he's ready to put down a deposit."

"So it's the same way with you, Brother Pak? Yep, some folks look crazy on the outside, but talk to them and you'll find they're perfectly normal. On the other hand, there are plenty of guys decked out in three-piece suits who are completely nuts."

"But what's that got to do with the fella who disappeared?"

"Come on, man! It's obvious, isn't it? In this troubled world of ours, sometimes it's easier to pretend you're crazy."

Chu erupted at Pak's putdown. He was quite drunk by now, and the liquor showed.

"Listen here, Brother Pak. How can you say such a thing? Who's gonna feed you if you act crazy? That's a foolish indulgence only rich folks with full bellies can afford. A bunch of nonsense . . . Why, people'll steal the spoon from your mouth if you're not careful."

"I guess you're right. You can act crazy, but make sure you don't lose out as a result."

It was only natural that Pak should say as much. He would get up in the middle of the night to settle a score if it looked like he was going to lose out on something. His guiding principle in life was, never harm others, because he hated being harmed himself.

"How could she stand it—watching her husband run off to the mountain morning and night? My wife would have done something."

Ŏm's wife had born him three daughters in a row, but he loved her dearly and cooked and cleaned for her whenever he could.

"What could she do? I'll bet she cried and pleaded with him in the beginning. They say she did everything she could to make him snap out of it—sent him on trips, invited his friends over—but he kept going up there."

"Come on, Brother Pak. The guy wasn't human. I'd have popped him one and still wouldn't have been satisfied. Why should his wife have to plead with him?" Chu pounded the platform with his fist, sending an empty bottle rolling.

"You mustn't get too excited," warned Ŏm as he filled Chu's glass. Kim then filled Pak's glass, carefully holding the bottle in two hands. "Fill her up. Yep, right to the brim, even if you have to wring that bottle dry." The two men joked at the newly emptied bottle, then Kim pulled out a new one, which had been leaning against the platform leg, and laughed heartily, as if he had known this was going to happen all along.

They weren't visible from the main trail, but if he went in the direction of the grape patch by the lower village, across the rice paddies to the mountain, he passed several well-kept graves in a sunny area. Old men and women returning from the spring stopped there to sun themselves, even in the middle of winter. On his hesitant return home, knowing that one more step would take him back into the neighborhood, he often sat on the grass next to the graves to pass the time. After he stopped going to get water from the spring, he spent even more time there.

Everyone who went to the spring used the trail. When summer came and the city began to ration water, the spring bustled like a marketplace. You had to stand in line for more than two hours to fill a single container. Where did all those people come from? The line started at dawn, just as darkness was receding, and continued until early evening, when darkness returned. It was only natural that he should abandon the spring water. Some time earlier he had begun to find the water container a burden. And he had once raised his wife's ire when he handed her the bottle of water that he had collected that morning while she was clearing the dinner dishes. "If it's because of this damned water, I'd rather not drink it," she said. But it wasn't because of the water that he went to the mountain.

He had come to resemble a person who had taken a wrong turn somewhere. The problem was, he lacked the resolve to find the right way. If not for the dense forest, the tiny blades of grass fluttering in the breeze, or the serenity of the birds flapping their wings, something more momentous might have awaited him. He couldn't say for certain what it might be. When surrounded by a noisy crowd, he felt he would suffocate from the animal scent. In the bustling cafeteria at work or on the streets jammed with traffic, he sometimes felt nauseated. He was even irritated when someone called out to him as he sat at his office desk. At the slightest provocation, he was overwhelmed by an unbearable hostility that he couldn't understand.

It was hardly a coincidence that he had that trouble on the subway coming home from work. The train was packed, without an inch of room to move. To him, it was nothing more than a sturdy steel crate that caged animals. He understood the bestiality hidden there.

That day, he was on the verge of suffocating by the time the train reached Namyŏng, the first station aboveground on the way home from Seoul. It was hot and humid, not a breath of wind, and the subway felt like a sauna. At every station, passengers swarmed in like ants. By Yŏngdŭngp'o, the cars were literally ready to burst. In this state, even a rolled-up newspaper, normally a harmless thing, became a weapon that struck him on the forehead. His own foot ground down on someone else's. The slightest movement brought him in contact with the sticky skin or sweat-soaked hair of the person next to him. The ceiling fan was useless; in fact, it made matters worse by circulating the hot air. He had to get off—it didn't matter where—and breathe the air outside. He had often done that.

But he was too far inside the car, and as the stations slipped past, he watched helplessly. No matter how deeply he tried to breathe, it seemed the air wouldn't enter his lungs. He couldn't even raise his arm to wipe the sweat from his forehead. He struggled to get closer to the door for a mouthful of fresh air, but it was futile. Each time he tried to worm his way toward the door, spiteful looks pierced him from all directions. *If I keep struggling, they'll strangle me,* he thought. Terror seized him, but he also felt a fierce hostility and wanted to smash them to pieces. The train was already moving through Oryu-dong Station. Then it happened.

"I'm going to blow it up! I'm going to blow this train up!"

At first, he, too, was surprised. Then he realized the shouts had come from his own mouth, and he clamped it shut. The passengers, joined together like links in a chain, rolled their eyes, searching for the culprit. The human chain surrounding him loosened slightly. He could have reached up and smoothed his hair if he had wanted to, but he didn't.

He didn't blow anything up, but he did feel as if a handful of something, some comfort, had flowed into his air-stricken lungs. It wasn't long before the train pulled into Puch'ŏn Station. Like a tidal wave on a tumultuous sea, a surge of people swept toward the exit. He was carried by the wave. And soon he was anonymous. No one paid attention to him as he slipped outside.

Once he had abandoned the mineral-spring water, Wonmi Mountain was all his. He found a new way to Changdae Peak, past the sunny gravesite, along a wooded path that no one else took. Steeped in the pleasures of wandering—scratching his arms on bushes and startling at the dull sound of caterpillars squishing underfoot—he had already missed several days of work. He had taken to carrying a small rucksack. Inside were a towel, some warm clothing, and a pocketknife. He also carried some bread, cigarettes, and a few crackers to toss to the birds.

The ground in the deserted parts of the forest was soft and spongy. The piles of leaves, accumulated over centuries, were the forest's food, giving birth to new leaves. Even the smallest crawling insect seemed precious. When he encountered a tiny caterpillar dangling in the air, he stuck out a finger and broke its thread. The fallen caterpillar struggled desperately, and he didn't step on it.

When he was hungry, he ate the bread; when he was thirsty, all he had to do was go to the spring for a cup of water. He didn't shed a drop of sweat in the forest, not even on those sweltering days. When he was tired, he slept in the shade of a tree, using his rucksack as a pillow.

It was different on Saturday afternoons and Sundays, however. People were everywhere, searching for a secluded spot to grill their marinated meat on gas burners. Young lovers crawled into the deepest parts of the woods, anywhere they could find privacy. The waves of people, buzzing like swarms of bees everywhere he went, made his flesh crawl in loathing. To avoid the crowds, he started visiting the mountain at night. Each empty bench became his bed. When he opened his eyes in the middle of the night, the stars twinkled down at him lovingly. The crescent moon floated between the branches. No matter how dark it got, Wonmi Mountain always welcomed him quietly.

Soon after he began visiting the mountain at night, a tent appeared in a clearing not far from the spring. It belonged to two young men. Their camp was well equipped, complete with a clothesline. Judging from the picnic table and chairs, bucket, and washbasin, they must have come from nearby. The tent was usually empty during the day, but after the two men finished their business in town, they returned, like commuters coming home from work, and cooked dinner. Whenever he passed the tent late at night, the orange glow of a lantern shone inside, and he often heard the strumming of a guitar.

While he didn't dislike the young men, he didn't go near the tent. He enjoyed listening to the guitar as he lay on his bench in the middle of the night. Because of the guitar, perhaps, he soon began to wonder how much longer they would stay or if they might leave. It somehow comforted him to know that someone else was watching over the mountain. He hung around the area so as not to miss their hearty laughter and the clinking of their dishes, and often he cried for no reason as he watched the single spot of light in the dark forest.

Other tents appeared in the woods from time to time. It was usually a young man and woman who stayed one night and left. The two young men remained, however. He was happy to discover they had brought a new wooden bench to their campsite. That meant the tent would be there a while. They might have bumped his arm or stepped on his foot in the subway or on a crowded city street, but he could easily forgive them as long as they remained near him in the deep of night.

He knew how human beings, who gathered in packs, could be cruel solely because they were part of a pack. He had learned this nearly five years earlier. At the time, he was in that southern city on a month-long business trip. In May of that year, he had been as deeply wounded as the citizens there—a deep internal wound that didn't show on the outside. His business in the city was left unfinished; that went without saying. However, he had seen the sharp claws that those packs of countless beasts with human faces used to protect themselves. He simply couldn't acknowledge the fact that all of them, when separate and alone, were ordinary neighbors who cried at simple stories from the past.

Perhaps that was when it had all started. His heart pounded whenever he went someplace where many people gathered. He was afraid of hearing the cries of the beasts hidden behind the smiling white teeth. And the image of himself, transformed into a wolf attacking a passerby who happened to poke him in the side to ask directions, rose again and again in his mind.

The previous spring, some beehives had been placed at the entrance to the woods to collect acacia honey. He had looked in a hive once, just out of curiosity. Astonished to find a black knot of hundreds and thousands of bees, he had stepped back in alarm. Each of the twenty or more square hives was clotted with countless swarms of bees. It was a frightening sight, like the armies of ants that throng in black waves over a child's lost candy or the clouds of day-flies that flit toward streetlights. Their numbers, simply their numbers, were enough to intimidate him.

As the stories of that fellow stretched endlessly on, the woman from Kohŭng came to get Pak, but she returned home without him. Then Ŏm's wife appeared, scolded her husband for drinking too much, and went back inside. The men owed their wives' rapid retreat to the television. The wives were watching an old Korean tearjerker and wringing their handkerchiefs as they debated which was more important—the love of a birth mother or that of the mother who had raised the child.

"They're all wrapped up in that TV show. My wife's eyes are so red. Didn't say a word, just looked at me like I was botherin' her. Silly woman," Chu chuckled when he returned from checking to see if his youngest, a son acquired late in life, was asleep. Then Kim emerged from his store with a small watermelon about the size of a child's head.

"What? Are you tryin' to run yourself out of business? You sure we're not wipin' you out?"

"What are you talking about? Bring it over. Let's have a party!"

"Hey! What's with you today? You must have some nest egg stashed away if you can serve up treats like this."

The men all had something to say. Chu, who had rolled up his undershirt to expose his stomach, pulled it down now, as if the almost imperceptible breeze was chilly. The scent of watermelon filled the air, and the mongrel from the supermarket came running. It lived in the street but was so scrawny no one thought of stealing it.

The dog poked its nose into everything and was quite the trouble-maker. Still, it recognized Kim as its rightful master and whimpered miserably, pretending to suffer deeply, whenever it was caught underfoot.

"Who knows? Maybe they'd have found him if they'd gone out as soon as he disappeared. But they let it go for a week. No wonder they didn't find him."

There was Ŏm, back on the subject of that fellow.

"You're right there. He spent so many nights on the mountain, I guess his wife didn't think much of it until she hadn't heard from him in three days."

"Why'd any woman put up with that crap? Weren't for the kids, I'll bet she wouldn't have gone lookin' for him at all."

"No, I heard she looked for him everywhere. It was pitiful to watch. Practically lived on the mountain for ten days herself. They combed the whole area, but there wasn't a trace of him. No corpse, no scraps of clothing torn in a fight, no nothing."

"The knife!" Kim interrupted Pak. "Remember! She found his pocketknife. Didn't you hear? It was lying on the ground next to a tree. She picked it up and went to the commander of the local reserve forces. It just so happened they had training the next day, so several dozen reservists went over the mountain with a fine-toothed comb."

"Really? You went along?" Pak's eyes opened wide in anticipation.

"No. I just heard about it."

"What? Then why are you acting like you were part of the search party?" Ŏm slapped Kim on the back.

"What's that about a pocketknife? You mean she really found one?"

"I'm sure of it. A red pocketknife. He kept it in his pack. When they found the knife and not the man, they figured something happened to him. That's when they organized the search party."

"And then?"

"What do you mean? He'd already been missing for ten days. There was no sign of him, of course."

"That's strange," Ŏm murmured. Then he threw back another drink. Chu, Ŏm's rival in *go* and drinking, gulped his own and let out a satisfied *"Ahhh."*

"Hey! And what about those poison moths? Did you hear about them?" Pak exclaimed suddenly.

The men jerked to attention.

"Poison moths?"

Ŏm and Chu crawled closer to Pak on their knees. Kim began collecting the littered remains of the watermelon, a look that said, "Oh, that old story!" on his face.

"You know, I get the creeps just telling the story. After it happened, I couldn't go anywhere near the mountain for quite a while. Even now, I'm none too happy when a house comes up for sale there."

"Get to the point, Brother Pak!" urged Chu impatiently.

"Ohhh, I think I know this story, but not all the details. Let's hear it," Ŏm said much more serenely.

"It was the day they sent out the search party from the reserve forces. The son of Mr. Sŏng down at Central Real Estate was among the fifty-some young men in the party. Anyway, it's about two in the afternoon and really hot. They're just hiking up the mountain, talking among themselves, kind of like they're going on a picnic. After all, they just had one man to find. And then they came to this garbage dump. You know, the one halfway up to the spring on this side? That big hole in the ground? That's when this cold wind started blowing."

"Must have been nice and cool."

"Are you kidding? This was no ordinary wind. It was real damp and creepy. Stopped that long file of soldiers dead in their tracks. It was strange. All of sudden the woods were quiet as a tomb. Couldn't even hear a bug, and that cold wind came surging toward them."

"So then what happened?"

Ŏm swallowed hard. Kim already knew the story, but he was holding his breath, waiting for Pak to continue.

"Well, they were scared, but what were they going to do? Fifty strong young men in broad daylight. So they just kept going, and gradually the wind got stronger. Seemed like it was trying to keep them out of the woods. And the leaves . . . The wind was blowing hard, but those leaves, even the blades of grass, were completely still. The men up front were whispering about how weird it was, but what could they do? They had to keep going."

"Several of the soldiers in the very front were actually pushed back by the wind. They fought it at first, then they just ran away."

Kim could contain himself no longer.

"Enough of the local news!" Chu poked Kim in the ribs.

"Well, they finally managed to push their way up to the ridge leading over to Changdae Peak. And then it happened. The soldiers out front started screaming and turned back."

"Why?"

Ŏm swallowed once more.

"Poison moths. Not just a few, but thousands of them! The woods were black with them moths. Flying everywhere. Why, they were so big, the soldiers thought they were bats. The soldiers couldn't go one step farther. The moths were going nuts, sprinkling their poison dust every which way. Why, none of those boys had ever seen or heard of such big moths before. Imagine! Black clouds of poison moths. Must have scared the devil out of them!"

The four men—Ŏm, Chu, Kim, even Pak—imagined the cloud of poison moths in the woods. A damp, disagreeable wind blowing down from the dark, thick forest. Dozens of young men pushing through the wind. The dark brown moths filling the woods, releasing poison powder each time they flapped their wings. A cloud of poison moths flying crazily in a quiet forest where even the bugs were hiding.

"The moths were swarming all over the place. A few of the braver men went into the woods, but they got driven right back out again. The moths darted into their eyes, their mouths, everywhere!" Kim mimicked the soldiers swiping at their eyes and mouths.

"I don't know about that," Pak said. "But it seems they couldn't do a thorough search because of those moths. No one went near the mountain for several days after that. People figured the poison had gotten into the spring, too, so no one went up for water. Anyway, the mountain was dead quiet for a long time after that. And why not? Every time someone went up there, that cold, nasty wind came blowing at them."

At that very moment, a cool breeze blew across the empty road. The four men's mouths dropped open as the chill air touched their skin.

When he rose from the wooden bench that had served as his bed for a night, the morning sunlight stung his eyes. Brilliant five-colored rainbows hung in each bead of dew poised on the leaves. The blades of grass stretched small and pretty, lifting heads bent low in the night. If he listened carefully, he could hear the new morning ringing through the forest. He felt he could almost understand the murmurs of the nameless black-spotted bug crawling past his feet. The ants that had crawled all the way to the bridge of his nose marched briskly, showing off their slender waists.

They all seemed so busy. When morning came, humans weren't the only ones bustling to prepare for the new day. Everything in the forest seemed to wake at the first ray of light and urge him to get moving. He felt he couldn't remain, and sure enough, human voices sounded in the distance. Who knows? Maybe some people had seen him lying there as they passed. He hadn't heard any of the early-morning hikers call *"Yahooo!"* from Changdae Peak yet, but it was only a matter of time. He had awakened several times during the night but thought he had slept quite well. Still, his head seemed heavy and he couldn't quite feel the freshness of morning. He would have to find a more secluded place and rest some more.

About a quarter mile through the woods from where he had slept, he found a small bare spot, invisible from the path. It was hidden by vines that had formed a tight web over the tree branches, and the ground beneath was surprisingly dry, with few biting insects. He knew of several secret resting places like this. He had carefully lined each one with flat paving stones lugged up from the neighborhood below, because he had ruined more than one pair of pants sitting on damp ground. On the eastern slope of Changdae Peak, he had another resting place. It was much cozier than this one, but he couldn't run the risk of being seen now. His wife might be out looking for him.

He hadn't been home for three days. She would think nothing of a day or two, but this morning would be different. He couldn't be sure, though. He didn't want to see her out searching for him. But, on second thought, perhaps that was just what he wanted. The feeling floated around him like a fogbank. He felt as if he was falling into a maze every time he thought deeply about anything. Maybe it was his heavy head. It might get better if he lay down on the cool stones and looked up at the sky. He propped his feet up on his pack and stretched out, head on the stone platform. Overhead, the sky was blue, and finally a hiker made it to the top of Changdae Peak and yelled *"Yahooo!"* at the top of his lungs.

How long had he been lying there? He must have dozed off because now the sun's rays were beating down mercilessly on his face.

He got up with a start. His clothes were soaked with perspiration, yet he didn't feel hot. It was as if all his energy had seeped into the ground and his body was lighter than a single sheet of paper. Hungry and out of cigarettes, he decided to look for a store. If he followed the ridge down to Yŏkkok, he could easily find one where they didn't know him. His greatest concern was his shaggy beard: One moment he longed for a disposable razor and the next a tired voice told him to forget the beard.

By afternoon he was sitting at his resting spot on the eastern slope of Changdae Peak. As soon as he arrived, he had encountered a mouse. It had preceded him to the resting spot and showed no sign of running away as it gazed up at him; then it dropped its tail and disappeared as if it had no choice but to leave. He sat down in the private nest that he had wrested from the mouse and took off his pack. The bottle he had filled at the spring coming up was heavy, and he sighed wearily in spite of himself. The mountain was quiet that day. There hadn't been many people at the spring. Several rambunctious boys had been shouting and playing nearby, but they were gone now. The sun had already dipped to the west of Changdae Peak, and the woods were silent like a secret room.

The thickest pine grove on Wonmi Mountain stood just a few steps from where he was resting. It was a verdant forest, several decades old at least. For some time, a bird had been chirping, its call short and high like a car horn. In between its cries, if he listened carefully, he could hear a low growling in the sky, as if an airplane was passing overhead.

As twilight settled, he cautiously entered the pine grove. The needles were golden brown in the reflection of the orange sunset. It wasn't just the needles; the entire grove had taken on a warm, snug glow, as if it had been covered with brown wallpaper. Soon darkness would come. The brown wallpaper would disappear, a black curtain would descend over the woods, and all living things would return to their nests. Decomposing pine needles crunched beneath his feet. He leaned against a tree trunk and looked up at the jagged fragments of distant sky. Goosebumps formed all over his body for no apparent reason. Even the bird had stopped singing. It was too quiet; the silence tormented him. He hit the tree trunk with his hand to break the silence.

He needed to hear something, if only the sound of his own footsteps. If there had been a well in his heart, he felt as if it would overflow at the slightest whisper of wind. Carefully, so as not to let the water flow from his heart, he wandered the pine grove. It stretched on and on like a deep, endless tunnel.

But in fact it wasn't long before he came to a clearing and was looking down on hills covered with tangled brush. He had to walk in circles to remain in the forest. And as he circled, he once again encountered the mouse he had seen at the resting spot. It gazed up at him blankly from about ten paces. He looked quietly back into the mouse's black eyes. A blue darkness settled over the hunched back of this lonely mouse, wandering alone and separate through the forest.

Strange little fellow, he thought as he turned to go. He took several steps, then glanced back, and the mouse was still there. A layer of darkness had settled over his own hunched back now. He leaned back against a tree again and closed his eyes. He didn't want to see the approaching darkness, but the darkness behind his eyelids was even more dizzying.

The night before he had discovered that the two young men who shared his campsite had gone. When did they pack up their tent and leave? He was sorry that he hadn't seen them go. The tent with its orange light and the sound of the guitar, amateurish but full of human warmth, were gone now. He had stared at the empty spot, swathed in darkness, and couldn't leave that place for the longest time. He wanted something to be there, if not the sound of the guitar, then a single ray of light, or at least the sound of the young men's wholesome breathing as they slept.

He had to leave the woods and find a place to sleep before it was too dark, but he couldn't move. It was as if he were glued to the tree trunk. He thought of his daughter with her long fingers and the piano she required. He thought of the wristwatch he had left on the bureau. *I wonder what time it is?* He tried to guess what time the hands on the watch with the long scratch across its face would indicate. He couldn't move from the tree, he couldn't tell what time the watch on the bureau said, he couldn't believe that night had come again, and finally he wept, alone in the middle of the forest.

"So in the end, he just disappeared," Ŏm said with a serious look. He seemed sober now.

"Who cares if he disappeared or dropped dead? His wife and kids are what we have to worry about."

Not surprisingly, Chu was interested in the family. Ŏm of the Happiness Photo Studio was known to be a devoted husband, but he couldn't compete with Chu, who, while sometimes brusque, adored his family.

"She waited and she waited, hoping to hear from him. And she kept searching for him, then she moved away. Now that the family's gone no one looks for him anymore. The whole thing's been forgotten. There's no way of knowing whether he's still in the forest or if he went back to his family. He could be dead."

Pak looked up at the mountain as if to see if the man was still there.

"Mr. Pak, did you ever see him?" Kim asked.

"Nope, never did. Just heard about him."

"And his family?"

"Nope. What about you?"

Kim shook his head.

"Hey, Chu, did you ever see him?"

Chu waved his hand no.

"How about you, Ŏm?"

"Me neither. I've heard about him many times, but I don't think anyone's actually seen him."

"Well, then what's the point of all this talk? Nothin' but nonsense. It's late. Let's turn in. You know, sleep's always the best investment."

"That's right," Kim said with a hearty laugh.

"Yep, I need to go in and get some shut-eye."

Pak slapped his arms and cursed the mosquitoes.

"They say there aren't many mosquitoes in the city nowadays, but we've got our share of the little bastards, thanks to Old Kang's land."

"Don't talk like that, Brother Pak. Why, those mosquitoes are just tryin' to make a livin'! You've gotta give creatures strugglin' to live a chance."

"If business keeps up like this, my bride will starve for sure. Profits are getting smaller and my expenses just keep going up," Kim complained.

"Still, you're a lot better off than us with our photo studio. Everyone says things are getting better, but nothing's coming my way."

"I tell you, these days I'm barely keeping my head above water. If I don't get something besides rentals, I'm going to be begging in the streets when I get old." Pak's real estate business had fallen off of late.

The drinking party wound down, and drunk as they were, the four men all scowled with worry about the next day's business.

"What did I tell you? Sleep's the best investment."

Chu stood up first. The bamboo platform tipped, sending his hefty body into Kim's arms, just barely.

"Darned thing's always givin' me trouble. I'm gonna fix those legs first thing tomorrow morning."

Chu gave the platform leg a kick, and just then an ambulance raced through the empty streets of Wonmi-dong, its siren shaking the sleeping neighborhood. Who could have died at this time of the night? The four men blinked and stared at the ambulance as it flew past.

On Rainy Days I Have to Go to Karibong-dong

THE TWO WORKMEN stormed in just after eight in the morning. The project began with the tearing apart. Ŭnhye's father grimaced at the racket as he watched the men pound and smash. Pieces of tile and fragments of concrete flew through the air with each blow of the hammer, so he couldn't stand there watching. The kitchen, right next to the bathroom, was just as chaotic. The things they had moved from the bathroom made the small kitchen seem even more cramped than usual. His wife stood in the middle of it all, washing greens for the workmen's lunch.

Ŭnhye was still glued to the television. She was watching a program for preschool children that he had never seen before, but he found it pleasant listening to her sing along and so left her and looked into the small room. Oblivious to the pounding in the bathroom, Ŭnhye's baby sister, still young enough to nurse, was sleeping peacefully. His mother hadn't said anything, but she was obviously very disappointed that another granddaughter had followed Ŭnhye. For years, she had prayed for a house of their own, and now that they had finally managed to buy one, albeit a small apartment in a multifamily building in Puch'ŏn, she had begun sneaking a line about a healthy grandson into her prayers.

"Mother went to Deacon Kim's to help them unpack," his wife said. From the way he poked his head from room to room, she assumed he was looking for his mother. Without answering, he looked back in the bathroom, which was fast becoming a complete mess. The man in the faded T-shirt, carefully hammering with a chisel to avoid damaging the bathtub, was Mr. Im. He was in charge of the day's project. Breaking the floor apart was a youth who looked at least ten years younger than Im. It was the height of summer, but the young man was dressed in a long-sleeved shirt and skin-tight blue jeans, trying to be stylish, no doubt. The outfit somehow made Ŭnhye's father wonder if the young man was up to this kind of work. Im, a self-described technician, made his living delivering *yŏnt'an* briquettes in winter, so there was ample reason to doubt his credibility as well. Mr. Chu of the wallpaper shop had recommended Im, who came from the neighborhood down the hill. Chu had observed Im at work on several jobs in the neighborhood and said he knew no one better with his hands or more honest. Until recently, Sora's father from Reliable Equipment had handled their household repairs, but he was down with a bad back and they couldn't find a suitable substitute.

He didn't learn about Im's background until after he'd taken Chu's advice and hired the man on the basis of his estimate on the job. According to Ŭnhye's mother, Im was actually a common laborer who took odd jobs during the summer months when he wasn't delivering *yŏnt'an*. This made Ŭnhye's father uneasy before work even started; something was bound to go wrong. As far as he was concerned, bathroom repairs required specialized skills, such as plumbing, sealing, plastering, and even tiling, so he couldn't help feeling that he had acted hastily in hiring Im.

Of all the rotten luck! Ever since this trouble with the bathroom had arisen, he had been cursing their "rotten luck" at every opportunity. Whenever something went wrong with the house and he had to spend more money, it was "Of all the rotten luck." And theirs was no ordinary bad luck. After bouncing from one rented house to another in Seoul, they had finally found their own place, this little apartment in Puch'ŏn, but they hadn't been there a month when the problems started popping up here and there. It was driving him crazy. Each problem meant a new home repair project for him, projects that could only be completed with money, and as a result, he had been hard-pressed for cash ever since becoming a homeowner.

The winter they moved in, water started seeping through the ceiling and walls. Soon the house reeked of mildew, and, with the spring thaw, water dripped from the ceiling like rain. *This is my place, so I have to fix it,* he thought and happily proceeded with the first repairs. The job was handled by Mr. Chu, who installed thick layers of Styrofoam to the walls and ceiling. Tiny particles of Styrofoam floated everywhere, and after the furniture was moved to make room for the repairs, the house resembled an open marketplace. But once the waterproofing was done and new wallpaper hung, the house looked quite nice.

This first job was simply a harbinger of things to come, however. Before long, the heating pipes burst under the floor in the small room used by his mother and Ŭnhye. It took several days of confusion, of course, and considerable expense to tear up the floor and restore the room to its original condition.

And that wasn't all. Soon the kitchen drain clogged, then the chimney collapsed, requiring the replacement of the boiler. The house was less than three years old, so it was hard to believe that so many things could burst, clog, and collapse. And if it wasn't that, it was the handle on the faucet in the bathroom stripping its threads or the water tank on the toilet failing. Money, in large sums and small, was constantly pouring into household repairs. When he finally heaved a sigh of relief, certain there would be no more trouble, the deadbolt lock on the front door broke, and he decided to have one of those newfangled computer deadbolts installed.

And then there was this trouble with the bathroom. It happened just yesterday. Because of his touchy appetite, he had been picking at his breakfast, as if his rice bowl was filled with grains of sand, when suddenly someone started pounding on the front door. The baby woke at the commotion and began crying. Furious because they had a perfectly good doorbell and the visitor could have knocked politely if he chose not to ring, Ŭnhye's father flung open the door.

Outside stood a balding man who must have been in his sixties. His eyes were round with surprise at the sudden opening of the door, and he seemed to have forgotten that he had been beating on it just seconds before. The old man looked so innocent that Ŭnhye's father naturally had to adopt a polite tone.

"May I help you?"

"Ah, er . . . the water, you see, the water . . ."

"Water? Do you mean the tap water?"

Ŭnhye's father thought the man was referring to their drinking water, which was supplied only every other day in summer, but the old man kept swallowing, seemingly in frustration, and began to rub his hands together.

"The water's . . . I mean water from the bathroom . . . water . . ."

Ŭnhye's father began to feel a growing irritation at what appeared to be a deliberate attempt at evasion, for the old man didn't have a stutter nor did he seem particularly inarticulate. Then he heard footsteps pounding up the stairs, and a young woman appeared.

"Oh, Grandpa, let me handle this. Excuse me, but it seems one of the pipes in your bathroom has burst. The water's running today, you know. Yesterday there wasn't any problem, but this morning, when they turned on the water, it started seeping through our bathroom ceiling. The leak's getting bigger by the minute. You better do something quick."

His wife, who was nursing the crying baby, stood up with the child in her arms and came to the front door.

"Oh no! I *thought* the water pressure was kind of weak this morning. What are we going to do?"

After their neighbors left, he shut off the main valve and returned to his breakfast. They had plenty of water collected from the day before, so he decided to put off looking at the bathroom until he returned from work that evening, but then he put his spoon down and could eat no more. The last few months had been relatively quiet, but now the thought of another major problem filled him with anger. Tomorrow was Independence Day, and he had planned on spending the holiday quietly, resting at home. That was out of the question now.

"Who was that old man?"

"That's the Old Screamer. You know. You've seen him before," his wife answered; then she burst out laughing, though it was hardly the time for levity.

"The Old Screamer? What kind of name is that?"

"Who knows? Captain Kim from Brothers Supermarket made it up. It really fits the old fellow, though."

Come to think of it, he *had* seen the old man before, coming home from work a few days earlier. There was something peculiar about the old man in front of him. He had been walking behind him all the way from the bus stop, and every thirty seconds or so the man screamed "*Uaaak!*" And that wasn't all: Each time he shrieked, the old man clapped his hands together and shook his arms as if he were trying to work something out of his throat. At first, he thought the man was coughing up phlegm, but clearly that wasn't it. According to his wife, the old man had rented the extra room from the family downstairs a couple of months earlier. He had no family of his own and often walked up and down the streets of Wonmi-dong shrieking in that manner.

Im removed the bathtub without mishap, despite his general air of incompetence. In Im's opinion, there was an 80 to 90 percent chance that the problem lay with the pipe that ran beneath the bathtub, connecting the sink and the toilet, and consequently the entire floor had to be taken up. Even if they managed to pinpoint the leak, by sheer luck, of course, there was still the problem of sealing the floor and replacing the old pipes. They had to begin work prepared to redo the entire bathroom. He never did anything halfway, Im explained, because if there was a problem with the re-pairs that he made around the neighborhood, his very livelihood was threatened. That's why his customers always called on him again. Im was a fast talker, but throughout his explanation his hands worked as quickly as his mouth. When he saw the wet spot where the bathtub had been, Im smiled with satisfaction and took out a cigarette.

"See, Boss? Look how damp it is over here at the end of the tub. We've found it. The problem is somewhere between this spot and the sink."

It was embarrassing that Im should call him "Boss." Im looked to be around thirty-eight, at most forty, and Ŭnhye's father was just a small-time office worker in no position to be anyone's boss. Im must have called all his clients that.

"Oh, Boss! Look at what those bastards did! I thought so. They used substandard pipes! Those contractors are all alike. They buy cut-rate materials just to save a few pennies."

Im tapped the rusted and discolored pipe with his hammer.

"Yeah," the younger workman blurted, "but we owe our living to them, don't we? And we're not the only ones. There are dozens of repair shops all over Wonmi-dong. Just think of all the people the contractors are keeping alive!"

Apparently exhausted from filling a sack with debris and carrying a couple of loads downstairs, the youth sat on the threshold of the bathroom and lit an Arirang. Come to think of it, Im still hadn't opened the pack of Arirangs that Ŭnhye's mother had given him when he arrived that morning; he was smoking the inexpensive Galaxy brand he had brought with him. Ŭnhye's father found the youth's shiftless tone irritating and scowled at the clouds of smoke he was producing. The youth, who looked to be at least twenty, dusted off his clothes as he sent smoke rings into the air. *If that kid installs the new plumbing, it's sure to burst again in a few months,* Ŭnhye's father thought and returned to his room, tortured by doubt once more. Im couldn't be much better if he hired help like that. And even if the new pipe didn't burst, they might botch the sealing, and the bathroom would soon be leaking again. In other countries, houses lasted for centuries, but not in Korea. "Stupid gooks." Without realizing it, he was cursing his own countrymen.

Of course, he hated the thought that he should indulge in such self-deprecation. It was a natural remnant of Japanese colonial rule, but he was amazed to find it lurking so deep within him. What's more, this spring he had been transferred from sales to the PR office and was now in charge of editing the corporate magazine for his company, a semigovernmental organization. It was his job to accentuate the good points of the Korean people—their diligence, sincerity, honesty, and so on. From start to finish, the hundred-page magazine was devoted to affirming, verifying, and reminding readers what a proud nation they were, so he couldn't help feeling it was strangely hypocritical to call Im and that young punk gooks, as if he were a member of a noble race of Koreans, while they belonged to a lower breed. He was preoccupied with such thoughts when Ŭnhye came running in from outside where she must have been playing.

"Daddy! Daddy!" Ŭnhye shouted. "Let's fly our flag, too. They already have the flag up at Sora's house. And Chŏngmi's, too."

That's right, he thought, it's Independence Day. He stuck his head out the window and there they were. Korean flags fluttered in the scorching sun on practically every balcony on the lower floors. He bowed to his daughter's urging and hung out their flag. Ŭnhye bounced proudly outdoors again. The demolition of the bathroom continued, and his wife rushed around the kitchen, repeatedly adjusting the direction of the electric fan. Simultaneously preparing lunch and conserving water seemed to be causing her to work up a sweat.

"They won't finish today, will they?"

She already seemed weary at the prospect of the project continuing into the next day.

"Probably not," he answered halfheartedly, shoving aside the bathroom paraphernalia that was spread across the floor. He had asked Im the same question and he, too, was vague.

"It could go on for days, but there's nothing for you to worry about, Boss. You pay only what I put down on the estimate. The rest is up to me. I'll get it perfect if it takes me a hundred days."

Apparently, Im didn't expect to finish by nightfall. The younger man was dragging things out, pausing to smoke a cigarette and drink a glass of cold water every thirty minutes or so. And Im, too, busy policing his assistant, carrying on with his own work, and providing a running commentary, seemed to be working at an agonizingly slow pace. It was true, of course, that this was hardly the kind of job where you'd expect quick results, like rolling noodles off a press. Still, when he looked in much later, to his eye there had been no progress with the tearing up, carting off, and scraping. That didn't mean he could stand in the doorway like a supervisor, making sure they weren't fooling around, however, and so he wandered through the house, looking in one room, then another.

"Stop pacing and keep an eye on them! Repairmen have a nasty habit of taking shortcuts when the owner isn't watching," his wife whispered as she mixed spinach greens for lunch. He would have taken care of the baby had she cried, but the child always slept soundly on a full belly and there was really nothing for him to do. Reluctantly, he returned to the bathroom, where he found Im sending the young man to the hardware store for a new pipe. It seems the curved pipe that connected the bathtub to the sink was the source of the problem. Im looked up, his face dripping with perspiration.

"Boss, could you turn on the water? I think the leak is right here."

When he returned from turning on the main valve, water was streaming from the spot Im had indicated.

"See? One tap of this trowel and it'll spout like a fountain."

As soon as Im picked up his trowel and tapped gently on the pipe, water gushed out almost uncontrollably.

"Rusted right through. Boss, hurry and close that valve. Now that we've found the leak, our work's as good as finished."

Im asked for a glass of cold water as he waited for the young man to return. Pleased with Im's prediction, Ŭnhye's mother poured him a large glass of soda.

"So you won't have to work on the sink or toilet?" she asked.

"No, Ma'am. There's no need to replace the rest of the pipe, so it should be fine. It looks like this spot got knocked around when they installed the tub." Im gulped down the soda, his Adam's apple bobbing.

Ŭnhye's father scrutinized the man. Im did a pretty good job for someone who only did repairs during the summer. His T-shirt might have been maroon once, but it was faded now from repeated washing, and the waistband of his black sweat pants, worn so thin that the elastic showed through, was held together by a jagged row of stitches. Despite his small frame, Im's shoulder muscles and the tendons in his wrists looked strong, and his face, flushed with the heat, was healthy looking, like that of a farmer who had just returned from plowing.

"You do very good work, just like Mr. Chu said."

Everyone's vulnerable to praise. And a simpleminded laborer like Im was sure to do his best after a compliment like that. Ŭnhye's father was secretly proud of his well-turned accolade, but Im reacted quite unexpectedly.

"Oh, it's nothing. Anyone would have done the same. You see, there's a certain order to bathroom repairs."

"But you . . ." He wanted to silence Im but was unsure what to say. "But you are the best" would sound strange, and "No one could do as good a job as you" would have been too obviously insincere.

"Ma'am, I'll make sure today's work is perfect, and you promise to order your winter *yŏnt'an* from me, all right? After all, I'm really a *yŏnt'an* deliveryman."

What could he say to that? His wife didn't make it any easier. She failed to make the promise and her face went hard for some reason.

"So where's your hometown?" he asked, confident that he was quicker on his feet than Im. There had to be a way to get to this fellow. Win him over with some smooth talk and he would work harder and do a perfect job, wouldn't he?

"Hometown?" Im smiled bitterly. "There's a song, isn't there? 'Don't ask me where my hometown is?' It hurts to talk about it. It's already been seven or eight years. I was a farmer in Ich'ŏn over in southeastern Kyŏnggi Province. Just a country bumpkin who sold his land, thinking he could make it in the city, and look at me now. If only I'd held onto that land . . ."

Just then, the young man returned with the pipe. He was sucking on an ice pop, the kind children eat, and had a bounce in his step as he entered. *A fool like that deserves to spend his life working as a common laborer,* Ŭnhye's father thought. *Ignorant punk.* After the men had returned to work, his wife dragged him to the far corner of the living room. She obviously wanted to be sure the workers didn't hear.

"So how's he figuring the bill? He told us he was going to have to rip the whole bathroom apart. That's how he figured the original estimate. He said it would be two hundred thousand won altogether, right?"

She had hit on an important issue. The estimate that Im had drawn up, all the time emphasizing how bathroom repairs must be done with the greatest exactitude, clearly assumed that the job entailed much more than the replacement of a pipe running between the bathtub and the sink.

"Go ask him. Now! Those people will say anything for money. I know what he's up to. He gives a high estimate, then he finishes off the job for half that amount. Ordinary people like us have no way of knowing how much it should cost. We have to take their word for it."

His wife was anxious. She would have gotten several estimates had she known better. They'd believed Chu and now they were getting ripped off. With a conscience like that, no wonder Im was only a *yŏnt'an* deliveryman. And on and on. In the end, she even implied that Im's slick talk was all meant to hide his dark intentions.

"And *you* had to compliment him on his fine work. Geez!"

She glared at him, then returned to the kitchen. From the sudden clatter of dishes, it was clear she was vexed at the thought of being cheated. He could hardly blame her, especially since he knew how carefully she balanced their bankbooks and watched real estate prices in Seoul. They wouldn't live in a dump like Wonmidong forever, she said. She had once complained of the pain she felt seeing the high-rise apartments looming in the distance along the Han River when she rode the train to Seoul. According to her, the feeling as you passed through Yŏngdŭngp'o, with all its factory soot, and crossed the Han to Seoul was completely different from the sensation you got crossing the river as you left the city.

They owned their own home with three rooms, if you counted the small room off the kitchen—which was useless, actually, except as storage—an open living area, a kitchen, and a bathroom. But the satisfaction of living in that home had evaporated within a year. Life was different now—none of the endless scurrying and wandering of Seoul—but somehow they found it difficult to sink roots in Wonmi-dong. The frequent household repairs prevented them from feeling anything resembling stability, and more importantly, he and his wife just couldn't give up their longing for Seoul. It was ridiculous, when he stopped to think about it. Even when he had first arrived in Puch'ŏn, after riding through Yŏngdŭngp'o and Kaebong in the back of that truck, he hadn't had any great expectations for a new life in a new place. Of course, he had felt a certain satisfaction knowing he finally owned his own house and wouldn't have to live in someone else's anymore. Otherwise, there would have been no reason to come all the way to Puch'ŏn. That's what was so silly. Of the twelve to fifteen million people living in Seoul, there were surely many who were less educated and poorer than they. He had the unreasonable feeling that those people were citizens of Seoul, while he and his wife had been driven all the way out to Wonmi-dong, and the thought was slowly suffocating them like *yŏnt'an* gas seeping under a door. Puch'ŏn was supposed to be a good place for people with no money, but he was a white-collar worker with a respectable job across the Han River, right in the center of Seoul. He had bar tabs ranging up to 200,000 or 300,000 won at the bars near his office, and he was as scared as the next guy when his boss gave him a dirty look; but he was hardly in the position of someone like Im, who delivered *yŏnt'an* in winter and had to take construction jobs in the summer.

His wife, convinced they were being fleeced, was still stone-faced when she brought out the lunch table. He was embarrassed when she didn't even bother to say "Enjoy your meal." What's more, there were only two rice bowls on the table. She hadn't set out a bowl for him.

"Give me my rice. I might as well eat with these gentlemen," he said in a deliberately carefree manner.

"You eat later with Mother. It's still early." They had eaten breakfast quite late, it was true, but he knew this was her way of saying he couldn't share a meal with the workers. Im paused, spoon in midair, and agreed.

"That's right. We're all messy and covered with dust. We can't eat with the boss."

"Nonsense," he said to Im. Then, to his wife, "Hurry up and get me my rice!"

She reluctantly placed a bowl of rice and a spoon on the table. His head blanketed with white cement dust, Im immediately began emptying his heaping rice bowl. The young worker ignored the side dishes except for the sliced sausages breaded in egg batter. Finally Im rapped him on the head. "Hey, cut it out! What are you, a ten-year-old kid, taking all the good stuff?"

"What do you mean? Other people give us pastries and milk for a morning snack. We didn't get anything today. I'm starving!"

Im knocked the boy on the head again, thinking perhaps that the "boss" was embarrassed by his comment. "You eat like a horse, but your work adds up to little more than sparrow's tears."

"The morning just flew by. We didn't have a chance to prepare a snack. Why don't you have a drink and rest before you go back to work this afternoon?"

His mouth full of rice, Im waved him off.

"No, Boss, no need for that. This is fine. We won't have time to rest if we're going to finish the job today. This kid just has an incredible appetite, that's all."

"Well, it's true. How will I have the strength to do a good job if I don't have a full stomach?" The younger man pouted.

People who have studied, graduated from college, and make their living pushing pens don't need to worry about full stomachs. In fact, overeating is strictly taboo for pen pushers, but for laborers like these men, eating one's fill is a way of recovering one's investment. Ŭnhye's father offered them this side dish and that, all the while secretly watching his wife's reaction.

"When did you start doing this sort of work?"

He was curious about Im's background. The man's hands were covered with huge calluses.

"I've done a little bit of everything. I thought if I worked hard and didn't slack off, anything'd be better than farming. At first, I took the money I got from the sale of my land and tried fish peddling, but I ran out of cash. And then I figured I'd be good at selling peppers, since I'd been a farmer and all, but that wiped me out completely."

Im was as skilled at emptying a rice bowl as he was at making repairs. He had put down his spoon and lighted a Galaxy before his host was half-finished.

"I didn't have any money after that, so I took anything that came my way. It's been six years since I lost all my money in Seoul and moved to Puch'ŏn. I've tried everything—peddling ice, vegetables, dogmeat, roasted silkworms—you name it. But you can't be a peddler without a little money to invest, even if it's only one thousand won, and I was always losing money. And when I did manage to make a little, I always needed more, what with all the kids, so I've been doing construction work since the year before last. I paint, plaster, and install boilers. I've done it all. If they need a handyman, I'm a handyman. If they need a wallpaper hanger, I hang wallpaper. And come winter, I pile *yŏnt'an* in an empty lot and deliver it."

Im's list of occupations was so long and varied, it reminded him of the lyrics of one of the breathless songs by the folk duo of Ha Ch'ŏngil, the short singer, and Sŏ Sunam, the tall one. If Im had done so much and was no better off than this, such despicable skills as overcharging on estimates and skimming off the top must have been recently acquired.

"Delivering *yŏnt'an* is the easiest. Least stress anyway. The price per briquette is set so I can figure how much I need to deliver to make ends meet. It's frightening to see your kids grow when you don't have any money. We live in one basement room and eat a one-hundred won package of instant noodles twice a day. Hard to believe I could afford a big box of rice cakes during the holidays when I was farming. Down home, we used to think all the money came from the city, but I've hardly seen a copper since I got here."

I wonder what he does with all the money he bilks from his customers, Ŭnhye's father thought, studying Im's face. Of course, few homeowners were foolish enough to put their repairs in the hands of an amateur like Im, as he had. The thought left a bitter taste in his mouth.

"You should have kept selling ice. At least it's nice and cool during the summer, right?"

The younger man burped noisily and smirked. *Miserable punk!* Ŭnhye's father thought when he saw that the younger man had left rice at the bottom of his bowl after picking only the most delicious side dishes.

"You don't know what you're talking about!" Im retorted. "I wasted so much money renting a truck and buying the refrigeration equipment. It looks like a good business at first. After all, you just freeze water and sell it, right? But I worked my tail off for an entire summer, and there wasn't a cent left in the end. I figured I'd get some regular customers if I undercut the other ice peddlers, but all I had to show for it was a backache."

"Well, you must have eaten a lot of dog stew when you were selling dogs."

The young man, leaning against the wall and smoking now, smirked once more.

"Boss, you eat dog stew, don't you? There's nothing like mixing a bowl of rice into a thick dog stew come summer," Im said.

Ŭnhye's mother screwed up her lips as she carried the lunch table from the room. She could sulk all she liked, but the story of Im's days as a dog peddler was interesting. Im had taken up the business when the mongrel that he kept at home had puppies. There wasn't much to it, he explained, just throw a sack over your shoulder and stroll through a quiet neighborhood with a few dried squid legs or herring heads for bait.

"There's never been much profit in dogs because the middlemen are so stingy. The only way to turn a profit is to catch stray dogs. All you do is throw the dog a dried fish head and wait for him to finish. Then you start walking. He'll follow you anywhere after that, drooling all the way. When you think you've got far enough away, you slip a chain around his neck and head home. It's that easy. You know the dog market in Yŏngdŭngp'o Market, don't you? Well, that's where you sell the dog, and if you come back the next day, he's dead meat, lying on a board ready to be sold. Can't keep doing it for long, that's for sure. Makes you feel guilty when you see the dog sprawled out with its eyes wide open."

Im gave up the dog trade after he had taken dozens to slaughter. It was around that time that he lost his taste for dog stew. And before long, the newspapers and television were filled with stories about dogmeat carrying some kind of bacteria. That relieved the suffering of dogs to a certain extent.

As the men rose to resume work, Ŭnhye's grandmother returned, pushing Ŭnhye ahead of her.

"What a nice place they have. I never dreamed there were such fine homes in Puch'ŏn." She was referring to the house Deacon Kim had recently moved into.

"Mother, time for lunch." His wife had set a new table.

"No, I just came to get Ŭnhye. They're preparing lunch now. The minister's going to perform a service at Deacon Kim's to bless the move. Ŭnhye'll just get in the way here. I'll take her with me. We'll eat lunch there and then help them for a while."

She changed the child out of her dirty clothes and set out. Left to eat alone, his wife poured water into her rice. That was a sign she was in a bad mood.

"What's wrong?" he asked.

"She didn't need to take Ŭnhye. Why didn't you stop her?"

"What's wrong with Ŭnhye having a tasty lunch with her grandmother?"

"They just moved in. They must be busy. They don't need a child underfoot. Besides, we're not beggars. It's not like we've never seen good food."

"Ah, come on! What's wrong with you? Can't stand the idea of Deacon Kim living in a house as big as a palace, eh?"

"I didn't say that. Besides, you can hardly compare our circumstances with Deacon Kim's."

At least she hadn't completely forgotten their circumstances. He could tell by the way she quickly returned to the subject of Im's estimate.

"Go straighten it out. From what he said earlier, the man's been through a lot. He's sure to have developed a lot of tricks over the years."

As he listened to Im's story, he had thought how hopeless the man's life had been. It was really no different from the lives of the dogs he had dragged off to slaughter. Neither Im nor the dogs had any hope of deliverance. But his wife, hearing the same story, saw a man who could be extraordinarily deceptive.

"I'll mention it when I pay him. There's plenty of time. If he's so tricky, how come he's still living like this?"

Whether he realized it or not, he had left his wife's side for Im's. Most likely though, his reaction was nothing more than a sliver of sympathy, having glimpsed the sad fate of an unfortunate man.

The plumbing project took on a new look in the afternoon. The young man, who had worked so reluctantly that morning, now stopped altogether, claiming he had an appointment to keep.

"Pay me for a half-day now. And you didn't pay me for yesterday yet. I can't afford a cup of coffee."

The young man stuck out his hand to Im, heedless of who was watching. Im grumbled as if he might whack the younger man on the head once more, then took out a 5,000-won bill and handed it to him. The young man looked in the mirror hanging on the wall, examining his teeth and combing his hair with a comb he carried in his pocket, then went to the kitchen sink and washed his hands with great care. It was obvious he planned to go out and spend his morning's wages.

"He hasn't experienced enough of life's hardships yet. That's his problem. The boy lives next door to me. I noticed he was just idling at home, so I've been sending him on errands and the like, but he's always goofing off."

"He doesn't look like the type for this kind of work."

"You're right. He'd make the perfect con man, slapping folks on the back and playing up to them."

At the mention of playing up to people, Ŭnhye's father couldn't help but recall Im's own dark tricks with the inflated estimate. The man probably thought he deserved understanding for his back-slapping deceit while he applied stricter standards to others.

With the young man's departure, Ŭnhye's father was reduced to playing Im's assistant. First, the bathtub had to be returned to its original position. He had thought lightly of the work that the young man had made such a fuss about, but now he realized it was quite strenuous. His shoulders ached from carrying sacks of broken tiles and cement down the stairs. After several trips, his undershirt was soaked with sweat, and he secretly fumed at the way Im called him "Boss" while ordering him around.

"You're working too hard, Boss. And today's your day off. Oh my goodness! Look at you sweat!"

Seemingly unaware of the perspiration dripping down his own face, Im marveled at the beads of sweat and chuckled. Hefting bags of cement and sand up the stairs and mixing the two were jobs for the "boss." As the "technician," Im simply poured the cement. When they ran out of sealant, the "boss" had to run to the hardware store; he had to stand, arms outstretched, pressing down on the tub to hold it in place while it dried.

It was after three when his wife brought a bottle of *makkŏlli* and some snacks, and he and Im were finally able to straighten up and rest.

"*Makkŏlli*. It's the best drink for a working man."

The bottle was soon empty and Im dashed out, saying he was going to get the tiles. Whether out of gratitude for the roast pork his wife had served with the *makkŏlli* or in anticipation of the coming winter when he returned to his job delivering *yŏnt'an*, Im had been solicitous as they drank.

"Now Ma'am, let me know if there are cracks in the cement anywhere else in the house. We'll be finished as soon as I get the tiles in, but with these long summer days, I'll be able to give you a hand with any other repairs you have."

When Im stepped out for the tiles, his wife pursed her lips.

"I guess he does have a conscience after all. Must feel guilty trying to take advantage of us like that."

"I don't think so. He's just thankful that I helped him. Why do you always have to think the worst of everyone?"

"So all of a sudden you're taking on a worker's mentality, are you?"

Anyhow, they agreed that as long as they were being overcharged, they might as well fix the leak in the roof over the bedroom. Whenever there was a heavy rain, they heard water dripping. All they needed to do was take up the part of the roof that leaked and seal it. They had put off the task because the leak hadn't stained the wallpaper yet.

After the tiles were laid and the tools gathered, the bathroom was finished. It was nearly six, but the summer day was long, and blue sky was still visible through the window. Im prepared to seal the leak in the roof without further discussion. The two men estimated where the leak was and set upon the spot with their hammers. Ŭnhye's father immediately regretted joining Im in this task, however, because after a few blows of the hammer, he pulled a muscle and felt a stabbing pain in his shoulder.

And that was only the beginning. They had only broken up a few square feet of roof, but it took three or four trips to haul away the debris and four or five more to carry up two sacks of cement and several loads of sand, all on his back. Each time he mounted the zigzagging flight of stairs, his legs wobbled. Darkness was fast approaching, however, and he couldn't make Im do it alone. For whatever reason, Im was doing something not included in his original estimate, so Ŭnhye's father carried the sacks, dripping thick beads of sweat all the way.

Boy, this work isn't for everyone, he thought, recalling Pak Ch'ansŏng, his coworker in the sales division. Pak had tried to console him when he was transferred to the PR office.

"They must be trying to sack me," he had complained. "Why else would they make a fool of me, forcing me to do something I've never done before?"

"Just do what you're told," Pak advised. "Play up to them. A wage earner's life may be miserable, but what would become of us if we got fired at our age? No money in the bank, no rich in-laws, not a scrap of land to our names. And we could hardly make a living doing physical labor. Our bodies are already rotten. Rotten from drink, rotten from bootlicking, rotten from worthless knowledge. Me? I'm so burned out, I can hardly lift my spoon to eat."

Pak was right, every word. Ŭnhye's father's head was spinning from work he had never done before. Im, on the other hand, was in fine shape, although he had been working since morning. He was perspiring—after all, it was hot—but he didn't look tired, really.

"That's it!" he murmured as he stared at Im's bulging calf muscles. "Today's Independence Day! Im's as brave as the soldiers of the anticolonial forces. A veritable Hercules! If he'd been born in the Koryŏ Kingdom, he would have been a heroic general, that's for sure." He shook his head; he had a useless habit of analyzing everything, and the long strands of thoughts, tangled like coils of taffy, made his head feel heavy. But what could he do? The thoughts kept coming, one after another.

Disgruntled workers often did a halfhearted job and deliberately messed things up when the boss wasn't watching. It was a form of rebellion. Before liberation from Japanese rule in 1945, Korean laborers must have messed things up on purpose, carefully avoiding the eyes of their Japanese supervisors, because the smelly Japs were always complaining about the gooks. And since liberation, social contradictions had driven workers to act this way. The rich enjoyed their wealth in grand fashion, never doubting their right to it, while workers like Im, equally confident of their own rights, ignored the rules of fair trade and cut corners whenever they had a chance. So . . .

Unaware of what was going on in the boss's head, Im deftly spread a combination of sealant and cement over the surface of the roof. The weather didn't affect the work done indoors, but on the roof everything would be ruined if it rained before the sealant dried. Ŭnhye's father looked into the darkening sky. It was a typical summer sky. A few dark clouds floated by; behind them wavelike wisps of clouds drifted on the south wind. *There's no stopping summer's fickle weather,* he thought as he dusted off his hands. He was thinking of smoking a cigarette now that Im's work seemed to be nearing an end.

"It often rains in summer. What do you do then?"

"Oh, I have things to do when it rains."

Im's dusty hands began to move faster. A dark blue light was descending around the two men.

"So you have another job when it rains?"

"On rainy days I have to go to Karibong-dong early in the morning."

"Karibong-dong? The factory district?"

"Yes. It doesn't concern you, Boss. I just go to Karibong-dong when it rains."

Im paused for a moment, and an enigmatic expression crossed his face. Ŭnhye's father was about to suggest that Im deserved to rest on rainy days if he worked this hard all the time, but he kept his mouth shut. As the head of a hungry family that had to survive on instant noodles twice a day, Im could hardly afford to loll around at home just because it was raining.

The roof patching, which he had thought so simple, was taking much longer than he had expected. It took a long time to get the angle right so that water drained into the downspout, and then they had to chip away a bit more of the roof to make sure water didn't seep between the patch and the roof. Night was fast upon them and lights appeared in neighboring windows. Still, Im seemed disinclined to lay down his tools until he was satisfied with the results. He measured here, then there, broke apart an area he had already sealed and spread a new layer of cement over it. He seemed completely oblivious to the passage of time.

Ŭnhye's mother, who had stuck her head out from time to time to check on their progress, finally seemed weary of the whole business.

"Just finish up as best you can. It's dark. Hurry and come down."

"Yes, Ma'am. I'm almost done. I have to finish the job properly."

Only after adding more sealant to the cement and spreading it over the patched area with his fingers to assure a perfect seal did Im straighten up. While Im worked, Ŭnhye's father watched in silence, practically holding his breath. He felt sorry that the payoff for the calluses on those ten fingers was nothing more than life in a basement room. He had noticed Im's hands when he was working on the bathroom, too. There was something remarkable about them. The fingers were more than fingers—the way they moved, so quickly, so attuned to the work he was doing. At first, he had thought Im was putting on a show because he felt bad about taking the full sum of the estimate. His wife had expressed the same thought when he came downstairs briefly while Im was still working.

"The roof's a lot more work than he expected, I guess. Serves him right. Now he'll see that nothing comes free in this world."

But if they thought it was all a show, the joke was on them. Ŭnhye's father had to play errand boy until well after eight o'clock, and his wife was beside herself with guilt for purposely concocting the project in the first place.

She prepared a tray of drinks while she was waiting for them to finish. Im washed his hands and feet and brushed the dust from his clothes in the stairwell. When he returned to their apartment and saw that it was after eight, he apologized. "I didn't realize it was so late. Ma'am, I'm sorry I've kept you up, and you, Boss, you really worked hard today. I'm sorry."

Ŭnhye's grandmother, who was looking after the children in the bedroom, praised Im's efforts in their stead.

"You do fine work for a young fella. You could have called it a day and finished up tomorrow, but you aren't afraid of hard work. That's for sure. Yep, you have a bright future."

Im listened politely, kneeling forward with his hands pressed to the floor.

"I'm a Christian, so I don't think much of men drinking, but you deserve a drink today. You just relax and enjoy yourself. I'll go in the other room."

As soon as the old woman closed the door, Im wrapped his hands around the glass Ŭnhye's father offered, then politely turned aside to drink.

"What are you doing? Relax and enjoy yourself! We're practically the same age. No need for formalities."

Despite saying that, Ŭnhye's father couldn't erase the discomfort he felt at the thought that Im might be much older than he was. When the cold winds blew, Im would have to go out to deliver the *yŏnt'an* that covered him with soot, and when summer came, he would have to get by, one day at a time, on the odd jobs he got from friends who owned bona fide repair shops that had signs out front. Knowing that, he could hardly say Im had a bright future.

"So how old are you, Boss? I was born in the Year of the Rabbit. That makes me thirty-five."

Im was thirty-five, born in the Year of the Rabbit, and he was thirty-four, born in the Year of the Dragon. His wife, who was seated next to them, fidgeting with her billfold, started to answer, "My husband is—" but he cut her off.

"Really? I was born in the Year of the Rabbit, too. We're the same age!"

His wife stared at him in astonishment, but he ignored her and poured Im's glass to overflowing in celebration of the coincidence. How lucky to have to lie about only one year.

"Men born in the Year of the Rabbit generally have a hard life, but rabbit women live quite well. Strange . . . How men our age have such a hard time, I mean. But you're doing pretty well for yourself, Boss. You're a lucky man."

Damn, he felt terrible.

His wife abandoned all artifice and opened her billfold, sensing perhaps that this talk of the Year of the Rabbit could go nowhere or realizing that the liquor she had served would soon run dry.

"We should pay you. But there's . . ."

She looked to her husband, unable to go on. He lifted his cup and pretended not to notice. Just like a woman—gets him to do the roof and now she can't stand the idea of paying him in full. He prayed that she would hand over the 200,000 won, minus 20,000, as the estimate stated. But Im waved his hand before she had a chance.

"Ma'am, could I see the estimate I gave you? I think the total will have to be changed."

His wife handed him the paper she was holding in her hand. It wasn't a formally printed bill, just a sheet of childish stationery with a pink background. Im studied it at length. The couple was nervous, fearing what he might say.

"It's hard figuring the numbers after a few drinks," he said, bending over the paper, adding and subtracting, then crossing out a line here and there.

Ŭnhye's father shook the near-empty bottle and poured the remaining wine into his glass, draining it quickly. He was disgusted with himself for worrying about the numbers rolling around in Im's head.

"That's it. Okay, Boss, now look here. In the beginning, I drew up the estimate figuring we'd have to tear up the whole bathroom, since we didn't know where the leak was. But like I told you, things turned out to be a lot less complicated than I expected. So, that means forty thousand less for labor, and I didn't use all this cement. Same goes for the sand . . . Oh, and we didn't need a truck to haul off the debris. Let's see. The sealant and tiles . . . I used only half of them, so I'll take that off."

Im explained each item, poking the paper with the tip of the pen, but Ŭnhye's father wasn't listening. The feeling that something was gravely wrong, that this wasn't the way it was supposed to be, pressed down on him like the pain in his shoulders.

"So it all adds up to seventy thousand won," Im announced, handing the pink paper back to Ŭnhye's mother. She was even more astonished than her husband was. It was clear she couldn't believe that he had really said seventy thousand won.

"Seventy thousand? But the roof—"

"I've included the cost of the materials I used on the roof right here. It didn't come to much."

"But really, this is too . . ."

She looked at her husband with imploring eyes. He had to intercede.

"Why don't you check it one more time? Didn't you say it came to one hundred eighty thousand in the beginning?"

"Are you saying you want to pay more? Oh, Boss! I didn't work for free, believe me. I figured it all out, item by item. And I threw in the labor on the roof as a favor."

"A favor?" he asked in amazement.

"Of course. I know when to give a little bonus."

What could he say?

"Ah, *now* I see why you have such a good life, Boss, even though you were born in the Year of the Rabbit. You wouldn't believe some of my customers, Boss. They're always finding fault with everything, just so they can knock a few cents off my wages. I'm an ignorant laborer, but let me tell you something, Boss. You mustn't be so softhearted. You'll never make it in this world. I've been paid for everything I've done, so you just promise me one thing: Be sure to order your *yŏnt'an* from me come winter."

Im shoved the 70,000 won into his pocket and stood up.

Ŭnhye's father decided to see Im off at the front door downstairs. Im's tool bag banged against the railing as they stumbled down the steps. The cool night air embraced them as they emerged from the front door. He tried to think of a way to say farewell to this man. "You did a fine job. Thank you." The words somehow seemed shabby after Im's "little bonus." Im turned and grabbed his arm.

"Hey, Boss. I'm feeling kind of low. How about a beer? I'm paying."

Im pointed to the chairs in front of Brothers Supermarket, lit now by an incandescent light.

"Sure, but I'll buy."

"No! It's on me."

"Okay. Who cares who pays? Let's go!"

They ordered three bottles of beer from Captain Kim.

"Whoa there! Where you all been drinking, gentlemen?" he asked. Kim was from Puan in Chŏlla Province, and when he was feeling good, he had a knack for teasing people in his native dialect. "Beer's fine, but it sure would be nice if you could pay off your bill first, Uncle Im."

Im promptly paid Kim the 1,300 won, then, with an air of bravado, told him to roast three dried filefish.

"Boss," he said turning toward Ŭnhye's father, "do you want to order something else to go with the beer?"

"Come on. Why do you keep calling me 'Boss'? We're the same age, remember? It's been bugging me all day. Boss, Boss, Boss. Let's treat each other like equals," he bellowed, holding out a frothy glass of beer. Im stared at him in surprise.

"All right, Brother. Drink up!" Im clinked his glass with bravado.

"Yes, yes! What's all this 'Boss' talk when we were both born in the Year of the Rabbit?"

He matched Im's bluster and soon the two men were exchanging glasses.

"You know, I've got a lot of kids," Im said. He had four children. His eldest son was doing well in fourth grade, and his younger daughter was on the school basketball team and handled the ball like the national team's star, Pak Ch'ansuk.

"I've always regretted it, Brother. Never been able to feed them so much as a bowl of beef soup. Next time I go to Karibong-dong I'm going to wring it out of that bastard."

Im sent a stream of spit through his teeth. Kim's mutt dashed over, thinking it was something good to eat.

"What? You get beef soup in Karibong-dong?"

Ŭnhye's father shook his head at the sudden wave of intoxication that swept over him. Im poured him another glass of beer. *I go to Karibong-dong when it rains.* Im's words rose in his mind with a drunken fever.

"Not just beef soup. There's a bike for my oldest boy and sneakers for our basketball star, and a permanent wave for the wife. All together it comes to eight hundred thousand won. Eight hundred thousand. Shit. You see, for a whole year I supplied *yŏnt'an* to this fellow who ran a sweater factory, then he ditched, in the middle of the night, without settling the bill. He made a big fuss about the factory going bankrupt, and I felt bad, but then, do you know what he did? The son-of-a-bitch ran off to Karibong-dong and set up an even bigger factory! Can you believe that? Of course, we working folk come from all over, so it didn't take me long to find out where he'd gone."

"You've got to get that money. It's your money."

Ŭnhye's father started to hiccup. His hand shook uncontrollably as he poured Im another beer. Im, by comparison, seemed in complete control.

"Yeah, it's my money, but that doesn't mean he'll give it to me. Brother, let me tell you something. The rich are just a bunch of thieves. Every time I go over there, he tells me these sad stories. About how he hasn't been able to pay the women who work in the factory, about how he had to sell off his wife's necklace to pay his debts."

"Bastard."

He could picture the owner of the sweater factory. He was sure to have a potbelly and a greasy mug.

"That was last year. And you know how much it's rained this

summer. So I've gone to Karibong-dong every time it rains. Yep, whenever it rains, off I go."

"Man, it rains all the time. Whatcha worried about?" Kim asked as he returned with more beer.

"Shut up, you. It has to rain for me to go to Karibong-dong. It has to rain."

"Sunny days earn some money, rainy days collect some money. Whoopee!" Kim chanted, tapping a pair of chopsticks on the table. Im slapped him on the rear.

"Brother, you've got a house, so there's nothing to worry about. What does it matter if you were born in the Year of the Rabbit? You've got a house, and real estate prices will never go down."

"You can hardly call that a proper house . . ."

He was about to say that it was a miserable dump that swallowed money right and left, that he didn't know what would go wrong next, but Im cut him off.

"You know, I . . . this man born in the Year of the Rabbit lives with four kids and a wife in a basement room with a one and a half million won security deposit and thirty thousand won a month in rent. While that bastard in Karibong-dong—he's got a condominium! It's a mansion!"

Im shook his fist at the word "mansion," but to Ŭnhye's father's ear, it sounded like *maenson*—bare fist.

"I never have the time to go get the money. My wife, she works in a brick factory, and I do this crap for a living. We can't even afford to sit down and enjoy a fried egg."

Im's voice had grown hoarse. Ŭnhye's father was afraid to offer him another glass of beer for fear he was getting too drunk.

"They say money goes round and round, don't they? Well, I'd like to meet the guy who's seen it come round. Folks like me, we live our whole life like this. Money? Ha! It's all a load of bullshit! Bullshit, that's what it is!"

Im slammed his fist on the table. The beer bottles teetered and rolled to the ground with a crash.

"Just try to hold on. Someday—"

"It's useless!"

Overwhelmed by Im's anger, Ŭnhye's father fell silent once more. He could hardly say that someday Im, too, would live in a condominium, that someday he would grow tired of fried eggs and hate beef soup because it was so filling, that someday he would grumble about gourmet food and guzzle expensive imported whiskey when it rained, because he knew that no matter how you held on, that thick wall, that insurmountable peak, wasn't going to crumble of its own accord.

Ŭnhye's father couldn't face Im's bloodshot eyes. Suddenly he felt himself sobering up. What if Im realized that he had spent the whole day thinking he was trying to swindle him with a trumped-up estimate? Im may have been healthy, but he could hardly hold all that alcohol if he was living on instant noodles. As he watched Im list further and further to one side, the effects of the alcohol left him.

"Some guys make hundreds of millions while others work their fingers to the bone and barely get two hundred thousand won. How do those sons of bitches do it? You know, the ones that drive around in imported cars and pay hundreds of thousands in tips at bars. I could kill 'em! I'd like to kill those bastards!" Im sputtered.

"Hey, why you raisin' such a racket when you're drinkin' that expensive beer? Come on, Uncle Im. Relax!"

Kim dashed over and cleared away the empty bottles and glasses. Im banged his head on the table. "I'll kill 'em, I'll kill 'em," he kept crying. Ŭnhye's father just stared helplessly at Im's pale face. A feeling of alienation prevented him from even touching the man's shoulder; he feared that he might be one of the "bastards" Im was so determined to kill.

"Come winter the wife and kids are covered in soot. I drag the kids along so we can deliver more *yŏnt'an*. Brother, don't you see what kind of person I am? I'm a good-for-nothing fool who covers his own wife and kids with soot."

Im's tongue, so fluent before, was finally soaked in drink. He kept grabbing at his mouth because the words didn't seem to be coming out right.

"I . . . Next time it rains, I'm going to Karibong-dong and I'm . . ."

Im stared at him, eyes empty. Even his voice had lost its vigor now.

"If only he'd give me the money . . . If only I had that money . . . If I had that money, I'd go back to my hometown."

"Your hometown?"

"Yeah. I'm going home, my hometown."

Im pulled his hair with those callused hands and began to cry. "Ah, Uncle Im! He always ends up crying in his beer. It's a habit, an old drinking habit," Kim called from inside his store. But Im kept crying, like a child driven from his home. Ǔnhye's father rose stealthily, feigning the need to urinate, and went to Kim to settle the bill. After paying, he really did need to urinate and slowly crossed the street to the empty lot, beyond the reach of the supermarket's lights. Someone brushed past him. "*Uaaak! Uaaak!*" A scream, a groan, accompanied by a clapping sound, echoed through the darkness. "*Uaaak!*" It was the Old Screamer. The old man lingered near the empty lot until Ǔnhye's father finished his business, repeating the pained sound again. "*Uaaak! Uaaak!*"

As he zipped up his pants and turned, Ǔnhye's father saw Im under the light of the incandescent bulb, slumped over and pulling at his hair. People from the neighborhood, people whose names he did not know but whose faces he recognized, stole furtive looks as they went to and from the supermarket.

It must be quite late, he thought, and the Independence Day holiday was now over. His heart tightened. All he had left to do was go home and fall into a deep, dreamless sleep, like a tree falling in the forest. The sky was full of stars, and it looked like it wouldn't rain the next day. The Old Screamer clapped his hands and cried, "*Uaaak! Uaaak!*" as if he, too, was looking up at the sky.

Bellfinch

AT THE ENTRANCE to the park was a shelter for lost children. It looked like a glass cylinder; its round roof was painted green, and large windows wrapped around its sides. She paused quite unintentionally and, with her daughter Kyŏngju, looked inside. Faces curious, Yunhŭi and her son Sŏnggu, who had been following behind, stopped, too. Five or six small children looked out at the passersby; some were sucking on ice-cream bars, others were crying halfheartedly, noses running and faces stained with tears. It was still early, but these children had already lost their parents in the crowded park, and now they pressed their noses against the windows and whimpered at the outside world.

People laughed as they passed. Some pointed and seemed to find the sight of the lost children amusing. Young children, still holding fast to their own parents' hands, stood on tiptoe and peered inside as if they had discovered something truly remarkable. The lost children looked all the more pitiful because they were imprisoned under that green roof, away from their parents. A girl's pretty dress, trimmed with lace, and the beret worn by a well-dressed little gentleman looked ragged and limp for the simple reason that their owners were separated from their families. The orphaned children were a source of entertainment for the people outside the glass.

It was some distance from the lost children's shelter by the main plaza to the entrance of the zoo. Yunhŭi struggled to hold on to Sŏnggu's hand, as if she had concluded from the four-year-old's rambunctious behavior that he was a likely candidate for the shelter they had just passed. Sŏnggu and Kyŏngju were the same age, but

Kyŏngju was overly cautious and timid in crowded places like this. She looked back repeatedly to make sure she hadn't strayed too far from her mother. Kyŏngju's mom felt a certain regret each time she saw Yunhŭi and her son. *If only Sŏnggu were a girl.* But whenever she told Yunhŭi that a daughter would be much easier for a divorcée to raise alone, Yunhŭi tried to laugh it off. "So you should have a girl just in case you get divorced?" she asked.

The two women had talked about coming to Seoul Grand Park for a long time. She and Yunhŭi were from Inch'ŏn. They had gone to the same middle school and high school, and now they both lived in Puch'ŏn. Yunhŭi, who ran a restaurant that closed its doors only one day a month, had been planning a special day with Sŏnggu for some time. When it came to her son's education, her well-defined sense of duty was no different from any other mother's. She had already decided that Sŏnggu was a problem child, simply because he was raised by a divorced mother and growing up in a noisy restaurant. Kyŏngju's mom was less enthusiastic about today's outing, but she'd had no reason to refuse Yunhŭi's suggestion, which was meant, in part, to roust Kyŏngju and her mother from their old tile-roofed house.

The two women were alike in that neither had a husband at home. Kyŏngju's mom's thoughts turned to her absent spouse, not simply because she and Yunhŭi were two women alone amidst a throng of families. Strictly speaking, she would have to say it was more the faint hint of fallen leaves on the distant mountains or perhaps the early autumn sunlight falling on the asphalt road. The sharp contrast of colors made her think of her husband. Most husbands were at the side of their wives and children, but hers had to spend an indeterminate period of time in an isolated world now. She thought of him as young fathers carrying picnic baskets and ground cloths brushed past with their families.

Gazing up at the mountains shrouded in yellow-green shadows, she suddenly felt her right eyelid twitch. Soon it began to twitch every three or four seconds, and the mountains, trees, and brightly colored souvenir shops in her right sphere of vision looked as if they, too, had been seized by a momentary spasm. She lifted her hand and gently pressed down on the eyelid. Because the tic was a familiar symptom that had been interfering with her life for some time, she could have walked forever with her hand pressed against her eye.

❖

She felt as if she had walked down an endless corridor. Then, too, the white walls and silent ceiling had trembled every few seconds, and her hand was pressed to her eye. But there was nothing resembling a corridor leading to the visitors' room; she had passed only a few steel doors and firmly fixed stares. Her husband's face was pale, and his forearms seemed so white as they poked out from the short sleeves of his prison uniform. In that perfectly square space, they were completely separate: husband on that side, wife on this. She laced her fingers together—fingers that could have ripped away the single layer of steel screen—and stared blankly at the gray wall behind her husband. It was covered with stains and fingerprints. He blew a puff of air at the floor and made a show of scuffing clean the spot, for no apparent reason.

The ticking of the wall clock, unadorned except for its large numbers, resounded sharply through the visitors' room. Finally she stopped staring at the stains on the blank wall and looked at her husband. Like a caged beast, but with eyes now devoid of any spark, he looked at her, too. "Has Kyŏngju recovered from that cold?" he asked. Only after a long pause did she answer. "It looks like summer's gone already." "Don't worry. Take it easy." His words passed through the screen. "Your cousin in the countryside sent some garlic." Her words passed back through the screen. Just when she had grown accustomed to the wooden chairs, polished from use, and the bitter taste of the repeated hand gestures, her husband was reminding her once again to take it easy and offering her a slice of a large but feeble smile. Then, with a final look that seemed to say that the empty gestures were finished, he left through the door he had come in by, and she pulled herself up and returned to the outside world.

When her husband was first cut off from his family and sent to the other side of the wall alone, she'd been completely unprepared. Later, she learned that contingency plans were of no help in such situations anyway, but at first she had despaired at her helplessness. Her husband hadn't always been the kind of person to simply exist inside the old tile-roofed house that they had inherited from his father, eking out a living off the rent from its many rooms. Her husband was a person who had once thought that all people should be equal, if possible, and live together in warmth and harmony.

At some point that thought had become a conviction to which he dedicated himself exclusively. She in turn had tried to master the task of living despite the absence of her husband; she had left his place vacant.

❖

Their first stop was an enormous monkey cage. It was the monkeys' exclusive stage, with steep man-made cliffs and rope ladders stretching from one side to the other. The animals performed their stunts happily, shrieking as they flew through the air; she could have watched them forever. Her husband held the simple expectation that, no matter what, he would turn out like Kafka's Red Peter; as long as his belief remained unshattered, that tribe of monkeys was a mirror of humanity for her.

The children didn't want to leave the monkeys' cage. It wasn't accurate to call it a cage; it was more like a deserted island taken over by dozens of monkey entertainers, who flashed their red anuses and taunted the spectators lining the wall. As they watched the monkeys battling on the rope ladders and dashing back and forth over the rocks, the spectators kept quoting the old proverb, "Even the monkey falls from his tree sometimes." But the monkeys never fell. Sometimes one pretended to, as if to reassure the humans with their proverbs, but when the cries of alarm passed, the monkey was invariably crouched safely on an artificial rock at the far side of the enclosure, spitting out apple peels.

Monkeys imitate humans and humans imitate monkeys, and as they left the monkey island, Sŏnggu insisted on mimicking their antics. He soon fell and skinned his knee but still showed no sign of tiring. His mercurial energy made Kyŏngju even more timid. The typical girl, she clung to her mother, mumbling under her breath, "I'm scared. I'm scared of Big Brother. He's scary like a bug."

Kyŏngju feared bugs more than anything. She steadfastly believed that there was nothing more frightening in the world than bugs, whether it was a squirt bug or sow bug crawling out from under the wardrobe, a cockroach, or a money bug. When Dracula appeared in a summer horror show, she screamed, "Mommy, Mommy, I'm scared. Look at that awful bug." But when her mother came running, she saw it was Dracula, chasing people with blood dripping from his fangs. It would be a long time before

Kyŏngju realized that there was nothing more frightening than the creatures that walked around on two feet. And it would be years before she understood that the only way to escape the anxieties of this society, where people were regularly exposed and attacked simply for being human, was to become an insect herself. It was no accident that the insects hiding in the dark recesses under wardrobes or in cracks in the floor were squashed in one brief defenseless moment.

Kyŏngju's mom realized this all the more clearly when she thought of her husband, who had left their side and was now focused elsewhere. If you are afraid of parting with the things you love, you must stand up proudly on your own two feet. That's what it means to be human. And the people left behind have to deal with the resulting loneliness.

Keeping up with the children as they searched for things to see was more tiring than she had expected. Not that there were any truly amazing attractions. They walked for a while and there were the giraffes, then they walked until their legs hurt and there were the wolves. That's how it went. People moved in waves, wandering this way and that, as if they had lost their sense of direction. They drifted aimlessly, then drifted some more. At the sight of an elephant, they let out a whoop and dashed toward the animal, like castaways grabbing for a floating board on the open sea. Then they regrouped and wandered off again in another direction. Sŏnggu scampered through the crowds like a squirrel. Yunhŭi perspired heavily trying to keep up with him, and when she managed to catch the boy, he shook her arm, begging for an ice cream or cola. The boy reminded Kyŏngju's mom of Yunhŭi's ex-husband.

She had only met the man two or three times, including the time she saw him before the wedding and at the wedding itself. She had never seen him again after they got married. The marriage had been so brief, and her own precipitous life hadn't allowed her to look beyond her own immediate concerns. After her marriage, she'd hardly ever had the peace of mind to see her own friends. She hadn't gone to her parents' home in Inch'ŏn, either, except when it was absolutely necessary. Puch'ŏn was where her husband was born and where he had grown up; she had never thought of leaving the town. He loved Wonmi-dong and thought the old house was a dream. She felt the same way. Oblivious to the neighborhood changing around them, they had locked themselves inside and lived their days nurturing an unreachable dream and futile hopes.

Later, when she heard that Yunhŭi had opened a restaurant—all on her own, with a small son just learning to walk—she was truly amazed. She had never thought Yunhŭi would also end up wandering the slopes of a precipitous life. What's more, Yunhŭi's decision to leave Inch'ŏn and move to Puch'ŏn, of all places, to pursue her independence seemed profoundly meaningful. For whatever reason, Yunhŭi felt the need to start a new life. It would have been nice to live in Seoul, but she didn't have the money, Yunhŭi explained. "They say a true friend will follow you to the ends of the earth, and *you're* in Puch'ŏn," she quipped. "Let's just say that's why I came to Puch'ŏn." Kyŏngju's mom readily accepted Yunhŭi's grounds for divorce. Never mind the fact that she had been thoroughly deceived by the matchmaker. With the countless lies, the wastefulness, and the gambling, the marriage was hopeless. She knew how realistic and practical Yunhŭi was in all things. In fact, Yunhŭi wasn't at all despondent; rather, as she focused her efforts on earning money, she looked more radiant than ever. All in all, her divorce seemed a success.

"This really is the largest zoo in East Asia. It'll take the whole day just to see the animals." Yunhŭi surveyed the park, shielding her eyes from the autumn sun with her hand. The camera hanging from her shoulder glinted metallically. Her necklace and bracelet, and the round earrings dangling from her ears reflected the sun in tiny fragments.

It was less than an hour since they had entered the park, but already Kyŏngju's mom found herself searching for places to sit down. Yunhŭi diagnosed this fatigue as a "lack of vigor." It was her pet theory that the secret to making money in the restaurant business was targeting men concerned about their "lack of vigor." She said she would never be satisfied with her present restaurant, which specialized in *samgyet'ang*, a medicinal soup made of chicken stuffed with ginseng roots and rice. The restaurant was located on the left side of the plaza in front of the train station and was doing quite well.

"Snakes or worms—what does it matter? If the customers feel like they're brimming with vigor after eating them, it's good for the customers, and I make money, so it's good for me, too." Then Yunhŭi lowered her voice to a whisper. "You know men. . . . They turn white as ghosts if they can't get it up."

Men seemed fixated on the fatalistic notion that if they no longer desired women, they were finished as men. That was why they chased after women and told dirty jokes without inhibition. Of course, women weren't any better. After all, while women seemed less aggressive, in the end, sex was impossible without them.

Now that she was living alone, Kyŏngju's mom was confronted with countless sexual innuendoes, suggestions practically announced in the streets, in the market, even from close neighbors, all making her keenly aware of the stark reality of her husband's absence. Yunhŭi was already adept at responding to such signals. Of course, she had guaranteed freedom and economic independence, so the advances on her came from a position of greater equality, and as time passed, even her gestures seemed to take on a certain seductiveness.

That was especially true in Seoul, Kyŏngju's mom thought suddenly. Though the city was crumbling and its residents might soon be buried, at present, Seoul was awash with money, lust, and a greed for power. People with a little bit less struggled to acquire one more thing, while the people who already possessed many things constantly searched, eyes bright, for something new. Very few believed they couldn't acquire something more. In the name of freedom and equality, they had been taught that resignation meant humiliation, so anyone who was human dashed ahead, gasping like an asthmatic for something more than they already possessed.

Sometimes when she rose at dawn and saw the gray strands of mist hanging over the city, she imagined the clouds were the residue from all the gasps of desire released through the night. And when she saw the breath of conspiracy, from the city's many secret rooms, basements, and dark street corners, steal away with the sun's appearance, she felt certain she was right.

There had been times, when the mist rolled in thick, that she imagined she had disintegrated and been swept up in it. She had once thought that the cycle of sleeping and rising was the very first respiration in the passive repetition of life. But those days were definitely more comfortable than recent days; each morning now she struggled under a vague feeling that she was gradually being drawn deeper into a bottomless well. Back then she had anticipated the future. Back then she had thought that the future was hers to realize and shape on her own—not someone else's. Marriage, too, was the product of that optimism. The first time she saw him, she was hopelessly in love.

As far as she knew, there was nothing wrong with marrying the person you loved. When she was beside herself in love, he had proposed; this didn't contradict the life she had predicted for herself. And her future continued to follow its predetermined course, as if it wasn't hers at all. But now, judging from her husband's repeated incarcerations, it appeared his future was not rightfully his, either. Their lives had been reduced to such chaos that she could no longer take solace knowing that his offense was not that of a common criminal. All she could do was stumble toward the precarious future visible beneath her twitching eyelid. This time her husband wouldn't be returning to her side for a long time. She might need to borrow a pair of padded prison trousers for him to wear come winter. And she wasn't sure if she should hold out any hope for spring, either.

The zoo animals lived in accommodations that made it seem almost as if they weren't incarcerated at all. Dig a channel just wide enough to prevent them from jumping out and that was that. As a result, the deer and sheep looked like they were frolicking alongside the people. A parrot sat on a perch above the grass, looking down at the humans. "How do you do?" it said. The elephants opened their mouths to reveal cavernous throats and waited patiently for someone to hit the bull's-eye with a cracker. An ad balloon announcing the dolphin show bobbed in the distance, and peacocks strutted toward the crowd, their ornate tails spread wide. The animals all acted like the closest of neighbors. They were so relaxed, as if they thought they belonged to the same club as the humans and would throw a party if not for the secret channel that separated them.

The elephants, the giraffes, even the crocodiles didn't leave the humans' side, hoping that they might throw them something to eat. They looked as if they would eat anything, even a stone, if only someone threw it. According to the television news, the zoo animals were fed a carefully balanced diet of beef, bananas, even yogurt, but they begged anyway, eyes wide with hunger. Their insatiable appetites were no doubt products of their imprisonment. One could hardly say they were free to graze simply because a secret channel that offered visual freedom had been substituted for iron fences and walls.

The surrounding area was noisy. Babies cried, a hearty-lunged woman bellowed to someone, rock-and-roll music blared, and as midday passed, the sun scorched. Each woman who passed by, out on a rare excursion, was accompanied by a man, bored and tired as he pushed a stroller or clicked a camera. Trailing slowly behind, lonely old men and women dressed in white gazed with tired eyes at this vast park. They felt forced to walk endlessly, on the pretext that it was the largest in East Asia. The men and the old people generally were bored and stood back from the excitement, while the children were completely content, despite the adults.

Women and men and old people and children. Their fleeting expressions, the scraps of conversation that collided and fell to the ground. As Kyŏngju's mom brushed past each sluggish response and winded breath, she felt lonely. She couldn't escape the boredom of the life that clung to her everywhere she went. They had embarked on this excursion because they were bored and tired, and now they were growing even more bored and tired. Their slow pace and increasing fatigue made her feel lonely somehow, and now her eyelid had started twitching again, adding to her emptiness.

Lunch took place on a plastic ground cloth spread out on a flat spot overlooking the park. The two women set out the rice rolls, marinated beef, fried sausage, and other delicacies prepared by the cook at Yunhŭi's restaurant and, for a short time, they were busy feeding the children. The children couldn't sit still for even a moment. Yunhŭi grabbed Sŏnggu and fed him a bite before he stumbled down the hill, then ran after him and fed him another bite. Finally, she threw down the chopsticks and sighed.

"Sometimes I feel like I was born to feed that kid. It's absurd, running around trying to get him to eat something. I feel good when I manage to get him to eat a full bowl of rice, but what about later? I don't know how I'm going to manage."

"Soon he'll be grown and able to feed himself. Then you won't have anything to do!"

So hurry up and remarry, she almost said but then swallowed the words. Already Yunhŭi looked like she half-dreaded and half-looked forward to the day when she would no longer have to feed Sŏnggu. Once the justification she was struggling to hold on to disappeared, she'd have no reason to put up with life by herself anymore. And when she no longer had a legitimate reason to reject the temptations that kept flying her way, it might not be right to live alone.

"It's bad enough being cheated once. I don't want to be cheated again. Besides, who would put up with a little troublemaker like Sŏnggu? No one, not in a million years. Men might as well be from a different species. They can go their whole lives without saying what's really on their minds."

Men are like this. Men are like that. And in the end, they are all the same. That was Yunhŭi's philosophy. As far as she was concerned, men's lives were so mixed up, they deserved pity.

"I don't want to remarry. Maybe I'll try having a little affair. You know, just have my fun and never look back. How about you? Don't you miss having a man?"

Kyŏngju's mom giggled. "So how is he? Is your husband any good?" Yunhŭi had asked before her husband had left. Whenever Kyŏngju's mom looked depressed, Yunhŭi asked, "What's wrong? Your love life isn't going so well?" For someone like Yunhŭi, who earned her own living and was gradually accumulating moneymaking experience, husbands may not have been much use by day. And now she asked, "Don't you miss having a man?"

Though he had lived with her at one time, he had spent more time away. While she may have missed having a man around, she didn't feel like it had to be her husband. She asked herself: If she missed something in life, why did it have to be a man? Why not the little stones buried in the yard of her childhood home? Or the old tennis shoe she had floated down the stream, the perfume of the young ladies who passed by, little bunches of lilacs, or faded diaries in the attic? The things she missed hovered at the edge of her ordinary memories, and when she looked at them after a long time had passed, the world seemed like a scribble of graffiti. She cradled Kyŏngju's slight body in her arms as she recalled the colorless scenes unwinding from the dark shadows of her memory.

Are there colorless recollections in this little head, too? she wondered. If there were, Kyŏngju's memories probably consisted of questions about her father. Kyŏngju's most frequent question was "Mommy, what do daddies do?" His presence was too faint to have left any impression in the child's mind. He was always so busy that he had never stayed long at Kyŏngju's side. She felt closer to Mr. Ŏm from the photo studio or Mr. Chu from the wallpaper shop, because they were neighbors, nearby when she opened her eyes in the morning.

Well, maybe not, but how many things do we forget in the course of living? She knew how memories so clear they seemed ready to expand in the air could start to crumble a day later; then another portion was gone after a few more days, until several months later, only a small portion remained. Except for a few moments from the past that pierced one corner of her heart like a dagger, she wondered whether she would ever hold anything so deep inside again. She knew the pain and frustration of trying to catch hold of nighttime's long, shocking dreams, which sank and disappeared beyond the darkness as soon as she opened her eyes in the morning.

Dreams. One dream was embedded in her heart. The night when she woke from that dream and sat up in bed, her husband was fast asleep, curled up in a ball, his face etched with fatigue. *I'll tell him in the morning,* she thought, but morning came and her lips wouldn't open. She hesitated, wondering if she shouldn't wait until tomorrow to tell him, but he was gone before tomorrow came. And so the dream remained hers alone. As a result, she could clearly recall it anytime, completely and without harming it at all.

There was a big, bright room. On the eastern wall was a large window that somehow seemed desolate and bare, perhaps because there were no curtains. In the corner of the southern wall was a door that opened into an attic. But it was an attic in name only; it looked like a deep, cavernous vagina. The room was completely empty. There was nothing left, no furniture or daily necessities, but she was standing there with a broom in her hand. That was the stage, the backdrop of the dream.

The pace of the dream began to accelerate with remarkable speed when she realized that the bare room was actually covered with thousands, millions, billions of maggots. Swarms of maggots cascaded from the attic, covering several of the wooden steps, covering the floor and the walls of the room. They wriggled stubbornly, the twisting of their white bodies coalescing in a certain rhythm as they pushed relentlessly toward the door. The procession of swarming, writhing maggots was so enormous that she shuddered. An ominous premonition—they might envelop the house and then the whole world—sent shivers through her body.

Soon she was enraged and began shaking her broom in all directions. She stomped on some of the maggots and tried to push them away with all her might. Then she tried to herd them back into the attic, but the lumpy sensation of their bodies under her feet made her feel faint. When she turned to look, she saw an immense river. A river of maggots. A white wave that caught the sunlight and reflected it. The white backs of the maggots formed a billow of wrinkles. She forgot her nausea and fear and shook the broom crazily. The maggots filled the room, flowing defiantly from the attic. They were unstoppable. She had only a broomstick to rely on, and she used it to attack the maggots; but now it appeared to be just another maggot, only slightly larger, drowning in the river.

Finally, the room reappeared, empty and clean. She stood with her broomstick held high and looked around, sensing her victory. The window to the east was as bare and desolate as ever, and the stairs leading to the attic and the walls of the room were clean. She looked about to collapse from complete exhaustion. Throwing the broom aside, she moved slightly; then, with difficulty, she lifted her skirt and shook it. Scores of maggots cascaded down. Bodies rolled tight, they tumbled to the floor. She shrieked in terror and snapped her skirt up and down. From the folds of fabric, from her neck, from her armpits, from inside her underwear, from her thighs, masses of maggots fell, and within moments they had multiplied to cover the room again. She yanked at the maggots embedded in her hair and finally collapsed into a bottomless pit.

"Now that we've eaten, I'm sleepy. It would be nice to take a little nap before we moved on."

After putting the dishes away, Yunhŭi stretched out on the ground cloth. A middle-aged woman approached them with a small bag clutched to her chest. "They're ice-cold," she said, opening the bag to reveal several frosty cans of beer. Some other middle-aged women watched carefully for park guards as they strolled among the picnickers; they must have had beer in their bags, too.

"We'll take two."

They poured the cold beer into their mouths little by little. Yun-hŭi finished hers first.

"There's nothing like beer on a day like this. Just washes the thirst away. You know, men—they're a whole different breed. They couldn't live without the pleasures of women and drink. The day before yesterday I watched an 'art' film at the home of someone in my loan club. The men in that movie didn't put their drinks down the whole time they were doing it."

According to Yunhŭi, blue movies were unbearably dull. Kyŏngju's mom knew such movies existed. Most women knew they were shown in secret, and the women of Wonmi-dong were no exception, of course—because Wonmi-dong wasn't the Wonmi-dong of old. The women were accustomed to swapping information about such things as if they were secret documents, and afterward they pretended with wide-eyed innocence that they never knew such films existed. An endless indulgence of base human instincts motivated their hidden curiosity, covering the city like a sticky fog. It hovered there like a smoke screen, and people rushed to hide themselves in it. Kyŏngju's mom knew that the fog would not soon disappear.

"Mommy, Mommy! Let's go see the dolphin show. Hurry! Let's go!" Sŏnggu ran up from where he had been playing nearby. "Dolphin, dolphin," Kyŏngju chanted. Sŏnggu had begged impatiently to see the dolphins earlier; someone must have reminded him about them.

A human wall surrounded the building where the dolphin show was held. The line of people trying to buy tickets tangled with the line of ticket-holders waiting to get in, and the announcements crackling over the loudspeaker inside were enough to drive anyone mad. Kyŏngju's mom left Yunhŭi and the children at the edge of the crowd and went to the ticket window to gauge the situation. They had just eaten lunch, so she hoped they might be able to purchase tickets for the last performance.

"No amount of money will get you a ticket to this show. I've been waiting in line since we got here this morning and I just barely got tickets for my family. Didn't even get to eat lunch and I haven't had a chance to see anything. Spent the whole day in this line."

An older man with graying hair showed her his tickets for the two o'clock performance. The dolphin show was sold out, except for a few seats at the five o'clock performance that were now being sold, so there was no need to stand in line. Of course, Sŏnggu was furious. Perhaps they could get scalped tickets, Yunhŭi and her son suggested. Kyŏngju's mom persuaded them to forget it, but as she left the crowd, pushing Kyŏngju by her thin shoulders, she looked back. There were still hundreds of people waiting.

Having given up on the dolphin show, they felt as if they had been dropped once more into the middle of a vast plain. It was midday, and the sun beat down on their heads with undeniable intensity. Families seemed frazzled by the crowds and sheer size of the zoo, and the men leading those families looked like they were getting tired. Their interest fading, Sŏnggu and Kyŏngju grew irritable and whined for cold drinks and ice cream. Yunhŭi began to rant about how the autumn sun hastened the aging process. Unable to walk any farther in the blazing sun, they all sat down in the shade of a tree and ate ice cream. There was a state-of-the-art amusement park nearby, with roller-coasters, rocket planes, and merry-go-rounds, but it would take more than thirty minutes to walk there. Their fatigue pressed down on them, so they didn't even consider the possibility.

They may have been tired, but it wouldn't be fair to go home now. That would be stupid after coming all this way with their elaborately prepared lunches. They'd seen only a few animals, Yunhŭi said, and that over the shoulders of other people. Kyŏngju's mom was reluctant to leave the shade, though. But wait! They hadn't even seen the lions or tigers. At the very least, they had to see as much as other people saw. No matter how insignificant the sight, Yunhŭi insisted that they see as much as they could.

The day wouldn't have been a total loss had they turned back. For Kyŏngju's mom, who spent her life confined in that house, just getting out was sufficiently meaningful. Missing the tigers wouldn't have been a disaster. They had seen more than enough for Kyŏngju to return home and brag to the children of Wŏnmi-dong for several days. But Kyŏngju's mom didn't say anything to Yunhŭi; she readily understood her feeling that the day hadn't been particularly special for Sŏnggu. They could never do enough for their children, it seemed.

Heat rose from the ground, and even the tree's shade wasn't entirely cool. The children were already squirming. There was an escape, however, because a short distance away the cool entrance to an indoor aviary beckoned. Lifting their tired feet, they finally got up to move from the animal kingdom to the bird kingdom. Kyŏngju's mom wiped the sticky layer of perspiration from her neck and arms and looked up into the sky; Kyŏngju looked up, too. Though the sun was hot, the sky wore the face of autumn. Then Sŏnggu and Yunhŭi lifted their eyes and looked at the sky. Seeing nothing but blue, Yunhŭi lowered her gaze and tapped her friend's hand and asked, "What's the matter? Thinking of your husband all of a sudden?"

As they entered the building, an unpleasant odor greeted them. Three-foot-square glass display cases lined the walls. The smell alone, whether from bird droppings or poor ventilation, clearly distinguished this world from the one outside. Suddenly Kyŏngju's mom thought of her husband. He had always had a strong reaction to smells, especially this kind of musty odor. He couldn't handle being where there were bad smells. He couldn't bear to leave garbage rotting or a drain clogged.

She didn't smell anything in the aviary now. In a matter of moments, her sense of smell was deadened. It was as if there had never been an odor. Her nose stopped its twitching. For those accustomed to giving in and being tamed, there is very little that can't be endured.

So many birds, but not a single one was singing. They stood packed together in rows, eyes glassy and claws cold, almost as if they were stuffed. The sparrows, the Korean hawkfinches, the larks—they all sat on dead tree branches, glaring at the human beings on the other side of the glass. Was it because of the heavy silence that the birds seemed so different from the ones outside singing cheerfully on the telephone wires or in the fields of barley undulating in a gentle wind? The branches were thick and leafless, hacked from the trunks of old trees and firmly affixed to the cement walls. The birds sat silently, then flitted up to another branch, where they perched without moving again. The children pressed their faces to the glass, waving their hands and chirping to attract the birds' attention.

Halfway through the aviary, she saw a bellfinch. She wouldn't have recognized it from its beak or the color of its feathers. She was terribly disappointed when she identified its gloomy eyes and gray feathers from the signboard. *Bellfinch, bellfinch, glittering bellfinch.* Where was the sensation of fresh morning dew she thought of every time she sang the song? For a moment, she didn't know what to do.

The bird's true self was revealed; it was no longer hidden or metaphorized. And then she understood. The song—maybe it was because the bird's song was missing. It was only a bellfinch when it sang in a clear, bright voice. A bellfinch that didn't sing was simply a bird with gray feathers.

"That's a bellfinch."

She had to tell her daughter. Just as she had taught her the song line by line: *Where did you get that bell last night? Where did you find that tinkling bell? Yes, where did you find that bell?* Kyŏngju asked where the bell was, and her mother tried to think where they might find it. Where could it be? And why doesn't the bird go find its bell now? Clearly it couldn't find its bell as long as it was trapped behind that thick glass wall, perched on a dead branch with a cement ceiling overhead instead of the blue sky.

Kyŏngju began to sing with enthusiasm. She had never seen a bellfinch, either. She sang in a clear, bright voice with the bird of the song sitting right in front of her. Kyŏngju had found the song here inside an aviary as deep as a cave.

"Oh, so the bellfinch lives in a cave." Kyŏngju nodded knowingly. Her mother looked at her, stunned. She thought her daughter had said, "Daddy lives in a cave."

From now on, Kyŏngju would be reminded of the bellfinch living in a faraway place whenever she sang that song. She would probably recall how she sang its song and moved her lips to try to make it sing. Her mother looked at the bellfinch again. A tiny life that moved its beak but never made a sound, the bird fluttered its wings and moved to another branch.

It was Yunhŭi who decided that they should hurry back before the buses got too crowded. Luckily an express bus operated between the Grand Park, which was in Kwach'ŏn, and Puch'ŏn, but it was horribly crowded and Kyŏngju's mom wanted to hurry, too. As they left the aviary, Yunhŭi insisted they use the last of her film and said they would have to come back next month to see the rest of the park. *Next month? What a novel idea,* Kyŏngju's mom thought, as if hearing the words for the first time. For her, tomorrow was an uncertain future; it was difficult to imagine something as distant as a month away. She knew what a month from now would be like, though—how she would long for the warmth of the heated floor in the morning and evening, how the garbagemen who swept the fallen leaves would be resting along the side of the street. She would have to dress Kyŏngju in long sleeves, and after ordering one hundred *yŏnt'an*, she would have to make white rice cakes from newly harvested rice and seaweed soup to celebrate Kyŏngju's fourth birthday.

On a ripe autumn day four years earlier, Kyŏngju was born in a shabby obstetrician's clinic near their house, after twenty-four hours of labor. Kyŏngju's mom remembered it all clearly. That night, when he came running to the clinic after hearing of his daughter's birth, her husband's gift to her had been a small plastic pouch of milk. Neither of them spoke as she drank the milk. Unable to offer a single word of happiness to the infant sleeping beside them, the young couple was silent.

Now, as they walked to the bus, they passed the giraffes again. Several people were gathered around an indentation in the wall and a large steel gate that they hadn't noticed in the morning. The people laughed as a giraffe hung its long neck over the wall and took the food they offered on outstretched palms. They placed crackers and candies in the giraffe's open mouth when it reached its neck down to them.

By the time they neared the wall, another giraffe had figured out what was going on and was stretching its neck over, too. Yunhŭi reached out and offered a cookie to the newcomer. A red tongue appeared, and Yunhŭi quickly placed the cookie on it. Sŏnggu jumped up and down happily, and Yunhŭi turned to give him a triumphant look. Then another giraffe appeared, and more people gathered. They stretched out their arms, offering the animals green apples, hard candy, ice cream. Some people even offered dried filefish or chewed gum. One person rolled up a candy wrapper and stuck it in a giraffe's mouth.

Yunhŭi wanted to stay until her cookies were gone. It could be fun, Kyŏngju's mom supposed. It was a sight to see the long necks stretching over the wall, so close you could pat the giraffes' heads if you stood on tiptoe. The crowd didn't give up easily. They were thrilled to be able to feed the animals themselves, looking into the open mouths with the red tongues and long throats. By now there were five giraffes. Kyŏngju's mom thought she saw tears, big as pine cones, in their black eyes as they stretched their necks out, desperate for one more bite to eat. Suddenly a man with a long whip and leather boots appeared. He snapped the whip, producing a loud *crack* against the steel gate. The animals didn't move away from the wall at first. Then the whip finally hit one of them, and the long necks disappeared in an instant. They could hear the giraffes galloping away. The giraffes had seemed insatiably hungry, no matter how much they ate, but now they had been chased away. The people brushed off their hands and turned to go.

Happy now because of the giraffes, the children scampered ahead, chasing each other back and forth. Kyŏngju was still singing the bellfinch song. *"Bellfinch, bellfinch! Where did you get that bell last night? Where did you find that tinkling bell? Yes, where did you find that bell?"* The song went on, and the two women followed it wearily.

That simple, merry tune kept their heavy feet moving. *"Bellfinch, bellfinch!"* Each time the child sang the words, her mouth grew sharp as a bird's beak and their footsteps faltered slightly. *"Bellfinch, bellfinch!"* Kyŏngju's mom adjusted her stride and felt her eyelid beginning to twitch again. Her twitching eyelid. *"Bellfinch, bellfinch!"* She felt as if she were slipping. Everything she saw was quivering, and her child was running, fluttering away.

She pressed her eyelid; she would visit her husband tomorrow, or perhaps the next day, she decided. This time she felt she wouldn't simply stare at the walls or make empty gestures with her hands. She could tell him about the bellfinch. She also wanted to tell him about the gaping mouths of the hungry animals. And she would ask him if he would like to hear Kyŏngju's bellfinch song.

If the conversation went well and they still had some time left, she would tell him about the river of maggots. She might even tell him she still felt as if hundreds of thousands of maggots were buried in the follicles of her scalp, even now when she thought of the dream. She would tell him how frightening it had been keeping the dream to herself. Once she screwed up her courage and spoke, the words would stretch on and on, long and resilient, like silk thread unraveling from a skein. If she just opened her mouth and pronounced the vowels and consonants, if she just opened her beak and let out the tinkling song, she felt she could bear it all.

At last they passed the shelter for lost children. That morning there had only been a handful of children, but now, as the sun began to set, the building was nearly full. The children squatted inside, whimpering like puppies, their eyes wide with concern. Dirty faces and hands pressed to the glass, the lost children were as limp as rumpled scraps of paper. Passersby stared at them without bothering to hide their amusement. The children were crying and the people outside laughed at them, enjoying the sight. She kept looking back as they headed for the bus stop. Was it because of the sight of those children? Her confidence had slipped away, and she now doubted whether she could talk to her husband on her next visit. It was hard enough just holding her daughter's hand and getting on the bus.

"Sŏnggu! Let's come again. Next time we'll see the dolphin show and ride the roller coaster. I promise."

Trying to console her son as he whined about his aching legs, Yunhŭi looked back, too. All that awaited her was a cold, empty room. She was leaving behind the sunshine and the trees and the animals in their cages to worry about tomorrow's business, to scheme of a way to collect from the customers who owed her money, and to fall asleep.

Sŏnggu kept whining. At her wit's end, Yunhŭi let him climb onto her back and carried him. She somehow looked older in the fading sunlight. With the heavy boy on her back, Yunhŭi walked on, stooped with fatigue.

Kyŏngju's mom lifted her hand and pressed her eyelid. The tic hadn't started again, but she continued to press down. Then, realizing that it had become a habit, she dropped her hand.

The Tearoom Woman

THE TAXI LET THEM off in the middle of the plaza in front of the train station. As always at year's end, there was barely room to move. Cars swung into the turnaround, oblivious to the crowds, and pedestrians precariously wove their way through the vehicles. The new department store to the left of the plaza meant even worse crowds. Before the store's construction, the plaza was already overflowing with passengers who streamed from an endless succession of trains arriving and departing on the Seoul–Inch'ŏn line, and with people trying to catch taxis. "It's packed," Ŏm muttered to himself as he headed purposefully for the waiting room, as if they had already agreed to take a train somewhere. The woman followed, one step behind. The waiting room was as crowded as the plaza outside. Long lines of passengers leaving Puch'ŏn looped back and forth in front of the ticket booths. Everywhere he looked, people were laughing boisterously and jostling each other. They all were infected with the year-end mood, rushing about as if they had important business to attend to, but all the while keeping one eye open for a little fun.

"Where should we go?" He glanced at the names—Chemulp'o, Songnae, Kuro, Chonggak—but at the same time tried to think of somewhere else. The trains ran constantly, shaking the waiting room, and people began running as soon as they had pushed through the turnstile. Like all well-prepared travelers, they were dressed in so many layers that they could have rolled in the snow and still kept warm. He looked at the woman beside him. Her hands were thrust deep in the pockets of her worn trenchcoat, and the toes of her frayed shoes, which should have been replaced long ago, tapped the cement floor. "Let's not go too far." She reasoned that they had to come back anyway, so there was no point going far by train. He listened to the jingle of coins at the ticket window and looked up at the train map again. Go to the left, and there was the sea; to the right, the glittering city.

Suddenly the ticket inspector seated by the turnstile exploded in anger. "Hey, you! Get over here!" he shouted. He was straddling a small electric heater and couldn't move quickly; all he could do was wave his hands. A boy dressed in a nylon windbreaker took a few steps backward, then turned and ran from the waiting room. The inspector didn't pursue him, sensing perhaps that there was no catching the boy. What a letdown, after the way he had shouted. He might as well have been just testing his vocal chords.

When Ŏm was the fugitive boy's age, he had pulled up the backs of his tattered sneakers and buttoned his shirt whenever he heard the faraway whistle of a train. He had spent whole days hanging on the iron gate of the local train station, waiting to catch a glimpse of the trains that passed through his remote mountain village.

As soon as quiet returned to the turnstile, a minor scuffle broke out at the ticket window. Ŏm watched the argument between a fellow who insisted he had been shortchanged and the clerk who swore he had handed back the right amount. Then he turned in the direction of the woman.

"We could go to Inch'ŏn for some raw fish . . ."

Actually, he didn't want to take her to the sea. It seemed like things would just get out of hand there. He had brought her downtown because he wanted to make her feel better, but he didn't want to make things any more complicated.

"Let's just eat dinner and head back," she said, but her face indicated that she wouldn't be able to work up an appetite.

"All right. Let's see if we can find some place decent."

He tried to smile. She looked at him, and he could see from her eyes that she would be more cooperative now. Again they were swept up in the crowd of the plaza. To the left was the department store, to the right the taxi stand. Vendors were encamped in both directions, their wares illuminated by bulbs hanging from a long electric cord. A cassette-tape vendor was selling pirated tapes from a pushcart, his speakers blasting as if they, at least, were the real thing, and beside him was a long row of tent bars on wheels. *Oh my hometown station where the cosmos flowers bloom! All the local girls will come out to greet me. . . .* The customers in the tent bars tapped their chopsticks to the beat of the song blaring from the speakers. Ŏm and the woman would have to go to the other side of the intersection if they wanted to find some decent food. As they waited for the light to change, he noticed a neon sign blinking up ahead.

"See that?" he said. The woman looked. Five syllables in a neon rectangle—Puch'ŏn Wedding Hall—blinked on and off at the top of a five-story building. First each syllable blinked separately, then the word "Puch'ŏn," followed by "Wedding Hall." After that, the rectangle blinked and the individual syllables flashed separately again. They stared at the sign. After the seventh interval, the whole sign, rectangle and letters, lit up the night sky. "I don't like it," the woman muttered after they had waited for the interval to finish and the whole sign appeared lit again.

"I think it's funny," he said, smiling as he watched the dark rectangle light up again.

"I've hated that smart aleck thing from the day I came to Puch'ŏn."

She stepped into the crosswalk ahead of him. So, her spirits hadn't lifted completely. He watched her march stubbornly ahead, and his face filled with worry. As they waited for the second light, she explained.

"What's the point except to tease innocent people? Not all of us get to have a wedding ceremony with a white dress and veil. It hurts enough already. Why does that stupid sign have to flash all the time?"

What could he say? *It hurts enough already.* Ŏm had said the same thing the night before when he was trying to smooth things over with his wife. "She hurts enough already. What's the point of stirring her up?" he'd asked. "Think about it. It's not like I'm going to marry her. I'm not going to run off with her in the middle of the night, so what's the point of going after her? I was just trying to help her. She's new in town. She doesn't have anyone. You know how much I love you." He had spent the whole night begging and pleading, but this afternoon his wife had dashed over to the tearoom and made a terrible scene anyway. When he left home, his wife was in bed, where she had retreated, proclaiming she was too ashamed to face the neighbors. He wandered the streets aimlessly for hours, returning to the woman's tearoom only a short time ago. Would she be lying down, too? he wondered, or would she be sitting under the red light, greeting her customers as usual? As dusk fell, he could contain his curiosity no longer.

The lights were out at the Han River Ginseng Tearoom. At the Seoul Beauty Salon, Kyŏngja was still working busily. Every evening at eight she pulled down the shutters and went home. He looked at his watch now and saw that it was only a few minutes past seven, but the sky was dark as ink. Next to the brightly lit beauty salon, the tearoom looked like an abandoned house, lonely and miserable. In the darkness, even the tinted blue glass was as somber as death. After all she had been through that day, she must have gone out somewhere. Worried the neighbors might see him, he headed quickly toward the Brothers Supermarket. The women who frequented Captain Kim's store for dinner fixings must have been home in their warm rooms, discouraged by the cold, because the streets of Wonmi-dong were empty. The only sign of life was an unfamiliar dog loitering on the icy street in front of the butcher shop.

Ŏm headed toward the dark tearoom once more. The sudden drop in temperature had caused frost to form on the beauty salon windows. Kyŏngja wouldn't spot him unless she was on the lookout. Ŏm hesitated a moment, then pushed on the tearoom door. He must have pushed too hard, unconsciously assuming that it was locked. The door, which he had thought was firmly bolted, flew open. "Oops!" He quickly pulled his hand back. The door remained open, however, refusing to swing shut. Leery of the inky darkness inside, he reached out to shut the door. A human voice drifted out of the darkness. "We're not open today. Come back tomorrow." It was clearly her voice.

The woman recognized him before he discovered her seated in the darkness.

"Go to the playground. I'll lock up and meet you there." Apparently she hadn't been crying. Relieved to hear her voice unchanged, Ŏm did as he was told. As he walked toward the playground, he glanced back and saw that the light in the show window of his photo studio was still on. The faces of a youthful Namgung Wŏn and Mun Hŭi smiled broadly into the street. He stared at the studio, thinking as others surely must, *Those two are the only happy people at the Happiness Photo Studio.*

They passed the Puch'ŏn Wedding Hall and walked for some time. There were several restaurants, but they ignored them. He didn't want to go to just any restaurant, since it was going to be their last supper. She didn't seem at all interested in food. They walked on aimlessly, following other pedestrians whose breath formed clouds of steam behind them. Ŏm ignored the woman's old shoes as they passed a shoe store. Beyond the shoe store gaped the entrance to a basement pub where a doorman dressed in a British cavalier's uniform bowed incessantly, welcoming prospective customers. Ŏm ignored this, too. If she wasn't hungry, a dark corner in an inexpensive beer hall might be a good idea. But he could hardly ask her to go to a drinking place. He didn't think he'd be able to look her in the eye if he did.

She had practically been a fixture in a tavern for eight long years. She once told him that in those eight years she had drunk more than the average man could put down in a lifetime. She always spoke of the past so bravely. She said that if she didn't act proud and firm, some know-it-all would jump on her, demanding to know why she hadn't made a new start in life. According to her, the best way to subdue the fine ladies and gentlemen who thought you could climb out of the gutter any time you wanted was to be frank about your past from the very beginning.

Her names were as numerous as her past lives. Oksŏn, Kyŏnga, Sŏngmi, Yŏnju—her pilgrimage was piled layer upon layer in those names. When she was called Oksŏn at the One-Heart Kisaeng House in Seoul's Myŏngnyun-dong, she had flown from room to room with such frequency that she had to change her white padded socks three times each night. She was happiest when she spoke of her days at the *kisaeng* house. There was a house rule: No one was to sell her body, no matter how much she was offered. Powerful gentlemen pulled out checks and quarreled over the women, but the proprietors never let them have one. She often said that if she had stayed at the *kisaeng* house, she could have turned herself around. Regrettably she had not. It was in a T'oegyero beer hall called the Stagecoach that she perfected her skills as a hostess. She then took over the Sŏngmi Corner of the Globe Stand Bar in Myŏng-dong, hoping to earn her independence. During that time, when she was going by the name Sŏngmi, she had a passionate affair with a fellow who was something of a gangster; they had ended up living together.

After that came a string of room salons on the outskirts of Seoul, and as she got older, she was reduced to working as a barmaid at a little dump in Ch'ŏngnyang-ni. Anyway, she now had enough experience to feel confident that she could sit at a table and sell her laughter, as long as it sounded youthful and flowed easily as a spring. With her experience and skill, the barmaid job wasn't particularly difficult. But when she found she was being pushed aside by younger women and was growing tired of being treated like a retired *kisaeng*, she decided to leave Seoul. It was remarkable that she had lasted until age thirty—it might as well have been sixty or sixty-one, in her line of work—but if she didn't start earning more money now, while she could still wear makeup, who would feed her later on? Each time she changed her name, the makeup thickened. She claimed she hadn't aged a day since she turned twenty-seven. Even now she insisted she was only twenty-seven.

There was nothing more foolish than asking the woman her real name. "It was Madam Hong, right? Hong what?" he had asked when he first met her.

"What name would you prefer?" she had replied. "It's not just my given name that I change. I've used lots of surnames, too—Chang, Kim, Yun—whatever's convenient. I've never used Hong before. I'd like you to call me Chuhŭi. What do you think? Hong Chuhŭi."

They passed a movie theater, a pediatric clinic, a furniture store, and a bicycle shop. And before they knew it, the street was dark and deserted. *How did we get this far?* he wondered. He decided to turn back the way they had come. There was no sign of a decent restaurant. That's the way it was in Puch'ŏn. The streets in the bustling commercial district were short, and the vacant streets were long. The crowds that had flocked to the short, bustling streets radiating from the train station milled near the lights in order to avoid the dark periphery.

They were greeted once more by the British cavalier and passed the soft lambskin rug of the shoe store. Next to the shoe store was a restaurant specializing in Chŏnju *pibimbap*. The woman stopped. "If we must eat . . . ," she murmured. Then she raised her voice. "We already feel lousy. Might as well have *pibimbap*." What kind of reason was that for having *pibimbap*? Did that mean that she was past feeling lousy? He wanted to say that they hadn't wandered through the cold streets just to have *pibimbap*. He wanted to insist they find a better restaurant. But he didn't.

Maybe he was the only one who thought this was going to be their last supper. He couldn't guess at the silent woman's thoughts. The Chǒnju Club—he looked at the sign again. It didn't look so bad; it wasn't a cheap place. He opened the door and guided the woman through. She squared her shoulders and walked inside. Her hair looked disheveled in the bright light. He liked the natural way she pinned up her long hair, but the strands that had escaped the pin looked messy. He imagined his wife pulling that hair. No, she couldn't have. Once they were seated, Ǒm scrutinized the woman's face. Eyes hard and cold, his wife had told him that she had gone to the tearoom and smashed everything she could get her hands on. He wondered if she had hit the woman.

"What are you looking at?" she blurted irritably as she took a sip of hot water.

"Nothing, just . . ." he hesitated. He couldn't ask her straight out.

"You're afraid she might have scratched me, aren't you?" She thrust her face forward for him to inspect. There were no scratches.

"My nails are longer than hers anyway," she murmured, then suddenly she looked serious. "I'm not much for fighting, but I've never lost to a woman who bragged about her devotion to one man. Your wife . . . she didn't look that tough, so I let her off easy."

She wore the triumphant expression of a bully who had conceded a toy to another child. No, that was what she was trying to look like. Still, Ǒm was grateful and proud of this woman for shaking off the incident earlier in the day, an incident that, depending on how you looked at it, could have been extremely traumatic. "Shall we have some grilled beef?" he asked, as if to suggest her haggard appearance was due to a lack of red meat. She shook her head, and Ǒm didn't push the point. Feeding her meat wouldn't compensate for what his wife had put her through. Actually, he was worried that she might think he was trying to pay her off with one lousy meal. At that very moment, the words "Wonmi-dong" burst from a private room where a group of men were dining. Hearing this, Ǒm and the woman shuddered and looked down at the table as they waited for their *pibimbap*.

She had become a resident of Wonmi-dong the previous autumn. Wonmi-dong's twenty-third precinct, simply described, was shaped like one of the ladles used in old peddlers' inns. Packed tightly along the ladle's handle were the Wonmi Wallpaper Shop, Ŏm's photo studio, Sunny Electronics, Kangnam Real Estate, Im's Butcher Shop, and the Seoul Beauty Salon. Across the street were the field where Old Kang raised his vegetables, the Rose of Sharon Apartments, and Brothers Supermarket, run by Captain Kim. The handle ended there, and from the point where the ladle's bowl started was the no-man's-land of the twenty-third precinct, where a variety of shops came and went, opening and then quietly disappearing before another new shop opened and closed once more. There was no getting around it, really, since the neighborhood had always had more little shops than houses, and there were no customers to be found in the empty lot across the street. The trouble began when the Han River Ginseng Tearoom opened for business in the triangular storefront right around the corner, just past the Seoul Beauty Salon. In the words of the women of Wonmi-dong, a "foxy tramp" had appeared on the scene, charging 1,000 won for a cup of ginseng tea and tempting the men stuck in their shops with little to do. The women of Wonmi-dong all hated her, almost as if they had agreed to do so.

After opening the tearoom, the woman frequently appeared on the streets of Wonmi-dong. Judging by the long hair cascading over her shoulders, she looked like a young miss—a hundred yards off, at least. Up close, when she passed on the street and offered a shy—well, at least not a bold—smile, you might think she was an old maid. It wasn't until he had focused his own camera lens on her that he realized she was well past the age that she could be called a young miss or an old maid.

The first time she opened the studio door and called out in a small voice, "Anyone here?" Mr. Ŏm somehow felt it fortunate that his wife wasn't in. He didn't know why. He hadn't been to the tearoom yet, but he had seen the woman on the streets of Wonmi-dong on several occasions and, impressed by her long hair, felt her appearance at his studio was not something to be taken lightly. Of course, she didn't have any personal business with him. All she wanted was a photo for her ID. He had expected her to be flirtatious in her eyes or gestures, out of habit if nothing else, but she wasn't much of a talker. She could have at least introduced herself as the proprietor of the new ginseng tearoom and invited him to drop by sometime, but she didn't. Ŏm liked that about her, too. What a remarkable woman, he thought, considering she came from a crowd who permed and dyed their hair, wore garish shades of nail polish, and used their sunken eyelids as canvases, painting them a thousand shades of eye shadow. While he prepared for the shoot, she smoothed her hair and straightened her collar like any other customer, glancing up occasionally at the camera, which stood its ground like a black monster. He seated her in a chair and carefully examined her face through the lens for much longer than necessary. She had tied her hair back in an unbecomingly tight ponytail, so only her face was magnified to fill the lens, and he was free to inspect her eyes, nose, and mouth in full detail. She looked much older than when he had seen her in passing. It seemed meaningless to try to label her as a beauty or not. Compared to the faces of other women that age, hers actually seemed cleaner, almost sharp looking. However, on closer inspection, he could see that the fearless round eyes simply softened the unusual shadow of experience along her prominent cheekbones and under her eyes. He turned on all his incandescent lights, pulled the black camera hood over his head, and focused on her handsome nose. He must have swallowed hard at least once as he stood under that black hood. For some reason, he was nervous. When he touched her head to raise her face, which seemed a bit too low, when he placed his hand on her shoulder to correct her posture, he felt as if the two of them—he giving instructions and she obeying—were creating a work of art together. He hadn't felt that way for a long time.

He may have been running a shabby neighborhood photo studio, but he had once dreamed of a bright future as a photographic artist. In his youth, he had wandered unfamiliar places for days, searching for green moss covering roof tiles, for the round age rings of trees, for wildflowers trembling in a gentle country wind. As a small boy, he lived near the train station and dreamed of leaving, and later, he did leave, without the slightest regret. He couldn't attend college or receive any formal training because his family was poor, but he cherished what he believed to be a unique artistic insight that rejected conventional shots of beautiful models and mountainous landscapes. He may have become a third-rate photographer who clicked at every face he saw now, but he wore the artistic spirit he had once possessed like a medal around his neck.

"Photography is much harder than I thought."

The woman had surely never endured such a long sitting for an ID photo, and when she expressed astonishment at the photographer's challenges, he discovered that she had an unusual gift. Her tone suggested that she grasped the joys and sorrows of the photographer's profession. Other people had said the same thing to him, but they spoke out of politeness, nothing more, nothing less. She said it sincerely, with a bare, unmade-up face. It was intriguing to find a sincere heart behind the bare face of this woman who made her living pouring whiskey and selling loose laughs under the red lights of the tearoom each night. *Perhaps only those who have lived a long time amid pain have such a perceptive eye,* he thought. On occasion when passing City Hall, he saw people sitting inside big black cars. They never walked through the gate. They rode their car to the main entrance and waited until their driver opened the car door before they placed their shiny shoes on the pavement. Their faces were hidden by thick masks, unfathomable and impossible to read. They looked angry, even when they were smiling, and when they were angry, they always wore a smile. To him, they were a riddle. There was nothing to be learned from their faces, even if he scrutinized them through his camera lens, nothing but the texture of their skin.

Throughout his life—and he would soon be forty—he had existed in two different worlds: the world that came to him through his retina and the world inside the camera's lens. Each world spoke in its own unique voice. Of course, he had abandoned the ideal world of his camera long ago. He had suppressed one of the voices. His third daughter was born, and with age he came to realize that a life devoted to his children was the only one left to him. The age of carefree optimism had passed.

When he first came to Puch'ŏn, there was a real estate office in every other storefront, and before long, beauty salons were opening with the same frequency. Now photo studios were popping up in every third storefront. He had brought in videotapes to rent in a desperate effort to survive and offered a free enlargement with every roll of film processed, because all the neighboring studios were doing so. The number of customers ordering baby pictures commemorating their children's first one hundred days or first birthday had dropped off dramatically. It wasn't simply because of competition from other studios. According to Mr. Pak from the Kangnam Real Estate Office, demand was down now that people had only one or two kids instead of four or five. It was only natural.

The Happiness Photo Studio owed its survival in large part to the Little Star Kindergarten out on the main road. Since last spring, when his wife's sister got a job there as a teacher's assistant, Ŏm had served as the kindergarten's in-house photographer. Whenever the kindergarten had a special event, he dashed over and took the children's pictures. He got 300 won a print, including the cost of the film and labor, and was always paid on time. His wife volunteered to handle publicity for the kindergarten whenever the opportunity arose, because it was an important source of income for them. Chasing after the children and clicking away with his camera, riding in the van with them when they went on field trips or picnics, consoling a crying child, sometimes even carrying them on his back, Ŏm could hear his artistic inspiration creak and crumble with rust. He knew that his own wife thought it was a joke, but he held fast to his belief that he had a unique artistic soul.

His wife hadn't always been like this, but he sensed she was standing up to him more these days. She must have forgotten the days of their courtship, when he had stroked her long hair. Later, despite his insistence that she wear her hair long, she chopped it short and wore it curled tight in a permanent wave, a style that he hated. As he watched her slap on makeup without the slightest thought to artistic harmony, he couldn't imagine what she, at the ambiguous age of thirty-four, neither old nor young, could be dreaming of. She was no longer the wife he had known so well.

After a long wait, the *pibimbap* arrived. The waiters looked busy with the customers who were drinking and smoking up the private rooms with barbecued meat. The stoneware bowls in which the *pibimbap* was served were too hot to touch, and the rice sizzled at the bottom. The circular arrangement of meat and vegetables on top of the rice was appetizing and enhanced the dignity of the heavy bowls. It was a simple table but substantial enough to make him feel that *pibimbap* wasn't such a bad choice after all. They mixed the contents of their bowls in silence.

Before picking up his spoon, Ŏm had thought of what would happen after dinner. She had probably thought the same thing. He had a nagging feeling: They had to go back sooner or later, but wasn't there something, somewhere, that could keep them busy for an hour or two? He also felt sorry for her because she was missing a day's business at the end of the year, when there were so many drinking parties. The Han River Ginseng Tearoom barely had enough customers to pay the rent. It was in such an out-of-the-way spot; hardly anyone passed except people from the neighborhood. She had put all her savings into the deposit on the place, but she seemed less concerned about this than he did. She felt free now, she explained. She had spent her entire life getting fleeced, but there was no one left to take her money. She didn't push the customers too hard since, as she said, she had enough to feed and clothe herself. Long ago after the initial terror of her arrival in Seoul had disappeared, she had been overwhelmed with despair. At the time, she was sure she had taken the wrong road. Her despair ran deep and far until she realized that it was much more comfortable to keep lofty words like "dignity" and "truth" at a distance. She said that as she grew older, she had grown sick of scrambling to make ends meet.

"Woman, you got a long way to go before you'll make a livin' at this. Ain't many folks who'll buy a cup of ginseng tea in the first place, even with the waitresses fawnin' all over 'em. And look at you, just sittin' there, not doin' a thing! This business is doomed— doomed, I say!"

Mr. Chu, her self-appointed older brother, voiced this conviction every time he visited the tearoom. He thought nothing of offering his frank opinions to anyone. Chu was forever lecturing his errand-boy Sŏngu on his business philosophy. Perhaps it was because of the pleasure of educating Sŏngu that Chu did not let the boy go even now in winter when business was slow. Instead he had the boy live with his family in their room off the wallpaper shop. Ŏm knew Chu well and was grateful that he hadn't figured out what was going on between him and the woman. Still, he prickled with anger when he heard Chu giving her advice.

"Why don't you try something like this?" Ŏm asked. He meant there were plenty of other businesses—like a restaurant, for example—that didn't rely on liquor sales the way her "tearoom" did.

"How did that come up all of a sudden? Why do you say that? Are you going to marry me if I open a restaurant?" she asked in a dry tone as she wiped her mouth with a napkin.

"'All of a sudden'? What, are you angry?"

"See, you can't even give me a straight answer. Don't you realize a leopard can't change its spots?" That was one of her favorite sayings. However, she also tended to say things like, "Do you think I wanted to be born a leopard?" in a belligerent tone.

A herd of young men and women who looked to be office workers heading for a year-end party walked in, and the restaurant was soon as noisy as a public market. The laughter from the young people's private room reverberated throughout the restaurant. In every clutch of diners there were always a few jokers. Ŏm didn't have that talent, and he despised his boring conversational style. If only he could make her feel better, entertain her with a few funny stories. The woman put up her hair again and rose from the table. She looked much neater now.

They had forgotten the cold, but it rushed over them when they stepped outside. The temperature must have dropped as night fell, and the woman's thin autumn coat couldn't have offered much protection. *Now where?* He looked around. If he went home now without offering her a word of comfort, he'd regret it. If the rumor had already spread through the neighborhood, starting tomorrow, they wouldn't be able to meet when they liked. He had never meant to prolong the relationship, but he hadn't expected it to end in this sudden disaster, either. Why had it ended up like this? He turned to look at her again. Her face, unprotected from the cold, revealed her age. Had she said she was thirty-one, or was it thirty-two? "I'm past my prime," she had once said when asked her age. "Too bad," Chu had replied, and that was the last she spoke of age.

They stood hesitantly outside the restaurant amid the stream of passersby. "You go ahead," she said, but he didn't move. She hadn't said where. His three daughters went to bed early. They had probably already dropped off to sleep, but his wife was certain to be seething with anger still. "Go," the woman repeated. *Where?* he asked with his eyes. She pointed to the taxi stand in front of the train station. Buses were lining up just across the street, but each one was packed with people heading home. *So many people,* he thought. No matter where they went, it was bustling with people. He couldn't stand it. The taxis, taking advantage of the holiday season, accepted extra passengers without hesitation, and the street vendors who jammed the edge of the sidewalk called tirelessly to their customers. The vendors looked as if they might sink into the ground under the weight of their clothing.

The woman walked toward the taxi stand. Lacking an alternative, he followed. So now he was supposed to go home and take care of his wife? Perhaps that was why the woman kept urging him to go: She was thinking of his wife. If his wife found out that the two of them were roaming downtown as if it was perfectly normal, today of all days, she might give him his walking papers. In the end, he would return to his wife and daughters. There was no place for this woman in his life, but he was still afraid of his wife.

Why doesn't she let her hair down? It troubled him to see her bare neck. He felt badly for this woman who didn't have the good sense to buy a decent winter coat. He was angry at her family, though he had never met them. There was no one left in her hometown, but she had two brothers, one older and one younger, in Seoul. Her aunt, who had taken care of them after their parents passed away years ago, lived somewhere in Sŏngnam, on the other side of Seoul. Before the woman had moved to Wonmi-dong, her few remaining relatives took turns asking her for money. Naturally, they'd had an easy life while she worked the bars. Whenever she had saved up a little money, someone always showed up needing it, she said. Besides, she seemed to have been born to help others. She had sacrificed her youth to help them, but not one of them lived well now. One woman's youth was no match for the tenacity of poverty. When she passed thirty, her family gave up on her. They realized she was a dried-up spring, a machine that had outlived its usefulness.

He had known that she had used all her money to set up the Han River Ginseng Tearoom, but still he was shocked when he stepped into her room for the first time, and he hadn't forgotten the feeling. He had sensed a mutual attraction, but since his house was only a short distance away, he dared not imagine going into her room. That night she had said she was going to lock up early because it didn't look like there were going to be any more customers. If only he hadn't gone into her room, if only he hadn't seen that cold, lonely room, things wouldn't have turned out as they had today. He felt a vague regret as he stopped beside her and waited for the streetlight to change.

The Seoul Beauty Salon and the Han River Ginseng Tearoom were in the same building; originally, neither had living quarters in back. Kyŏngja rented a room elsewhere and commuted to work. She looked up to Ŏm's wife as an older sister and often said how inconvenient it was having no room in the back of the beauty salon. A back room had been added to the tearoom by the young couple who had run a noodle shop there before the woman's arrival. After going to all the trouble of building the room, they had left the shop after only a few months. Since then, he had heard they were running a tent bar near South Puch'ŏn Station. Anyway, the room was across from the cramped kitchen, which consisted of a gas stove and a sink. He was amazed at how cold and empty the tiny room was, and the ceiling was so low, Ŏm couldn't even stand. It wasn't a room; it was a dog kennel!

She had glanced up at him as he stood by the door awkwardly, stunned by the bleak room and unable to sit; then she plugged in the electric blanket that covered the floor. Come to think of it, the floor was cold as ice. Apparently they had never installed an underfloor heating system. The only furniture was a large beige cosmetic case. Ŏm crouched in this room, where even a cosmetic case seemed luxurious, and realizing they would be sitting knee to knee when she returned from the kitchen, he felt terrible. He looked around: a roll of toilet paper, a wastepaper basket with no lid, and on a stained pink pillow, one strand of long hair and a foil wrapper of pills. Later, the woman told him they were liver pills; she took them with beer. Her clothes were hung on nails and didn't cover even one small wall. Though brightly colored, none of them looked expensive.

That night the woman had treated him to three large bottles of beer. She said that she had run out of money after decorating the tearoom, and so the room might seem a little shabby, but she claimed she found nothing lacking. Still, she looked embarrassed. She brought in the large stereo cassette player from the tearoom and started going through her tapes, but the cassette player made the room seem even smaller, so she decided to take it out again. That was the night she said she wanted him to call her Chuhŭi. Unwilling to leave her alone in that empty room, he kept telling himself, *Just a little longer, just a little longer.*

They ended up drinking *soju*. She drank a lot and kept slumping into him. There was no avoiding it—the room was so small—and when he caught her in his arms, he felt sad that she was so thin. Her fragile, rounded shoulders felt like a child's plaything as they touched his chest briefly. He took her shoulders in his arms once more, those shoulders that had supported her through more than thirty difficult years. "Yes, you'll always be Hong Chuhŭi to me," he said as he stroked her hair.

She wouldn't be so cold if she let her hair down. He looked at her bare neck once more and felt helpless. When would she earn enough at that little tearoom for a decent coat?

"I need to go to the pharmacy," she said, pointing across the street as they headed for the taxi stand.

"Indigestion?"

"No, I ran out of my pills."

He recalled the pills wrapped in foil but kept silent. He knew she bought many different medicines at the pharmacy—all of them for her liver, she said. Some time ago at a high school reunion, he had casually asked a classmate who ran a pharmacy about the pills she had been taking.

"You know these barroom hostesses? Doesn't all the liquor affect them when they get older?"

"Of course, are you kidding? Men can hardly stomach the stuff. How could a woman take it night after night? It doesn't take long to hit them. After a couple years hostessing, their faces get yellow. They often look fine on the outside, but their guts are worse than a seventy-year-old grandmother's. They try to get by on this medicine and that, but they suffer for the rest of their lives."

Ŏm recalled his friend's words as he watched the woman step into the brightly-lit pharmacy. She said something to the pharmacist, who frowned, hands thrust deep in the pockets of his white coat. She raised her hand and said something else. Only then did the pharmacist move slowly to the display case and return with a small box. The woman paid and came out. The pharmacist stuck his hands back in his pockets and stared blankly into the street—as if he wondered what the world was coming to, as if he couldn't have understood even if he tried.

Ŏm tried to look as impassive as the pharmacist as the woman approached. She didn't spot him immediately, however, and headed toward the parking lot, then stopped and looked around as she stuffed the medicine into her pocket. Dozens of pushcarts filled with fruit lined the sides of the parking lot, and pedestrians fumbled their way between the pushcarts. She seemed to be having trouble locating him. He watched her for a moment as she stared into the distance, then started walking slowly toward her. When she discovered him, happiness and relief flashed in her eyes, then disappeared immediately. At that moment, a man in an old felt hat appeared like a shadow behind her. He had a dirty muffler wrapped around his neck and wore an old overcoat with wide lapels, the kind most people would have thrown out ten years ago. "You let Chŏngja go! Where's Chŏngja?" The woman pushed the man's clenched fist away.

"Old man's a nut. Let's get out of here."

Ŏm glanced back once or twice as he followed her through the crowd. The man in the felt hat was frightening young women; their screams pierced the air. He scurried around the square, the hem of his overcoat dragging on the ground. People waiting in the taxi line clucked at the sight. "Living's no better than dying," sighed some-one at the front of the line. Taxis carried away passenger after pas-senger, but people kept attaching themselves to the tail of the line. Ŏm and the woman inched forward; the north wind assaulted them, clawing at her throat. The line behind them was long, but there were still many passengers waiting ahead of them.

He regretted their decision to take a taxi. She would have warmed up on a crowded bus. What's more, since one pocket was occupied by the package of medicine, one of her hands was left defenseless in the freezing cold. He took her hand. Her icy fingers squirmed in his. A train shook the ground as it passed through the station, and the fruit vendors called out for customers. "Thirty tangerines for a thou-sand won," they shouted as they stuffed the fruit into plastic bags.

Under normal circumstances, he would have bought some tan-gerines or apples to take home. He found it difficult to ignore the fruit carts whenever he passed the station. His daughters pouted if he returned from one of his rare visits to Seoul without a bag of something to eat. Chu from the wallpaper shop had two sons to Ŏm's three daughters, and the men often boasted to each other of the joys of child-rearing. Ŏm carried the trash and heavy *yŏnt'an* cin-ders out to the street when the garbage truck came, and when his wife was busy, he even brushed and tied his daughters' hair. He was happy to do it. At least his daughters still had long hair! And yester-day afternoon, just before his wife found out about the woman from the tearoom, he had even run an errand for her, dashing out to the market to buy salted mackerel for dinner. He believed that he always put his daughters and wife first, despite seeing the woman on occasion and treating her with more than casual feelings. It was only a guess, but he was almost certain that Kyŏngja was responsible for telling his wife about the woman. She must have looked out her window at the beauty salon and seen him going to the tearoom. Had Kyŏngja told anyone else before she talked to his wife, he wondered. The line for the taxis grew shorter, and as their turn approached, he thought of his predicament once more. Maybe the rumor had already spread among the neighborhood women who hung around the beauty salon. He had tried to be careful, visiting the tearoom only occasionally, though he would have liked to go every day. It was no use. There were already more than enough reasons for rumors to inflate around them like so many balloons.

Whether they were aware of it or not, the women of the neighborhood had reined in their husbands from the moment the Han River Ginseng Tearoom opened its doors. When they saw this woman, who was hardly in her prime, running the place on her own without the help of a single young waitress, they were the first to cluck in disgust. They were the first to recognize the doomed destiny of the tearoom wedged in that isolated corner. The building's owner said that he had been getting angry looks from the neighbors ever since they found out the tearoom had been transformed at night into a bar, with partitions between the tables. Even Captain Kim from the supermarket pretended to be angry. Why should a bar find its way into a residential neighborhood when there were plenty around City Hall? Kim was the one who regularly visited Kangnam Real Estate whenever a storefront came on the market, for fear that a new grocery store might open in the area. He supplied the tearoom with soft drinks and beer, but from early on, he was disappointed with the size of the orders. Ŏm cringed at the thought of all those people he saw every morning as soon as he got up. He also wondered how the woman felt. She hadn't said a word the whole time they were waiting. What was she thinking?

A whistle screeched from beyond her stiff shoulders, and everyone turned in the direction of the sound. A boy with a wool cap pulled over his ears quickly hid a whistle behind his back. People looked nervously at the green riot police bus with barred windows that stood stubbornly in the station plaza. Young people dressed like university students routinely had to open their book bags. He had once been searched for no reason at the entrance to the underpass. Suddenly he recalled the ID photograph he had taken of the woman. "Where are you planning to use this photograph?" he had asked when she came to pick it up. He was proud of the photo, because it had turned out as he had expected, but she didn't show much interest in the result of his efforts.

"I was thinking of getting a new ID card."

"Oh, so you've lost your ID? That can be a real bother. You'll have to make several trips to the ward office."

She smiled ambiguously.

"I didn't lose it. I just wanted a new one."

Then she paid for the photo and turned to leave. His wife must have been watching from the back room, for she observed sarcastically, "I guess she doesn't have anything better to do. What difference does it make if your ID card's old or new?"

He thought of asking if she had gotten a new ID card yet, but didn't. He could imagine why she had wanted a new one. She probably was sick of the mess on the back of her old card. He guessed that she wanted to erase the address register that shackled her each time she moved. "I hope the twenty-third precinct of Wonmi-dong is my last address," she had once said. "I don't have the energy to move to another place where I don't know anyone," she had added with a wilted smile. When he was a child, every time he saw a train he had longed to get on it and go. After getting into photography, he was forever thinking of places to go in search of subjects. And now he dreamed of moving the Happiness Photo Studio to a better spot, a nice corner in Seoul, if possible. She probably felt the same way. She was forever leaving in search of someplace else, failing, then leaving again, only to fail once more. That must have been how she ended up in the twenty-third precinct. What seemed a trap to one person could be the start of a new tomorrow for another. He never was able to ask her about the new ID, because just as his feet were beginning to feel permanently frozen, a taxi stopped in front of them.

The taxi was warm inside. The driver flicked on the meter, and Ŏm told him to go to Wonmi-dong. The woman pressed her hands to her cold cheeks, then spoke at last, almost as if the warmth of the taxi had melted her lips.

"Back there, I saw a beggar in front of the entrance to the underpass."

He didn't know what she was talking about. "A beggar? So you've been thinking about a beggar all this time?"

"Didn't you see him?"

"I'm not sure."

"He had a piece of paper stuck on his back. And it said . . . well, he was a beggar."

He asked her what the piece of paper said.

"It went like this: 'I'm a truly pitiful person. Help me.' "

He smiled, not knowing what else to do. She carefully repeated the words: " 'I'm a truly pitiful person. Help me.' "

"And it didn't say why he was pitiful?"

Then the driver interrupted.

"The man's a nutcase. Retarded or something. Someone made the sign for him."

"I guess so. Why would anyone in their right mind go around with a sign like that on their back? Even a beggar . . ."

The woman looked out the window without finishing her sentence. The driver signaled for a right turn and turned onto the road leading to Wonmi-dong. As they passed City Hall, she asked him to pull over. They still had a way to go, but Ŏm paid the fare and they got out. The woman turned down the dark road that followed the back wall of City Hall.

"Let's part here." She tried to smile instead of saying goodbye.

He looked into the distant darkness. They had wandered the cold streets all evening without a word about what had happened. He couldn't speak. There were so many things in his head all of a sudden.

"You take the main road. I'll go this way," she said eventually, turning him in the direction from which they had come.

What about tomorrow? he almost asked. He didn't want to confirm the fact that there was no tomorrow for them to share. No, maybe he wanted her to confirm it. Her seeming lack of concern bothered him and he couldn't speak. He was the one inconvenienced by the rumors, not her. As long as she remained in Wonmi-dong, he would never escape his neighbors' wagging tongues. He thought she was cruel for not even pretending to understand his predicament. Earlier, when they had left Wonmi-dong, he had felt sorry for the abuse she had taken from his wife. But this woman seemed as solid as a rock, and now, as they returned, he wanted her to make him feel better.

"I don't want Ŏm Chi's mom coming after me again, so let's pretend we don't know each other from now on," she said before darting down the road. He stood listening to the dizzying sound of her feet, then started after her. She was already some distance ahead of him. The electric sign outside the Seoul Beauty Salon was off, but she used the faint light streaming from the Brothers Supermarket across the street to insert the key in her door. Ŏm hid in the darkness, then slipped into the tearoom only after he had checked to make sure no one was around. "Don't turn on the light," the woman said in a low voice. She must have known he would follow her; she was right beside him. He fumbled his way across the room, kicking aside the things in his way, and lifted the curtain that concealed the kitchen. She locked the door of the shop behind him.

More accustomed to the darkness than he, she found the door to her room without much difficulty, opened it, and turned on the light. He followed without hesitation. Once they had closed the door, no light escaped. The room was like a wooden box, without a single window. They stood looking at each other, both stooped because of the low ceiling. They were still shivering, even though they were inside now. The woman plugged in the electric blanket without a word, her hands visibly shaking. It was cold—even colder than outside. The cold seeped from the walls and made his shoulders shake and his ears ache. She squatted on top of the quilt that covered the electric blanket and stuck her hands in the folds behind her knees. So he had come back to this room after all. He lifted the quilt and draped it over her shoulders. Then he embraced her, quilt and all.

"It'll be warm soon."

He pulled her a little closer. She buried her face in his shoulder and murmured something. *She must be telling me to go*, he thought. He squeezed her tighter. "Come inside. It's much warmer." She lifted the folds of the quilt and he sat beside her, the quilt pulled around the two of them. Slowly, warmth spread through the electric blanket. Her breath touched his neck. He wrapped his arm around her shoulder again, and the quilt slipped down. Soon the woman took off her coat and tossed it to the other side of the room. She was wearing a violet sweater. She nestled in his arms, and he searched for her cold lips. He wished she would turn off the light. He didn't want to see the room, the dirty walls pressing in on them, the low ceiling. Her forehead touched his cheek. She had closed her eyes. She looked as peaceful as a tiny infant.

They lay side by side and listened to a dog barking in the distance. She spoke first. "It must be late. You should get going." His face ached where the wind had chafed it. He was afraid to get up. She turned to him and heaved a low sigh.

"Do you know what Ŏm Chi's mom said?"

He couldn't answer.

"She told me to leave the neighborhood. She said she didn't care if I sold tea or booze, just do it in Seoul, not here."

His wife was capable of that and more. *Pack up and get the hell out of here. You meet my husband one more time and that'll be the end of you,* she must have snarled. Was this woman going to follow his wife's orders? Only then did he understand that a realistic solution was right in front of him. If one of them had to leave, he had no doubt that she was the natural choice. Then the woman spoke.

"Why should I leave? I'm not going anywhere. What does a woman like me have to be afraid of, just because they're gossiping about me and some man? I've put everything I own into this business. I'm not going to walk away from it now. I mean it. I'm not going to go, no matter what."

"But . . ." She paused and thought for a moment. He held his breath, waiting for her to continue. The neighbors' whispers, his wife's incessant surveillance, the unrelenting stream of stories he would hear about the woman whirled through his head. Now that he thought about it, he had expected her to leave. That's what he thought would happen, wasn't it? He tried to convince himself that he hadn't wandered the dark streets and followed her to her room just so he could get a firm statement that she would leave, but now he waited in silence for her to go on.

"I am not going to say that I wouldn't have anywhere to go if I got pushed out of Wonmi-dong. I'd find a place. But I don't want to sink any lower than this. I've felt so thankful that I've been able to live this well . . . but you mustn't ever come here again."

She was telling him that she could never give up this life. *She's right,* he thought, trying hard to agree with her decision. No one needed her. Those many people who had clung to her in the past clearly would ignore her now. Her only resource was her ability to pour drinks and sell laughter while gulping pills that she didn't even know the name of. If someone told her to give up the Han River Ginseng Tearoom, the result was clear as day. She would lose the measly deposit she had put down on the tearoom and end up living in the streets, an ugly raven. Or her sickness might worsen and she would slowly die away in the back room of a house somewhere. He stood up decisively and began putting on his clothes. No sooner had he slipped out of the quilt than goose bumps covered his body. He spread the woman's coat on top of the quilt and turned the electric blanket up a notch, but still he couldn't leave the room. He felt as if he was casting her into a desolate plain and abandoning her.

Wasn't there some way of warming the room up? Then he recalled the kerosene heater in the tearoom. He waited for his eyes to adjust to the darkness, then groped around the tearoom. It was only a couple meters wide, but somehow she had managed to fit four tables in the triangular space. Partitions had separated the tables, but, in the darkness, he saw they had been knocked over, and the chairs and tables had been pushed out of place. It was his wife's work, no doubt. Perhaps that was why the woman had insisted he not turn on the lights. His heart pounded as he searched for the heater, which he found in a back corner. He carried it to her room and turned up the wick. The woman didn't move; she simply lay there, watching him. Only after the musty smell of kerosene soot had filled the small room did the old heater seem ready to function properly. Nothing she owned was shiny and new. He waited for the flame to come alive, then turned up the heat. The handle, stiff with age, creaked with each turn. The woman turned to face the wall. "Hurry up and go," she said.

Ŏm's wife spent that night awake, with her back to him, and the next morning even his three daughters acted coolly toward him. It hurt to see the girls following after their mother and ignoring him like this, but what could he do? His wife made the children cry for no apparent reason and wore an icy expression that sent chills through his body. He choked down a few spoonfuls of rice and went straight to the studio.

The studio felt empty, like an abandoned house, though he had only left it for a day. He opened the lid of the *yŏnt'an* stove and found some red coals left. He sat down and warmed himself. From his seat by the stove, the outside world was clearly visible through the window. The weather was cold, just like yesterday. There were fewer people on the street, and even the sun was reluctant to show its face, making the day especially gloomy. Ordinarily he would have thrown the door open to air out the shop and mopped the floor, but today Ŏm was in no mood to rush outside. Inside, his wife and daughters glared at him coldly, and outside his neighbors would laugh at him with scorn. He wanted to cry at the hopelessness of it all. Then Mr. Chu from the wallpaper shop flung open the door and walked in. A curious smile played on his lips, and from his restless movements, it was clear that he had been waiting since dawn to make the visit. Ŏm was right.

"So tell me, is it true? You know, that business about you and Madam Hong?"

Chu spoke in a whisper in case Ŏm Chi's mom was listening, but to Ŏm his voice sounded like rolling thunder. "Oh, come on. Not you, too?"

"Hey! You still think it'll just blow over if you play dumb? The women are all stirred up about what Ŏm Chi's mom did yesterday."

Ŏm just looked at him.

"So when did it start? Ŏm Chi's mom's in bed with the covers over her head, right? Boy, are you in a fix! And we thought you were such a devoted husband."

It wasn't long before Mr. Pak from the real estate office sauntered in, as if he had just dropped by for a visit.

"You lucky son-of-a-gun! So when did you start building that Great Wall? You've just got a natural talent with women, yep, a natural talent."

"Why are you all—"

"Yeah, he's got talent but one thing's missin'. How come you let the wife catch you?"

Chu winked at him, and Pak lowered his voice.

"Anyway, you're a naughty boy. Having all that fun without giving us a piece of the action. It's not fair."

"No, it wasn't like that."

"Then what's all the talk about? You're the one who told us about all the ass you were gettin' before you got married. So how can you deny it? Habits ain't that easily broken. Still, it's kinda low. Don't you agree, Brother Pak? There are plenty of fresh young things down at the Prairie Coffee Shop. Why'd you pick Madam Hong? She's just a worn-out old barmaid."

Chu had gone too far. Ŏm should have gotten angry for the woman's sake, but what could he do in the face of the two men's teasing?

"So what do you say? The day after tomorrow's New Year's Eve. Why don't we go over to the tearoom and have a New Year's Eve party? She can hardly overcharge us if her boyfriend's with us. You're buying, aren't you, Ŏm?"

"Please stop."

Ŏm grimaced and fortunately, Chu left.

"Do you think you'll last till New Year's with Ŏm Chi's mom breathing down your neck? She still looks pissed." Pak clucked disapprovingly as he left the studio.

The sky grew ominous as the day wore on. By afternoon the sun, which had shown itself at intervals, was hidden behind the clouds, and a north wind had swept in. Ŏm stared out as he listened to the wind rattle the windows. What was she doing at that moment? Did she have many daytime customers? There'd have to be customers for her to turn up the wick on the heater and drive the cold air out. He worried about her sitting alone and lonely. His wife gathered their three daughters together and went out, as if she were leading a demonstration. Her sister rented a room nearby; perhaps they had gone there. Or maybe she was hanging around the Seoul Beauty Salon, watching the comings and goings of the tearoom. Chu must have been busy; he hadn't shown his face again since morning. Though Chu teased him mercilessly, the time wouldn't have dragged like a cruel punishment if he stopped by. Ŏm considered going to the wallpaper shop but quickly discarded the idea. How could he endure the stares of Chu's wife?

If only the tearoom woman would leave Wonmi-dong, then everyone would forget the whole business, but as long as she remained, nothing was left for him except the hopeless flogging of time. He understood the woman, but at the same time resented her. He hated himself, too, for his own weakness. If he liked her, shouldn't he have acted less cowardly? He should have protested when Chu spoke so crudely of her. A worn-out old barmaid, a sick old barmaid? Why did he have to call her that? Ŏm then recalled what his wife had said. *Have you no shame? What do you see in that filthy tramp? How could you touch her? Who knows what she's been up to!*

Pak poked his head in the door, though Ŏm would have preferred a visit from Chu.

"This weather really sucks, eh?" Pak wrapped himself around the heater and shook his head. "Boy, is she tough. Yep, she's one tough woman."

He was obviously referring to the tearoom woman. Ŏm didn't know what to say.

"Someone wants to set up a discount cosmetics shop in the tearoom spot. You know, now that I think about it, that's the perfect spot for a cosmetics shop."

"Who is it?"

"A friend of Kyŏngja's. Looks like Kyŏngja's going to go in with her, but Madam Hong just won't listen." Pak shook his head again.

I'm not going to go. Ŏm recalled what she'd said.

"You know, it looks like you're gonna have to talk to her. I just spoke to her myself. I went to the tearoom. I told her to take her deposit while she can and go someplace else. I said you'd look like a fool as long as she stayed in the neighborhood. And you know what she said?"

Ŏm hung his head.

"She said, 'What does Mr. Ŏm have to do with me?' According to her, you chased after her of your own free will. She didn't even bat an eyelash in your direction, so why should she leave? She made a big fuss. Holding her head up high. Why, she came at me with this blue fire in her eyes. Nope, she ain't no ordinary woman, that's for sure."

"That's because you're telling her to leave before the lease is up." That was the only excuse Ŏm could muster.

"The lease ain't the problem. If nasty rumors start spreading through the neighborhood, it won't do her any good, either. The building owner agrees. He wants to get rid of the tearoom and replace it with the cosmetics shop. It's only a matter of time before they get rid of her. Everyone would be better off if she left now, while we're asking her nicely, but it looks like she's gonna cause trouble till the bitter end."

Pak frowned and complained how hard it was to get even the smallest commission. A new tenant had appeared and Pak had intervened, so it really was only a matter of time before the woman was thrown out. *Why should I leave? What does a woman like me have to be afraid of, just because they're gossiping about me and some man?* He recalled the stubborn look on her face. The outcome was clear, now that Pak was bent on getting his commission. So what would happen to the woman? She had said that she didn't want to sink any lower, but it wasn't Pak's hand that was shoving her toward the cliff's edge. In his fear, Ŏm saw his own dark hand pushing her.

"Why don't you have a word with her? To tell you the truth, I set up the deal to help you out, Ŏm. After all, it's best for everyone if we get rid of her kind as soon as we can. Understand? Well, I'll be going now."

As he pushed through the door, Pak said, "Oh," and turned back. "On my way in, I noticed something had fallen off of your sign. Don't just sit there brooding. Go out and fix it."

Wind rushed noisily in the door as Pak went out. It would be a long time before darkness fell, but the studio was gloomy inside. What was Pak talking about? Ŏm opened the door cautiously. Scraps of trash blew through the street. Even the bare trees seemed to be rubbing their arms, howling from the cold. He looked up at the sign. HAPPNESS PHOTO STUDIO. The "i" in "happiness" had blown away. A chill ran through him, as if what he knew as happiness would be lost forever if he didn't find that letter and put it back in its place.

HAPPNESS PHOTO STUDIO. All that remained of the "i" were traces of the glue that had once held it. Where had it gone? He searched everywhere for the scrap of plastic. He looked under every piece of trash lying in the street. Tangled clumps of dust floated through the air like swarms of butterflies.

In this wind, the letter could have flown miles by now. He abandoned his search and looked up at the sign again. HAPPNESS PHOTO STUDIO. The woman's face came to him from between the letters. Whether she left or not, he would never find that letter. Shoulders sagging, he dragged himself into the studio. And the wind blew relentlessly.

Our Daily Bread

FOR THE PEOPLE LIVING in Wonmi-dong—no, to be precise,
for the people of the fifth subprecinct of Wonmi-dong's twenty-
third precinct—a particularly thorny problem arose this winter. Depending on your point of view, you might think it a trifling matter,
easily overcome with a little common sense, but in any case, it was
clearly a most unfortunate situation.

It all began at the end of last year. In summer the streets of
Wonmi-dong bustled until midnight as residents escaped the sweltering heat of the one-room living quarters attached to their shops;
but once the cold came, things were different. The neighbors all
hunkered down on their heated floors and were perfectly content
watching television, without a thought to the dark streets, where a
chill wind whistled. Circumstances weren't much different during
the day, when temperatures rose only slightly with the sun. Because cable television, a recent fad spreading from house to house
through the neighborhood, showed movies at all hours of the day,
the local people remained glued to their sets, carefully budgeting
their time in the bathroom and banishing noisy children to the outdoors. Some families said they received the broadcast without ever
connecting a line, no doubt because of the forests of antennas on
every roof. The weather was cold, the floor was warm, and the television took care of the entertainment. As winter deepened toward
the end of the year, the neighbors whispered about the love affair of
Mr. Ŏm of the Happiness Photo Studio every time they got together, but once the Ginseng Tearoom closed its doors, Ŏm's relationship with the tearoom woman lost its appeal.

And then, as if timed to coincide with their fading interest in that affair, the new situation arose. As with all things, no one thought much of it at first. The Kimp'o Rice Shop simply changed its name to Kimp'o Supermarket. Originally the rice shop had sold only rice and *yŏnt'an* briquettes, cornering the market on those commodities in the twenty-third precinct, and the proprietor, Kyŏngho's dad, appeared to have amassed quite a fortune. He and his wife had expanded the shop to include the empty lot next door, and now, as Kimp'o Rice Shop made the leap to Kimp'o Supermarket, it was only natural that its shelves were filled with all manner of staples as the new name implied. The former rice shop's conspicuous success, with the bags of rice on one side, the "mini" supermarket on the other, and the neat stacks of *yŏnt'an* out front, astonished the neighbors.

Dreaming of a better life, Kyŏngho's parents had first moved to the capital from a mountain village in the heart of Ch'ungch'ŏng Province. With money earned working as day laborers, they had come to Wonmi-dong and set up the rice shop four years ago. At first they sold only rice, which they brought up from their home village, but they were an honest, hard-working couple, and the next year they began delivering *yŏnt'an* as well. They were also gentle-natured people, respectful to elders and always smiling, and consequently everyone in Wonmi-dong thought highly of them. So on the day Kimp'o Supermarket opened, many people made a special trip to encourage the diligent couple by buying something, if only a package of cookies or a cake of tofu. And afterward the neighborhood children all ran around with mouths smeared with red bean crumbs as if to prove that the proprietors of the store really had handed out two whole steamers of red bean cakes to commemorate the opening of their new business. It wasn't a large, fancy supermarket on the main road, but it wasn't shabby, either, and the couple was so happy, smiling all the time, that the woman from the dry cleaning shop next door told everyone she felt rich just watching them.

The woman from Kohŭng who ran the Kangnam Real Estate Office with her husband, Mr. Pak, envied the success of Kyŏngho's family, as did others in the neighborhood, and felt sure they would make even more money now that they had such a large store. It was a rare sight—someone actually expanding a business in Wonmi-dong. No matter how cold the weather, none of the shopkeepers would have spent the day watching old kung fu movies on cable if there had been customers to attend to. The proprietors of the Wonmi Wallpaper Shop, which did a brisk business briefly in spring and fall, the Happiness Photo Studio, which did little more than develop film, and Sunny Electronics, whose business consisted of the occasional sale of batteries and fluorescent lights, all left their shops unattended now and stayed in their warm rooms for good reason. Im's Butcher Shop may have complained, but they were never short of money, thanks to the stream of customers who came in around sunset each day for a half-pound of pork, if nothing else. The Seoul Beauty Salon, on the other hand, was dependent on a handful of customers who wanted only a blow-dry, since winter was said to be a bad time for permanent waves. Kyŏngja's proceeds barely covered the cost of the *yŏnt'an* used to heat the place. That was true for every shop in Wonmi-dong these days, but Kangnam Real Estate was in especially bad shape. For the Paks, the good times were gone. Flies were the only things buzzing around their place, and business didn't look like it was going to improve any time soon.

"The market's in such a state, we can hardly pay our own rent! Who'd even think of opening a real estate office at a time like this? I'm at my wit's end. The kids are growing up and ready to get married, but we don't have any money coming in. I don't understand how Kyŏngho's family does it. They're raking it in. It's just plain luck, that's what it is. You can run around, working your tail off, but it won't do you any good without luck."

As the woman from Kohŭng said, the future of Kyŏngho's family looked bright indeed. Kyŏngho's mom, a pleasant woman, gave a puffed-rice cracker to every child who came into the store, even if the youngster bought only a 100-won candy. *Welcome! Have a nice day! Thank you!* Friendly greetings were always on her lips, and she offered an amiable smile to even the most disagreeable customers, catering to their every whim. Kyŏngho's father was busy from dawn until dusk, filling the *yŏnt'an* orders that poured in during the winter heating season. Between deliveries of *yŏnt'an*, he delivered rice, without delay. The sight of him furiously pedaling to the big market downtown for vegetables heartened everyone. The supermarket seemed to be making a tidy profit selling all kinds of vegetables and fruits as well as everyday staples. It was only a matter of days before word spread among the women of Wonmi-dong, who tended to buy their groceries at the local shops because the market was so far away: Kimp'o Supermarket was cheaper than the public market, and its fruit and vegetables were fresh and of good quality. Around this time, the women observed Captain Kim of Brothers Supermarket stacking several hundred *yŏnt'an* in the empty lot next to his store. They also noticed sacks of rice and other grains piled in the tent that he used for temporary storage and, whirring beside them, a winnowing machine, which removed stones from grain. Of course, Brothers Supermarket had not dealt in rice or *yŏnt'an* before. It called itself a supermarket but was really nothing more than a hole-in-the-wall store that sold fruit, vegetables, fish, and other daily necessities. The sudden appearance of rice and *yŏnt'an,* and Captain Kim's fine red sign advertising them, were clearly an attempt to keep pace with Kimp'o Supermarket.

"We deliver *yŏnt'an,* too, and ours is two won cheaper because we've got a special deal with the supplier. As for rice, well, you all know my hometown produces the very best. We carry only top-grade, new and improved Chŏlla rice, so come on over and try it. It's the best there is."

Captain Kim recited this speech to everyone he met. He stood in front of his store, face cheery and voice brimming with confidence as he tried to persuade the neighbors to buy from him. Only then did people realize that a distance of less than one hundred yards separated the two supermarkets. And they realized that everyone had done their grocery shopping at Captain Kim's Brothers Supermarket when Kimp'o had sold only rice and *yŏnt'an.* They had been so dazzled by the success of Kyŏngho's family that they had forgotten about Captain Kim.

He was twenty-seven now, a charming bachelor, and, as the head of the fifth subprecinct, Kim had the neighborhood in the palm of his hand. There wasn't a local event that he wasn't involved in, and the shrill Chŏlla dialect most frequently heard on the streets of Wonmi-dong invariably belonged to Kim, the neighborhood spokesman. Four younger siblings, his father, unemployed because of a leg fracture, a nagging mother, and a hunchbacked eighty-year-old grandmother all depended on Kim's supermarket. The store was as chaotic as his extended family and was said to carry everything, except what it didn't carry. However, having had a monopoly on the local market for so long, Brothers Supermarket tended to be untidy and the groceries weren't as fresh as they could be. And so people started going to the neat and well-organized Kimp'o Supermarket, without really thinking about what they were doing. After all, new is better.

No one had expected Captain Kim to start selling rice and *yŏnt'an* so quickly, though. Everyone knew that he had bought a small van last fall and was still trying to pay off the debt resulting from an accident less than a month later. He had exhausted the funds that he had saved for his marriage to buy the van for transporting goods and bringing vegetables and fruit straight up from the countryside, but then he hit someone while he was driving. They had come to a settlement, and Kim had paid damages to the victim, but everyone knew that he had run up quite a debt in the process. He also had to pay off the van. Borrowing more money to start a rice business and selling *yŏnt'an* on top of that were simply foolish—like digging his own grave, according to Mr. Chu from the wallpaper shop. Especially when Kim knew that Kyŏngho's father had cornered the rice and *yŏnt'an* business in their neighborhood.

"Kimp'o Supermarket? They have nothing to do with me. We deliver *yŏnt'an* and rice, too. I know what I'm doing. I got a license from the city."

From that, everyone could imagine how anxious Captain Kim must have been after Kimp'o Supermarket opened. Whenever a storefront came up for rent, he always rushed over to the Kangnam Real Estate Office for fear another grocery store would move into the neighborhood. He had probably never imagined that Kimp'o Rice Shop would come to strangle him in the guise of Kimp'o Supermarket. No matter where you go, there is an unspoken rule that every little grocery has its own territory, and Captain Kim's conviction that basic etiquette required maintenance of a certain distance when a competing store opened was obviously correct. "What do they think they're doing, setting up a shop like mine right across the street? This neighborhood can hardly support one supermarket. I guess they want to pull me down with them, but I ain't dying. Nosiree! You folks have to buy your rice and *yŏnt'an* from me, for old time's sake, if nothing else. Besides, our prices are cheap and the quality's lots better."

Kim stood on the corner and shouted until he was hoarse. His mother and grandmother called out to the local women, too. "Please buy our *yŏnt'an*. Buy from us this time. Please!" Though stooped with age, his octogenarian grandmother followed on the heels of the women scurrying to escape the cold and recited her pitch: "I tell you, you simply must buy from us." More pitiable, however, were the women of Wonmi-dong. They could hardly turn their backs on Kyŏngho's family and go back to Captain Kim, since they remembered their own casual promises when Kimp'o Supermarket first opened. "Don't forget us. You come back now! We'll do our best to serve you." Kyŏngho's family had bowed and handed out foil trays of red bean cakes the day their new store opened, and everybody had something nice to say in return.

"Why, of course! After all, you can live without a lot of things but you can't live without rice and *yŏnt'an*. We won't forget you."

If that had been all, things might have been different. Everyone knew that kind words won't fill your stomach, so they could shrug off the well-wishing as mere courtesy. However, every time they visited Kimp'o Supermarket, they all received something extra, like a cake of laundry soap pressed discreetly into their hands as the proprietors thanked them for coming, and that made it especially difficult to turn their backs on Kyŏngho's place and return to Captain Kim's.

Around this time, some people began to blame Captain Kim for selling rice and *yŏnt'an*, and others criticized Kyŏngho's parents for transforming their shop into a supermarket. Neither side was guilty of any serious crime, however. They were all simply trying to make a living, just trying to survive, and now the innocent neighbors were caught in the middle.

"Captain Kim's got a point, you know. We'd better buy our next load of *yŏnt'an* from him." The wife of Im, the butcher, was the first to buy *yŏnt'an* from Captain Kim. Their shop was right across the street from Brothers Supermarket. She said she felt terrible. After all, she was running a small business, too.

"There's no other way," Shinae's mom from Sunny Electronics said with a frown. "We bought fifty pounds of rice from him, without Kimp'o knowing. I always worry about what Kyŏngho's father might think, but you know, why should I feel like a criminal for buying rice with my own money?"

"So take turns. This time you buy from Kimp'o, next time from Brothers. It's easy."

The new bride who lived in number 64 seemed to have come to a reasonable conclusion, but the woman from Kohŭng shook her head. "You mean, you're gonna divide your shopping between the two stores? How will you keep track? Eggs, tofu, instant noodles, once here, once there. I'm too old for that. My memory's bad—I'll just get mixed up."

She had a point. If they went to Captain Kim to buy the rice and *yŏnt'an* that they used to get at Kimp'o, then they would have to buy the groceries and other provisions that they had once bought at Brothers Supermarket from Kimp'o. That would only be fair. Wherever they went, a dirty look was sure to follow. It was truly a thorny problem, for one wrong move could ruin their neighborly relations.

And that wasn't the end of it. The couple at Kimp'o Supermarket couldn't sit back doing nothing, so they put their heads together and came up with a plan to undersell Kim by 10 or 20 won per item. A package of cookies that sold for 180 won at Brothers Supermarket went for 170 won at Kimp'o. Cookies that sold for 300 won at Kim's went for 280 won. They even cut the price of vegetables sold by weight, piling produce on the scale. And there was more. Buy two dozen eggs and you got one egg free. And when Brothers Supermarket sold twenty tangerines for 1,000 won, Kimp'o Supermarket gave twenty-three. Somebody even returned three cakes of soap she had bought at Brothers Supermarket for 500 won when she heard Kimp'o was selling them for 450 won. The women could ignore the dirty looks. If it meant extra change in their pocketbooks, there was no question that they would head straight to Kimp'o Supermarket.

Now Captain Kim could hardly sit on his hands and watch, could he? In no time, he cut his prices 10 won below Kimp'o's and began heaping more vegetables onto his scales. He gave twenty-five tangerines instead of twenty and so began a price war in which either store was lucky to break even on a box of fruit. As the battle escalated in the New Year, the neighborhood women were the ones to strike it rich. In the old days, they took the bus to the public market three stops away when they had a lot to buy, but in the New Year, they rarely went. The two supermarkets carried just about everything, and both undersold any ordinary bargain sale.

"Wow! You paid two hundred won for all those bean sprouts? And I thought Kimp'o was cheap. Captain Kim gives a lot more." No wonder the woman from Kohŭng gasped at the bag of bean sprouts that Sora's mom was holding. It would have cost at least 500 won at the public market.

"Yes, but Kimp'o's *yŏnt'an* are cheaper. I bought one hundred yesterday, and they gave me a five-hundred-won discount and a plastic bowl for free."

After discreetly relaying this information, Sora's mom left, and the wife of Mr. Chu from the wallpaper shop came along with new information gleaned from a trip to buy chocolates for her children.

"What's up with Captain Kim? He's selling two-hundred-won chocolates for one hundred fifty won. That's less than what he pays for them. He says it's kill or be killed."

That's when the woman from Kohŭng started to get really mixed up. She had boasted of saving 30 won at Kimp'o Supermarket, but moments later Brothers Supermarket was selling the same thing for 50 won less. She didn't know where to go. After all, she was the one who had become fodder for the neighborhood gossips by demanding a refund on the soap she bought at Brothers Supermarket and going straight to Kimp'o Supermarket for a cheaper price. To put it bluntly, they criticized her for being too blatant in asking for a refund to save just 50 won. She could, of course, go back and forth between the two stores, but more discreetly. The woman from Kohŭng got the message. No one was going to blame her for going to the cheaper place, but she should figure out which was cheaper *before* she went into action. Still, it made her angry because she always seemed to be one step behind the others. Take the bean sprouts, for example. That morning she had heard that Kimp'o was extremely generous with their sprouts, so she had gone and bought a bag for 200 won. They had given her a lot and she felt great until she saw Sora's mom with an even larger bag from Captain Kim's. She complained that she had lost out again, only to get a sound scolding from the wallpaper shop woman.

"What on earth are you talking about? Lost out! How'd you lose out? At Kimp'o Supermarket, you already got twice what you paid for, didn't you?"

Come to think of it, the woman was right. If she had been quicker and gone to Captain Kim, she would have profited more, but that didn't mean she had lost out.

"Yep, that old proverb's all wrong. Who says it's the shrimps whose backs are broken when whales do battle? We shrimp are doing pretty good while those two whales fight."

This interpretation seemed plausible enough at first, but toward the end of January, things slowly began to change. The weather was unseasonably warm, and everyone's winter kimchi reserves were bubbling over. There were several vacant storefronts next to the Seoul Beauty Salon. The neighborhood was lined with deceptively attractive shops with live-in rooms, but many of the shops were vacant, with only the rooms rented. It was as if the contractors had all agreed to make space for two shops on the ground floor and an apartment upstairs whenever they built anything. They even remodeled the first floor of existing single-family homes and multifamily buildings to make room for shops. Only recently had people come to realize that the prospects for shops were worse than those of single rooms for rent; but still, in the last four or five years, buildings with shops on the first floor and apartments on the second had been the rage in the twenty-third precinct of Wonmi-dong. Expectations for a development boom, which had seemed inevitable given the proximity of City Hall, had completely evaporated. It might have been different had they been at the front gate of City Hall, but the chances of a commercial area developing this far away were dim.

A few shops had opened elsewhere in the neighborhood, small ones, of course, but the storefronts with attached living quarters next to the Seoul Beauty Salon remained unoccupied because of the empty lots next door and across the street. The beauty salon, on the corner where the fire road met the main road, had the advantage of visibility, but the shops set away from the main road almost always went bankrupt, no matter what they sold. A variety of businesses appeared, then disappeared, with the regularity of migratory birds. Then one day a sign appeared outside one of the storefronts, announcing the arrival of Freshee Fruit.

If one were to explain the location of Freshee Fruit, it would go like this: The Seoul Beauty Salon was across the street from Brothers Supermarket, and to the left, along the fire road, was the Cosmetics Discount Corner, a joint venture by Kyŏngja from the beauty salon and a friend that had opened at the beginning of the year and sold cosmetics at a discount to the neighborhood women. The ginseng tearoom used to be in that spot. No one knew what happened to the tearoom woman after she was forced to leave because of her passionate affair with Mr. Ŏm from the Happiness Photo Studio, but whenever someone entered the cosmetics shop, they invariably discussed Ŏm's dalliance. On the other side of the cosmetics shop was a vacant storefront where Myŏngok's family lived upstairs. To its left was the storefront that Chinman's family had used to store the cut-rate toilet paper that they bought wholesale. Chinman's father had finally been reduced to peddling toilet paper from a cart, and then, at the end of last year, they had moved to the countryside. A pants factory that operated like a cottage industry soon moved into the storefront that Chinman's family had occupied. Apparently the owner worked right alongside three or four employees. Through the tinted glass the neighbors could see young men bent over their machines, the fabric piled high around them.

Freshee Fruit was next to the pants factory, and beyond it were two more vacant storefronts, a few empty lots, and, across the street, Kimp'o Supermarket. The storefront where Freshee Fruit appeared had been rented out as living quarters, but the tenants moved away without anyone knowing, and the fruit shop appeared, quite unexpectedly. Apparently they had gone through another rental agent, for if Kangnam Real Estate had handled the deal, Captain Kim surely would have known about it.

The fellow who ran Freshee Fruit had just moved in and seemed to know nothing of the neighborhood. If he had only sold fruit, there might have been no problem, but unknowingly the man stuck a sign in his window advertising "a full stock of groceries" and began selling, if not a full stock, then at least scallions, bean sprouts, tofu, lettuce, onions, and other groceries. It was an unfortunate move on his part. There he was, with a sign proclaiming his full stock of groceries, smack-dab between Brothers Supermarket and Kimp'o Supermarket, which were still locked in a desperate struggle to attract more customers themselves. No way was this man going to emerge unscathed.

At the time, Kyŏngho's family and Captain Kim were beginning to feel the effects of their price war, which was eating into their profits. The face of Kyŏngho's mom, once smiling and kind, was now creased with worry, and Kyŏngho's parents often argued at night— at least that's what the woman from the dry cleaners said. On Captain Kim's haggard face was the obvious evidence of his drinking, which he now claimed had increased to a daily intake of at least four bottles of *soju*. Indeed, his drunken antics were becoming somewhat extreme, causing his neighbors to scowl with disapproval. A few drinks and he would declare that he was going to give up the business, or he would get mad and sell things at absurdly low prices. And why did he have to run up debt stocking rice and *yŏnt'an* that didn't even sell? It was breaking their hearts, his mother and grandmother whined daily. His bent-over grandmother was especially upset. "My oldest grandson's losing everything and he hasn't even gotten married yet. The poor boy's suffered so, putting his brothers through school in his parents' stead," she lamented tearfully.

"I'm going crazy! What does this guy think he's doing? Bad enough he's selling fruit, but 'a full stock of groceries'? I don't need this kind of trouble." Captain Kim was livid, and the couple at Kimp'o Supermarket didn't look too good, either.

"I declare. They're trying to kill us off. They are. Captain Kim's already bleeding us dry, and now Freshee Fruit's after a piece of the action." Kyŏngho's mom, who used to smile so easily, heaved a sigh.

The fellow at Freshee Fruit must have been oblivious to the turmoil, for another sign soon appeared in his window: NEW SHIPMENT OF WANDO DRIED SEAWEED.

A few days later a rumor swept the neighborhood: Kyŏngho's parents and Captain Kim had agreed to a ceasefire. And sure enough, prices at the two stores synchronized, and the produce scales returned to normal. The local residents now paid the same price no matter which store they went to. No one said anything, but the neighborhood women secretly felt let down. Still, only the woman from Kohŭng was of sufficient age to speak frankly without becoming the target of criticism.

"Should have been this way from the beginning, but I must say I am a little disappointed."

It wasn't long, however, before the women learned a new fact. Kyŏngho's parents and Captain Kim hadn't simply arrived at a ceasefire; they had agreed to a temporary alliance. And, of course, the target of these new allies was Freshee Fruit. According to a reliable source, Captain Kim had suggested the alliance. Someone claimed to have seen him having a drink with Kyŏngho's father late one night at the pork rib restaurant near the industrial complex. Someone else said that while Captain Kim had suggested the alliance, it was Kyŏngho's father who came up with their ingenious scheme. There were even rumors that the two men had become quite friendly, lamenting their shared fate and calling each other "Brother" in conversation.

All that remained was the manner of Freshee Fruit's demise. Now that there were three whales, the shrimp could hope for more to eat, just as the woman from Kohŭng had suggested. Not surprisingly, the principal tactic was price-cutting. The two stores drastically lowered their prices, but only on items carried at Freshee Fruit. The rest of their merchandise was sold at the original price. In response to Freshee Fruit's shipment of Wando seaweed, Captain Kim brought in a load of Wido seaweed and sold it at the price he'd paid in Wido. Kyŏngho's industrious father went to the wholesale fruit market in Seoul and brought back apples and tangerines, which he divided with Captain Kim and sold at low prices. The women of Wonmi-dong had no reason to risk a grudge by going to Freshee Fruit when fruit and groceries were much cheaper at Kimp'o or Captain Kim's, and they knew the familiar proprietors of these shops were watching the newcomer's store.

It was then that the man at Freshee Fruit quietly removed the sign advertising groceries from his window. He also removed the sign for Wando dried seaweed, and, as if to announce that he was only going to carry fruit, he put up another sign declaring FRUIT AT WHOLESALE PRICES. Kyŏngja told her customers at the beauty salon that she had seen the man spit in disgust and growl about how he'd just sell fruit, as they wanted, since there wasn't any money in bean sprouts or scallions anyway. The alliance brought results, and now the local people wondered about the future. Captain Kim and Kyŏngho's father no longer had any reason to maintain their alliance. What would happen next? But the assault on Freshee Fruit was not over. According to Kyŏngho's mom, the couple considered the alliance finished, but Captain Kim was still hopping mad.

"We sell fruit, too, you know. I'm not giving in till I see him closed down."

The reactions of the neighborhood women upon hearing Captain Kim's bitter vow varied.

"He's vicious. And why is Kyŏngho's father going along with him? Captain Kim's younger. Kyŏngho's father has to calm him down when he gets nasty like that."

"What are you talking about? How can he go against Captain Kim now? They agreed to the alliance, so they have to be loyal till the end."

"Loyal? Ha! I can't be sure, but I think Kyŏngho's parents plotted with Captain Kim because they also want to see Freshee Fruit ruined."

"Then they figured wrong. The fact is, Captain Kim really wants to see Kimp'o Supermarket closed down. Do you think he'll be satisfied getting rid of little old Freshee Fruit?"

"That Kim, he's so bullheaded. I don't understand how a young man can be so heartless."

"I know, and he's so rude to his mom. He smiles and plays up to everyone except his own parents. Haven't ever seen him smile at them."

"That's how incompetent parents get treated. If we keep up like this, our kids will treat us the same way."

Freshee Fruit, which seemed to assume there would be no problems now that they sold only fruit, began stocking up on boxes of apples, tangerines, pears, Chinyŏng sweet persimmons, and hothouse strawberries for the lunar New Year. The solar New Year holiday stretches over three days, but it's no match for the lunar New Year when it comes to sales. Im's Butcher Shop was also preparing for the holiday business, filling the streets with the smell of ripe meat. And the displays of fruit at Kimp'o and Brothers supermarkets were splendid. Captain Kim rented a van and went to Seoul to buy fruit wholesale. They set their prices according to Freshee Fruit's. If Freshee Fruit was selling a box of Grade A apples for 15,000 won, they sold it for 14,000, and if a customer tried bargaining the price down, they lowered it even more. At the New Year, most fruit was sold by the box. And that wasn't all. If he saw a customer haggling for a lower price at Freshee Fruit, Captain Kim grabbed a scratchy old hand-mike from who knows where and interfered with the sale.

"Bargain sale on fruit! Yes, we have a new crop of fresh tangerines. And we're selling delicious Fuji apples straight from the orchard at rock-bottom prices. Yes, it's a fruit sale!"

Sometimes he even advertised Kimp'o Supermarket. "Fruit sale! We're having a sale on apples, pears, and tangerines. Go to Kimp'o Supermarket or come to me, whatever you like. Everything's on sale!"

It was only natural that the fellow from Freshee Fruit should come running to Captain Kim. However, he was at a disadvantage from the very beginning. His first incautious remark landed him in Captain Kim's snare. The man made the mistake of talking down to Kim, simply because Kim was younger.

"From your tone of voice, it seems you think I'm young enough to be your lousy son," Kim replied. "How are you going to run a business with eyesight like that? Do you think money's so blind it's just gonna lie there waiting for you? You gotta learn to talk right before you try your hand at earning a living."

The man from Freshee Fruit simply stood there at a loss for words. He hadn't even had a chance to complain about Kim's interference with his business when Kyŏngho's father butted in. Sensing an opportunity, the man from Freshee Fruit started shouting.

"What are you people after? Everyone knows the prices. Why are you selling below cost to ruin my business? Huh? What do you have against me?"

Kyŏngho's father wasn't about to back off. "Since when is it a crime to buy cheap and sell at a discount? What are you talking about?"

His face red now, the fellow from Freshee Fruit simply raised his voice. "Listen, you bastards! I see what you're doing. You two are wicked. 'Since when is it a crime to buy cheap and sell at a discount?' Tell me! What have I ever done to you? Why are you bastards trying to wipe me out?"

With that, Kim struck back with anger. "What's your problem? Haven't been eating properly? Every other word a curse! This guy needs to be taught a lesson."

The fellow from Freshee Fruit grabbed Captain Kim by the collar and began shaking him. Slightly built, the man was no match for Captain Kim, who easily threw him off. Without thinking, Captain Kim raised his fists at the cursing man and began showing off his boxing ability. "I don't know where you came from, but it makes my blood boil to think of you horning in on my business," Kim snarled. His voice was cold as a knife blade.

Even Kyŏngho's father paled at the force of Captain Kim's fists as they pounded the man's swollen face, which was already covered with blood dripping from his nose. And what murderous language!

"I don't care who it is. Ain't no bastard gonna ruin my business.

I've worked hard to get where I am. Why should I let some bastard bring me down? Not on your life!"

Kyŏngho's father finally snuck away, and if the other neighbors hadn't pulled the two men apart, who knows what would have happened to the fellow from Freshee Fruit. It was partly his own fault, recklessly placing himself beneath Kim's fists and attacking him so vehemently.

"What's wrong with you fellas? What are you doin'? How can two neighbors beat up on each other? Look here, mister, you stop that. There's nothin' to be gained by gettin' beaten up. And you, Kim! When did you turn into a thug, huh? This ain't right. No matter what he done, you can't go around beatin' an older man like this. Get your hands off him! If you don't do as I say, I'll never talk to you again. Come on! Get your hands off him!"

Mr. Chu from the Wonmi Wallpaper Shop ripped the two men apart, but Captain Kim continued to kick blindly at the other man's ribs.

Witnesses to the fight spoke of it for a long time. Two days later, they all shuddered at Captain Kim's brutality as they watched the fellow from Freshee Fruit trying to sell his remaining fruit from a cart. That was the only way the man could get rid of all the fruit he had stocked up for the New Year holiday.

"That Kim, he's cruel. I'm not going to buy anything from him anymore. Not even a cake of tofu."

Shinae's mom shook her head in disgust. Though Shinae, an only child, was already three, her mother looked younger than the new bride at number 64. From the soulful music that seeped from their shop in the dark of night, it was clear that she and her husband, who ran Sunny Electronics, lived a romantic life.

"I'm going to have to look at Kyŏngho's father in a new light, too. How could he turn tail and run like that? He's so tricky. I think he's meaner than Captain Kim."

The new bride from number 64 was angry at Kyŏngho's father, but the women generally agreed that Captain Kim was the worse of the two. They all pursed their lips in anger and declared that they had never imagined him to be so vicious. It takes a long time to really know someone, the women exclaimed.

And so Freshee Fruit closed its doors, only a month after opening. None of the other businesses had ever lasted long at that spot, because it simply wasn't a good location. The dumpling shop, the pork rib restaurant, the pinball parlor—none of them had lasted more than two or three months, so it was no surprise that Freshee Fruit closed. At least the fellow from Freshee Fruit hadn't put any money into decorations and his family could eat the fruit and groceries that hadn't sold, so they were better off than the others were, the women whispered. Still, they were all amazed and a little disturbed that the alliance had finally accomplished its goal.

Shinae's mom felt especially bad about the demise of Freshee Fruit.

"He must have been really hard up to come all this way to open a shop. I mean, who ever made any money in this neighborhood? He's just trying to make a living. Why'd they have to be so cruel?"

"I'm sorry to see him go, but it couldn't be helped. Everyone's scrambling to make a living." Generous by nature, Chu's wife defended Captain Kim.

The weather was unseasonably warm, over ten degrees Celsius, for several days into February. There was no telling when the spring cold snap would come and freeze everything again, but if the weather remained this warm, one could say that spring had arrived. The streets of Wonmi-dong bustled again after a long silence. Children streamed from their homes, pedaling tricycles and dashing up and down the street. A crowd of women gathered to watch from a sunlit spot in front of Sunny Electronics.

"Look!" one of the women chuckled. "I guess that means spring is here. It's been quiet all winter but it looks like we're going to be hearing from the old man again."

Sure enough, after a long winter without a trace, Old Screamer was standing on the stairs in front of the Rose of Sharon Apartments. He must have let out at least one shriek already, because now he was engrossed in the slapping motions, first his elbows, *"Uaaak!"* then his hands, *"Uaaak!"* The old man spit out the cries that had accumulated within him, rubbed his head, then headed up the stairs to disappear into the apartment foyer.

"I wonder what's wrong with him. Some kind of sickness, I guess. Breaks my heart to watch him. Imagine how the old man must feel."

"I know. I've never seen such a thing, though I once heard there's a disease that makes you laugh all the time."

"Yeah. It would be a lot nicer listening to laughter all the time, wouldn't it? That old man sounds like he's coughing up something or getting stabbed in the back."

"Oh, gross! You know, I've heard he's very neat and clean. They say he does more laundry than the family he rents from. He's not a bad old fellow, except for shrieking every once in a while."

The women of Wonmi-dong changed the focus of their discussion with the appearance of the woman from Kohŭng. They had just been wondering where she was, for they rarely had a conversation without her, when suddenly the door of the Kangnam Real Estate Office flew open.

"What? Is there some good news?" the butcher's wife asked. It might have been the weather, but the Kohŭng woman's face seemed brighter than usual.

"Good news? What good news? Nothing's good in the real estate business these days."

"What do you mean? Spring's just around the corner. That's when everybody moves. So tell us! Did you just clinch a deal, or what? What is it? A rental?" Sora's mom did the asking now.

"You hit it right on the button. We found a tenant for Freshee Fruit. Just signed the contract."

"Already? Well, I guess it's in his best interest to get out as soon as possible," Shinae's mom said, glaring in the direction of Captain Kim's supermarket.

"Well actually, your family's not going to be too happy about this one," the woman from Kohŭng said in an ominous tone. The women all turned to look at Shinae's mom.

"What do you mean?" she asked, eyes round with curiosity. "Why should we care?"

"Well, they haven't decided for sure, but they say it's the only trade they know, and they have to do something."

"What? Do you mean there's going to be another electronics store?" The younger woman's face darkened.

"They haven't decided for sure yet. They said they were going to look into it . . ."

The woman from Kohŭng didn't finish. She felt bad taking the commission without discussing it with her neighbor first.

"They must be really hard up to come all this way to open an electronics store. They're just trying to make a living, right?"

When the butcher's wife mimicked Shinae's mom, the women

all laughed. Shinae's mom was pale, though, and she hardly smiled at the joke.

"So what happens now? Will they keep fighting? It doesn't look like Kyŏngho's family will give up without a struggle," said the young bride from number 64. She couldn't control her curiosity, it seemed. Now that the alliance had succeeded in eliminating Freshee Fruit, they had only to wonder what direction the two supermarkets would take. The ceasefire had served its purpose, and now the question was, what would happen next.

"Oh, they wouldn't start fighting again, would they? They should let bygones be bygones and come to some sort of compromise."

The compromise suggested by the woman from Kohŭng seemed to be made with Shinae's mom in mind.

"Do you really think Captain Kim will let it go? In this little neighborhood, two shops in the same business are both bound to fail."

The women were cautious now, knowing that Shinae's mom had changed her views from black to white in the space of a few moments. An ill-placed word would only drive a wedge between neighbors.

"All we have to do is sit back and enjoy the show," Sora's mom quipped.

"Yep, when whales fight, it's the shrimp who grow fat," said the woman from Kohŭng, twisting the proverb once more.

"That Captain Kim doesn't give up easily. I'm worried." The woman from the wallpaper shop understood best that desperation was all her neighbor Captain Kim had left after feeding so many mouths.

"I don't see why everyone has to start up their own shop," the butcher's wife remarked foolishly.

"Because it's hard making a living," answered the new bride wisely.

And then they fell silent. As they contemplated the prospect of living day to day, the women of Wonmi-dong each looked troubled in her own way. And Shinae's mom was the gloomiest of all. The youngest child of the wallpaper shop, playing among the other children, soon stumbled and fell, and the sound of him bawling, gapemouthed, signaled the women to disperse, heading in their separate directions. All that remained was the early spring sun, beating down on the spot where they had stood.

The Underground Man

HE OPENED HIS EYES, but he didn't look at his watch. Even without turning on the light and looking at the watch, he knew it read four o'clock. It was about five minutes fast. He had to wait five minutes for it to be exactly four. Of course there was no reason he should wait until four, but he held his breath and listened anyway. At the stroke of four, the bell at Sŏg'wang Temple on the lower reaches of Wonmi Mountain produced its hollow toll, and the neighborhood's ubiquitous churches launched into a confused chorus of electronic chimes. He always woke five minutes early and waited for these sounds. Those five minutes passed slowly. It was dawn, but the basement room weighed with a heavy darkness, bereft of light. He tossed in the gloom, turned toward the wall, and scowled at the musty odor of mildew from the damp wallpaper. It wasn't just the walls that smelled but the damp bedding as well. The room didn't leak water, but it was dank and humid. When had he last fallen asleep wrapped in crisply starched linens that rustled when he turned? He tried to hold on to memories of days gone by as he slowly pulled his legs to his chest. He tried to ignore it, but the urge to empty his bowels gradually intensified. He buried his face in the smelly bedding, body tight as a bow. The musty quilt cover clung to his face, and he grimaced again. And then, as if it had been waiting for this moment, the bell from Sŏg'wang Temple began to ring. It almost sounded as if it were ringing from underground. If he hadn't known the temple was there, he would have thought the bell was ringing from somewhere inside the earth, calling the spirits for the early morning chant. He rolled himself into a tighter ball and strained to hold out as long as he could. His body had cooled through the night, but now a fever coursed through him, and a cold sweat collected on his lower back. He couldn't stand it anymore. Finally, he jumped up and slipped on the work pants he had flung on the floor the night before.

Today, as usual, a truck and a chocolate-brown sedan were parked side by side. The cars blocked the view from the road, and the other side was completely obscured by the outer wall of the Rose of Sharon Apartments where his room was situated. Careful not to step on other deposits of excrement, which were sure to be his, too, he walked around the back of the car. The darkness had lifted somewhat, but it was still too murky to see what was beneath his feet. He squatted by the back wheel of the brown car and glanced up at the sky. Faces freshly washed, the morning stars were gathered there, gazing down on him. As he finished his business and emerged from behind the car to walk past Sunny Electronics, a bicycle rolled silently toward him. Morning newspapers filled its freight rack. The legs of the boy riding the bicycle were too short, and his buttocks hovered precariously in the air as he pedaled. The boy stopped in front of him, pushed a newspaper through the closed gate of number 64, and mounted his bicycle, glancing at him nervously. Then he rode into the distance, glaring at the man loitering in the dark empty streets at dawn.

There was no ignoring the fact that the gate to number 64 was locked. On the first floor were the Wonmi Wallpaper Shop and the Happiness Photo Studio; on the second were two or more households. The gate hadn't always been locked. He had been able to push it open and go inside anytime he wanted and had used the downstairs bathroom on several occasions. Then one day they started locking the gate late at night. Number 65, home to Sunny Electronics and the Kangnam Real Estate Office, started locking its gate, too. It was the same with the inner gate of Im's Butcher Shop and the Seoul Beauty Salon. He knew the reason. After checking each iron gate along the streets of Wonmi-dong, he turned toward home.

The stairs leading into the basement were steep and cramped. He had once tumbled down them as he groped his way through the dark. At the bottom was a narrow corridor where discarded furniture from his landlady's apartment was piled. Sometimes as he fumbled for his door, the chimney from the *yŏnt'an* stove, which stuck out in the corridor, poked him in the ribs. Right next to his door was a single water spigot. Lacking a drain, he drew only the water he needed because he had to collect the water he had used in a pail and dump it outside when it was full. And there was the added inconvenience of water rationing: He had to remember to fill a container in advance because water was supplied only every other day.

As soon as he opened the door, the dank, musty smell assailed him. His nose grew accustomed to the smell when he was in the room, but each time he returned from the outside, the stench of mold was the first thing to greet him. There was a small window in the outer wall by the ceiling, but it was too small to provide any real ventilation. From outside, the window was practically at ground level. It was always caked with dust and streaked with rain and took considerable effort to open. The first thing he did when he moved into this basement room was climb up on a chair and glue white paper over the windowpane. Outside was a hedge of Chinese arborvitae and beyond that Old Kang's vegetable patch, so no one would be looking in his window anyway. Still, he thought it necessary to take some measure against exposure. Every night he climbed up on the chair and closed the window. In summer the room was stifling, but he didn't want to sleep with the window open. After all, the stray cats and fearless mice of Wonmi-dong might frolic over his face as he slept. And there was no telling when some drunken passerby with a dulled sense of direction might urinate through his window.

After calculating that he could sleep at least two more hours, he lay down on top of the musty bedclothes. Upstairs someone must have turned on the tap. Directly overhead a loud splashing issued from the ceiling as if someone was running water. Sleep, once interrupted, did not come easily. He lay in the darkness, trying to decipher every sound overhead. He even indulged in futile thoughts: *Who is this woman cooking breakfast at dawn?* The sound of running water came from right above, but it couldn't be the first floor. The apartment directly above his bed, that is, number 102 of the Rose of Sharon Apartments, belonged to his landlady. The first-floor apartments all had basement rooms as large as his. Most people used them for storage, but sometimes a large family would use the space as an extra room. Some turned it into a children's study; others rented it out to factory workers who slept there and bought their meals elsewhere. If you rented the room, you needed the key to the landlord's front door because there was no bathroom in the basement. Of course, no one liked the idea of a tenant flinging open their door at any time of the day or night, and when they went out, they naturally were concerned that the stranger in the basement had the key to their home. For this and other reasons, people didn't rent out their basement unless they were desperate for money.

When he first moved in, he insisted on the right to use the bathroom. He met the landlady when he signed the rental contract. She dressed in such a youthful manner that it was difficult to tell how old she was: the skintight jeans, the round, dangling earrings, the scarlet fingernails counting his deposit. The woman said she lived alone with her daughter. Combing back her short curly hair with her fingertips, she assured him that he wouldn't be needing a key.

"Don't worry. I hardly ever go out."

However, she never opened the door for him. Not that she wasn't home. Even though she was home and knew perfectly well the urgency of his business, she didn't open the door. It was wrong of her to rent the room because she needed money and then ignore his needs. Suddenly he shuddered at the thought of her red lips and phony smile. If he wanted to sleep, he couldn't indulge in such hateful recollections. He struggled to turn his thoughts elsewhere. Today, yes, today was payday. Conjuring up images of crisp 10,000-won bills, he closed his eyes, but the balance sheet of his future passed through his head like subtitles in a movie, only to reignite his depression. Reminding himself that he nicked his hand with the tailoring knife when he didn't get enough sleep, he stretched out flat on his back with his hands folded on his chest like a child.

When sleep comes late, waking is that much more difficult. Work started earlier these days because orders had backed up. When he finally managed to shake off sleep, it was already half past seven. It would take twenty minutes to wash and get going. If he ate breakfast in ten minutes or less, he'd make it, just barely. He had made an arrangement for meals at the restaurant in front of the factory: 500 won for the house special, breakfast and dinner. It wasn't cheap, but lately he was working nights more frequently. That meant the boss paid for dinner, and his food expenses were cut in half. He washed in a flash but couldn't find a towel. When he finally did find one, it stank. His room was dark, but he was in the habit of not turning on the lights in the daytime. Still, when morning came, the shabby landscape of his room was relentlessly exposed. He kicked the bedclothes to one side as he put on his clothes. There was no choice but to wear the socks he had worn the day before. He hadn't had time to do the laundry because they kept working nights. If there were an easier way of throwing out the wash water, he could have washed his socks and towels anytime he wanted. *I've got to find a better place to live,* he thought, but as he looked around the room, he knew that he was in no position to do so.

The stairs leading down to the factory where he worked were steep and cramped. It was the same everywhere. Stairs leading aboveground were designed to be wide and safe, and stairs leading underground were designed as if they were meant to send people tumbling. They said the factory was once a supermarket storeroom. The building had been constructed with the supermarket in mind, and naturally a supermarket would need a basement storeroom. However, business had not gone as well as expected. The supermarket owner couldn't afford to stock up in advance when the merchandise on the shelves was already gathering dust. The supermarket was surrounded by old factories that should have been razed long ago, in a strange neighborhood, neither industrial nor residential. His room was in Wonmi-dong, and the factory was in the administrative district of Wonmi-dong. Each day he commuted to work by foot, about a ten-minute walk. In other words, he walked the length of Wonmi-dong twice each day. His life was spent sleeping curled up in a basement at one end of Wonmi-dong, and then, after barely managing to crawl aboveground, he had to descend once more into a basement where putrid air collected.

Really, there was no other way to express it: The air in that factory was putrid. When he stepped inside, a smoky haze hung over the room from the cigarettes the men all smoked before starting to work. A single fan labored furiously, but it was no use. He was thankful that the acrid smell of the fabric somehow managed to escape the room. It was a little better lately, now that they were using only transparent vinyl. When they worked with thick carpet cloth or artificial leather, his nose was constantly dripping from the smell.

He checked to be sure the boss hadn't arrived yet, then went to the faucet and brushed his teeth. It looked like Mr. Mun and Motorcycle Chŏng hadn't come to work yet. Mun, married and busy with his new family, was often late, but Motorcycle Chŏng was rarely tardy. Chŏng was always grumbling about something, so you would expect him to be late or absent, but he rarely was. He looked at his watch. It was 8:10. That meant it was really 8:05. By this time, Pak should have been standing in front of the new shipment of material, he and Na should have been at the cutting board, and Mun and Pae should have been sitting at the fusing machine. With orders piling up, everyone did what they were supposed to do without any nagging from the boss.

"Aren't we going to work?" he asked to no one in particular as he sat down to the cutting board. Pae was the only one sitting at the proper workstation. He looked like a dignified college professor with his thick, black-rimmed glasses. Even his demeanor suggested it, and they all called him Doctor Pae. His skill at the fusing machine qualified him for the nickname as well. But Doctor Pae hadn't started work, either. He lit another cigarette, seemingly unconcerned that the boss might walk in at any moment. Young Pak, a baseball and soccer fanatic, was actually lying down, with his back against a bundle of material, and Na was idly squeezing his pimples in the small wall mirror, as was his habit. The atmosphere was different somehow.

"Aren't you going to work?" he asked Pae.

"They're upstairs. The boss, too." Smoke slithered from Pae's nostrils.

"It's a strike. We've decided to go on strike," Young Pak said.

"How come you weren't there yesterday?" Na asked in a reproachful tone. After working late the night before, Motorcycle Chŏng had organized a drinking party; apparently they had come up with the scheme then. He didn't like drinking. He had never learned to smoke, either. Since childhood, he had been the solid type who knew he would never make a decent living if he indulged himself as others did.

"But why now? We're so busy—" he began, when Na cut him off.

"Listen to him! You gotta hit 'em when it's busy. Otherwise you don't have any clout. Motorcycle Chŏng's a smart fellow. All we have to do is follow his lead. We're sure to get something out of it." Then Na thrust his face in the mirror once more.

He reached for his knife, then paused to confirm they really were striking. "So we're not going to work?"

"I told you. Chŏng'll come down with a report in a minute. We've got to wait until he gets here." Pae leaned back, relaxed. Then the telephone rang. It was the first order of the day. When orders started pouring in first thing in the morning, it was sure to be a busy day. Na took down the order on a piece of paper.

"Okay, that's thirty sets for the Excel. I've got it. I'll tell the boss as soon as he comes in. Huh? No, we don't have any LeMans in stock right now. Well, maybe four or five . . . Yes. All right. Then ten for the LeMans . . ." Na shrugged as he hung up. He took the order, but no one knew if they would work today.

When he thought of the dark face of their boss, who was constantly harassed by clients' demands, he felt uncomfortable. He couldn't be certain, but he thought the boss might do the cutting and fusing himself if he had to. But there was no way the boss could satisfy the whining clients if he worked alone. The telephone rang again. Twenty more Excels. For some reason, Excel orders hadn't dropped off, although new cars had come on the market. Only a few minutes passed before the telephone rang again. It was like that every morning. Na shook his head as he answered the phone.

Without realizing it, he picked up his knife, and Young Pak, who was responsible for the preliminary cutting, slowly got up.

"Who drives a Pony nowadays?" Na complained as he put down the receiver. "Hey, Pak. Go look and see if we have any Pony covers left. The guy's desperate. He says five'll do. Doctor Pae, we can sell them if we got them in stock, right?"

This was their first strike, so no one was sure what to do. Even Pae, an old hand, sat up at his machine with his feet on the pedals as the orders came in. "We don't have any. We've got a lot of Maepsies, though, and plenty of Stellars." Pak waved his hand as he emerged from behind the partition.

There hadn't been any orders for Ponies or Maepsies lately. The factory made floor mats for passenger cars. The mats, which kept dust down and enhanced a car's interior, were now considered necessities. As a result, whenever a new car came out, their work changed. Until recently, they had been busy making mats for Stellars, but since the LeMans was introduced, Stellars were out. LeMans and Excels were the main items these days. Excels didn't require much material, and the work was relatively simple, so productivity was high. Who knows what kind of car would come out next? But whatever it was, they were sure to cut their hands more than once as they tried to follow the new pattern.

Na's face was bright red as he answered the telephone; there was no time to squeeze his pimples now. Na must have been twenty-five or so, but he looked like a high school student with that acne-covered face. The men chatted deliberately among themselves, unconsciously trying to relieve the stress caused by the telephone's ring. "Have you seen those red LeMans? Women seem to drive them a lot. With sunglasses on. They look really cool." Pae pretended to twist the beard he didn't have. He was actually two years younger than Mun, but looked so much older and more experienced, that even Mun, a picky fellow, watched himself around him. For all intents and purposes, Pae, who had married early and already had a child in middle school, was the factory headman. The factory had started out with the boss operating the fusing machine and Pae doing the cutting.

"Some guys buy their wives a red LeMans, while we work our asses off making floor mats and never even get a ride in a car. It just ain't fair," Na grumbled, rubbing his face.

"Oh, I forgot. The woman from the supermarket told us to keep the bathroom clean. Otherwise, she's going to lock it up. She was hopping mad," Young Pak said.

There was only one toilet in the three-story building. It was coed and someone was always using it. The woman had already complained that the men from the factory used the toilet too often. There were seven of them, including the boss. In summer, it was embarrassing having to clamber upstairs to the toilet, with the woman from the supermarket watching their comings and goings. The bathroom was located just up the stairs from the supermarket cash register. With so many people using it, you could hardly expect it to stay clean. But that didn't mean they could set aside their work to go clean the toilet while the orders piled up.

"You use the bathroom most. You should take over cleaning it every night," Na snickered. It was true: He made a point of using the toilet at work. He was trying to adjust his body clock so he could avoid the cramps that wrenched him each morning at dawn. Strangely, though, it never worked. He always woke up at daybreak, whimpering for a place to shit. Whimpering? His choice of words stunned him. He didn't want to whimper like a dog. Suddenly he loathed the red-lipped landlady all over again.

He thought back to the time he had lived in the room off the gate at the boss's place. Those were the days. It may have been the boss's house, but it was no different than anyone else's. The boss had kids to raise and a sickly wife, plus a pile of debts that he had run up as his company's fortunes rose and fell. *We'll have to get a load of orders before the boss pays off all those debts,* he thought, shaking his head. Then he recalled what Motorcycle Chŏng had once said.

"Bosses always gripe. You can't believe what they say. Remember Yun? He used to work here, then he set up his own factory, remember? Lately, his factory's really busy, too. They need more people, so if we get sacked there's nothing to worry about. Yun said he'd take as many as we got. As many as we got."

It had been some time since Motorcycle Chŏng told them of Yun's offer. That explained the strike. But he had lived in the boss's house for several months, and from the goings-on there he knew that the boss had reason to gripe. He couldn't accept Motorcycle Chŏng's claim so easily.

It was Chŏng's job to package and deliver the mats that Mun and Pae made. Because of his deliveries, he was rarely in the factory. His motorcycle skills were legendary. His predecessor was always getting stopped by traffic cops and ended up costing the boss quite a bit in fines, but not Chŏng. Compared to the rest of them, who were stuck in the basement working all day, Chŏng heard a lot of rumors. And naturally, the more rumors you hear, the more complaints you have. Motorcycle Chŏng was always grumbling—about everything. At that very moment, he was probably sitting in the Chinese restaurant on the second floor, grumbling to the boss. And Mun was probably nodding in agreement, without saying a word. The two of them had always gotten along well. One could safely say that all of Chŏng's statements represented Mun's opinions as well.

Enough of those two, he thought. *I wonder what the boss thinks of this strike.* The boss had always believed that he treated his employees no better and no worse than any other business that manufactured floor mats. And he was right. He had started out as a day laborer himself and was simply doing what he had seen and experienced. Like Yun, who only a few months ago had been operating the fusing machine, the boss believed there was nothing special about being the president of a company in this field. He was probably just sitting there, frowning as he puffed on a cigarette. After losing a joint off his right pinkie when it was crushed by a press in his youth, the boss had always smoked with his left hand. He offered toasts with his left hand, too.

"What are they doing? Why don't they make a decision and get on with it? The work's piling up, and I'm feeling kind of itchy," Na said after taking another round of orders.

Actually, they were all feeling itchy, wondering what was going on upstairs.

"Go have a look. Doctor Pae, why don't you go up and see what's happening?" Young Pak said, but Pae waved him off.

"Whoa, not me," he said. "I couldn't stand to see the boss's face. He's sure to be angriest at me. He'll think I betrayed him."

At that very moment, they heard loud footsteps coming down the stairs. The footsteps echoed down the steep staircase, shaking the basement. But it was only Motorcycle Chŏng and Mun. The men in the basement craned their necks to look around the two men, but the boss wasn't with them.

"So how did it go?" asked Pae.

Chŏng shook his head. Mun brought his hand to his neck and made a chopping gesture.

"He told us to do as we like. He says he won't give in to our demands, even if it means he can't keep up with the orders, his credit's wrecked, and the whole business is ruined. Damn, it's hot, and it's still morning. Whew, it's boiling."

Chŏng looked unexpectedly subdued.

"What were our demands?"

Now that he thought about it, he didn't know what they had demanded. "Regular bonuses of three hundred percent!" Young Pak said in a loud voice, as if the pressure had gotten to him. All of a sudden his mind lit up, as if a tiny light bulb had flashed on, then off.

"The boss went out. He said he was going to find some other workers. He just won't listen. You should have heard him start up that motorcycle."

Mun sounded discouraged, too. "What are we going to do?" Young Pak looked at the others with a worried expression.

"What do you mean, 'What are we going to do?' We've got to hold out to the very end," Chŏng declared in a loud voice. After all, he had organized the whole thing. "Let's get out of here. We'll leave one person behind. The boss said he'd pay us this afternoon, so we might as well play hooky till then. Don't worry, fellas. It's not easy finding help these days. Let's meet back here by six."

"I'll stay," he volunteered.

"You're not going to work, are you?" Chŏng warned.

"Why don't we all go?" Na asked.

"We can hardly leave the place completely empty. We have to leave someone behind. You stay here and answer the phone." Pae had made a decision.

"Let's go play billiards," Na suggested. The other men agreed.

"Motorcycle Chŏng, are . . . aren't you going over to the factory that Mr. Yun set up?" Young Pak asked. He looked as if he was going to cry.

"Shut up, kid. You think this is the only place we can earn a living? I told you I'd take care of everything." Chŏng raised his voice.

"He's right. Let's take a rest while we've got the chance. My shoulders and back have been killing me lately," Pae said as he headed out the door.

After the others left, he looked around the empty factory and sat down in the chair by the cutting table. For some reason, he felt comfortable there in his usual place. It was already lunchtime. The boss supplied lunch. They usually ordered out, alternating between the Chinese place upstairs and the restaurant across the street. He wasn't sure what would happen today. He hadn't done any work, and accepting a meal without working for it was intolerable to him. During the lunch hour, even the phone was quiet. Missing a meal was nothing to him, he thought, as he sat down at the fusing machine, just to see how it felt. Fusers earned a lot more than cutters. All cutters needed was flexibility in the wrists. Any strong young man could cut several layers at a time; youth was the only prerequisite. Everyone started out doing the simple scissor work, cutting the material to the right width; then when new rookies came in, the more experienced workers moved on to the cutting table. They followed the patterns for each model, pressing down on the cloth with the tailoring knife.

The boss had wanted to buy another fusing machine for a long time because he was worried about the work piling up. If he didn't hire another fusing technician, he or Na would be promoted to operate the new machine. Na had a lot of experience as a grease monkey, but he was little more than a rookie in this field. He, on the other hand, had been working around here for two years already. As far as he was concerned, there was no reason why he shouldn't man the fusing machine pedals. *Then I'd bring in more income,* he thought as he pressed his right foot on the pedal that lowered the mold, then pressed the left pedal, which sent the current through the machine. With a raise, he could save more at the bank. Or at least he could send a little more money home to his mother for her arthritis medicine. No, maybe he should use the money to get out of that basement and find a better place. A room where he could use the toilet whenever he liked.

It had been a mistake to believe the landlady in the first place. Of course he had no choice but to believe Mr. Pak from the Kangnam Real Estate Office. Pak was the one who had introduced him to the woman.

"The room isn't cheap because it's in the basement. It's cheap because of the bathroom situation, but that's just an inconvenience, nothing more. You've seen enough rooms to know that a place like this is hard to find. Good rooms cost money. You'd be lucky to get a room like this so cheap. The landlady says she hardly ever goes out, so you'll be able to use the bathroom whenever you like. It's a lot better than carrying around a key and having her suspicious of you all the time."

The morning after he moved in, he went upstairs and rang the bell, though it was still a bit early. The woman had a daughter who looked to be nine or ten, so he figured she must be up, getting the child ready for school. There was no sign of life, though. *Maybe the bell's broken,* he thought, pressing his ear to the door, but the bell was clearly ringing through the apartment. *They must be sleeping late, or maybe they're out,* he thought. He had no choice but to turn to go. However, he couldn't ignore the habit of relieving himself before breakfast, and in desperation he recalled the toilet at work. Clutching his abdomen, he ran to the factory, only to find the supermarket's shutters still drawn. There was nothing he could do. The supermarket had to open if he was to use the toilet. The entrance to the factory was separate from the entrance to the toilet. Sweating, he managed to hold on, but then the same thing happened the next day. His landlady's apartment was locked like an ironclad fort. The door didn't budge, no matter how long or hard he pushed the bell. Thinking she might have left town for an extended period, he tried the bell on his way home from work, too, but there was still no answer.

It was in the evening a few days later that he finally got a verbal answer, though nothing else. He had thought the apartment was empty that day, too, when after a long pause, the landlady's voice came through the door. "Who is it?" she asked.

"It's . . . the new tenant from the basement."

"Yes, what do you want?"

What do I want! He was stunned. And she hadn't even thought to open the door.

"The bathroom . . ."

As soon as he mentioned the bathroom, the woman feigned astonishment. "Oh, and I'm right in the middle of a shower."

He blushed in spite of himself. Didn't that mean the only thing separating him from a naked woman was a door?

"It's all right now. But in the morning, around seven or eight, I'd—"

"Okay. Come by then."

The next morning he stood clutching his belly in front of the door that still would not open. He couldn't figure it out. Had she forgotten her promise, or did she simply sleep late? He stood at her front door on several occasions after that, but to no avail. Fortunately, as people say, there is a way around just about everything, and they were right, for he soon discovered that he could use the ground floor toilets in some of the two-story commercial units found throughout Wonmi-dong. Once he had mastered the trick of sneaking into other people's bathrooms in the dead of night or early morning hours, he no longer thought of going upstairs to number 102. And the urge to relieve his bowels naturally shifted to night or early morning. The public toilets in these buildings were shared by the shopkeepers and were generally located near the main gate, so if he moved quickly, he didn't run into anyone. If there was one thing that bothered him, it was the fact that he couldn't flush the toilet for fear of waking someone. This, no doubt, was the reason for his neighbors' horror and their decision to start locking doors that had remained open until then. Once, he had hinted of his plight to Mr. Pak from the real estate office. When he told Pak that the woman never opened the door, even when she was at home, the older man erupted in anger.

"It's just like those people, changing their minds at the drop of a hat. There must be nearly a dozen people living in the basement of the Rose of Sharon apartments, but not one of them can use their landlord's toilet in peace. And thanks to the people down in the basement, the folks on this side of the street are always complaining about the shit. Everyone's talking about how the people living in the basement over there use our bathrooms as if they were their own. That's why they started locking their doors at night."

Pak was the one who had found him the room, so he had expected some kind of solution from him. The man's sudden outburst stunned him. Pak's wife, the woman from Kohŭng, overheard their conversation and offered her own opinion. "The woman in number 102, she never opens the door for anyone. That's just her way. From the way she dresses, you wouldn't expect her to stay put at home, but everyone says she just sits around the house and never opens the door. Still, she promised when she signed the contract. She shouldn't go back on her word like that."

"Anyway," interrupted Mr. Pak, scowling still, "she promised when you signed that contract, so you'd better go and have it out with her, don't you think? A person can't go around saying one thing and doing another, can they?"

Mr. Pak clearly had no solution. By the same token, he knew he couldn't expect anything from the landlady, who had so firmly decided not to open her door. She probably loathed the idea of letting him into her house, and she certainly didn't want a dirty man in her sparkling clean bathroom. She rented the room because she needed the money, but she was clearly uncomfortable about sharing a toilet with him.

There was only one solution. He would have to change his schedule and do his "business" during the day. That was the only way, he decided, and so he set about the task of training his digestive system to perform its business in the bathroom at work. Of course, it wasn't easy. In fact, the harder he tried, the less he needed to go when he was at work. Then no sooner had he returned to his basement room, telling himself that he absolutely must not feel the urge there, than his lower abdomen began to churn. He couldn't figure it out. His metabolism had a life of its own, constantly doing everything backwards. What was he supposed to do? If he couldn't find an open gate, he had to squat in some dark corner along the streets of

Wonmi-dong. And if he was going to relieve himself in the streets, it had to be at an hour when few people were around. There were several vacant lots in the neighborhood, but they lacked adequate cover. He had to find some place that was enclosed on all four sides, but there weren't many of those around. Usually, parked trucks, cars, or vans offered the best protection.

Yep, cars were his savior wherever he went. He smiled bitterly as he looked at the fusing machine. He fed himself with the floor mats of cars and dumped what he ate using cars for cover. He scowled as he recalled the shameless face of Pak from the real estate office. If it hadn't been for the problem with the bathroom, he wouldn't have thought ill of Pak. A room in the basement suited his needs perfectly. He was accustomed to the underground life. Some day he would come aboveground, but right now, a room in the basement and a job in the basement were as precious as life itself. His dream was so simple: Since he had to eat in order to work, he should have the freedom to relieve himself at will.

It was one-thirty when Chŏng telephoned. On any other day they would have finished lunch and been working by then.

"You mean the boss didn't call? That's strange . . ." He could hear Chŏng pursing his lips.

"Are you having fun? Where are you?"

"Mun went home to render his services to the wife, and the rest of us are sitting in a tearoom by the train station. We're bored. You must be going nuts, stuck in that basement all by yourself. It's not right."

Chŏng acted so natural, as if he made his living aboveground. Shortly after he finished talking to Chŏng, the boss walked in, his face swollen with anger. Seeing that only one man had remained, he looked around the factory with despair. His faded shirt clung to his back. It must have been awfully hot outside. He hadn't heard the boss's motorcycle. Did that mean he had run back to the factory? He didn't know what to say, so he simply watched the boss to see what he did next.

The boss went to the faucet, filled a cup to the brim, and downed it in a single gulp. Then he sat at the fusing machine and began pressing down the mold in silence. "If you have anything cut, bring it over here," he said in a dry tone. Some fifty LeMans mats and one hundred Excel mats were already cut. He picked up the material and took it over to the fusing machine. He didn't know if the boss had seen the orders on the blackboard, but he arranged the material so the boss would work on the LeMans mats first. If only the boss finished them. That would shut up the client who had called again earlier, gasping as if the mats were a matter of life or death.

The boss handled the machine skillfully. He hadn't used it for some time, but he seemed to move more quickly than Pae himself. No one would have guessed that he was the boss. His hair bathed in sweat, his dark face scorched by time, his shabby clothing—he didn't look any better than Pae or Mun. As the noise of the machine filled the room, the basement air seemed to stir again. His chest tightened. He didn't know whether he should work or simply watch. He didn't like watching other people work while he stood by with his arms at his side. He was the type who had to work until they wrapped him in his shroud and sent him to his grave. If he was going to starve, he would rather do it working. He stood hesitating, fingering the tailoring knife; then the telephone rang. He was sure it was another client asking them to hurry an order, but the boss answered before him.

"Put it off till tomorrow. Well, if you're in such a hurry, get them in Hwagok-dong. We can't get the goods out today."

He put down the tailoring knife. After all, a promise was a promise. Who knows? Maybe the boss had a new crew coming to work the following morning. One thing he had learned moving from factory to factory was, you can't break a promise to your coworkers. It would be wrong to harm simple and gullible coworkers who were sensitive to betrayal.

Why was time moving so slowly? It was barely three. His stomach felt empty since he had skipped lunch. At daybreak, when he had whimpered like a dog because he had no place to shit, he had arrogantly thought about going without lunch, but now he could see that the effects of one skipped meal went deep. The stubborn heat was hard to take on an empty stomach. He turned on the fan, and the boss took off his shirt. The fan must have reminded him that it was hot. Thick beads of sweat rolled down the boss's face.

"Have you eaten?" the boss asked.

He shook his head.

"Order two bowls of noodles with black bean sauce. Doubles." The boss must have missed lunch, too. When the noodles arrived, the two men sat down on either side of the cutting table. As he peeled the paper wrapper off his chopsticks, the boss signaled him with his eyes to eat. That reminded him of the time he lived at the boss's house. He would sit at the breakfast table, waiting for the boss to finish washing up; then the boss would come, face still dripping, and give him that look. The telephone rang twice while they were eating.

"Don't answer. The day's ruined anyway."

The boss's lips were smeared with black bean sauce, but he didn't say anything as he wound noodles around his chopsticks. *Where are the others?* he wondered. Suddenly, he thought of his coworkers walking up there, outside, somewhere aboveground. Then he looked at the boss. At any other time, the boss was aboveground and they were stuck down here in the basement. He'd always thought of the boss as someone with no connection to this place, to this underground world, and now he was surprised to realize that the image of their boss mopping sweat from his brow with one hand and twirling noodles onto his chopsticks with the other wasn't the least bit unfamiliar.

The boss emptied his bowl first, and soon he laid down his own chopsticks. After setting the empty dishes by the door, he took a handful of toilet paper and went upstairs. He had already developed a habit of heading straight to the bathroom after putting something in his stomach. Of course, it was a habit limited to hours spent at the factory. The thought of returning to his basement room with something to digest left inside himself was frightening. For nearly twenty minutes he was ensconced in the bathroom, pushing with all his might, testing chants and magic spells, but he returned to the basement with his toilet paper. The boss was dozing with his head against the back of his chair; the noodles must have made him sleepy. The chair wasn't designed with comfort in mind. Its back was too low to support the boss's head comfortably, and he had propped one foot up on the cutting table, so his posture was a mess. If he really wanted to sleep, he could have pushed several chairs together or leaned against a roll of material.

The boss just can't fight off the fatigue, he thought, as he sat down on the bottom step. He didn't want to wake him. His coworkers would be back in an hour or so. He looked over at the boss's haggard face, wondering if he had come up with a solution to their sudden strike. The boss's mouth hung open, and beneath the creased forehead, his eyes were squeezed tightly shut. He looked as if he were frowning at the world even as he slept. Was there some way of helping him sleep a little more comfortably? He rose to look for something to prop up the boss's head. That's when he heard plastic slippers slapping down the stairs. It was Mun. Without even realizing it, he put his finger to his lips.

"He's back?" Mun asked, lowering his voice.

He nodded and moved up several stairs to sit. "Where are the other guys?"

"I went home . . . and to Yun's factory."

Apparently Mun had been worried. Maybe he had planned to get a job at Old Yun's—no, Mr. Yun's—factory before the others had a chance. Mun had always been closer to Motorcycle Chŏng than the rest of them, but now he attacked him in a barbed tone.

"I knew he was taking a few sets for himself every time he went out on a delivery. We've been so busy lately, and it looks like he's taken advantage of that. He knew the boss was on to him. He was just marking time before he staged this strike and dragged us into it. He's trying to shut the boss up. There aren't any jobs at Yun's factory. He never said they were short on staff."

As he listened to Mun whisper, he calculated his finances in his head: his bare-bone living expenses, the money he sent home to his mother, the bills he had run up at the store. He could probably find another job if he put his mind to it, but his immediate plans clearly would be as tangled as thread off a skein.

"So what did he say? Did he find a new crew?" Mun looked as if he was about to cry. It was hard to remain calm when Mun was on the verge of tears.

"He didn't say anything. He seems really tired. He pressed out a few mats and has been sleeping ever since."

The boss had always been a man of few words. He had been with him for almost a year now, but he had never seen him really laugh. The past had been difficult, but lately, with business so good, he could afford to laugh. The grim expression never left his face, though.

"It's almost time, isn't it? Did he go to the bank and get the money? I hope it's not our last paycheck here." Mun stood up and brushed the dust from his pants. He rose and did the same.

Motorcycle Chŏng led the others back around twenty minutes

before six. The boss had awakened and smoked several cigarettes by the time they arrived. He looked around at the assembled workers. The men, who had escaped the cavernous basement and spent the afternoon wandering around doing nothing, stared at the walls self-consciously and waited for the boss to speak. They seemed exhausted after spending half a day in the outside world. Pae's drooping shoulders told the whole story. Clearly there was nothing outside that filled him with the pride he derived from his skill at the fusing machine. Finally the boss took their pay envelopes from the small black bag he carried. No one said a word as he handed them out.

"You're getting a little extra this month since you've all been working overtime. And I just want you to know, I added a little bonus—not much, of course."

No one looked inside his envelope. The boss scratched the back of his head as he always did when he was embarrassed.

"You know, I was finally getting out from under my debts. Of course, we're all in the same boat, I guess."

He spoke in a low voice, as if to himself, but they all seemed to understand. Chŏng cleared his throat and avoided the boss's eyes. Young Pak and Na just stood there, blinking.

"We could work for a few hours now if you like. I'll bet you got a lot of calls today," Mun said.

"Oh, that's nice of you to offer but . . ." the boss said, scratching his head again, "but there's no point really. The day's a bust."

Pae straightened up, and the other men turned to him.

"Curse me if you like, but I say we go back to work tomorrow morning. And, Boss," he said, turning to the owner, shoulders straight and proud now, "when you've paid off your debts, you have to give us the taste of a real bonus."

As he returned home after the dinner the boss treated them to, the sun, still visible in the summer sky, stained the antenna on top of City Hall a rusty gold. He had gone to the toilet in the restaurant, struggling to excrete the food he had eaten that day, but to no avail. When he glimpsed Captain Kim from Brothers Supermarket in the distance, he couldn't hide his apprehension. He was unable to erase the feeling that his abdomen was already boiling, and he recalled what Na had said in the restaurant. "You've been chanting in the bathroom again, huh? What an idiot! Just have it out with the landlady. Have it out with her! What's the point of having a mouth if you don't use it?" Then Na lowered his voice and said, "Look what happened today. We didn't do any work, we got a couple ten-thousand-won bills extra, and now we're eating pork ribs! It pays off."

Perhaps Na was right. Yes, he would do as Na said. He'd sit in front of her door until she answered. And when the door opened, he'd push his way inside and stay put until she gave him a key.

He went straight to the landlady's apartment, without stopping at his room in the basement. *Ding-dong, ding-dong.* In contrast to his own dark mood, the doorbell rang brightly through the apartment. The door didn't look like it would open easily. He pressed the doorbell repeatedly and rattled the doorknob, but the door didn't budge. Finally he formed a fist and pounded, but that, too, was useless. He did have a mouth and he was determined to use it, but she had to open the door if he was going to negotiate or plead with her. He glared at the solid steel door once more, then went downstairs to his room. As soon as he opened the door, the musty smell greeted him, almost as if it had been lying in wait. He climbed up on the chair and opened the window, then lay down, using the rumpled bedclothes as a pillow. It was the first time he had come home early in a long time, and the water was running that day, so he should have washed the pile of laundry, but he didn't feel like moving. Though the rainy season had not yet arrived, moisture seeped through the linoleum floor. *I'm going to fall asleep if I'm not careful,* he thought as he dozed. Then suddenly there was a racket outside his window. He opened his eyes with a start. He must have fallen asleep.

"Who's the bastard that keeps doing this? If you don't have a place to shit, then stop eating!"

He jerked upright at the piercing voice. They must have been talking about him, but he couldn't tell who the voice belonged to. He hadn't heard it before.

"You're right, there. It stinks to high heaven. I can hardly bear it. No use cleanin' up, either, 'cause they just do it again. You can't win."

The second voice was clearly Mr. Chu's from the wallpaper shop. Come to think of it, the sound of water running from a rubber hose was coming from somewhere nearby. He leaned his ear toward the window, trying to catch every word. The jet of water seemed to soak into the basement and dampen his heart.

"You wouldn't believe the flies. And it's not like it's happened only once or twice." It was a woman's voice now. From the high soprano, he could tell it was Shinae's mom.

"Well, anyone with an ounce of humanity won't do it again after we've taken this water and cleaned everything up so nice." Then the sound of water grew louder.

"It's like this every morning when I come out to get my car. This morning I stepped on something soft. It was disgusting. What a way to start the day."

The unfamiliar voice laughed. It must be the owner of the chocolate-brown sedan. After his misstep that morning, he must have waited all day to bring out his hose.

His face burned, and he sat down heavily.

Please, he begged and begged again, but it was no use. He tossed and turned, and then the bell from Sŏg'wang Temple tolled through the morning air. Soon the church chimes rang. Just like the day before. Even the slow twisting in his bowels was the same. He pulled his legs to his chest and took a deep breath. There must be other private spots, besides the curb behind the brown car. He suddenly regretted choosing a spot so close to home; he should have gone a little farther afield. In a real pinch, he could try Old Kang's vegetable patch. He could hide behind the cucumber vines or even the pepper plants, since they had grown quite tall. *If you don't have a place to shit, then stop eating!* He would have gone to the old man's field if it hadn't been for that knife-sharp voice. Old Kang was a tall curmudgeon of a man who would surely curse him even more. As he weighed his options, a cold sweat began to collect along his spine. *Anyone with an ounce of humanity won't do it again.* Chu's deep voice made his face redden again. Whose fault was it that he couldn't act like a decent human being?

He clutched his abdomen and sat up. Perspiration covered his forehead, and tiny goose bumps broke out on his arms. He tried pressing his face into the musty covers. He stood up and paced the tiny room, but it was all useless. Why did his bowels insist on acting up here in his room, when they didn't do a thing all day long? He couldn't understand his own gut, and that was immensely discouraging. With an intense hatred, he imagined the landlady's red lips. If he made it through the rest of this night, just through the rest of this night in peace, he would go upstairs and kick her door in. Yes, he was going to confront her, even if it meant knocking her door down. He rubbed his cheek against the mildewed wallpaper and prayed for the murky darkness to recede.

He wasn't sure how he had fallen asleep, but when he awoke, he was curled up on the bare floor by the door. At first, he wasn't even sure he had slept. The struggle, the intense pain returned to him as soon as he opened his eyes. Six-twenty. The room was bright enough to read his watch. That consoled him. *I've finally managed to act like a normal human being,* he thought. Then he heard glass breaking. So that was why he had awakened. Or maybe it was the sound of glass fragments showering down in front of his small window. He held his breath. For a brief moment, he thought it was a stone aimed at him. He visualized a jagged stone in the hand of the car owner who had snarled, "Who's the bastard?" Then he heard another pane of glass shatter. Glass fragments cascaded like hail, some bouncing off his window.

"Open this door! I'm telling you, open this door!" a woman screamed. She sounded so close he felt as if he could reach out and touch her. A moment later, the walls began to shake as someone pounded one of the apartment doors upstairs. "Open this door! I know everything, so open the damned door!"

It sounded like she was kicking the door. The violent thumping went on for some time. It was hard to believe that it was a woman. He doubted his ears for a moment. She was clearly kicking the door of number 102. And it was the clatter of her heels that he heard in front of the apartment. In front of the door that only a few hours earlier he had vowed to kick in with such fierce antagonism. What on earth could have happened? The early morning intruder dashed from the front to the back of the apartment, pounding on the door and throwing stones at the balcony window, but there wasn't even a squeak from inside the apartment. The silence was so complete that most people would have thought the apartment empty. Even he was having doubts, despite his own experience with the formidable silence of number 102. But the intruder acted with confidence.

"Open the door! I know everything! Open up!"

The walls shook with her pounding, glass broke, and another hail of fragments hit the ground outside.

"Did you think you'd get away with stealing another woman's man? Open this door, you little bitch!"

Finally the intruder's identity was revealed. The violent woman must have been the wife, and the woman quaking inside, the mistress. He recalled the red fingernails of the woman who opened the door to no one. Because of her personal circumstances, he hadn't been able to live like a normal human being. "Aren't you going to open it? Open up! Right now!" The next stone sounded like a big one. With a loud shatter, glass fragments rained to the ground, longer this time. He shook his head, thinking there was probably nothing left to break.

He was right, for then he heard the intruder scrambling over the iron railing onto the balcony. The railing was just to the side of his window. It was about the height of an ordinary adult, and without the glass, it wouldn't be difficult to climb over. Now what was going to happen? His heart pounded as he waited for events to unfold. Was his landlady inside, pale with fear as she clung to her lover? Soon the sounds of a woman shouting, things breaking, and loud crying flowed from the apartment. Hadn't she realized that the wife would climb in through the balcony once the windows were broken? If she had opened the door in the first place, there wouldn't have been such a scene. He felt sorry for the landlady's foolish obstinacy. The whole neighborhood was sure to be watching the spectacle. It was strange: All of a sudden his antagonism toward the landlady had dissipated like a cloud of dust. He simply felt sad at the thought that he no longer had anyone to hate, that it was his misfortune to have encountered the wrong landlady.

On his way to work he saw number 102 in ruins. The wife, who had caused the commotion, must have left, and the apartment was ominously quiet. The windows facing the street were all broken—not only the windows on the balcony, but the bedroom window as well. There was a pile of glass shards in front of his window. They glittered, reflecting the sun's sharp light. Passersby craned to peek inside, and neighbors came out and gossiped about the racket. He hurried on his way, fearful that Mr. Ŏm and Mr. Chu, who stood in front of the Happiness Photo Studio looking at the destruction, might glance in his direction. The brown sedan was nowhere in sight, and at a glance he could see its parking spot was much cleaner than the surrounding area.

After walking some distance, he looked back. Old Kang's field was lush with green vegetables, but across the street the shell of the ravaged apartment stood cold and lonely. Was it because the sun was so bright and strong? The apartment sent shivers down his spine. He felt empty when he realized that number 102, which had denied him for so long, was nothing more than a dark cave. He stood in one spot for a long time, staring at it; it was no different from his own basement room now. The sunshine pouring down his back was hot, though it was still morning. Try as he might, he couldn't see his room below the ground. He couldn't even see the window. He couldn't grasp the solemn fact that there was another cave beneath the gaping number 102.

He stood there for a long time, then turned and looked at the road ahead. The factory was to the left at the intersection visible in the distance. He was heading toward another cave, but he hurried on, uncomprehending. The weather was sweltering despite the early hour. His neck was already sticky, and when he moved, the musty smell of mildew rose from his clothing. It was a smell only underground men knew.

Cold Water Pass

THE WOMAN'S VOICE flowing from the telephone was dreadfully thick and hoarse. At first it was difficult to tell whether the owner of the voice was a man or a woman. The moment I heard it I spread open the pages of my memory and began searching for its owner. I had received telephone calls from two husky-voiced women in the past. One was the editor of a corporate newsletter, the other, a publisher. While I had met neither, I had a preconception that both were active, no-nonsense career women.

Of the two, I hastily concluded that it must be the editor and replied to her polite inquiries in a halfhearted tone. Something was cooking on the stove, and I was in no mood for idle conversation. Oblivious to my impatience, the woman paused in silence for a moment after confirming once more in that husky voice that I was indeed the person she was looking for.

"Did you . . . By chance did you ever live next to the railroad tracks in Chŏnju?" she asked in a diffident tone.

I had assumed she was going to ask me to write an essay or short story, something along those lines, so the question was completely unexpected. However, she was right. I was from Chŏnju, and I had lived in the neighborhood by the railroad tracks. The railroad, which in my childhood passed through a residential area, had been relocated to the outskirts of the city several years earlier, but scenes from the old neighborhood remained clear in my mind. When I said yes, I had lived there, the voice on the telephone paused once more.

"You may not remember me, but my name is Pak Ŭnja, Ŭnja from the steamed dumpling shop by the train tracks."

The voice was even more diffident now, as if she could hardly expect me to remember the name of a playmate I hadn't seen for well over twenty years, as if she were resigned to the possibility that I might not remember at all.

Pak Ŭnja. I remembered the name clearly, so clearly that by the time the voice on the phone mentioned the dumpling shop I had already smelled the cellophane noodles and pork lard used in the dumpling stuffing. However, I didn't tell her that. The years had taught me to disguise my pleasure, and I tried as best I could to control my voice as I said, "Yes, I remember the name quite clearly." Even so, my delight must have flown over the telephone lines because the husky voice immediately jumped several octaves. It was naturally hoarse, and now it fairly crackled as the words gushed forth.

"I'm so pleased! How long has it been? I didn't think you'd remember me. I was afraid to call . . . but your name is popping up everywhere! You know, I've been showing people the newspapers and bragging how you're my friend. I knew you'd make it, way back when you liked reading all those comic books. I phoned the newspaper and they gave me your number. I've had it for more than a month but I didn't have the courage to call till now. Wow! So, how long has it been, anyway?"

It was exactly twenty-five years since I had last heard Ŭnja's voice. It was in second grade when I had made friends with the daughter of the couple who ran the steamed dumpling shop, so it was exactly twenty-five years. Since my name comes up on bylines here and there, on occasion I receive telephone calls from names buried deep in the past, names I can easily live without hearing again. Of course, I am happy to hear from them, and we reminisce, but that's it. They are invariably one-shot reunions, always ending with the ritual promise to keep in touch or get together, although we are all too aware of the solemn fact that we have taken quite different paths in life.

But never had I imagined a call from Ŭnja, the girl from the dumpling shop.

She may have discovered my name and face in a newspaper somewhere, but to tell the truth, I was the one who couldn't believe that she remembered me. And even if she did remember me, there was no reason she should call the newspaper for my address and telephone number. We simply had lived in the same neighborhood for one year in the 1960s. As I look back now, that year was a great comfort to me, but it must have been a terrible bore to her.

It took a long time for the unexpected telephone call to untangle those twenty-five years. More than anything else, I wanted to ask why she hadn't become a singer. I wanted to tell her I had never heard anyone sing "Deep Dark Blues" as well as she had. But she didn't gave me a chance. Over and over she described reading something I had written, the stupidity of those around her who refused to believe I was her friend, and her happiness at discovering my name in the paper. And then she revealed her profession.

"I still sing for a living. But wait a minute! Do you mean you live in Puch'ŏn and you haven't heard of Mina Pak? That's my stage name. Your hubby must be really straitlaced! He's never taken you to any of the nightclubs or bars? Mina Pak's mighty popular on the night scene around Kyŏnggi Province and Inch'ŏn. I've been singing in the clubs there for years now. You can tell from my voice. It's completely shot. Sometimes I can't even talk. I sing solo, and I sing in the chorus. Yep, I've done it all."

Only then did I consider other aspects of that husky voice flowing from the telephone. Professional singers' speaking voices are generally much hoarser than their singing voices. My heart ached at the thought of her singing herself into such a state. I had secretly feared that I might remember nothing about Ŭnja except her singing. How would I have felt if she had simply been a housewife, having nothing to do with singing? It's true: She was a nameless singer going from nightclub to nightclub, not a star who frequently appeared on television, but the fact that she hadn't given up singing was important to me. I subtly reminded her of a few things from the past, of "Deep Dark Blues," the little performances she held under the willow tree, and the tales of the professional singing world she had told on rainy days in the cramped watchtower by the railroad tracks. Ŭnja chortled with delight at each memory, just as I had expected. She marveled at the depth of my friendship and thanked me profusely for remembering such minute details. In the end, we slipped back into the friendship we had shared so long ago.

I recalled many other things. The sad eyes of the pig that floated down the stream during the rains that summer; Ŭnja's mother, who always seemed to be in her petticoat; the smooth calves of Ŭnja's older sister, who had gotten a job waitressing in a tearoom—I could have told about all that and more. It was perfectly natural. After all, I had published a short story about my childhood. Ǔnja was the main character. The story had helped me realize, for the first time, that fiction writing can bring back the past and that the job of writing can be quite sweet. Never had I so abandoned myself to my writing. I cast out my line and reeled in word after word, from a time in my childhood when the intersection between life and death was as startlingly clear as the contrast of darkness and light in a black and white photograph. As I emerged from my parents' protective embrace into a world of alternating hunger, greed, hatred, and love, the confusion that assaulted the sharp new leaf of my consciousness often caused me to cry. At the time, Ǔnja was already one step ahead of me, out in the world. Her pop songs, the railroad tracks, and death kept pushing her deep into the world; indeed, she was so accustomed to the ways of the world that my mother called her the "baby witch." For decades now, I've been living in that world, the one I found as frightening as the fiery chaos of hell back then. But am I really living or just surviving?

I didn't tell Ǔnja about the short story. Actually, I didn't get a chance. She took a long time to explain how she had ended up a nightclub singer and to relate a general account of the many complications she had faced in her struggle to make ends meet. I barely had a chance to ask a single question: Hadn't she been in the national singing contest on TV about ten years earlier? I had heard something about that.

"You're right. I was a runner-up—got the consolation prize. A songwriter told me he'd help me cut a record. So I followed him around, but you've got to have money to get the right song. I told you I once had a gig at the Chǒnju Tourist Hotel nightclub, didn't I? I was twenty at the time. I just did it to make money for a recording, but I ended up a nightclub singer forever! Anyway, let's get together. I'm dying to see you. What do your brothers do? Oh! A long time ago I heard your oldest brother was a big success. That's great. And what about you? I can't wait to see you!"

She insisted that we meet, as if to say we couldn't possibly unravel twenty-five years over the telephone. And I could hardly refuse when she told me she was singing every night at a club right here in Puch'ǒn. She performed two sets a night, one at eight and another at ten, which meant I had to go to see her around nine. She said we could meet somewhere else, if a nightclub wasn't the place for a dignified writer, but then she encouraged me to come there. After all, writers are supposed to explore drinking establishments for their work, aren't they?

I wanted to meet her, of course, but I couldn't give in to her impatient demands that we get together that day or the next. My daughter had to be in bed by nine o'clock, and after she went to sleep, I had a couple of essays that needed to be finished by that day or the next at the latest. We hadn't seen each other for twenty-five years, so what was another day or two? And besides, she was singing every night right here in Puch'ŏn. We were sure to get together some time. Ŭnja was adamant, however.

"Today's Wednesday, right? My contract ends this Sunday. After that, I won't be working the clubs in Puch'ŏn or anywhere else in the Kyŏnggi area for a while. I've managed to save some money. Yep, the dumpling shop girl has made a success of herself, and she's opening a cabaret in Shinsa-dong in Seoul! It opens in two weeks. If we don't get together this week, when will we? Don't you want to see me? I can't wait to see you! Let's get together and talk. Stop by, just for a minute, so I can get a look at you. Can't you do that? Did you say you live in Wonmi-dong? Why, you could walk! It's no farther than the walk from my house to the five-way crossing in Chŏnju. Remember how we used to run back and forth along there?"

Don't you want to see me? My heart ached at Ŭnja's hoarse voice. Before our conversation could end, I'd promised to go, at nine one night that week. As I hung up, I heaved a long sigh, quite in spite of myself. The journey across those twenty-five years had exhausted me. Only then, as I returned to reality, did I remember the blue flame of the gas stove and the boiling pot. I rushed into the kitchen, but the contents of the pot had long since turned to ashes.

It was strange. Lately, even before that unexpected call, I had often recalled scenes from my childhood in Chŏnju. And then Ŭnja, a figure from that time, had suddenly appeared. Those frequent recollections were probably caused by news of my eldest brother, who lived there. The stories, relayed from start to finish in the most minute detail by my sister or mother, were, like those of all families, quite tedious and always the same: My eldest brother, as constant and unyielding as bamboo and meticulous to the point of intimidating all his siblings, was slowly falling apart. At first, the only news was that he was gradually becoming more taciturn. We thought it simply an indication of age. After all, his children were in college, and he had plenty of white hair. That was last spring. Sometimes my mother would call, anxious that her son often spent the entire day staring into the distance, speaking to no one. Then his old drinking habit returned in full force. He had quit drinking some years earlier because of poor health, but now he sometimes wandered off for days on drunken binges, without a word to anyone. And just when the whole family was frantic with worry, he would suddenly return and start weeding the garden as if nothing had happened. He had worked so hard on his business, but now he ignored it, his gaze fixed on some distant, bewildering place. According to Mother, "It's as if he's exhausted by it all." My sister said her eyes filled with tears when she saw him stare off into space like that. In fact, on the telephone, it sounded as if Mother, too, was exhausted, and my sister's voice was choked with tears. I also felt a certain emptiness, almost as if I had been told the solid levee that we had relied on for so long was now leaking.

Daily life was hard enough as it was. Naturally I couldn't help longing for the strong, trustworthy levee that had protected us. I also felt that I understood the source of his anguish: He could no longer be called young, and he had suffered from poor health ever since he'd had major surgery some years earlier. Sometimes I felt as if I didn't understand him at all, though. Just a few years earlier he had finally escaped the burden of the eldest son that had weighed so heavily upon him. Our father had passed away early on, but we had all managed to grow up to become productive adults, climbing on the shoulders of our eldest brother. Back then, when we clung to his shoulders and back, he had seemed like a strong and ferocious Hercules. Ŭnja would understand how magnificent my oldest brother had been. I felt a sudden comfort as I recalled her hoarse voice, as if she had reappeared suddenly to bear witness to that fact.

However, I didn't go to the club where she was singing that night or the next. That didn't mean I had forgotten about her phone call. Hardly. Every spare moment, I was strolling the old neighborhood by the railroad tracks. In the distance, I could see Unicorn Peak. The sunlight shone bright and smooth off the two ribbons of rail stretching from Five-Tree Lookout. The coal yard was just across the stream, which, filled with dusty weeds and sewage, extended past the railroad station to the west. Along its banks was the red-light district where heavily rouged women sauntered in broad daylight. Around the neighborhood, our family was known for its wealth of sons—five sturdy boys all in a row. And two daughters taking up the rear. We had so many mouths to feed: Mother made two batches of winter kimchi each year and still worried that we would run short. When we gathered at the circular table, heads together and spoons flying, dawdlers were left with nothing but rice, for the side dishes were soon gone. My eldest brother, the family's sole source of income, was served at a separate table. As the man of the house, responsible for our large family, he barely touched his meal, leaving delicacies for his brothers and sisters to savor after he had left his table.

With the exception of the cornbread they handed out at school, our only snacks were pancakes made of sugar and flour and steamed rice cakes mixed with mugwort, so Ŭnja's steamed bread and dumplings were ambrosia to us. Her parents were oblivious to the concept of hygiene, so Mother explicitly forbade us from eating anything from their shop, even if given free of charge, but my brothers frequented Ŭnja's place in secret. On rainy days, they sent me on two types of errands financed by what meager spending money they could collect among themselves: buying dumplings from Ŭnja's shop and borrowing comics from the local comic book store. Since I didn't contribute any money, it was my job to run the errands. When I went to buy the dumplings, Ŭnja always gave me two extra, without her mother's knowledge, then grabbed her umbrella and joined me on the trip to the comic book store. Under that umbrella, she warmed up her voice and sang. On the walk home with my brothers' war comics and my ballerina tales by Ŏm Hŭija, I listened to Ŭnja's songs over and over again. And if a song wasn't finished by the time we reached our gate, I was obliged to stand and listen to the end before I went inside.

On the surface, Ŭnja's circumstances were much poorer and more squalid than ours were, yet she always seemed to have some loose change and therefore was the wealthiest child in our crowd. I had often seen her father beat her for stealing from the till. Ŭnja wasn't his only victim. It wasn't unusual to hear bloodcurdling screams coming from their house, for the man beat her older sister, a full-grown woman, and their mother, as well. By the time Ŭnja escaped in the dark of night, determined to become a singer, her father was dead. Had he lived, she never would have dared to sneak off at so young an age. Ŭnja vowed to come back when she was a star, but her glorious return was not to be. The dumpling shop closed before she became a success. As I recall, a dressmaking shop, a stationery, a noodle shop, and a bookstore took turns in that spot, and now it has disappeared altogether. After the railroad tracks were moved, the neighborhood was paved and transformed into a four-lane road. Only by tearing up the asphalt could you hope to smell the rich earth of the old days.

Ŭnja called again around noon on Friday. She insisted that I come that evening. It was her second call, and she acted like a pushy old friend, unreserved and familiar.

"I just got up. Last night I ordered out for fried rice in the green room at the club so I wouldn't miss you. You're coming tonight, aren't you? Won't your husband let you? Bring him along. I'll buy him a drink. You know, one of the waitresses at the club, she read your novel. Everyone's so excited. A real novelist is coming!"

She then told me about her two sons and the expensive apartment she shared with her musician-husband. Since her first call, all I could think of was the dumpling shop where the flies buzzed all day. Now, almost as if she knew what I had been thinking, Ŭnja offered a detailed account of her income at the peak of her career when she worked ten different places at once. It was nice to know she lived comfortably now. Well, she couldn't be that rich, but it would have been awful if she still smelled of the rancid pork fat they used in the dumpling stuffing.

"You *have* to come tonight. You've got a car, don't you? Just drive over . . . What? So what do you do with all the money you earn? A famous writer has to have a car! Well, then grab a taxi and get over here. I'll be waiting."

She had turned me into a famous writer all by herself and clucked in disapproval when I admitted having no car. It is only a guess, but I think she had begun reevaluating my financial status. She had asked if I had a car because she was certain I would have one. Or maybe that was her way of telling me that she was a car owner. It troubled her to think I might remember her as nothing more than the old dumpling shop girl. The hoarse voice was sincere as it told me how much had changed, how she had risen to a certain status. And if only we met, I would know for certain how her reality had changed. I felt renewed delight at her eagerness to meet me. I had thought she might avoid seeing me because I recalled what had happened at my first high school reunion a few years before. More than half of the alumna in the Seoul area were absent. Of course, in some cases it couldn't be helped, but it seemed most were absent out of shame. They weren't in the position to make a proud appearance at our reunion.

After Ŭnja hung up, I received a long-distance call from Chŏnju. It was my mother. Like the mothers of all married women, she was more interested in the contents of her daughter's larder than her daughter's health or well-being. *Do you have enough red pepper powder? Have you been airing your bean paste jar regularly?* I told her about Ŭnja's call. She didn't recognize the name at first, but when I said the dumpling shop girl, she immediately asked, "Pak's daughter?" Her voice was weak, however, and it didn't sound like the call would end with the usual inquiries after my refrigerator's contents. I could hardly talk of Ŭnja at length. For a moment, we were silent. As I waited for Mother to say something, I read the notes on the memo pad that I kept by the phone: *20 pages by the 3rd, 15 pages by the morning of the 4th—at the latest! Don't forget a photo.* My life was embedded in those scrawled notes. A low sigh from my mother, who once had been the driving force in my life, seeped through the telephone lines that crossed over Ch'ungch'ŏng Province and Seoul from a place in faraway Chŏlla.

"You can't make it for your father's memorial service, can you?"

Mother barely managed to get the words out. We were all busy, and she knew she could no longer orchestrate her children's lives, so as May drew near, she always took this approach. Still, that wasn't her sole reason for calling today. I knew that. Last night my oldest brother must have unloaded his suffering, heavy as chunks of iron, into Mother's lap again. He must have despaired of the drunkenness, which his body could no longer bear, and begged her to join in his reminiscences of past journeys when the two of them had worked so hard. He wouldn't have hesitated to cry as they recalled the bone-breaking hardship of a more difficult era, as they dug up that bleak time when the long, cold winter nights were spent worrying about the future. Mother's heart must have ached because of her oldest son, but I said nothing.

"Your brother said he went to your father's grave yesterday. I don't know why he keeps going there. It's been nearly thirty years since he died. Says he finished a whole bottle of rice wine with his drunkard father before coming home."

My eldest brother had long since moved our father's body from the public cemetery where he was first buried to a grave site in his home-town. When we were children, I used to follow my five brothers to the public cemetery at the far end of the city every Harvest Moon. My eldest brother policed our ranks and asked, "Can you find Father's grave?" But there was never an answer. Whether they could find it or not, my other brothers offered nothing in response except sheepish smiles. When we entered the sloping cemetery covered with its tight rows of identical grave mounds, our eldest brother went straight to the spot where our father lay, never pausing to look for landmarks.

Time passed, and when holes began to form in our ranks as my other brothers left home one by one, our eldest brother hastened to move our father's grave. In recent years, our siblings had never man-aged a single visit to Father's grave together. After all, living means building a fence of unexpected excuses around oneself. Only once a year, at the end of strawberry season, on the occasion of Father's an-nual memorial service, was the entire family required to come to-gether, although even that gathering was sometimes marred by absences.

"So why did Pak's daughter call?"

Mother was about to hang up when she finally expressed an in-terest in Ŭnja. She had become a singer and was actually making a success of it, I said, but Mother cut me off: "Success? How could she be a success when her father died like that?" Pak had been mur-dered by a young man who worked at the railroad watchtower. He was angry at Pak, who might have become his father-in-law, for hiring Ŭnja's older sister out as a tearoom waitress. The incident sent the entire city into an uproar that autumn. Apparently Mother still considered the family from the dumpling shop a pack of witches. Perhaps she believed that the ladder of salvation from the sulfurous fires of hell would never be extended to them. But since she, more than anyone, knew how fierce the struggle to survive could be, I wondered if she wasn't just saying that.

Mother's phone call upset me as usual. Recently, calls from home, like the ringing of the telephone late at night or early in the morning, made my heart jump with foreboding. The telephone was my only connection to the outside world since I tried to stay home as much as possible. If not for the telephone, I probably wouldn't have been able to live in such isolation. Like it or not, I would have had to go out and meet people. In that sense, the telephone was a link to the outside world, and, at the same time, a wall, cutting me off. My hometown was no exception. Thanks to the telephone, I didn't feel out of touch, although I visited only once a year at best. And it was the telephone that stepped in so that I didn't need to visit.

I couldn't work after Mother's call. I tried reading the morning papers, which I had skimmed earlier, but they only made my head hurt more. Every paper contained an orderly list of signatories on political petitions, and in the first or second column a few meaningful phrases flickered before my eyes. It was hot and humid for spring, but by the window, the breeze was cool. From our second-floor apartment, I could see all of Wonmi-dong. There was Mr. Ŏm from the Happiness Photo Studio, leading his three daughters up the road to the market. Shinae's father, who ran Sunny Electronics, had a new motorcycle and was all smiles lately. Even now, he was circling the neighborhood with Shinae. Brothers Supermarket was bustling with housewives who had gathered to buy the frozen squid that Captain Kim had shipped in by the box. Who could resist his smooth tongue? It looked like everyone in Wonmi-dong would be eating squid tonight. The street would have been noisy even without the women. The children, who would grow up to call Puch'ŏn's Wonmi-dong their hometown, little kids who would someday find comfort in their memories of this neighborhood, shouted, cried, and cavorted everywhere.

I stood at the window for some time, but the mood to wrestle with my manuscript didn't return. If the telephone rang now, it would certainly be my faithful editor, desperate for the piece. That didn't matter, though. I dashed to the bookshelf and began searching for the collection of short stories that included that account of my childhood. The story began with me waking from a nap. I thought it was time for school and ran out of the house with my shoes on the wrong feet. The stories of those times, when I carried a bundle of tears with me everywhere, when I was terrified of the world for no reason, and at the same time, had an undying trust in that world, were always of comfort to me. I don't know how to explain it. Why do people who write for a living find comfort in reading their own stories? Late at night when I was trying to work but things didn't feel right, I would read the story about Ŭnja. I'd turn back time, run into the past, and there were the railroad tracks. My eldest brother was young and handsome. My other brothers were students with crewcuts. I opened the wardrobe, and there was the makeup brush my father had bought me. When I think about it now, I wonder why he bought a makeup brush, of all things, for a daughter so young. I guess it was meant to be a toy.

"Weren't for your big brother, we would have starved." Mother often recalled her eldest son's labors, and it was true. Like a cloud drifting in the sky, Father cared only for otherworldly things and died suddenly, leaving behind intense poverty, debt, and seven children. He was one of a handful of survivors of the misfortune that had struck his home village so much harder than others during the war. At that time, Father hung on to his life by hiding in a pile of barley stalks and in the root cellar behind the house, but he lost it soon after moving to the city. As Mother said, we have no control over life, yet Father's death was an unforgivable act of betrayal to her. At least I had the makeup brush he had given me; my sister lost her father when she was barely a year old.

While Father was alive, my eldest brother attended university at night and worked to support the family during the day, but after Father's death, he and Mother struggled to feed the children. Each morning we would pause, speechless for a moment, before sticking out our hands to our oldest brother. So many things required money—school fees, books, charity campaigns, gym suits—and there was only one person to provide it. My other brothers took advantage of the eldest's generosity toward his two sisters by asking me to get money from him. They would gather on the corner waiting for me—my third brother in the sack-like school uniform destined for the siblings beneath him, my fourth brother with his ankles sticking out of the pants he inherited from the third, and my fifth brother with the ragged crewcut, who complained of never having worn new clothes. I recited the list of needs, just as my brothers had instructed: PTA dues, lunch money, and fees for school materials. We could have printed the money in a factory, but it wouldn't have been enough. Still, my eldest brother always took out his wallet.

As we were growing up, I wasn't the only one who felt uncomfortable around him. My other brothers lived in awe of him, too. They all agreed with my second brother when he said that no matter how delicious a dish was, his taste buds went dead when our eldest brother was around. I remember the summer Sundays when all five sons ate watermelon together, but only the eldest spat out his seeds with gusto; the rest munched the fruit halfheartedly, swallowing their seeds. When the boys bathed at the well, only Mother could scrub the eldest's back. The rest took turns, scrubbing and pouring buckets of water over each other: The third brother scrubbed the second's back, the fourth scrubbed the third's, and so on. When our eldest brother finished and asked someone to pour water over him, no one knew what to do. Our neighbors were no different, because they didn't know how to treat him, either. Even Ŭnja's mother, who rushed around the neighborhood with her nylon petticoat flapping as she poked her nose in everybody's business, always thought of an excuse to duck back into the dumpling shop when my eldest brother passed.

"I'll be waiting," Ŭnja said as she hung up. She emphasized the "waiting," and conscious of that, perhaps, I finished with dinner earlier than usual that day. I could have gotten to the New Puch'ŏn Club, where Ŭnja was working, by nine, even if I hadn't hurried. My husband, who was reading in the spare room, said he would put our daughter to bed and urged me to go. He was curious about Ŭnja. Imagine, the heroine of one of my stories actually singing in a club nearby. Time ticked away. As nine o'clock approached, my daughter began to yawn. I didn't need to put her to bed; she would soon collapse and head off to dreamland on her own. In the main street out front, empty taxis turned around after dropping passengers in the neighborhood. All I had to do was get up and leave the house. All I had to do was tell the taxi driver, "Downtown." But I couldn't seem to move.

Her eight o'clock set finished, Ŭnja would be staring at the entrance now. I did nothing until the clock struck nine and the evening news began. My daughter was asleep, and my husband was leafing through a fishing magazine, envious no doubt of the grin on the face of a fisherman who had reeled in a large fish. He had bought some gear and never missed any news of fishing, but his own outings always seemed to fall through. He had only gone deep-sea fishing once, but that was enough to whet his appetite. There were so many things tying him down, so many knots to be undone before he could take a weekend off and dangle his line in the water. At times, he seemed to covet nothing more than the wonder one feels just before becoming a true fisherman. Like mountain climbers who have set one foot toward the summit, whenever he was exhausted by the world, he wanted to join the ranks of anglers gathered at fishing spots. I glanced over his shoulder at the color photographs in the magazine and imagined the fish he would catch. The fish flopped about, scales glistening, and the clock ticked toward the opening of Ŭnja's second set.

The next morning she called, as expected. It was Saturday. There were only two nights left. She emphasized that fact.

"You're not going to skip it altogether, are you? Heavens! Who'd have guessed meeting an old hometown friend would be so hard? What's the matter? A novelist can't meet an old friend who makes her living as a nightclub singer? Is it bad for your reputation? Come on! I may seem pathetic to you, but I've worked hard to become Mina Pak! I don't know how many times I've had to pick myself up and start over again."

She had reason enough to say such things. There are those who would say a nightclub singer is hardly an appropriate friend for an author skilled at choosing just the right words to run in the newspaper, so certain that this is the right way and that is the wrong. I didn't know how to reply. Our conversation was going wrong, but I was helpless. Apparently she had stumbled more than once in her transformation from Pak Ŭnja to Mina Pak. But that's true of everyone, isn't it? Since moving to Puch'ŏn, I have heard the same tired stories over and over. And it's not only Puch'ŏn; I've just heard Puch'ŏn's stories because I live here. If I sat down at the window right now, I'd hear the stories of the people of Wonmi-dong, of the scars they've incurred in their struggles. No matter how many times they stumble, they always pick themselves up and resume their march over the passes to the summit. The stark reality that there is little room at the top is simply a ruse in their eyes. And they refuse to admit that, even if they do manage to crawl all the way to the top, they will only be met by the path down on the other side. To the owners of lives spent desperately struggling to survive, truth by any other name is useless. For them, life isn't something to examine or ponder; it is a steel door, bolted shut, a door that you have to throw your weight against, that you have to beat on with all your might. It is a mountain peak towering in the distance.

Ŭnja was one of those people who believed that she had finally conquered the mountain peak. She said that she had once given up singing because she simply couldn't make a living at it. After that first phone call—no, actually, after she realized that I wasn't going to rush out to see her—Ŭnja began revealing episodes from her past one by one. Was it the second call? She told me about her experiences wandering alone in Japan. She had somehow managed to join a third-rate entertainment troupe headed for Japan and ditched the troupe on the day of their last performance, hoping to find another job in that foreign land. However, today she told me an even more painful story. After setting up housekeeping with her present husband, a former band conductor, it seems she bought into a small concession at a theater-restaurant and ran up a pile of debt. She was forced to juggle several jobs from Chu-an to Pup'yŏng to Puch'ŏn and on, while her husband was stuck in an exclusive contract that kept him strumming his guitar until dawn. Ŭnja was pregnant with her first child at the time, but she could hardly go on a nightclub stage with her belly sticking out. To fit into her costume, she had to bind herself up in a corset and strips of cloth. After a month or so, the fetal movements stopped. She thought it strange but kept singing with her belly bound tight for two more weeks. Only then did she go to the hospital and learn that the fetus had long since died.

"To a famous writer like you, it probably sounds like a novel. I've read plenty of sad novels, but they're nothing compared to the story of my life. Sometimes I can't figure out what writers are talking about. Are you one of those authors who writes stories that make you sleepy? You know, I haven't read any of your stories yet. But I'm going to! Hey, have you made any money?"

It was fortunate that Ŭnja hadn't read my stories. Last night I was up all night, struggling to write one "that makes you sleepy." Then this morning I made a big show of getting some sleep, as if I had achieved something of importance the night before. Ŭnja informed me that she, too, had to sleep a few more hours. She never got home before dawn. I smiled bitterly at the realization that we did have something in common: We both worked nights.

In a drowsy voice, Ŭnja made another appointment for that evening. On the weekends, the program was different; she was on call from eight o'clock. There was a chorus, she explained, and she sometimes sang backup, too. On Saturdays, customers liked flashy spectacles, so the management switched the performers around for variety. "I'm only on stage for a few minutes at a time. I'll be there till midnight, so come whenever you like. Tonight and tomorrow are my final performances. Don't you want to hear me sing? You used to love to listen to me. Oh, and if you tell them you've come to see Mina Pak, they'll take good care of you, so don't get shy or chicken out on me."

I hung up without having assured her that, of course, I would go that evening or explaining that I hadn't had a spare moment the day before. Somehow, the unthinking pleasure I had felt when she first phoned had been replaced by a mysterious hesitation.

Ŭnja was a road sign at the center of my memories. Especially since I had written that story about one year in my childhood, in which she was the main character. I hadn't consciously planned to remember only what I had put down on paper, yet my memories revolved around the space created in that story. My hometown was almost unrecognizable to me now. If not for the road signs visible from the express bus that I took to attend my father's memorial service in Chŏnju once a year, I wouldn't have known where I was. The family home was completely different now, alone amid the inns and stores that had sprung up after the roads were widened. In fact, the old house had been torn down and replaced by a Western-style home, and the lot had long been coveted by a man who wanted to build a motel. After the stream that ran in front of the house was covered by a road, our neighborhood was rapidly incorporated into the city. The transformation was complete with the rerouting of the railroad tracks. The old neighborhood was gone. The willow tree where Ŭnja held her little concerts had been cut down long ago, and cars raced past the spot where the dumpling shop once stood. It was no longer a residential district. In the old days, we had lived there happily, surrounded by friendly neighbors, but not now. The Ŭnsŏng Motel, the Mirim Inn, and the Kŏbu Hotel couldn't be neighbors. And the children were growing. My nieces and nephews begged their father to move, as all our siblings did, but my eldest brother wouldn't think of selling the house. The more we urged him to sell, the more he invested in repairs. He was the last of the old-timers in that neighborhood.

Going home once a year, only to confirm the unfamiliar faces of strangers, left me feeling lonely, nothing more. And now, even that loneliness would no longer be mine. No one could go home again. Home existed only in the past. Someone once wrote that man lives by confirming the existence of his family home in the willow trees at the entrance to a village, in the salty smell of a seaside town, in the long river that wraps around the old neighborhood. For me, Ŭnja was the last road sign pointing home. Everything, even my eldest brother, had changed, but Ŭnja remained the same. When I thought of her, the old memories, the very breath of the old neighborhood, came back to me, so close it felt as if I could reach out and touch them. The image of my eldest brother, still strong, remained unscathed there. But if I went to the New Puch'ŏn Club and met Ŭnja, I might lose the last road sign home.

I couldn't imagine what she looked like now. I was afraid I wouldn't recognize her, even if I did go to the nightclub. In my memories she was a little girl with short bobbed hair, bruises on her grimy neck from her father's stubborn grip, and a frayed undershirt peeking through a rip in her blouse. How could I picture a woman well over thirty in that child? After nurturing the old hometown in my heart for so long, I didn't want to encounter it in reality. I couldn't shake off the fear that once I met her, that era in the story, which had given me such comfort, would disappear. But what about Ŭnja, who had already appeared in reality? She remained an unsolved problem as I spent that Saturday night at home in Wonmi-dong.

I stayed near the telephone all day Sunday. Ŭnja's sharp tongue was sure to impugn my indifference, but I was ready to accept her criticism. I waited for her call, imagining the words she would throw at me. The phone didn't ring that morning, not once. Sundays were like that. I could have an overdue manuscript, but editors never called to remind me on Sunday. If the phone rang, it was sure to be Ŭnja.

The phone finally rang in the afternoon, but out of the receiver came my sister's familiar voice, not Ŭnja's hoarse one. The voice of a family member from home chased away my foreboding, and I was glad. Of course, all she had to report were gloomy anecdotes about our eldest brother. He had finally decided to sell the house and had affixed his seal to a sales contract. In a month's time, our father's memorial service would be held at the house for the last time. My brother had sealed the contract the day before and spent the rest of the day drinking alone, she said. They all had wanted to sell the house, but now they were uneasy, seeing their brother so unsettled.

Brother may have sold the house, but he had the means to move to a much better one, so no one worried about that. The problem was, our brother had spent the entire day drinking alone, drinking so much that neither my sister nor I could help but worry.

"Everyone has to show up for the memorial service this year. I'm going to call all of them. He's having a hard enough time as it is. Big Brother wouldn't have sold the house if the neighborhood hadn't turned into a forest of motels. He drank so much *soju* yesterday he couldn't get up this morning. He can afford good liquor. Why *soju*? I don't get it. Give him a call. And you've got to come to the memorial service! We've been selfish. We only get together once a year, at best. I think he's disappointed in us."

He had raised his siblings and his own children in that house. The most important years of his life had been spent there. He had created a legend educating his six younger brothers and sisters, but now he was a remnant of a bygone era that had lost all meaning. A young, handsome man twenty-five years ago, he was over fifty and showing his age. In the course of those twenty-five years, one of our siblings had left this earth. The third son had betrayed his eldest brother by throwing his life away, but the rest of us lived on, tending our eldest brother's legend. My second brother, still in awe of the eldest, silently served as his brother's right arm in the family business, while at the same time becoming something of an expert on flowers. My fourth brother, an internist with his own clinic, and my fifth brother, who had passed the national administrative examination and was now a high-level government official, hadn't turned their backs on our eldest brother's legend. Even I, nose forever buried in a book and adept at little but weaving lies in the eyes of my mother and eldest brother back home, hadn't strayed from the path. And my younger sister, just a year old when our father died, was a music teacher and already a mother of two.

However, our eldest brother was shackled by the legend he himself had created. In the days when he was responsible for our survival, even if it meant printing the money himself, we had been his purpose. Each time he started a new business, the livelihood of the large family he led was what kept him going. But now his brothers and sisters had made lives for themselves. They had all earned a fair amount of money. With youthful resilience and vigor, his siblings were making a place for themselves in society, just as he had once done. He didn't want to remind us who had made that independence possible, but the deep hole of his gradual decrepitude was causing him to fall apart. His life had begun to waver noticeably since the surgery from which he had narrowly recovered a few years ago. Life's rules—you must not do this, that is dangerous, this or that is forbidden—were choking him. Every time I heard him lament that only emptiness awaited him when he reached a goal that he had worked so hard for, I couldn't help wondering what my brother had lost. Perhaps he wanted to forget reality by turning back the pages of the past, just as I found comfort in rereading the account of my own childhood. Perhaps he was practicing to distance himself, one step at a time, from the present.

When I thought of how hollow Brother's heart must have been as he drank the bitter *soju* with nothing on the side but memories of a life spent in that house, soon to become a motel, I was frustrated by my own helplessness. I thought I understood how he had felt when he made sudden visits to Father's grave to share a bottle of *soju* with a dead man. The living couldn't relieve one man's bone-wrenching loneliness; only someone buried in the ground could understand. I knew that was deeply significant. My sister ended the call telling me of our mother's decision. In a sense, it was the only thing she could do for her eldest son.

"Mom started an abstinence prayer this morning. She's going to skip breakfast and pray for him every morning until he goes to church. It could take months, even years, but you know how stubborn she is."

Mother believed that our eldest brother could endure this empty world unscathed if only he went to church and embraced the Lord as she had. There was nothing for me to do but hope that Mother's abstinence prayer ended in the near future. After my sister's call, I turned the page on the calendar and drew two red circles around the date of the memorial service.

The afternoon wore on with no news from Ŭnja. I began to

worry: Had she decided to forget her disloyal friend? The realization that I might never hear her songs if I missed tonight's final opportunity made me anxious. I tried to figure out a way to answer her urgent call by going to the club, listening to her sing, and coming home without her knowing.

My husband returned from a walk to Wonmi Mountain with news of spring. "The azaleas are in full bloom," he said, "and the new leaves are so green, it was like bathing in a pool of green water." Wonmi Mountain was visible throughout the neighborhood. The long ridge, stained crimson with spring blossoms, was immediately apparent from the window. There was no need to climb the mountain to see the azaleas. I took out the binoculars that I had bought for my daughter and adjusted the focus. The mountain stepped toward me. Through the lenses, the azaleas were in full bloom and the mountain's skirts, covered with new sprouts, were as soft as green velvet. One cup of the mineral water that he had brought back from the spring and the person who had gone to Wonmi Mountain and the person who had stayed home looking at it through the binoculars would be equals. If only I could hear Ŭnja's songs from a distance, as I had seen Wonmi Mountain through the binoculars.

Finally, I decided I couldn't miss Mina Pak's last set. I wanted for nothing more than to hear "Deep Dark Blues" again, but I couldn't be sure what songs were in Mina Pak's repertoire. I could only guess. In nightclubs, old pop songs were the thing, weren't they? My ears wouldn't suffer. I liked those kinds of songs. Not long ago, I had taken such pleasure in the endless medley of old foxtrots I had heard in a taxi; I regretted that the ride from Puch'ŏn Station to Wonmi-dong was so short. I even asked the driver the name of the tape. I haven't bought it yet, but now I understand why those old songs are sung at every drinking party and always demanded for encores.

I was surprised to find the New Puch'ŏn Nightclub on the second floor. Somehow I had imagined the dank darkness of a basement; the lights glittering at the entrance were disconcerting. The band's blare and the garbled noise of the crowd inside made me suddenly long for home. It was funny. I didn't know it would be like this. As I was leaving our house, I had told Mr. Chu from the wallpaper shop that I was going "someplace nice." He had been moving the rolls of wallpaper displayed in front of the shop inside when he saw me. Surprised that I should be going out so late, he asked, "And where are you going?" I hadn't seen him recently. It was spring, so business must have been booming. He always wore Bermuda shorts, except in the dead of winter, but beads of sweat glistened on his brow. Sweat shimmered on the foreheads of the drunks emerging through the nightclub's leather-bound doors, too. I counted the steps they took reeling down the stairs, then pushed through the doors and went inside.

The club was dark, as I had expected. No one seemed to notice my entrance, perhaps because I had sneaked in so quietly. I hid in a corner and looked at the stage. A woman was just stepping into the spotlight. I had no way of knowing whether Ŭnja's set was over or if this, in fact, was Ŭnja. I was standing some distance from the stage and the colored lights distorted the woman's features. Besides, it was impossible to guess her age because of her heavy makeup and cascading hair. I tried to remember what Ŭnja had looked like twenty-five years before, but my mind was a murky blank. *Maybe I'll recognize her voice,* I thought, and stared at the woman's lips anxiously. Slowly, the music began to flow. The band's accompaniment was dark, slow, solemn. The buoyant mood of the club disappeared immediately, and a dark, heavily colored music seized the audience.

Then a clear voice began to flow from the woman's red lips. *"The mountains are telling me, Don't come, Don't come! The valleys are wet and slippery beneath my feet . . ."* As the deep, lonely voice seeped into every crevice of the room, the band's music faded. Without realizing it, I stepped forward to meet the song. A strange feeling moved down my spine, and goose bumps spread across my arms like a sheet of lightning. My whole body shivered; I took another step forward. The singer carefully modulated her breathing and continued, eyes closed. *"The mountains tell me to forget. Forget, forget they say . . ."* Her voice was so lonely, so deep. Only then did I realize I knew the song. I had heard it many times before. But I was absorbed in it, as if this were the first time. No, I wasn't absorbed. The song was sweeping me along. It was flowing toward me, a swift current, giving me no time to think. *"Oh, that I could live and die like a breath of wind, like the wind that stirs these mountains' clouds of tears . . ."* The veins in the woman's neck stood out as she sang, and the band's music grew stronger. I took a deep breath. Suddenly I saw my eldest brother in the song, his back stooped in loneliness and exhaustion. I closed my eyes to escape the image, and when I did, a single tear rolled from my eyelashes down my cheek.

The song was called "Cold Water Pass," for a spot high in the Sŏrak Mountains. But there was a big difference between the "Cold Water Pass" I knew and the one I was hearing now. If I had come to this place to hear a song, I was hearing a remarkable one. It didn't matter if the singer was Ŭnja or not. I listened with my whole being, and she never let me go, not for an instant. It felt as if an electric current, flashing sparks, was surging through the bottom of my feet, into the floor, deep into some distant underground. With a tearful gaze, I embraced the drunken guests seated at their wobbling tables. They, too, would have times best forgotten, moments when they wished they could live like a breath of wind. My brother wouldn't be the only one. My throat tightened once more. Then a man wearing a bow tie stepped in front of me and bowed politely.

"May I show you to a table?"

He was right. I had to sit, but where? I looked around, feeling so alone. Behind me, beyond the lights' reach, was darkness, a dank, stained wall, perhaps. I tried to say something to the waiter, but nothing came out. *"The mountains are telling me to go. Go down, they cry, shoving these tired shoulders . . ."* As I stood there groping for words, the final verse of "Cold Water Pass" flowed toward me like an incoming tide.

It was only after returning home that I was convinced the woman singer was Ŭnja. Like she said, Ŭnja had worked hard to become Mina Pak. How many times had she picked herself up and started over? It was only then that I was sure it was Ŭnja singing of the tearful climb up those mountains, of the towering peaks telling her to forget, of the exhausted loneliness she felt looking down those mountain slopes.

That night I met a song in my dreams. It was the first time I realized that you could dream in songs. In that song, I met a group of people climbing a barren mountain under a dark gray sky. They were exhausted, and each carried a heavy load on his shoulders. Their backs bent under their burdens. The slope was steep and the tree branches thick and unyielding. There was no spring to quench their thirst, no grassy spot to sit and rest their legs. They could only march, plodding heavily, one step at a time, through the thick forest.

My brothers and sister were among them. My eldest brother led the way, and the younger brothers followed. After each step toward the mountain peak, the weeds and brush closed behind them, erasing all trace of their passing. Awaiting them would be the echo of the mountains, saying *Forget,* or perhaps it would be a breath of wind urging them down again with a push on their sagging shoulders. If there was more, it would be only the gray sky and a scrap of yellow earth. Still they trudged on, backs bent under their burdens, with my eldest brother among them, on toward the summit.

Three days passed. Then late one morning Ŭnja called in that husky voice again.

"Down in Chŏlla Province, you know what we'd call you? One lousy excuse for a human being! You didn't come, did you?"

As befit the road sign to my hometown, Ŭnja reproached my indifference in a Chŏlla twang. I just laughed. I didn't tell her that I had gone to the club on Sunday night. And, of course, I didn't ask if it was her singing "Cold Water Pass."

"If I weren't so busy, I'd run over there and curse the hell out of you, but I can't. Anyway . . . you come see my cabaret next time you're in Seoul. It's right by the rotary in Shinsa-dong, so you'll have no trouble finding it. It opens next week. Oh, and I decided on a name for my club. I don't know if a fine writer like you will approve, but I'm calling it 'The Good Country.' It doesn't matter if you approve or not. I've already put up the sign.

"Just look for 'The Good Country.' Don't forget, 'The Good Country,'" she said before hanging up. I wasn't the least bit unhappy with her choice of names. "The Good Country." It was a wonderful name. Only I wasn't sure I could find that good country. No, I simply wasn't sure I'd be able to go inside and meet her.

About the Translators

KIM SO-YOUNG is a freelance translator living in Seoul. In addition to literary translation, she translates for Newsweek Korea and the Foreign Broadcast Information Service attached to the U.S. Embassy in Seoul.

JULIE PICKERING is a translator and editor living in Seattle. Her literary translations include *The Prophet and Other Stories* (1999), a collection of novellas and short stories by Yi Ch'ŏngjun, and Hwang Sunwon's *The Descendants of Cain* (1997), translated with Suh Ji-moon.